His betrayal
leads them into
temptation…

"I suspect you would very much like to waltz with the devil first."

"You're wrong."

"Prove it."

Before she could respond, he settled his mouth over hers. It was softer than she'd expected, hotter. With an insistence that should have frightened her, he urged her to part her lips. His tongue slid through, gliding over hers, velvet and silk. Inviting her to explore, to know the intimacies of his mouth as he was discovering hers.

She was entranced, drawn into sensations such as she'd never experienced. He was so terribly talented at eliciting delicious responses that began at the tips of her toes and swirled ever upward, a tingling of nerve endings, a lethargic warmth, that weakened her knees, her resolve to push him away.

She heard a deep groan, felt a vibration against her fingers, and realized she was clutching the lapels of his deep blue morning coat. Clinging to Drake Darling was all that was keeping her from melting into a puddle of pleasure at his feet.

This was merely a kiss, an ancient dance of mouths, yet it was proving to be her undoing.

By Lorraine Heath

Once More, My Darling Rogue
When the Duke Was Wicked
Lord of Wicked Intentions
Lord of Temptation
She Tempts the Duke
Waking up With the Duke
Pleasures of a Notorious Gentleman
Passions of a Wicked Earl
Midnight Pleasures With a Scoundrel
Surrender to the Devil
Between the Devil and Desire
In Bed With the Devil
Just Wicked Enough
A Duke of Her Own
Promise Me Forever
A Matter of Temptation
As an Earl Desires
An Invitation to Seduction
Love With a Scandalous Lord
To Marry an Heiress
The Outlaw and the Lady
Never Marry a Cowboy
Never Love a Cowboy
A Rogue in Texas

Lorraine Heath

Once More, My Darling Rogue

AVON

An Imprint of HarperCollins*Publishers*

This is a work of fiction. Names, characters, places, and incidents are products of the author's imagination or are used fictitiously and are not to be construed as real. Any resemblance to actual events, locales, organizations, or persons, living or dead, is entirely coincidental.

AVON BOOKS
An Imprint of HarperCollins*Publishers*
195 Broadway
New York, New York 10007

ISBN 978-0-06-227624-7
www.avonromance.com

First Avon Books mass market printing: September 2014

Printed in the U.S.A.

10 9 8 7 6 5 4 3 2 1

In loving memory of Pooh Bear,
who lumbered into our lives eight years ago—
large, clumsy, and awkward—always searching
for an idle hand. A sweet lummox who
enthusiastically welcomed visitors,
eagerly anticipated the arrival of the
pizza delivery guy (because *someone* in this
household shares his pizza with the dogs),
and loved greeting trick-or-treaters.
We miss you.

Once More, My Darling Rogue

Prologue

From the Journal of Drake Darling

I was born Peter Sykes, the son of a murderer, the son of a woman murdered, a heritage that has always haunted me. I do not know how many lives my father may have taken, but I do know that he killed my mother because she sought to give me a better life. Unbeknownst to anyone, I attended his hanging. I was eight at the time. The crowds jostled me but I managed to make my way to the front. He wept, my father. He soiled himself, he begged for mercy. Words I'd heard my mother utter, words that had done her little good.

Neither did they serve my father well, for they slipped the noose about his neck and released the trapdoor. All that I saw and heard after that I buried in the darkest recesses of my mind, but I could never bury the stain of his blood coursing through my veins. Nor the anger that simmered just below the surface—his legacy to me, one I feared I was destined to embrace. For it was always there, hovering, wanting to be let loose.

My mother had entrusted me to the care of a Miss Frannie Darling, who eventually married Sterling Mabry, the Duke of Greystone. They took me into their home, raised me as one of their own. As Miss Darling no longer had use of her surname, I took it in an attempt to wash off the sins of my father.

One night the duke pointed out the constellation Draco and in the stars, I saw the fierce dragon that nothing could touch. I became known as Drake, once more attempting to separate myself from my past and the destiny handed to me by my father. With the duke's family, I traveled the world, saw amazing creatures and creations, experienced wonders beyond imagining.

But no matter how far I journeyed, I could not escape my sordid beginnings. I could not be anything other than what I was born to be.

Chapter 1

London
1874

At times Lady Ophelia Lyttleton found herself quite disgusted with those of her gender. Tonight, unfortunately, was turning out to be one of those occasions. The young ladies—the old ones as well for that matter—were making spectacles of themselves as they all vied for the attention of one of the most notorious gentlemen in attendance at this evening's ball.

Drake Darling didn't often frequent Society's elite functions, but the gentlemen's club overseer could not very well have avoided this affair when its purpose was to celebrate the marriage of Lady Grace Mabry to the Duke of Lovingdon. After all, Darling had been raised within the bosom of Grace's family even though he was not related to them in any manner, not a distant cousin or long-lost nephew. Nor was he of the aristocracy and his blood most certainly did not run blue.

Yet the ladies tittering about him and dangling their dance cards in front of his nose seemed to have forgotten those little facts. He would not elevate their standing in Society. He would not pass on a title to his firstborn son. He would not sit in the House of Lords.

The only thing he could be guaranteed to achieve was turning ladies' minds to mush. It was his smile. The sublime way his lips parted ever so slightly to reveal straight white teeth, and then one corner of his luscious mouth hitching up a little higher to form a tiny dimple in his right cheek that winked with the promise of wickedness.

It was his eyes. The manner in which they, black as midnight, sparkled knowingly as though he could not only decipher a lady's dearest wish but deliver it to her in a manner that would far exceed her expectations.

It was his hair, so black as to look almost blue when captured by gaslight. The rebellious way he kept it longer than fashionable, the inviting manner in which it brushed against the collar of his blue jacket, tempting fingers to ruffle through the curling strands.

It was the breadth of his shoulders and the width of his chest that hinted at solace offered to any woman who rested her cheek there, his height that put him half a head taller than most of the men in the salon. It was his laughter, the ease with which he gifted it to one lady after another. It was his courteous bow, his incredible solicitousness, the seductive manner in which he lowered his head to hear more clearly, leaned forward to whisper in the delicate shell of an ear.

He made them fall in love with him. So effortlessly. Without care. Without considering consequences.

She hated him for it. They would follow him into gardens where he would kiss them senseless. She had once caught him doing exactly that with a young servant at the duke's estate. Behind the stables, the girl had been fairly clambering up the long length of him striving to capture all his mouth had to offer. While she'd been only eight, Ophelia had been disgusted by the display, had known it was wrong, sinful. She didn't think they'd seen her, but even as she ran away she heard his low laughter, and loped all the faster. She knew his sort, knew he had no regard for a woman's reputation.

Thus far this evening he'd danced with a dozen ladies. Not that she was keeping count.

She'd had her fair share of attention from earls, viscounts, marquesses, and dukes. From men who held courtesy titles but would one day hold far more, and from those who had already ascended to their proper rank. She hardly needed to beg for notice like the silly chits who surrounded Darling every time he came off the dance floor or returned from fetching a bit of refreshment for some ogling miss on the verge of a swoon. He certainly played the role of gallant well, was master of it. He made them all forget what he was, from whence he'd come. A man of coarse origins.

"They make such fools of themselves, fawning over Darling as they do," she muttered.

Standing beside her, Miss Minerva Dodger gave a start. "You can hardly blame them. He's a curiosity. I don't think he's attended a ball since Grace's coming out."

He'd dared to ask Ophelia to dance that night, but she had ignored his invitation. Someone had to maintain the high ground, had to adhere to socially acceptable standards. Her father had beat that fact into her often enough. Her lineage could be traced back to William the Conqueror. She was not even allowed to dance with the spares, let alone any sons who came after. She was expected to do him and her ancestors proud, to carry on the noble tradition of marrying well. If she did not obey his strictures, her impressive dowry would be forfeit, and along with it any chance she had for happiness. She was dependent upon what the fortune in her trust would eventually provide: freedom.

"He's a commoner," she reminded her friend.

Minerva arched a brow. "As am I."

Ophelia released a quick huff of air. "Your mother is nobility."

"My father is of the streets."

And one of the wealthiest men in Christendom. "He made something of himself."

"Could not the same be said of Drake?"

"Can one truly ever escape his past?"

"You can't have it both says. You can't on the one hand acknowledge that my father escaped his and then not give Drake the same consideration."

She could, she did. Her father had been an incredibly moral man. Since their father's passing, her brother had strayed a bit from the straight and narrow, spending far too many nights lost in gambling and drink, but she felt an obligation to honor her father's teachings. Sin was drawn to her, and if she did not remain ever vigilant, it would have its way with her. She'd never told anyone that ugly truth about herself. Her father would have been terribly disappointed, might not have provided her with a dowry, might have left her to her own means.

"My father has no complaints with the way Drake manages Dodger's Drawing Room," Minerva continued on, referring to the infamous gentlemen's club as though she had Ophelia's undivided attention. "Being raised by the Duke and Duchess of Greystone and garnering the same devotion that they give their sons, I daresay he could have avoided working altogether if he wished. I think he's to be admired."

She'd been unwise to mention anything at all as Minerva couldn't possibly understand how Ophelia managed to see Drake Darling for exactly what he was: beneath them all and not to be well-regarded in the least. He was no gentleman. He encouraged sin, tempted ladies with that wicked, wicked smile.

"He always manages to bring out the worst in you," Minerva mused. "I've never understood that."

"Don't be ridiculous. I give him no thought whatsoever."

"Yet here we are discussing him."

"No, actually, I was pointing out the ladies' improper behavior, how badly it reflects on all of us."

"My father has told me countless times that we are not a reflection of others' behavior, only our own."

But when that behavior touches us . . .

She broke off the thought, shoved it back into its hidey-hole, would not dignify it with voice. Although she did have to admit that Minerva had the right of it. Darling brought out the worst in her. Always had. Sin called to sin.

Just that morning she had been the envy of every female in London because Darling had escorted her down the aisle of St. George's following the ceremony that had united Grace and Lovingdon. She had served as Grace's maid of honor while Darling had stood as Lovingdon's best man. But on the long stroll from the altar to the vestry, she'd spoken not a word to him, and he'd barely acknowledged her. He hadn't bestowed upon her his remarkable smile. His eyes hadn't twinkled. She knew he wished to be with anyone other than her just as she wished to be with anyone other than him.

The ladies were dancing with the devil as he led them merrily into temptation. It was time someone put an end to the charade, that someone reminded them—and him—of his place within their ranks.

At that precise moment Drake Darling wished to be anywhere other than where he was, but he was well aware that in life one did not always get what he wished for. On occasion, he didn't even get what he deserved.

So he relied upon what he'd learned during his formative years about deception and he pretended that he was positively delighted, beside himself with joy, to be the center of attention. He much preferred the shadows to glittering ballrooms. He was most comfortable when not noticed, but he was at best a chameleon. He knew how to blend in even when the blending in took place within a room with mirrored walls, gaslit chandeliers, and the finest personages the aristocracy had to offer.

The one thing he was not feigning was his happiness for Grace and Lovingdon. He considered Grace a sister, even though their blood could not have been more opposite. For many years now he had been close to Lovingdon, a confidante on occasion, but more often a hell-raiser of late. Until Grace had captured the duke's heart.

Therefore, Drake couldn't very well not attend the celebration of their marriage. Only minutes earlier he'd caught sight of the happy couple escaping the ballroom. Normally the bride and groom didn't attend the ball held in their honor, but Grace was far from conventional. She'd wanted to dance with her father one last time. The Duke of Greystone's eyesight was deteriorating, although only the family was aware of his affliction. Another reason Drake was here: to acknowledge his debt to the man and woman who had given him a home. His presence was expected, and so he gave no outward sign to the six young ladies surrounding him that he wished to be elsewhere. He always did whatever was required to ensure the duke and duchess had no regrets about taking him in.

They were so young, the ladies who smiled and batted their lashes at him. Even the ones who were on the far side of five and twenty were too innocent for his tastes. They were all light and airy as though burdens were unknown to them, as though life encompassed nothing more than enjoyment. He preferred his women with a bit more seasoning to them, savory, spicy, and tart.

"Boy."

An exception to his preference for the tart had arrived. The haughtiness of the voice set his teeth on edge. He should have known he'd not escape her notice for the entire evening. That Lady Ophelia Lyttleton was one of Grace's dearest friends was beyond his comprehension. He didn't understand why the sister of his heart associated with such an arrogant miss when Grace was the sweetest, gentlest person he'd ever known. Stubborn to be sure, but she hadn't a mean bone in her body. Lady Ophelia could not claim the same. Her presence at his back proof enough.

The ladies who had been gifting him with their attention blinked repeatedly and went silent for the first time in more than two hours. Because they were there, because he was striving to give the appearance of being a gentleman, he would spare Lady Ophelia the embarrassment of ignoring her. Even though he suspected he would pay a price for his generosity. He always paid the price. The lady was quite adept at delivering stinging barbs.

Slowly he turned and arched a brow at the woman whose head failed to reach his shoulder. And yet in spite of her diminutive size, she managed to give the appearance of looking down on him. It was her long, pert, slender nose that tipped up ever so slightly on the end. She had been a constant aggravation whenever she visited with Grace and crossed paths with him. But devil's mistress that she was, she was very careful to slight him only when Grace wasn't about to witness her set-downs. Because he loved Grace too much to upset her—and she would be appalled to know he and her friend were not on particularly pleasant terms—he had borne Lady Ophelia's degradations, convinced that he was walking the high ground while she was slogging along in the muck.

It made no sense to him that such a beauty could be such a resounding termagant. Her green eyes with the oval, exotic slant were challenging him with a sharpness that could slice into one's soul if he weren't careful. While he was twelve years her senior, as she had grown toward womanhood, she had mastered the art of making him feel as though he were a dog living in the quagmire of the gutters again. Not that others among the aristocracy hadn't made him feel the same from time to time, but still it irked more so when she was the one responsible for the cut to his pride.

"Boy," she repeated with a touch more arrogance, "do fetch me some champagne, and be quick about it."

As though he were a servant, as though he lived to serve her. Not that he found fault with those who served. Theirs was a more noble undertaking and their accomplishments far outstripped anything she might ever manage. She, who no doubt nibbled on chocolates in bed while reading a book, without thought regarding the effort that had gone behind placing both in her hand.

He considered telling her to fetch the champagne herself, but he knew she would view it as a victory, that she was hoping to get a rise out of him, wanted to prove that he wasn't gentleman enough not to insult a lady. Or perhaps she simply wanted to ensure that he knew his place. As though he could ever forget it. He bathed every night, scrubbed his body viciously, but he could not scrape the grime of the streets off his skin. His family had embraced him, their friends had embraced him, but he still knew what he was, knew from whence he'd come. If he told Lady Ophelia the truth about everything that lurked in his past, she would no doubt pale and the moonbeams that served for her hair would curl and shrivel in horror.

From the ladies circling about, he sensed their anticipation on the air, perhaps even the hope that he would put *her* in *her* place. He'd never understood the cattiness that he sometimes witnessed between women. He knew Grace had received her share of jealousy because her immense dowry had made men trip over themselves to gain her favor. But Lady O for all her dislike of him had remained loyal to Grace, had served as his sister's confidante, had been a true friend. She didn't deserve his disdain or a set-down in front of ladies who might have wished Grace less attention.

He tilted his head slightly. "As you desire, Lady Ophelia." He turned to the others. "I'll be but a moment, ladies, and then we can continue our discussion regarding the most alluring fragrances."

For some reason they had devised a little game that resulted in his striving to name the flower that scented their perfume. It required a lot of leaning in along with inhaling on his part, and soft sighs on theirs.

Lady Ophelia had arrived on a cloud of orchids that teased and taunted, promising forbidden pleasures that in spite of his best attempts to ignore, lured him. Of all the women, why the devil did she intrigue him? Perhaps because she offered such a challenge, had erected walls that only the most nimble could scale in order to gain the real treasure behind them. He was adept at reading people, but for the life of him he'd never been able to read her.

Twisting on his heel, he headed to the table where champagne and sundry other refreshments were being poured. He was acutely aware of her gaze homed in on his back. He suspected if he looked over his shoulder, he would see her whispering with the other ladies, warning them off. Little did she realize that she would be doing him a favor if she could ensure that he was left in peace. He had committed to three more dances, and wouldn't disappoint his soon-to-be partners by heading to the gaming salon before he'd completed his obligations. Nor was he going to give Lady Ophelia the satisfaction of ruining his evening by sending him on errands. One glass was all she'd garner from him.

He didn't know why, two years ago at Grace's coming-out ball, he had asked Lady Ophelia to dance. He had thought she had grown into an exquisite creature, and she was Grace's friend. While she had often looked down her nose on him, she'd been a child then and he'd assumed she'd outgrown childish things. He couldn't have been more wrong. With a horrified look, she had given him a cut direct. Turned her back on him without even responding to his invitation. It had not spared his pride to realize that others had witnessed the rebuff.

Snatching up a flute of champagne from the table, he wended his way back through the throng, not at all surprised to find that she had moved on. He considered downing the bubbly brew but hard whiskey was more to his liking, and then he heard her seductive laughter. How the devil could an ice maiden have such a throaty, sensual laugh, a siren's song that arrowed straight to the groin?

Irritated with himself for being drawn to the sound, he glanced back over his shoulder to spy her flirting outrageously with the Duke of Avendale and Viscount Langdon. Their families were well-respected, powerful, and wealthy. He was not surprised to see two other ladies in the group. The gents were sought-after, but just as he tended to avoid social affairs, so did they. Marriage was so far in their distant future that they wouldn't be able to see it with a spyglass. They were here only because they were close to both Grace and Lovingdon. But now that the happy couple had departed, he suspected Avendale and Langdon would be headed elsewhere for their entertainment.

Unlike Lady O they would invite him to join them.

Ophelia's laughter reached him again, only this time when the sound went silent, her gaze landed on him like a huge stone, then dipped to the champagne, and her lips tipped upward in triumph, just before she wrinkled her nose as though she smelled something quite unpleasant. Her face settling once more into deceptive loveliness, she shifted her gaze back to Avendale, summarily dismissing Drake in the process.

Unfortunately for her, he was no longer quite so easily dismissed.

Ophelia knew a quick spurt of panic. Darling strode toward her with purpose in his step, his large hands—a workman's hands—dwarfing the flute he carried. His expression shouted that he was tossing down the gauntlet and she feared she might have misjudged his mood tonight, that managing him might be more challenging than she'd expected, but manage him she would. She would not be cowed, not by him, not by any other man for that matter.

He was a commoner who came from common beginnings. He might wear the outer trappings of a gentleman, but she had no doubt that deep down he was a scoundrel, with a scoundrel's ways, and a penchant toward sinful behavior.

She didn't know why that thought caused her to grow uncomfortably warm. It was the crowded room, the gaslit chandeliers, the layers of petticoats, and the tight corset. She certainly wasn't imagining those hands exploring her body. She was not of the streets. She was a lady. And ladies did not contemplate such things.

But as he neared, something within the black depths of his eyes twinkled as though he knew precisely where her errant thoughts had journeyed and was more than willing to serve as her companion on a sojourn into wickedness. He was not handsome, at least not classically so. His features were rugged, craggy, as though shaped by an angry god. His nose was too broad, his brow too wide. His jaw too square. She could see the beginning of shadow, bristles that hadn't the decency to wait until later to appear. Why was she wasting her time cataloguing each and every inch of him when she had lords aplenty willing to give her attention?

As he came to a halt in front of her, he gave his gaze free rein to take a leisurely stroll over her person. Breathing became difficult, and she had a horrid fear he would find her lacking. She drew back her shoulders. What did she care regarding his opinion of her, when his opinion was of no worth?

"Your champagne."

His rough, deep voice wove something dark and sensual around the words. She suspected he wasn't a silent lover, that he whispered naughty things into a woman's ear.

"You were so remarkably slow in retrieving it that I'm no longer of a mood to drink it."

"Surely you'll not deny yourself the pleasure of allowing these bubbles to tickle your palate."

He wrapped a wealth of meaning around the word *pleasure*. That he would be so bold as to speak to her with such disregard while others were near . . . it was not to be tolerated. But for the life of her, she could think of no witty rejoinder because he was studying her as though he could well imagine *her* tickling *his* palate.

"With your tarrying, I believe it has gone flat," she said, before turning her back on him. "Avendale, I believe you were discussing—"

Drake Darling had the audacity to wedge himself between her and the duke. His eyes were narrowed, his jaw taut. "Lady Ophelia, I must insist that you take the champagne."

"You, *boy*, are in no position to insist on anything where I am concerned."

His gloved finger tapped the side of the flute, while his gaze bored into hers, and she could fairly see the wheels of reprisal turning in his mind. She didn't know why she sought to provoke him, yet something about him unsettled her, always had. She wanted to put him in his place, to remind him—and herself—that he was beneath her. Her father had taken a belt to her backside and bare legs when he once caught her speaking with Darling. She'd been twelve at the time, but it wasn't a lesson easily forgotten. She was not to associate with anyone not of noble birth.

"So be it," he murmured, lifting the glass. He tilted back his head and downed the golden liquid in one long swallow. She could see only a bit of his muscles at his throat working, because a perfectly tied cravat hid the rest from view. But his neck, like the rest of him, was powerful. Moving aside the glass, he licked his lips, satisfaction glinting in his eyes. "Not at all flat. Quite pleasant, actually, like the kiss of a temptress."

Anger, hot and scalding, shot through her. He was mocking her, ridiculing her. It didn't matter that she had begun this little drama with her earlier request. He was supposed to scurry away when he realized she no longer had an interest in the champagne. He wasn't supposed to make her wonder if any lingered on his lips, if she might taste it there. "Boy—"

"It's been a good long while since I was a boy."

She angled her chin. "*Boy*, perhaps you would fetch us all some champagne."

"When hell freezes over, my lady."

He took a step toward her. She took a hasty step back. Triumph lit his eyes. Blast him. She would retreat no further.

A footman passed by, and without removing his gaze from hers, Darling set the flute on the silver tray the servant carried. Then took another long step forward.

She fought to hold her ground, but she could inhale his intoxicating fragrance now. Earthy and rich, the scent of tobacco or perhaps sin. He eased closer—

Half a step back.

"Dance with me," he said.

"I beg your pardon?"

"You heard me."

She angled up her chin. "I don't dance with commoners."

"What are you afraid of?"

"I don't fear anything."

"Liar."

She darted her gaze to the left, the right. Without her noticing, he had managed to maneuver her into the shadows of an alcove and was now barring her way. Those she had been visiting with earlier were nowhere about. She should have known that Avendale and Langdon would side with this blackguard and escort her friends onto the dance floor, into the gardens, or off for refreshments. Blast them! Still, she'd not be intimidated by the likes of Drake Darling. "You, sir, are despicable."

"And you're a haughty miss who needs to be taught a lesson."

"I suppose you think you're the man to do it."

His eyes darkened, his gaze dropped to her lips, and she found herself taking three quick steps back. "Don't you dare," she whispered, hating that her voice sounded more like a plea than a demand.

"You've been poking the tiger for some years now. You can't always expect him to remain docile."

He had the right of it there. She didn't know why she had continually singled him out. Perhaps because she sensed a darkness in him, one that called to her, one that was dangerous to welcome.

"You're making a spectacle of us," she pointed out.

"We're in the shadows. No one is paying us any heed at all."

Like some great hulking predator, he advanced on her. While she knew it to be unwise, she retreated farther into the alcove until her back hit the wall. Her heart beat out an unsteady tattoo. Within her gloves, her palms grew damp. "If you do anything untoward, I'll scream."

He laughed darkly. "And risk being caught with a guttersnipe? I think not."

"You're a black-hearted scoundrel."

"Which is exactly why I intrigue you. You're bored with all the fancy gents hovering around you. They'd never think of touching you with ungloved hands."

She caught her breath as his warm, rough hand cradled the left side of her face. Such a massive hand, his fingers easing into her hair, the edge of his palm against her jaw, the pad of his thumb stroking her cheek.

"You're bored with gentlemen running about doing your bidding," he continued.

"I'm not bored." She hated how breathless she sounded, as though she'd been running up a never-ending hill. Her chest felt tight, painful.

"You're spoiled because everyone gives you what you want. You've never had to work for anything. Not even a gentleman's attentions or affections."

"You know nothing at all about me." Her voice came out small, frightened. In her heart of hearts, she knew he wouldn't physically harm her, nor would he do anything to damage her reputation. Grace would never forgive him, and if she'd learned anything over the years, it was that he desperately wanted to please Grace and her family. But she feared he had the ability to glimpse into her shattered soul. Like called to like, dark to dark.

"I know more than you think, Lady Ophelia. Understand more than you can possibly imagine. You'll marry some proper lord, but I suspect you would very much like to waltz with the devil first."

"You're quite mistaken."

"Prove it."

Before she could respond, he settled his pliant mouth over hers. It was softer than she'd expected, hotter. His thumb grazed the corner of her mouth, over and over, as though it were part of the kiss. She felt his tongue outlining the seam between her lips, before tracing the outer edges. Once, twice, then returning to the center, but no longer content with the surface. With an insistence that should have frightened her, he urged her to part her lips. His tongue slid through, gliding over hers, velvet and silk. Inviting her to explore, to know the intimacies of his mouth as he was discovering hers.

She should have been repelled, horrified. Instead

she was entranced, drawn into sensations such as she'd never experienced. He was so terribly talented at eliciting delicious responses that began at the tips of her toes and swirled ever upward, a tingling of nerve endings, a lethargic warmth, that weakened her knees, her resolve to push him away.

She heard a deep groan, felt a vibration against her fingers and realized she was clutching the lapels of his coat. Clinging to Drake Darling was all that was keeping her from melting into a puddle of pleasure at his feet. This was merely a kiss, an ancient dance of mouths, yet it was proving to be her undoing.

He drew back, triumph glittering in his eyes. "Five more minutes and I could have you divested of your clothing and on your ba—"

Crack!

Her gloved palm made contact with his cheek, startling him, startling herself as well, but she would not allow him to make her feel as though she were a whore. "You are not only disgusting but you overvalue your talents. I didn't enjoy your touch, your kiss, not in the least."

"Your moans implied otherwise."

She lifted her hand to deliver another blow, but he snagged her wrist, his long, thick fingers wrapping firmly around her slender bones. He could snap them so easily. She was breathing heavily, while he seemed to have no trouble at all finding air.

"One slap is all you get, my lady. I would have ceased my attentions with the slightest of protest from you. You can't now be angry because you wanted what I was offering."

"I want nothing at all to do with you. Now unhand me."

His fingers slowly unfurled. Snatching her hand free,

she fisted it at her side. "You are no better than the muck I wipe off my shoes."

"Methinks the lady protests overmuch."

"May you rot in hell." She sidestepped around him, greatly relieved that he didn't attempt to stop her, slightly disappointed as well. Whatever was wrong with her? It was an odd thing to realize that with him she'd felt . . . safe. Completely, absolutely safe.

Which was ludicrous. He didn't like her. She didn't like him. He was simply striving to teach her a lesson. She could only hope that she'd taught him one: she wasn't a lady to be trifled with.

Chapter 2

"What were you doing talking with Drake Darling?" Somerdale asked as the carriage rolled through the quiet streets.

The ball would no doubt continue on until dawn, but Ophelia had been more than ready to leave after her encounter with Darling in the alcove. It appeared their little tryst had gone unnoticed, thank God. She'd lost all her enthusiasm for dancing, and had asked her brother to escort her home. He had gladly accommodated her request, no doubt because he was equally anxious to be off to his club.

Looking across the way at him, Ophelia couldn't read his expression yet his voice hinted at his disapproval. "I was thirsty. I asked him to fetch me something to drink."

"You would have been better served giving your attentions to a lord. Father placed an ungodly sum in a trust for you so that you would possess a dowry to entice the most influential lords. You need to set your sights on someone like Avendale. He's a duke for God's sake."

"With no plans to take a wife. He was only in attendance tonight because of his friendship with Lovingdon. And you need not worry. I have no interest in Darling as a suitor."

"See that you don't. I like the fellow well enough, but Father would roll over in his grave. He entrusted me with ensuring that you married well. I intend to see to that duty."

"Would you not be better served by seeing to your duty of marrying an heiress?"

It had been two years since their father's death and she knew the coffers were not as flush as they'd once been.

Somerdale glanced out the window. "I'd hoped for Grace. Now I must begin my search anew. It is a bothersome task."

Somerdale marrying Grace would have been a disaster. He needed someone not quite so rebellious.

"You don't think I find the search for a husband equally bothersome?"

"Bothersome it might be but it is a condition of your trust. Pity you can't gain access to it before you marry. We could have some jolly fun with the money." He turned his attention back to her. "But your husband will take it over once you're wed, and that will be the end of it."

"The funds become mine if I don't marry by my thirtieth birthday." Which was her plan. Much like Avendale, she had no wish to tie the marital knot. Oh, she made noises about it, even had both Grace and Minerva believing she wanted to marry for love, but the truth was that she wanted to be a spinster, never accountable to a man. No man would ever love her enough to forgive her for what she'd once done, and it was a secret she could not forever keep from a husband.

"If you want gowns for next Season you'd best

marry during this one," Somerdale said, cutting into her thoughts.

Her heart gave a little start. "Are things truly that dire?"

He shrugged. "Investments haven't turned out as I'd hoped. I considered taking a loan from your trust to see me through until my situation improves, had my solicitor look over the details, but your funds are locked up tighter than a drum. Only your marrying a commoner or your death would release them into my hands."

A shiver went through her. She was disconcerted to know he'd been searching for a way into her trust fund. That money was hers, her dowry, the key to her future, her freedom. Her father wanted her to have it. Somerdale would simply have to find a way to make do. "I most certainly am not going to marry a commoner. I doubt I'll marry anyone at all. And I certainly don't intend to die anytime soon."

"If you want to have pin money before you're thirty, you will marry some lord, even if he's on his deathbed. Honestly, Ophelia, I'm in quite the pickle here."

"That's why you were interested in Grace, because she had such a large dowry."

"Well, yes, of course."

He said it as though she were an idiot to think otherwise. "She wanted to marry for love."

"I assure you that if a woman puts coins in my coffers, I shall love her very much indeed."

"That's not the sort of love Grace wanted," she told her brother. "I'm ever so glad she didn't take your suit seriously."

"Well, I'm not glad at all. Lovingdon didn't need her fortune. He's got a bloody fortune of his own. It's not fair."

She could certainly enlighten him about things that

weren't fair. But surely he was exaggerating concerning his financial state. "How dire are things really?" she asked.

"Just don't purchase any new gowns," he said wearily.

"I don't see that I should be inconvenienced because you've mismanaged things." The carriage pulled to a stop in front of their residence. "Besides, I'm sure something will turn up."

Surely an heiress somewhere would take his suit seriously.

Somerdale chuckled low. "It had best happen quickly as creditors will soon be knocking. And you're quite right, sister, we wouldn't want you inconvenienced, now would we?"

Before she could respond, the footman opened the door and handed her down. Her brother followed.

"Aren't you going to the club?" she asked as they walked up the steps.

"Our conversation dimmed my desire to make merry. I think I'll simply drink myself into oblivion."

He opened the door and they entered the foyer.

"It won't make your troubles go away," she pointed out.

"But it will make me forget them for a time." Leaning in, he kissed her cheek. "Sleep well, Ophelia."

He'd taken two steps before she called out, "Somerdale?"

Stopping, he glanced back over his shoulder.

She released a long put-upon sigh. "I shan't purchase any new gowns, but I won't be happy about it."

He gave her a small smile. "I wouldn't expect you to be. And I'm quite sure you're right. Something will turn up. I simply need to give some thought to it."

She watched him head down the hallway. For a mere second she considered going after him, but she had her own troubles. Uppermost was how to make Drake Darling pay for the kiss he'd stolen. When next their paths crossed, she would give him a proper set-down. She would publicly snub him. She would tell Grace exactly what sort of rogue he was. Perhaps her family would boot him out, the scoundrel.

She made her way upstairs, and it wasn't until she reached the top that she realized she'd been searching for any lingering taste of him on her lips. How could someone so sinful taste so utterly delicious? Had he kissed others tonight? Probably. She hated the thought of it, of him in a shadowed corner with another lady, thrusting his fingers into her hair, taking possession of her mouth as though he would die without it.

Marching into her bedchamber, she decided she would need a bath tonight to get the scent of him off her. After jerking on the bellpull to summon her maid, she paced. She wasn't in the mood for a bath, yet it had to be done. Otherwise she would carry his aroma into her dreams. The last thing she wanted was to have him visiting her in sleep.

Turning at the sound of footsteps, she scowled at her maid. "Why must you dally? Assist me with my clothing. I feel a headache coming on. I'll want some warm milk before retiring."

"Yes, my lady."

It was nearly an hour later before Ophelia was in her nightclothes and curled on the settee, staring into the flames of a low fire. Colleen was having the warm milk prepared. Why was it taking so long? Staff moved as slow as honey around here. She would have to speak with the housekeeper about the matter again. Honestly, since her father's death the staff had gone to ruin. Somerdale really needed to be a bit more forceful, more along the lines of Darling.

She doubted Darling's servants lollygagged. If he even had servants. She doubted that he did or ever would. He no longer resided with Grace's family. From what she understood he lived in that gaming hell that he managed. She wondered if that was where he entertained ladies. She shook her head. She was not going to think about him entertaining.

Where was her warm milk? She came to her feet just as Colleen entered the room—empty-handed. "What the devil, Colleen? Do you not value your position here?"

"My apologies, my lady, but His Lordship sent me up to begin packing your things. He says you'll be leaving within the hour."

"It's half past eleven. I'm not going anywhere."

Colleen appeared terribly apologetic when she murmured, "He seems to think you are."

"Well, we shall certainly see about that."

Ophelia fairly flew down the stairs. Her brother was no doubt in a drunken stupor. Traveling this time of night made no sense at all. Even if he were in some sort of trouble with the creditors that resulted in a hasty departure, it could wait until a decent hour. And why should it involve her? She wasn't the one in a spot of difficulty.

As she neared the library, a footman opened the door. She stormed through—

Staggered to a stop as fear fissured through her. The door softly snicked behind her, closing her in with her worst nightmare.

Chapter 3

With his hands shoved into his coat pockets, Drake walked along the path that bordered the Thames. When a lad, he would come here and dig through the mud, searching for little treasures that might bring in some coin: a fancy button, a bit of silk, a shoe—which hadn't been much good without its match—a watch. The pocket watch had been his most precious find, but he'd made the mistake of showing it to his father, who had snatched it from his grasp. He often wondered how it had come to be in the sludge along the river.

He hadn't been the only child with hopes that the mud would reveal something of value. Mudlarks, they were called. Sometimes he still felt as though the mud clung to his skin, clung to his clothing.

Perhaps that was why Lady Ophelia Lyttleton managed to irritate him so, because when she gazed on him, he felt as though she saw the filthy child he'd been. The child who had been starved so he would remain thin enough to ease in through basement windows or climb down chimney flues in order to gain entry into a fine residence. He would slip carefully through the dark and open the door for his father—a great hulking brute.

Sometimes when Drake looked in a mirror, he saw his father standing there. He didn't possess the polished elegance of the aristocracy. No matter how well tailored his clothing, how refined his speech, how impeccable his manners, he could never forget that he came from the mud.

Although tonight, more so than usual, he was in danger of it sucking him back in.

What the deuce had he been thinking to kiss Lady O? She irritated the devil out of him, to be sure. Perhaps it was because she disliked him so much that he wanted to give her a satisfactory reason to think him unworthy of her. As far as he knew, he'd never treated her poorly. He could think of no reason for her dislike of him other than the fact of his birth. In her circles, he supposed that was enough.

Within that small alcove the shadows closed in around them, effectively creating an intimacy that hid differences. He and she were simply a man and a woman. And she had smelled so blasted enticing. He had been surrounded by assorted fragrances all evening, and yet her orchid scent called to him as no other did. He imagined her skin heated with passion, damp with desire causing the scent to bloom, unfold. Her skin had felt so silky beneath his roughened fingers. And those eyes, those damned green eyes that hinted at secrets.

He'd bet his soul she was a lady of complicated layers, and for some unfathomable reason he'd been tempted to unwrap them, to see what happened when he unsettled her calm façade, when he melted the ice.

What happened was that she slapped him. Deservedly so.

Now if he could just forget the flavor of her he might manage to ignore her in the future. Unfortunately, forgetting events in his past had never been his strong suit.

Stepping over the low barrier that marked the path, he walked down to the water's edge. Distant streetlamps barely illuminated this area. Wisps of fog were swirling about. He refrained from falling into old habits, of crouching down and digging his fingers into the cold, slimy muck. Tonight his soul felt as black as the river. All because of her. *Boy, fetch me some champagne.*

Boy. He'd wanted to demonstrate to her that he wasn't a boy, but in his approach to showing her, he hadn't exactly revealed himself as a gentleman either. Stupid pride, stupid—

A slight moan caught his attention. He immediately went on alert. It wasn't unusual for people to sleep out of doors. Not everyone had a roof over his head. Nor was it uncommon for thieves and troublemakers to be lurking about. But they didn't usually make noise to gain notice. Had someone been attacked before he arrived?

The mewling came again.

He took a cautious step in the direction he thought it came from, but the fog could distort sounds, disguise their origins. "Hello?"

He listened more intently. The water lapping at the shore. The splash of a fish. The scurry of tiny feet. A hard, rattling cough.

Taking two more steps toward the last sound, he cursed himself for not bringing a lantern, but he was familiar with this part of London. He could walk it blindfolded. Besides, he preferred being part of the darkness. As much as he might wish otherwise, he wasn't one for shedding light on things. Lady Ophelia had the right of it: his was blackguard's soul.

Catching sight of a mound that looked at odds with the surroundings, he quickened his pace. The weak moaning came again. It was a person, a woman, partway washed ashore, her skirts billowing behind her as the water rocked with the tide. Kneeling beside her in the darkness, he could tell only that her hair appeared to be pale, although it was difficult to know for certain as she was covered in mud. He touched her shoulder. It was ice-cold. He gave her a small shake. "Madam?"

Nothing. Not a sound, not any sort of reaction or response.

Glancing quickly around, he saw no sign of anyone else in the vicinity. Pressing his fingers just below her jaw, he felt her thready pulse. If she were to stand any chance at all of surviving, he had to get her warm as soon as possible.

Quickly, he removed his coat and draped it over her, hoping some of the warmth from his body would seep into hers. Working his arms beneath her, he struggled to stand with the mud sucking at her, seeking to reclaim her, to hold her captive. He'd not have it. He'd rescued a good many trinkets from the banks of the Thames, but he'd never rescued a woman. He wasn't about to let her die now that he had recovered her.

She was soaked through. How had she come to be in the river? It was a question to be answered later, when she was recovered, and by damn she would recover. He cursed himself for not having a carriage about, but he'd been in the mood for a long walk. Fortunately, his residence was not too far, but with the water and mud, she weighed as much as an elephant. He considered taking a moment to divest her of her clothing, but how would he explain a naked woman should he be stopped by a constable? And where was a bloody constable when he needed one?

He could only hope that his chest was providing her with some much needed heat. She murmured something unintelligible.

"It's all right, sweetheart, we're almost there. Won't be long now."

He quickened his pace, lengthened his stride, for once grateful for his size and bulk. In spite of the weight, in spite of the distance, he had the stamina to cover the ground rapidly. Because of the late hour, no one was about. They were on their own: he and she. He'd not let her down.

Concentrating on the task at hand, rather than the great distance he needed to cover, he began mapping out his plan. Get her to his residence, get her warm, send for the physician William Graves. A woman found in a man's residence would be compromised but Graves would be discreet. He was an old friend of the family. He could be trusted.

The residence came into view and Drake released a sigh of relief because she was still breathing, although tiny shudders had begun traveling through her. Hastily he opened the gate, strode down the short path, and ascended the small set of steps. With some difficulty, he managed to retrieve his key and open the door. Once through, he kicked it closed behind him and climbed the stairs to the next floor where four bedchambers awaited. Fortunately, he'd left the gaslights burning low before he'd gone out. Having only recently purchased the residence, he'd found little time to set things to right. Only one room contained a bed: his.

He went into it now, crossed over to the massive bedstead, and gently laid her down. "Sweetheart?"

He patted her muddy face, but she failed to respond. She was cold, so damned cold. As impersonally as possible, he shed her of her clothing, surprised by the fine quality of the material and handiwork. She was no commoner, no resident of the streets. A lord's mistress, perhaps. One who had fallen into disfavor.

As petticoats, chemise, and stockings were flung to the floor, he noted a few bruises but nothing appeared broken. To look at her, it might seem that she'd merely gone for a swim.

When every stitch was removed, he covered her with sheets and blankets. He marched over to the fireplace and set about preparing a blazing fire, in hopes of warming the room and her. It seemed to be working for the room, as he found himself beginning to perspire. He removed his jacket and waistcoat, tossing them onto the floor, before returning to the bed. It didn't appear she'd moved at all.

He should fetch Graves, but he was loath to leave her alone. He could awaken a neighbor, he supposed, but his odd hours had prevented him from meeting any of them. He had yet to hire any servants because he didn't spend enough time here to warrant the expense. Most of his time was spent at Dodger's Drawing Room. He had apartments there, and they served him well when he worked long hours. But he'd purchased this place because he'd felt a need to own something that spoke of permanence.

He walked over to the washbasin, picked up the pitcher, and set it before the fire so the water could begin warming. Then he grabbed a cloth and the washbasin and returned to the bed. Carefully he sat on the edge, dipped the linen into the water already in the basin, and wrung it out. Gently moving aside her snarled hair, he began to wipe the mud from her face. An oval face, not round or square, but long and slender. A dainty, delicate chin. High cheekbones and a narrow nose that tipped up slightly at the end.

His hand stilled as he stared at the features his ministrations had revealed. He knew those features, he knew that face. What the devil?

He had just rescued Lady Ophelia Lyttleton.

Gently, he patted her cheek. "Lady Ophelia?"

"No," she murmured. "I don't want you to touch me. No. Don't!" She began flailing about.

Quickly, he stepped back. "No, I won't touch you."

His words must have reached wherever she was, because she instantly calmed, her breathing growing shallow, her face easing into soft lines that camouflaged the arrogance that usually marred what would have otherwise been pleasant features. Even in sleep, she seemed capable of recognizing his voice, remembering that his touch revolted her, that he was beneath her, something to be scraped off the bottom of her shoe.

The disgust that fissured through him almost had him contemplating the pleasure he would derive by tossing her back into the Thames.

Shifting his gaze to her pile of clothes on the floor, he realized that he needed to try to get some of the mud off them. She'd not be able to get back into the stiff skirts and petticoats if he didn't wash them. Ophelia would no doubt throw a tantrum because he'd touched her underdrawers. Blast it! He did wish that he'd already hired a servant to see to such mundane tasks, to put his house in order. Of course, if he did have a servant, as soon as Ophelia awoke, she'd be ordering the poor girl about—issuing commands, finding fault with the temperature of the bathwater or the crispness of the toast or the softness of the egg. So simple to judge when never having walked in a servant's shoes.

He turned his attention back to Ophelia. She lay as still as death, as quiet as a grave. He should fetch Grace, see if she could determine what her dear friend was doing rolling around in the muck, but it was Grace's wedding night, and while she might be happy to help him, he suspected her husband would spend his time without his wife in his bed by contemplating inventive ways to make Drake suffer. No, one did not disturb a couple on their wedding night for a spoiled lady who had no doubt simply carelessly slipped from a pleasure barge into the Thames. Probably full of drink, lost her balance, and over she went.

Tomorrow morning would be soon enough to bother Grace. Except they would be leaving for their wedding trip at first light. Heading to the continent for a couple of weeks, as he understood it. No, this matter wasn't so dire that he needed to upset their plans. But perhaps he should risk fetching Graves.

It had never bothered him before to reside in solitude here, but suddenly he found himself wishing he had an entire army, or at least someone who could deliver a missive for him. He contemplated shaking her, but he didn't want to upset her again. Probably best just to let her sleep.

Quite suddenly her eyes fluttered open, and he stared into the green depths, expecting a slap, a screech, a horrified outburst at finding herself in his bedchamber.

Instead she blinked, blinked, glanced around slowly before bringing her gaze back to his. In spite of her prone position, she managed quite well to tilt up that pert little nose of hers. "What am I doing here?"

Her tone fitted her so well: demanding, entitled, accustomed to being answered.

"I fished you out of the river," he stated, very much wishing that he'd left her there. He doubted she'd appreciate his rescuing her—which begged the question: Why the deuce had she been in need of rescue? "How did you come to be there anyway?"

She pressed the fingertips of her left hand to her temple and squeezed her eyes shut. "I don't know."

"How can you not know?"

Shaking her head slightly, she opened her eyes. "My head hurts."

"I haven't had a chance to examine it."

"Are you a physician?" she asked pointedly.

He scowled at her. Her attempt to bring him to task was quite annoying at a time such as this when he was striving to be helpful. Could she never put the differences between them aside? "Of course not, but I can feel a bump if it's there. Let me see."

The haughtiness seemed to drain from her. "All right. Yes."

Yes? She was going to willingly let him touch her? He supposed she realized she really hadn't a choice. Carefully he moved his fingers through the tangled mess of her hair, gently kneading his fingers over her scalp. He grazed a knot. She winced. "Sorry," he said. "You do have a lump there. A small one." He withdrew his fingers. "It doesn't appear to be bleeding."

"That's good, isn't it?"

"No blood is always good. I've hit my head before. I should think you would be fine after a bit."

She glanced around again, more slowly this time, as though she were cataloguing each and every imperfection: the faded and peeling paper on the walls which he had yet to replace, the crack in the mantel which he had yet to repair, the absence of rugs or draperies or paintings. Everything he planned to set right when he found the time. Her eyes narrowed, and he braced himself for her caustic comment regarding all that was lacking. "This room . . . it doesn't feel right, doesn't seem as though it would be mine."

Staring at her, he tried to make sense of her words. Perhaps the knot he'd felt was more dangerous than he'd surmised because she seemed terribly confused. "Of course it's not yours. It's mine."

Jerking her head toward him, she stared at him, her brow so deeply furrowed that had her head not already been hurting, he was fairly certain it would have been now. "Why would you bring me here? Who are you?"

What game was she playing? "You know who I am. Drake Darling."

"I fear you're quite mistaken. I don't know you," she whispered.

"That makes no sense. You've known me for a while now."

Slowly she shook her head and tears welled in her eyes. He was not one to be generally disconcerted, but a weeping female tended to be his undoing. Neither of the most important women in his life—the Duchess of Greystone nor her daughter, Grace—tended to weep. They were strong, courageous women, so when it came to dealing with tears, he was at a loss. He was especially at a loss when it came to offering comfort to Lady O. The last thing he'd ever envisioned himself doing was wanting to console her, but at that precise moment it was all he wanted; he wanted it more than anything else in the world because he could not abide the tears. He wanted her to feel safe and secure. While she would no doubt castigate him, he decided to use a form of her name that he had on occasion heard Grace use. Surely she would find comfort in the familiar endearment.

"Phee—"

"Phee?" A question. "Phee." An answer. A distance in her expression as though she were striving to snatch on to something that was just beyond reach. "Phee. It's familiar." She nodded, then looked directly at him. "That's my name, isn't it?"

Something was terribly amiss. Very slowly he came

off the bed and moved to its foot, putting distance between them as he tried to decipher precisely what was going on here. "What do you remember?"

A crease between her brows, she lolled her head from side to side. "I don't remember . . . anything."

Chapter 4

Drake Darling studied her as though she were some sort of curiosity, an odd contraption discovered in a curio shop that he wanted to pick apart and examine. He wrapped a large hand around the bedpost. From her position, he appeared to be a giant of a man. He furrowed his brow, his lips set in a grim line. "You're no doubt simply disoriented from your plunge in the river. Take a moment. Think. You can't have forgotten everything."

He spoke with such authority, as though he had the power to draw her memories from the dark abyss into which they'd fallen. He was correct, of course. She should be able to recall something, anything, but it was as though she were knocking on a tin wall that did little more than echo through an empty chamber. "I recall waking up."

"This morning?"

He sounded so incredibly hopeful, but she couldn't share in his hope. "No, just now. Here, in this bed."

"Before that?"

Shaking her head, she thought she should have been frightened of this man. She didn't know him, yet something about him was familiar, and she instinctively knew that she was safe with him. But how did she know that? How did she know this wasn't her bedchamber when she didn't remember what her bedchamber looked like?

How could she know things—bed, window, blankets, fire—and yet not know her own name? But she knew she should have a name. Phee had sounded right—and yet it didn't. She was confused and terrified and flummoxed. It appeared he might be experiencing the same emotions—well, other than the terrified. He didn't look to be a man who would be afraid of anything and it had little to do with his immense size. He just had that air about him, a man who understood who he was. She wanted the same knowledge regarding herself. Who the devil was she?

He said she'd been in the river. Why would she be in the river? A cold shiver went through her and her head began to throb unmercifully. She didn't want to think about the river. She didn't want to think about anything beyond the man standing at the foot of the bed.

He possessed such large shoulders that she thought he could carry a heavy burden with no trouble whatsoever. She thought about how he might have carried her here, cradled within those strong arms. Quite suddenly, she realized that beneath the covers she was without clothing. She clutched the blankets to her chest. "My clothes."

"I had to remove them. They were drenched and muddy."

"You took liberties."

"Would you have preferred to catch your death?"

No, but she didn't bother to voice the word. She was certain his question has been rhetorical. How did she know that word? How did she know any words? How did she know that it was wrong for him to remove her clothes? How did she know him? In what capacity? What was he to her? What was she to him? And why was she not certain she wanted answers?

She plowed her fingers into her hair, stilled when she encountered something sticky that caused her skin to crawl. "What is this?"

"Mud. I was striving to wipe it off but you seemed to prefer that I not touch you."

His voice contained a hard edge, as though she'd offended him. She was not up to determining his moods. She barely understood her own. Yet she became incredibly aware now of the muck on her face and neck. Holding out her arms, examining her hands, she saw the black filth clearly. "A bath. I must have a bath. See that it's prepared immediately. Hot water, a shade past warm."

He arched a dark brow. "A shade past warm."

Yes, that was how she liked her baths. She knew that. What else did she know? "My clothing. Have someone scrape off the mud and get it dried as quickly as possible. As you seem to know who I am, I assume you can see me to my residence." She glared at him. "Why are you still standing there? Tend to matters posthaste!"

His shadowed jaw tautened and a muscle jerked in his cheek. "As you desire."

Her stomach quivered. He'd said those words to her before. Dark and dangerous, a promise that had her looking away. What was he to her? A lover? Why else would he seem so comfortable with her being naked in his bed? Why was she so comfortable with it? Why wasn't she trembling and shaking?

She was acutely aware of his footsteps echoing through the sparsely furnished room. Heard the rustle of fabric as he swept up her clothing from the floor. The slam of the door as he exited.

No, he wasn't her lover. If he had been, he would have held her hand, caressed her brow, wrapped his arms around her, and held her close. He would have done all in his power to comfort her. She would have been grateful for his touch. She wouldn't have implied anything else.

She rubbed her brow. How could she know all of that, but not know *who* she was? It made no sense whatsoever. What was she doing in the river? Did she know how to swim? Yes, she believed she did, but the windows revealed the darkness beyond. Why was she out alone at night? Had she been alone? Had there been someone else?

The pain in her head sharpened, was like a knife jabbing, jabbing, jabbing. She didn't want to think about it, try to figure it out now. It would come to her eventually. She was certain of it. Once she was returned home, ensconced in familiar surroundings, wrapped in the bosom of her family—

Another sharp pain at the thought of her family. Family, family. Who were they? Were they out looking for her? Did they care? Of course they cared. She was loved . . . wasn't she?

Everything would be answered soon enough, once he took her home. All would become clear and make sense. She wouldn't have this dark void of nothingness, she wouldn't feel as though she were moving through a dense fog. Her head would cease its abominable throbbing.

Casting aside the covers, she felt a shiver course through her as she caught sight of her legs, caked in mud. He had put her in the bed filthy, dirty. What sort of man was he not to care about basic cleanliness?

And how was it that she supposedly knew him but had no memory of him?

He did not strike her as someone easily forgotten. Nothing about him appeared soft and gentle. She suspected he was a hard man. He had been quite short with her, at first anyway, until he'd realized that she was having difficulty remembering. Then he'd been a bit more sympathetic until she'd asked for the bath. She didn't understand him, wasn't certain she wanted to.

She crossed over to the wardrobe and opened the door. It contained hardly anything at all. Was he a beggar, this man? No, he possessed a residence, knew her. She would not consort with someone of a lesser station.

Stilling, she wondered where that thought had come from. Lesser station. Who was she? A princess? A queen? Perhaps he was a guard. He'd rescued her from the river because he was required to do so. It didn't matter who he was. It only mattered that she arrive home as quickly as possible and strive to figure things out.

From a hook, she removed a coat. A large, heavy coat. His coat. She slipped it on, and it provided immediate warmth, made her feel as though she were now shielded. Gliding over to the fire, she welcomed the heat toying with her toes. She could hear activity in the next room. The servants no doubt preparing her bath.

She tried to latch on to an image of servants, but she couldn't. Some things she seemed to know, to instinctually understand. Why couldn't she recall everything about her life?

Tears stung her eyes and she blinked them back. She would not cry. She was not allowed to cry. It indicated weakness, allowed others to take advantage. She'd not cried in years, not since—

Oh God, her head. That horrid insistent throbbing again. Exhaustion suddenly claimed her. But there were no stuffed chairs, no sofas for curling in. Spotting a hard-backed wooden chair against the wall, she dragged it nearer to the fire and sat with a heavy thud. Not at all ladylike to drop down like a sack of flour.

She didn't want to think, didn't want to question the things she knew and the things she didn't.

She focused instead on the man. He was quite beautiful, in a rough and rugged sort of way—like the Cornish coast. How did she know the Cornish coast?

She fought down the fear that threatened to bubble up and consume her. She mustn't show fear—ever. She knew that much as well.

Be strong. Never show any weakness, any doubt, any shortage of confidence.

Concentrating on the writhing flames, she struggled to regain her bearings. A masculine scent wafted around her. She'd been near it before, surrounded by it. It elicited a strange fluttering in her stomach, a wild pounding of her heart. Lifting up the collar, she pressed her nose against it. Drake. What was he to her that she could be at once wary and yet trust him implicitly?

She wanted to remember his role in her life. He seemed the only tangible thing at the moment. Why was he taking so long to return to her? A thousand questions were popping up in her mind. He could answer them all.

A quiet rap sounded at the door. Slowly she rose, drew back her shoulders, and angled her chin. She refused to display in any manner that she was frightened. That this big gaping hole where her life had been was threatening to swallow her. "Come in."

The door opened, Drake stepped in, and the room shrank. Just like that. He dominated it with his presence. Not only his size, but his bearing. He was not one to be trifled with. He owned this room, this residence, but more than that, he owned himself.

How marvelous would that feel not to answer to anyone?

She furrowed her brow. To whom did she answer? An image flashed through her mind but she couldn't snag it long enough to examine it, to identify it.

"I have a bathing room." He pointed toward a door near the fireplace. "The bath is ready."

"It took the servants long enough," she said, walking over to the door and opening it. "I daresay you mollycoddle them."

Assailed by the scent, the masculinity of it, she hesitated a heartbeat before strolling into the room. It was prudent to never hint at one's doubts with a misstep, sloping shoulders, averted eyes. Rules beaten into her until they were second nature and demanded that they not be forgotten, unlike other aspects of her life.

She was astounded by the enormity of the tub awaiting her. Had she ever seen one so large? But then it would have to be to accommodate his form. She didn't want to imagine his long limbs sprawled over the expanse of copper or his movements causing ripples in the water.

She didn't know why she was suddenly hesitant to bathe. It seemed obscene to sit in a tub that belonged to someone else. Surely she had her own, but it wasn't here, and she couldn't very well travel through London caked in mud.

Her head came up. She spun around and came up short. He was leaning against the doorjamb, his arms crossed over his broad chest, his shirt unbuttoned to reveal a light sprinkling of hair. He'd rolled up his sleeves. His forearms were bronzed and sinewy, muscles bunched, veins ropy. She saw strength there. Power. She wanted to run her hands over those arms, have them close around her as she rested her head on his chest.

Comfort. He would provide immense comfort. But it would be entirely inappropriate.

"Are we in London?" she asked.

"Yes."

"It's strange—the things I know and the things I don't."

His brow furrowed. "You still don't recall anything about your life?"

Slowly she shook her head. "No, but I'm certain it will all become clear when I'm returned to the bosom of my family."

Another pain ricocheted through her head. They were becoming quite bothersome. Doing her best to ignore it, she tiptoed her fingers through the water. "It's too hot. I shall have to wait for it to cool. Rather inconvenient. Have the girl removing the mud from my clothing bring the items up as soon as they are ready. Meanwhile, fetch a girl to help me wash my hair."

Glancing over her shoulder, she saw that he'd not moved a muscle, other than the one along his jaw, which looked as though it had turned to granite. "Don't just stand there as though you have all day. Fetch the girl, and then have a carriage readied."

"You're the *girl*."

"I beg your pardon?"

He unfolded his arms, inch by inch, before prowling over to her like some big hulking cat. "To put it bluntly, Phee, you're the servant here."

Chapter 5

Her eyes widened in horror. Her jaw dropped. For a moment there, he was afraid she might swoon, and he'd have to lunge for her before she hit the floor.

God help him, but it took every bit of control he could muster not to burst out laughing and ruin the moment. The startled look on her face . . . he would have paid a hundred quid to see it. No, a thousand, a million.

He didn't know what had possessed him to tell her she was the servant. He'd been worried about her as he'd prepared the bath, working as quickly as possible to get it done, so she would be more comfortable, so she could be clean once again, so he could deliver her to her family—

And for his trouble, not even a thank-you. Not a hint of gratitude. Only more demands. *Fetch this, fetch that. The water isn't to my liking. Why are you so slow? I am far too important to have to wait for anything or anyone.*

She kept her nose stuck in the air and never looked down long enough to notice the masses, to appreciate that the luxury in which she lived was provided by the hard work of others. She awoke to draperies drawn, fires crackling, heated water waiting. Clothes were pressed, beds were warmed, food was served.

Suddenly he'd had quite enough of her. Spoiled, pampered, entitled. Bored.

Because she might have very nearly drowned earlier, the unkind thoughts now pricked his conscience, but only slightly, certainly not enough to cause him to retract his words. Let her mull on them for a bit, let her rethink her place in this world for a few more hours, until morning, and then he would return her home. It would take that long at least for her clothing to dry sufficiently so she could put it back on.

Although it would be somewhat damp still so she would complain about it. He didn't have a carriage to be prepared for her comfort so they would have to walk for a bit and find a hansom. She wouldn't be pleased about that. He doubted she had ever ridden in one. She might not remember who she was, but it seemed, by God, that she remembered *what* she was.

"What do you mean?" she asked.

"It means, sweetheart, that you are my housekeeper."

She skittered away from him, around the edge of the tub, stopping on the other side as though putting distance between them would change his words. He didn't want to consider how vulnerable and innocent she appeared with his coat draped around her, that his body would swallow her up as easily. He wasn't going to think of bare, tiny toes or how he might have rubbed them if she weren't such a shrew. Shakespeare would have adored her.

Dazed, she shook her head. "That can't be right. I would know—"

"You don't even know your name. Why would you know you're a servant?"

She took in her surroundings, and he could see her striving desperately to remember them. Then her chin came up so quickly that he was surprised she didn't snap her neck. "Why was I telling you to fetch things if I'm the one who does the fetching?"

"Wishful thinking on your part? Perhaps this entire I-can't-remember business is your attempt to avoid what you gave your word you would do: see after the care of my residence."

He didn't know why he was continuing this charade, only that he was taking perverse pleasure in unsettling her. Not very gentlemanly on his part, but then hadn't she accused him earlier of being a blackguard and a scoundrel? He was only striving to meet her expectations. She didn't seem to be suffering physically from her swim in the Thames. As for her memory, she didn't seem to be suffering from the loss of it either. He was fairly certain it would return any moment. She was suffering from temporary confusion. Nothing more.

"A *servant*?" she repeated, sounding as though she were on the verge of casting up her accounts at the mere utterance of the word. "*Your* servant?"

"Quite right. I suggest you carry on with your bath. You may sleep in my bed for the remainder of the night as it's more comfortable than yours. In the morning we'll discuss the matter further." *In the morning, I'll confess to you my wickedness and take you home.*

Before he changed his mind and confessed all now, he spun on his heel to leave.

"No, wait!"

Glancing back, he refused to feel guilty at the sight of her distress. He knew she cared only for her own needs, never worried about anyone else's suffering. He was quite certain he wasn't the only one she'd abused with that tart tongue of hers. Besides, it wasn't as though he were taking a lash to her.

With a huff, she shoved up the sleeves of his coat. They fell back into place, which apparently made it extremely awkward to wring her hands, although she managed. "I can't be a servant."

"Why not?"

"It doesn't feel . . . right. Yes, that's it. It simply doesn't feel correct. What are my duties precisely?"

"Everything. You scrub my floors, prepare my meals, polish my boots, press my shirts, make my bed, prepare my bath. Do anything else that I determine needs doing."

"Little wonder I leaped into the Thames," she muttered.

"Did you leap in?" he asked, taking a step toward her, wondering if the shock of his earlier words had brought her memory back. "Do you remember it now?"

"No, but I must have. How else might I have gotten in there?"

"An accident. You slipped."

She rubbed her brow. "It doesn't matter. That's the past. It's now that's important. This"—she swept out her arms—"can't be my life."

"Why not? It's a good life. As I'm sure you'll remember once you're properly rested. Sleep as late as you like. Under the circumstances I'll not dock your pay. As it appears you need reminding of your duties, we'll discuss them later tomorrow."

He walked out, closing the door behind him. He didn't want to contemplate her removing his coat and climbing into his tub. The water would no doubt be less than warm by now. Perhaps he wouldn't take her home when she awoke.

Perhaps he would treat her to one day of walking in a servant's shoes. Only for a day. No reason for her family to suffer overly long, worrying over her absence.

Chuckling darkly, shaking his head, he headed down the stairs. He would have to do what he could to remove the mud from her clothes. He stopped. If he returned her clothing to her, its quality would alert her that she wasn't a servant. She seemed to recall the basic things. He would have to make a hasty trip out to the missions at first light to locate some appropriate clothing.

Was he really going to continue the farce?

It was ludicrous to even consider it. She was the daughter of an earl. Grace would never forgive him for heaping misery upon her friend. But then no one ever need know. Understanding Lady Ophelia as he did, he knew she would never reveal what had transpired during her absence from Society. Even if her memory never returned full force, once he returned her home and she realized the truth about her place in the world, she would once again embrace it with the arrogance that so characterized her existence.

Where was the harm in giving her a glimpse into another sort of life?

As she lowered herself into the water, Phee discovered it was less than warm now. She regretted that she'd been distracted by Drake's revelations and delayed her bath.

A servant. She was a servant. Worse, she was his servant. His sole servant apparently. It seemed so terribly . . . not quite right. She couldn't see herself scrubbing floors and dealing with filth.

Gathering up the long tangled strands of her hair, she wondered how one went about washing it. Shouldn't it be a task that she would instinctually know how to accomplish? Surely she had washed her hair numerous times. Yet she envisioned hands washing it for her. Perhaps it was merely a dream she had—to be pampered and spoiled. As he'd implied, wishing for a very different life than the one she had.

She immersed herself completely beneath the surface. Water lapping. A roaring in her ears. Panic took hold. Air, no air. She was going to die!

Springing up, she gasped, greedily gulped air into her lungs until they ached, until she couldn't fill them anymore. Tucking her bent knees against her chest, wrapping her arms around her legs, she fought to squelch the shivering. She wasn't cold, but she had been. In the water, in the Thames. How had she come to be there? Shouldn't she know? Had something horrid happened that resulted in her being there? Was that why she didn't remember, because she didn't want to remember? Did it have anything to do with Drake Darling?

What sort of name was that anyway? Harsh on the one hand, soft on the other. A name that rather seemed to describe him. He was gentle and concerned one moment, harsh and unyielding the next, as though she'd done something to anger him, or at the very least irritate him. She had the sense that he didn't much like her. Then why not dismiss her? Why keep her on as a servant?

Because her work was exemplary? It had to be. She wasn't one to settle for less. She knew that. Shoddy work was not to be tolerated. It was the reason behind her pique for having to wait so long for the bath.

Snagging the soap, she began scrubbing at her hair, her body. Now noticing a bruise here and there. And aches, so many aches. As though she'd been battered. She supposed she had been by the river currents and banks. As the bathwater darkened, became filthier, she started to call for a servant—

And stopped. Why did it seem a natural thing to do? To order someone to empty the bath and replenish it with clear water so she could bathe again? And again and again. Until all the grime had been scrubbed off.

But according to Drake there was no one to call. She certainly didn't want him coming to assist her. She didn't feel quite clean, but it would have to do. Stepping out of the tub, she grabbed a towel and rubbed it vigorously over her body, striving to make herself feel cleaner. Why couldn't she feel clean?

She wasn't quite certain that the sense of uncleanliness all had to do with the mud. It was her, something about her. Something she had no desire to explore.

Clutching the towel around her, she approached the mirror cautiously, not quite trusting what it might reveal. She spied the hair first. It was wrong, so terribly wrong. Tangled and wild, the blond locks cascading past her shoulders. She couldn't recall ever brushing it, but surely she had. It should be pinned up. Yes, that was how it should look. Neat, tidy, with a few curls left free to frame her face.

Leaning in, she studied her features more closely. She recognized the green eyes, the nose, the chin, the cheeks. Why couldn't she remember more? It seemed the harder she tried to recall the facts about herself, the more elusive they became, weaving in and out like fog that couldn't be grasped.

Glancing down, she spied the silver brush. His brush, no doubt. She could see a few stray black hairs woven through the bristles. Such an intimacy, to use his brush on her hair, but she didn't see that she had a choice. She didn't know where her brush might be or if she even had one. She thought the not knowing so much might drive her mad.

Wrapping her hand around the brush, she lifted it. It

was a good solid weight. Certainly not cheaply made. How did she know that?

Using it, she struggled to work out the tangles. It felt odd to be the one doing it. She had no recollection of ever managing her hair before. But surely she had. She wasn't a barbarian to run around unkempt. When the tangles were conquered, when the brush finally slid easily through her hair, she plaited the long strands into a single braid. She wore her hair in a braid when she went to bed, that she knew. She also knew with absolute certainty that she did not sleep in the altogether. Where would she find a nightdress?

After slipping on the heavy coat, she cautiously opened the door and gazed out. He wasn't lurking in the bedchamber, thank goodness. Relief, as well as exhaustion, slammed into her. Then something more. The bed she'd left in a rumpled state was now tidy, one corner turned down. As it should be, waiting for her to slip between the covers.

Lifting the blankets, she examined the sheets. No mud or muck remained. He'd replaced the dirty linens with clean ones. Unfortunately, he'd not left a night-dress for her. She feared if she went in search of one and encountered him that she would become unsettled all over again.

She padded over to the bureau, opened a drawer, and peered inside, grateful to find what she'd been searching for. Considering his immense size, compared with her smaller one, she decided that one of his neatly folded shirts would suffice. Shrugging off the coat, allowing it to fall to the floor, she slipped one of the linen shirts over her head. The material was incredibly soft. It was not the attire of someone from the lower classes.

Where had that thought come from?

Of course it made sense. He owned a residence, had

a servant. She was that servant. That admission refused to take hold. It seemed to go against any rational thought. Yet he would have no reason to lie.

With a sigh, she wandered over to the bed, climbed onto it with a bit of effort—why didn't he have steps? He didn't need them with his astonishing height. Did women never visit his bed? She supposed if they did, that he lifted them up and set them on it. Yes, she could see that.

He would have carried her, would have set her in the bed. Had she been standing, she might have lost her balance as her knees went weak. Instead, she brought the covers over her and curled onto her side. He'd removed her clothes, had quite possibly touched her, and yet . . .

She didn't believe he'd taken advantage. Something about him spoke of honor. Or maybe it was all simply wishful thinking on her part. She was weary of striving to make sense of all this. She wanted only to sleep.

When she woke up, perhaps she would discover it was all just a dream.

It wasn't a dream. She awoke in the same bed within the same bedchamber with the same man standing at the far bedpost. She wanted to object with outrage at his intrusion, but it was his room, his bed, his house. And she was his servant. He was well within his rights to do as he pleased.

"How are you feeling?" he asked.

Lost, confused, terrified, not that she would confess any of that. Instinctually, she knew that she needed to keep all her feelings to herself, was in the habit of doing just that, of never revealing anything beyond a confident façade. "Quite well, thank you."

"No hurts, no pains?"

"A bit of soreness here and there, but nothing with which I cannot live."

"Your memories?"

She furrowed her brow, wished she could keep that bit of information to herself as well, but she needed him to help her remember. "It's as though I didn't exist before I awoke in your bed."

He didn't move, simply studied her, and yet she thought she sensed hesitation in him. Concerning what, she hadn't a clue, but then that seemed to be the norm for her. Not having an inkling regarding anything of importance. How could her existence, her past, be wiped clean? She considered hitting him with a barrage of questions, but she wasn't certain she wanted to learn the answers.

"Are you hungry?" he asked.

Now that he'd asked, she realized—

"Quite famished actually. Do fetch my breakfast as quickly as possible."

A corner of his mouth curled upward before settling back down, and she thought she detected satisfaction in those black eyes. Familiar eyes. She could see herself gazing into them, becoming lost in the obsidian depths. Her own eyes were such a vivid green, a pretty color, but there was nothing beautiful about the shade of his. They spoke of dark secrets and darker journeys. A harsh life, even.

"I suppose I can't be in a pique," he drawled, "that you forget you fetch *my* breakfast."

Her stomach growled, no doubt protesting the words as sharply as her mind was. "Haven't you a cook?"

"I'm a bachelor. I have no need for an abundance of servants. You suffice quite nicely."

If she weren't still abed, she'd have sunk onto a chair or the floor. While he'd told her last night that she was the servant of the residence, she hadn't realized the true extent of her duties. She prepared meals?

"However," he continued, "as you endured some sort of horrendous ordeal last night, I took the liberty of preparing a repast for you. I wasn't quite certain if you'd have recovered enough to resume your duties today. I'm quite relieved to see that you appear up to snuff. Unfortunately, the clothing you wore last night was not salvageable. I brought some others in here for you." He indicated the chair and she saw the pile of clothing, folded neatly, stacked high. "While you get dressed, I'll wait in the hallway, then give you a tour to help familiarize you with the residence and your responsibilities once more. Don't dally. The food grows cold."

He spun on his heel and headed for the door.

"Wait!" Everything was happening too fast, and it all seemed so frightfully wrong.

Coming to an abrupt halt, he faced her. "Do you not remember how to put on your clothes? Do you require my assistance?"

An image of him lifting his shirt over her head flashed through her mind. Him handing her each item, holding them out when she needed to step into them. His hands following the path of drawers and chemise being placed over her body. His long fingers tying the laces. His knuckles skimming over the swells of her breasts. Heat, scalding heat, infused her, and she suspected she was blushing as red as an apple.

"No, I'm quite certain I can manage," she said, her voice sounding far too small. She cleared her throat. "I just . . . I don't know if I'm up to resuming my duties."

"Take it slowly today. Rest when you need to. I'm not a brute, but I do expect some results. So hurry along now. I should think you would be most anxious to surround yourself with the familiar."

He left the room, closing the door in his wake. He did have the right of it: she was most anxious to surround herself with the familiar. Clambering out of bed, she approached the pile of clothing as though it might bite. She lifted the scratchy and rough chemise. Nothing about it felt familiar, nothing about any of this seemed familiar.

She feared she wouldn't find the answers within herself. She wondered why she didn't think she would find them with him either.

He was going to burn in hell.

As Drake leaned against the wall in the hallway, that thought reverberated through his mind, along with images of Ophelia lying in his bed. What sort of scapegrace was he to have been arrested by the sight of her wearing his shirt, as though they'd shared an intimacy that had resulted in her being naked before covering herself with his attire? While he had fought not to notice the bare skin of the woman he'd undressed the night before, he was a man and his mind had captured images of her that tormented him now because he could see that flesh brushing up against the fabric of his shirt.

She'd appeared so innocent, nestled deep in slumber. In spite of all his preparations, he had decided to forgo his nefarious plan to give her one day to live the life of a servant. But then she had ordered him to fetch her breakfast . . . and it had grated on his nerves, had brought forth images of other moments when she had ordered him about, when he had seen her commanding servants. Even with no recollection of who she truly was, she managed to lure her true self to the fore and embrace the haughtiness that so characterized her.

He'd made a very generous donation to the missions for the clothing that he thought would mold itself to her body. It irritated him that he knew her well enough to determine her height, her width, her curves, to know approximately what sort of clothing would suit the shape of her torso. But then he'd been a keen observer of women since he reached the age of sixteen and discovered the delights of their bodies. So it wasn't she, per se, who garnered his attention. Merely the fact that she was female.

A female who would rue the day that she ever called him boy. Provided that her memory returned and she could recollect how she had snubbed him.

The door opened. He straightened. Her hair was still braided, but her face was pink, as though freshly scrubbed. Although the dress fit her quite well, it seemed out of place on her, the material faded and worn. It made her appear faded as well. He didn't want to consider that she belonged in the finest of gowns rather than something so humble and plain. It buttoned up to her throat, the sleeves were long. She rubbed her hands over her arms as though bothered by the linen. Or perhaps she simply sensed that she didn't belong in such simple attire. Or she was cold.

He should ask, but he didn't want his resolve weakened by sympathy or compassion. He could do much worse by her than giving her a day of walking in a servant's shoes. Pushing himself away from the wall, he asked, "Does any of this appear familiar?"

Her green eyes wide, her brow furrowed, she shook her head. "How long have I worked here?"

"A fortnight." Before she could ask more questions, he began walking toward the end of the hallway. "This way."

Her light footsteps echoed between the barren walls. He had yet to purchase carpeting for the wooden floors. He had yet to do a great deal. After reaching the last room on the right, he swung open the door. "Your bedchamber."

She hesitated as though fearing walking into the great maw of a beast. "My quarters are on the same floor as yours?"

"I'm a kind employer. The rooms here have fireplaces. The rooms above—where I know servants would normally sleep—do not."

"Kind. I suppose I shall have to take your word on that as I don't recall what it is like to be in your employ. To be in any employ. I can't imagine it. In truth, I can't dredge up the tiniest memory of servitude."

"I'm certain it'll all come back once you're engaged in the activity again."

"I shall hope so."

With cautious steps she approached and peered into the room. He could not mistake the horror that crossed her features. The space contained little more than the bare cot that he had used until his bed had been delivered and a pile of clothing that he'd hastily grabbed for show. He doubted she would be using any of it before he returned her home on the morrow.

"I sleep on a cot?" she asked.

"You are a servant, after all."

Walking through the doorway, she glanced around. "I would have thought that I would have made it appear more welcoming."

"I doubt you've had time, what with all your chores."

"I'm truly your only servant?"

"You're all I require at the moment. Come along. I'll explain your duties as we head down to the kitchen, so you can get some sustenance." Marching toward the stairs, he heard the patter of her feet behind him. "The floors need to be swept and polished, of course. Shelves and mantels dusted."

He hurried down the stairs and turned into a hallway, bypassing the front parlor, which contained only a fireplace with a mantel to be dusted. As he pointed out empty rooms, he became suddenly self-conscious regarding what was lacking in the residence. Even the library, his sanctuary, had been furnished with only a large desk and chair. He had ordered a few pieces that would be arriving soon, but for the most part he'd yet to decide what he was going to do with all the space. Sometimes he thought it pointless to purchase furniture, paintings, and statuary when he never intended to marry. He knew the cursed darkness that ran through his blood, had no desire to expose it to a woman who might love him, to pass it on to their children. He had long ago accepted what he was, and this latest effort on his part only confirmed what he and she alone understood about himself: he was a rotten bastard.

He strode from the library with hardly a backward glance, Ophelia traipsing behind him like an obedient puppy. Fighting to quiet his conscience, he reminded himself that this little ruse would be for only a day.

When the truth came out, Ophelia would be furious—whether or not she regained her memories—but then he'd long ago learned to ignore her rants. Perhaps with this little lesson, her servants would have to suffer through fewer of them.

He almost laughed at his convoluted justification. He'd always been honest with himself. He should be honest now. He wasn't doing this for the servants. He was doing it because Lady Ophelia Lyttleton had been a thorn in his side since she was old enough to speak coherently.

Coming to a halt, he spun around to face her. "The kitchen, of course. I hope you'll enjoy your breakfast."

It was paltry: boiled egg, toast, porridge, milk.

Her nose wrinkled as though he'd offered her cow dung. "I like creamed eggs."

Leaning against the counter, he crossed his arms over his chest. "I don't know how to prepare creamed eggs." He indicated the stove. "You're welcome to prepare them yourself."

With three slender fingers, she rubbed her brow. "I know I prefer them, but I don't recall how to make them." She met his gaze. "Why do I remember some things, but not everything?"

On that particular matter, he suspected she had no earthly clue how to prepare creamed eggs. "I'm not familiar with all the ramifications of your condition, although you don't seem to be suffering physically." For which he was grateful. It eased his conscience.

She swept her arm in a wide circle. "None of this—none of the rooms through which you walked me—appear familiar. Shouldn't they, if I've been attending to them?"

"You've only been here a short while. You should eat. Perhaps if you regain your strength, you'll regain your knowledge."

Cautiously, as though she didn't quite trust it, she approached the table and stood by the chair, no doubt an ingrained habit of waiting for a footman to jump to do her bidding.

"You pull it away from the table to sit in it," he told her.

She did as he instructed, her brow furrowing. "It seems odd—as though I've never done it before."

Lifting a spoon, she cracked the top of her egg.

"It seems you do eat boiled eggs sometimes," he pointed out.

She scowled. "This one is overcooked. I like the yolk soft."

"You're quite particular, aren't you? Bath water just past warm, soft yolks, creamed eggs."

She jerked her head up. "Is that a fault? To know what one likes?"

"It can be if you disparage those who don't prepare things exactly to your liking."

"But if I don't tell you how I prefer things, how will you know?"

"In the future, I won't be preparing your bath or your breakfast. You shall handle that yourself. You will also be preparing my bath and my dinner. For tonight's meal, you'll find pheasant in the icebox." He shoved himself away from the counter. "I generally awaken around five. Bath first and then dinner."

He began striding toward the door. She came up out of the chair as though he'd lit a fire beneath it.

"Hold a moment!"

He stopped, studied her. Doubt flickered across her face, washing away any lingering signs of haughtiness, of entitlement.

"You're leaving me?"

"Yes, I've been up all night. I'm ready to be abed."

Her features seemed to fold into amazement, into gratitude that had his stomach tightening, his resolve weakening.

"You went without sleep to tend me," she said softly.

"No, in order to tend you, I did not see to my business. I'm a creature of the night, dusk is when I come to life. During the day I sleep."

The softness dissipated. "What is your business?"

"I manage a gentlemen's club."

"A place of sin?"

"Quite right."

Her brow furrowed once again. "How do I know that?"

"I'll leave you to ponder it. If I tell you all the answers, you may never regain your memory. I think you need to exercise your brain. Wake me at five, after you've prepared my bath."

This time as he left she didn't call out to him, and he wondered why he was hit with a stab of disappointment. He'd spoken true. If he allowed her to ferret out the answers to the questions herself, her memory would no doubt return. He quite envisioned himself awakening to a shrew determined to have her own revenge against him. His bath would be scalding, his pheasant laced with arsenic.

He bounded up the stairs, strode into his bedchamber, and staggered to a stop. The bed remained rumpled, his shirt pooled on the floor. She wouldn't tidy up after herself, now would she? When he'd first come into the room this morning, he'd retrieved his coat from where she'd abandoned it the night before and hung it back in the wardrobe.

He picked up his shirt, folded it, and set it on the chair, to be washed later. He preferred order and routine, and was quite obsessive about cleanliness. Came from spending the first few years of his young life living in squalor. He remembered the first time that the duchess had scrubbed his body clean. He'd feared that she'd take his skin with the brush, and while he'd complained mightily, he'd felt reborn.

His tired mind was journeying into odd musings. No doubt the reason that his plan to tell Ophelia she was a servant had seemed like such a splendid idea. Still, little harm in it really.

He removed his shirt, folded it, and set it with the other one. After tugging off his boots, he added his trousers and undergarments to the pile. Then he crossed over to the bed, stretched across it, brought the covers over his body, and settled in. The fragrance of his lemony soap wafted around him, but mixed within it was the scent of her, her skin warming beneath the blankets, her unique bouquet of womanhood. His body reacted swiftly and painfully. He cursed it for having no taste whatsoever. It cared only for breasts and thighs and the sweet haven that resided between them.

Striving to tame his needs, he brought up images of her gazing down her long, aristocratic nose at him, of her ordering him about, of her snubbing him—publicly and privately—any chance she got. *Keep your distance*, she had telegraphed frequently and accurately. *You're not good enough.*

What did he care what she thought of him when her thoughts so accurately mirrored his own? Perhaps that was the ironic twist. That she saw him more clearly than anyone else, and he didn't much like that they agreed on something.

Chapter 6

She couldn't recall how to cook creamed eggs, but she was supposed to know how to prepare pheasant? Dear God, she didn't even know how to heat the stove.

She nibbled on the dry toast. She liked it with more butter, so where would she find that? In the icebox, she supposed. Sliding off the hard-backed wooden chair, she wondered if a more uncomfortable piece of furniture existed in all of Christendom. She could not be expected to sit in it for every meal. It required pillows. She required pillows. Softness, comfort. Why would anyone settle for less?

She wandered over to the wooden box, released the latch, opened the door, and screeched.

The bird stared accusingly at her.

Slamming the door closed, she stepped back, her breathing harsh and shallow. It was dead, she knew it was dead, but it still possessed its eyes, its entire head. She couldn't cook something that had the ability to glare at her, to make her feel guilty about preparing it.

Drake Darling was going to have to make do with something else for dinner, because she had no desire whatsoever to touch that creature. Shivering, she rubbed her hands up and down her arms, then wished she hadn't because the material itched. It was incredibly stiff and scratchy. She thought of Mr. Darling's shirt—how soft it had been—and she longed to be wrapped in it once more. She didn't care that it was his. The linen was much more to her liking. She would put it on as soon as he left this evening.

As for dinner, well, it was late morning so she had several hours to decide how she would handle that. Bread and butter perhaps. Only retrieving the butter meant dealing with the pheasant's beady eyes again. Bread only then.

The man needed to hire a cook. She could not be expected to manage the house and the kitchen, although apparently she had. She sank back down onto the chair. None of this made sense, none of it felt right.

She supposed she could sit here all day in the uncomfortable chair, pondering, but perhaps he had the right of it. Once she began seeing to her duties, everything would fall into place.

Rising, she glanced around for her apron. She peered behind doors, examined the pantry, looked into drawers. It was not to be found. In her bedchamber perhaps. As she was truly in no hurry to begin scrubbing and polishing, she ambled through the hallways and rooms, searching for anything familiar. She failed to find it as well, but she could see the potential in the rooms, imagined the furniture that should inhabit each one, the paintings that would delight, the sculptures that would add ambiance. How did she know art?

Where was she before she came to work for him? Who was her family? Did she still see them? Did she send them her wages? How much did she earn? Obviously not much when her clothing was so terribly prickly and didn't fit quite right.

She wandered up the stairs and came to a stop outside Darling's bedchamber. He was sleeping in the massive bed. Was it appropriate for her to be alone in the residence with him? Did no one care about her reputation?

The longer she was awake, the more she wondered, the more questions arose. She carried on down the empty hallway, her footsteps echoing between the walls. He needed carpets, wall hangings, something to absorb the sound. She couldn't be expected to creep around all day. Still, she lightened her footfalls. As he had apparently saved her from drowning, she supposed she should show more consideration.

Walking into her bedchamber, she was once again taken aback by the simplicity of it and lack of anything personal. Sitting on the edge of the cot, she was struck by how hard it was. Surely she should remember sleeping on it. On the other hand, its discomfort was cause for not remembering.

Reaching down, she examined each piece of clothing that seemed to be awaiting her inspection. None of it seemed to be to her taste. Other than the fact that everything was quite plain, it was not made to her standards. Sitting back, she stared into space. What precisely were her standards?

Her head began to ache. Blast it all! Not remembering was quite a nuisance. She couldn't imagine where else she might have placed an apron. Had she been wearing it last night when she'd tumbled into the river? Had Darling tossed it with the remainder of her ruined clothing?

It didn't matter. It wasn't as though she was going to get filthy with her chores. As far as she could tell, she didn't have a great deal to keep her busy. Dust, he'd told her. She'd begin in the library where furniture and shelves would attract motes and cobwebs.

After returning to the kitchen, where she found a rag, she went to the library. In spite of the room's sparse furnishings, it contained a masculine quality. She could see him working behind the large, dark desk, his head bent in concentration as he wrote diligently in ledgers. The lamp on the desk would cast a glow over his work. Did he seek her advice on matters? Did he care about her opinion? She couldn't see herself not offering it if she had one.

Edging around the desk, she sat in the thick leather chair and sighed with pleasure. Lovely. Just like his bed. It seemed he didn't skimp on his own comfort. In the future she would take her meals in here. Or perhaps she would eat in his bed.

She furrowed her brow. She'd eaten in bed before. Probably when he wasn't here. She could get away with a lot when he wasn't about. If she cleaned up after herself he would never know that she made use of his possessions.

Walking over to the shelves, she slapped the rag halfheartedly at the shelves that were empty of everything except dust. She couldn't say much for her housekeeping skills, although to be fair she found it rather difficult to take battling dirt seriously. No joy was to be found in the action. No fun. However had this become her life?

She narrowed her eyes as an image flashed through her mind. Leather volumes. Dickens. Austen. Shakespeare. She could see them lined up, one after the other. Gold embossed lettering. She lifted her fingers as though she could touch them. She'd read these authors and more. She liked to read. No, she loved to read! She enjoyed being carried away into a world different from her own, with characters who did not sit in judgment of her.

As she considered what her life was, she could well

imagine wanting to escape it. But who judged her? Those better than she. But who were they?

If books were so important to her, why weren't any in her room? Because they were costly. Again, another tidbit that she knew.

She swung away from the shelves and the room seemed to circle around her in a blur. Her life contained other blurs. She began to hum a familiar tune. Lifting her arms, she swayed, then began moving her feet in time to the music that only she could hear. She knew the song, knew the movements, knew that a gentleman had swept her over a floor.

And she was convinced with every fiber of her being that she did not belong here.

"I know how to waltz."

Squinting against the sunlight pouring into the room, Drake stared at the woman standing near the end of his bed. She'd awoken him with her pronouncement. Why was he not surprised that she would think nothing of interrupting a man from his well-deserved rest? "Pardon?"

"I know how to waltz. I can hear the music. No, it's more than that. I *know* the music. I daresay, if you had a pianoforte, I would be able to play it. Chopin. Beethoven. Mozart. I can see my fingers flying over the ivory keys. I can see myself dancing with a gentleman. I can read. Dickens. Austen. Browning. I can quote passages."

He shoved himself to a sitting position, not caring that the covers fell to his waist. "Your point?"

She blinked, stared at his person, somewhere along his chest, he thought. Her lips parted slightly, and he didn't know why he felt a need to inhale deeply, expand his chest and beat on it like some great ape in the zoological gardens. He'd never cared about impressing her. He wasn't about to start now.

Swallowing, she grabbed hold of the bedpost as though she needed its sturdiness to support her so she could remain upright. "I don't believe a servant would know all those things."

"You don't think a servant could watch others dancing and pick up the steps? Memorize the music? Read? I assure you that valuable servants can in fact read."

"I'm not doubting that a servant can read, but that one would have time to read as widely as I have."

"You haven't been in service all that long."

She narrowed her eyes. "How did I come to work here at all?"

"You were recommended."

She tilted up her chin. "By whom?"

"I don't remember the names." *When lying, keep the lies as honest as possible. Don't create a lie that requires you remember something.* "You came with letters of reference."

She shoved herself away from the bed, balled her hands into tightened fists, and jerked up her chin. "As they aren't in my bedchamber, as there is nothing in that hideously ill-furnished room that feels at all familiar, I assume you have these letters of which you speak. I should like to see them."

"They're in my office at the club."

"Fetch them."

He ground his back teeth together. "It is not your place to order me about."

"But they might assist me in remembering."

"Has it occurred to you that there may be a reason you don't want to remember?" Even as he asked the words, it struck him that perhaps they held more truth than he'd intended. Except for a few bruises, physically she appeared fine. The lump on her head hadn't drawn blood, so how hard could something have truly hit her?

Gnawing on her lower lip, she appeared innocent, almost sweet. Her shoulders softened, her back relaxed. "Why was I in the river?"

"I don't know." Honesty.

"How did you know I was there?"

"I was taking a walk. I saw a form huddled at the water's edge. I didn't know it was you until I brought you to the residence. You were coated in mud." Truth.

She shuddered. "Yes, I remember that, washing off the awful stuff." She furrowed her brow. "Obviously we weren't being robbed, as there is nothing here of value, so I wasn't running from a thief. Would someone wish me harm?"

"I shouldn't think so, but then there is a good bit about you that I don't know." *A good deal that I do know, but that is to be revealed tomorrow.*

She wandered to the window, gazed out onto the street. He wasn't concerned with anyone spying her, identifying her. This part of London was not frequented by those of her station in life. "It all seems so strange. I just don't feel as though I belong here."

"Again, wishful thinking."

"Perhaps." She faced him. "We do seem to keep going over the same ground, don't we? Isn't it the sign of madness to keep asking the same question and expecting a different answer?"

"You're not mad."

"Perhaps I am and all this is simply an illusion. Will you retrieve the letters?"

"Tonight, when I go to the club."

"When do you return?"

"Generally I stay out all night. Yesterday was an exception. So I'll be here sometime after dawn tomorrow."

Scowling, she twisted her lips into a moue of displeasure. "But that's hours away."

"Nothing will change between now and then."

"Except I might remember. I could go to the club—"

"No." That would result in disaster. If anyone saw her . . . a good many of the members knew her. "That's not possible."

"You're a rather harsh employer."

"You're my servant, Phee. I'm striving to get some sleep here so I can see to my responsibilities tonight. You should be seeing to your duties now. I'll bring you the letters in the morning. Meanwhile, leave."

"What is the name of your club?"

He gave her a pointed look. He was too familiar with all the times that she and Grace had broken rules, and he suspected that little part of her character had not been lost. If he gave her the name of the club, she'd no doubt make her way there. He knew her well enough to know she could be quite conniving and resourceful. Little witch.

She released an impudent sigh. "Am I a prisoner here?"

"No, but until your memory is more dependable, it would be unwise to travel about London."

"I think I could make out quite well without my memory."

"I must question your judgment on that score. You're in the bedchamber of a man who is not wearing a stitch of clothing, a man who is tired and wishes to sleep, and is growing increasingly irate. You think that's rational behavior?"

Her eyes widened slightly, her mouth formed a soft O. "I know you're not wearing a shirt. Are you saying—"

"Yes, quite. Nothing at all rests between my flesh and the sheets."

"Oh. Oh, I see. I should leave you to rest."

"Yes, you should." Before he was tempted to shock her by clambering out of the bed, grabbing her arms, and kissing her senseless. He didn't want her asking questions about her past, didn't want her heading out on her own to try to answer the riddle of who she was. He would tell her tomorrow, right before he returned her to her family.

Bowing her head, she scurried from the room, closing the door quietly in her wake. With a sigh, he lay back, shoved a hand beneath his head, and wondered why he was continuing with this sham. It wasn't nearly as deliciously rewarding as he'd expected it to be.

But that was only because she didn't yet know the truth. Everything would change then, and her memory would return in full force. He wanted one moment with her that she would never forget, one moment that he could take out and examine on occasion. A moment that contained a task that would speak of servitude as no other would.

An image entered his mind—an evil, wicked image, one in which he would derive great pleasure, one that she would think of whenever their paths crossed, one that would prevent her from being quite so arrogant in his presence. One that would cause her to do his bidding, lest he tell the world what had transpired.

The more he thought on it, the more he wanted it. Just one little thing to hold over her, to topple her off the pedestal upon which she gloated, gazed down on him, and deemed him worthless.

Dark laughter circled around him as satisfaction took hold. He'd have his fun tonight. Tomorrow he would return her to her world, just a bit humbler.

Chapter 7

Drumming her fingers on the table in the kitchen, Phee could not have been more bored if she were lying in a coffin. What did she do with herself all day?

The hours dragged by. She considered going for a walk, but she didn't trust her memory. Drake had the right of it. She couldn't guarantee that she would recall how to make her way back here. Earlier she stood on the front stoop and nothing beyond looked familiar. Oh, the horses and the wagons, the occasional dog—she knew what they were. She could name objects. But the street itself, the buildings that lined it were as foreign as preparing pheasant for dinner.

And there were so many more eyes, staring at her, knowing things she didn't. So she retreated back into the house, wandered aimlessly, striving to unlock the secrets of her life, wondering why the thought of secrets unsettled her. Maybe there was indeed a reason that she wasn't remembering, that her past seemed to have vanished.

It would be a couple of more hours before Darling awoke. She tried not to think of him lying upstairs in the same bed in which she'd slept. Thank goodness she had her own bed as she didn't want his scent permeating her dreams. He smelled delicious, so masculine, so earthy. And he was naked. She should be appalled, but she wasn't. She was curious more than anything. Had she ever seen a naked man?

She expected Drake Darling was quite gorgeous.

How did she address him? Drake? Darling? Mr. Darling? Master Darling? The last was too formal, the first too personal. Darling. Just Darling. That seemed right. She would of course confirm it when he awoke. Meanwhile, she decided that the house could use some flowers to brighten it up. But when she went through the back door, she discovered no gardens. Only tall grass and weeds that pulled at her skirt as she walked through them. No orderly flowers lined up to reveal a rainbow of colors, nothing that emitted comforting fragrances. Nothing to pluck. Nothing to bring delight. Everything was so drab and boring. How did he not go completely mad?

How did she not? Perhaps she was in the beginning stages of madness. Perhaps that was the reason that she remembered none of this. Why would anyone want to remember it?

She heard a smack, something hitting something else. Again. Again. Coming from the other side of the brick wall. Was someone engaged in a fight? Should she fetch Darling, have him put a stop to it? She had no doubt that he could, if not with his very presence, then with his fists. She sensed leashed violence in him. She could see him prowling . . .

Yes, he could handle whatever was happening on the other side of the wall, but it really wasn't her business, now was it? People should be left to handle their own affairs. Still, she couldn't deny her curiosity. And what if someone was being hurt? Didn't she have an obligation to step in?

Glancing around, she spotted a wrought-iron chair in the corner of the terrace. Surely Darling didn't sit there to gaze out on his weeds. Where would be the pleasure in that? She decided that she must have a rather inquisitive mind as questions bombarded her, and she seemed to constantly want to ferret out the answers, especially where her employer was concerned. But the answers remained elusive so she grabbed on to the back of the chair and dragged it over the ground until she reached the wall, where she set it against the brick. With careful balancing, she stepped up onto the seat, grabbed the edge of the wall to steady herself, rose up on her toes, and peered over.

The gardens weren't particularly showy but they were well manicured, with shorn grass, hedgerows, roses, and absolutely no weeds. Off to the side, a rug was draped over rope strung between two poles. A woman in a black dress, full apron, and white mobcap covering her brown hair was slapping a broom against the carpet. With each whack dust floated upward.

Suddenly Phee was quite relieved that Darling had no carpeting.

The woman ceased her movements, hunched her shoulders slightly, and sneezed. Taking a handkerchief from her apron pocket, she wiped at her nose before putting the linen back. Then she raised the broom again, glanced back, and squeaked.

"Oh, I'm sorry," Phee called out. "I didn't mean to startle you."

Pressing her hand to her chest, the woman laughed. "It's all right."

Phee could see now that the servant was more girl than woman, close in age to herself perhaps. Still holding the broom, the girl walked over and stared up at her with wide blue eyes. She smiled broadly, revealing teeth that were slightly askew. "Are you the lady of the house?"

Now it was Phee's turn to be taken off guard. "Why would you think that?"

"There's a fanciness to your speech."

One that was lacking in the girl's Phee realized. Darling had the same sort of fanciness when he spoke. It was odd, but it did sound rather elegant, more so than the girl's, which seemed to have harsher sounds. "You don't know me then?" she asked, suddenly realizing that what had prompted her curiosity was the hope that someone on the other side of the wall might be able to help her remember.

The girl shook her head. "No, haven't met anyone from over there. Knew someone was in residence, a'course, but it all seemed rather mysterious, comin's and goin's all hours of the night."

"There's really no one to meet except for me and Drake Darling. He owns the residence. I'm his housekeeper."

Once again, the girl appeared astonished. "Oh, yes, I suppose I can see that, you being so tall. I wager you have no trouble at all reaching the top shelf in the linen cupboard."

Phee couldn't stop herself from laughing. "I'm standing on a chair."

The girl turned as red as beet. "Cor! Course you are. I wasn't really thinking it out, 'cuz I know employers like their maids to be tall so they can reach things." She scowled. "I'll never work in a fancy house or climb to a high position. Never grew into my height. So here I am beating rugs." Angling her head to the side, she studied Phee for several long moments. Finally she said, "You don't strike me as a housekeeper."

"Yes, well, apparently I am. I took a bit of a tumble and am having difficulty remembering things."

"Sorry to hear that. What sorts of things?"

"Almost everything, it seems, except my name. I'm Phee."

"Marla." She puffed out her chest. "The housemaid."

"Are there other servants?"

She nodded. "The cook's in charge. Mrs. Pratt. Then there's the footman, Rob."

"Is it possible they might have met me?"

"Not likely or they would have said." She blushed prettily. "We was always gossiping about who might be living there. Caught sight of the gent a time or two. Ever so easy on the eyes."

"Is he?" Yes, of course he was. She didn't know why she'd asked, but she didn't like the notion of others ogling him, finding him interesting.

Marla nodded enthusiastically. "He is rather."

Phee didn't want to discuss Darling and his appeal. So she changed the topic by asking, "For whom do you work?"

"Mrs. Turner. She's a widow. Gets lonely. Shame you're not the lady of the house. You could come visit her."

"I could visit her anyway."

Marla shook her head. "Oh no, that wouldn't be right. Domestics don't socialize with the lady of the house."

"Why ever not? I have plenty of time. There's nothing to do over here."

Appearing skeptical, Marla said, "I suspect you're just not remembering all you need to do. Perhaps I could come over tomorrow and help you get a bit more situated. Don't want you to lose your post."

She wasn't certain that would be such a tragedy but if she lost it, where would she go? How would she eat? "That would be lovely, thank you."

Marla looked apologetic. "Sorry. I've got to finish up with the rugs before Mrs. Pratt comes to scold me for dawdling. Ever so nice to meet ya."

Then she was gone, back to beating on the rug. Phee thought she could take some delight in that chore, after all. Beating out her frustrations. Surely she had met someone around here, someone who could tell her more than Darling could. It was inconceivable that they were so isolated from their neighbors. On the other hand, he didn't seem to be very social, and his hours seemed incredibly long. Out all night, sleeping all day. When did he have time for fun, the theater—

She loved the theater. Stage, opera, concerts. She relished them all. She was rather sure of it. How could she afford to go? Obviously she spent little on her clothing so she could spend her coins on entertainment. What plays had she seen? Shakespeare? *Midsummer*—

"What the devil are you doing?"

The deep voice boomed behind her, startling her, causing her to jump back, lose her balance—

The chair toppled—

She was falling—

Landed more gently than she'd expected, caught in those powerful arms that had rescued her the night before. Her own were entwined around his neck like some clinging vine that would never be ripped from its purchase. Her heart raced like a mad thing, her lungs fought for air. She could feel the warmth of his skin radiating through his loose linen shirt. The buttons were undone at collar and cuff, and the untidiness made him appear more masculine, more dangerous.

"You're not spying on our neighbors, are you?" he asked, one thick dark brow arched.

Angling her chin, she refused to be chastised for her actions. "I was meeting the housemaid, Marla."

"Marla?"

She nodded.

"What did she have to say?"

She didn't know why he appeared so displeased. Surely she was misreading him. She could hardly think, clasped so tightly against him as she was. "Would you mind putting me down?"

Very slowly, he released her, her body sliding down his as though it were striving to interlock with his, as though it belonged nestled within the planes and hollows. Her mouth suddenly dry, she stepped back, aware of his studying her as though he didn't quite know her, but then speaking with the neighbors, meeting the servants was obviously not something she'd done before.

"Marla mentioned that my speech is one of refinement. Although even without the mention, I would have noticed. She seems to have misplaced her G's and H's. Her vowels contain a coarseness that is lacking in mine. She rather thought I was the mistress of the household. And I must confess that I can more readily see myself in that role than in the role of servant."

A corner of his mouth curled up and the tiniest dimple appeared in the folds. She almost reached out to touch it. It was familiar, so very familiar. Had she skimmed her fingers over it before or merely contemplated doing so? "Can you?" he asked.

Could she? Could she touch it? Yes, she rather thought she could. But before she took the action, she regained rational thought and realized he was referring to her comment about her roles.

"Yes. Yes, I can. Quite well in fact. And don't say it's wishful thinking or daydreams." She began to pace. "I can't explain it, but I don't belong here. I know that with every fiber of my being."

"Perhaps you didn't once upon a time, but you do

now. And I need my bath prepared. Come with me." He headed for the house, his long legs eating up the ground. She hurried after him.

"But I have more that I wish to say."

"Your wishes are not my concern."

Good God, could she have found a more irascible employer? How desperate must she have been for work to have settled for being within his employ? Piqued beyond measure, she followed him into the kitchen and nearly rammed into his back when he came to an abrupt halt. "I'm not smelling the aroma of pheasant cooking."

"It has eyes."

With his own widened, he faced her, and for a moment it appeared he might choke. "I beg your pardon?"

She edged past him. "I can't cook something that can watch me while I'm doing it."

"It's dead."

"Well, yes, of course I know that," she said sharply. "But there is accusation in those eyes."

"Then chop off its head."

She thought she might be ill. "No, I don't think so. Besides, I don't know how."

"You pick up a cleaver—"

"No!" she cried, slicing her hand through the air, not wanting those images described in detail invading her mind. "I meant that I don't know how to prepare the blasted thing for eating."

He studied her as though she had said something of monumental importance. "Of course you don't."

"Yet I remember how to waltz. Do you not find that odd?"

"That you would prefer memories of fun over work? No."

Plopping down onto the uncomfortable chair, she

placed her elbows on the table and leaned forward. "Am I not a satisfactory servant then? Why keep me on?"

"We'll discuss all this later. I need to get to the club, and the journey there begins with a bath, which you failed to prepare. I'll assist so it gets done quickly."

He heated water, easily carted it upstairs, quickly dumped it into the tub, all the while insisting that she follow him and observe. As though she hadn't the wherewithal to comprehend how one went about filling a copper vessel. She considered informing him of such, but she held her tongue because, quite honestly, she had no desire whatsoever to carry and pour. Besides, she rather liked walking behind him and watching the play of his muscles over his back and shoulders as he occasionally shifted the weight of the buckets. Still, she had no desire to perform the same service. Whatever had possessed her to seek this occupation?

She couldn't have had a choice because there was absolutely nothing about it that appealed. She could read and write. She could tutor. She could hire herself out to write letters. She should have been able to find something better.

"Why would I choose a life of servitude?" she asked as they journeyed up the stairs for the third time.

"You didn't have a choice."

Just as she'd surmised. "Why? Was I poor? Never mind. Of course I was. Based on the smattering and quality of my belongings I'm still poor. Practically destitute."

"You have a roof over your head." He turned into the bathing room, set down one bucket, and upended the other. Steam rose up. Apparently he enjoyed his bath several shades past warm. "That's more than many have."

"What is my salary?"

"Twelve pounds," he said distractedly, setting down one bucket, picking up the other to add its contents to the nearly full bath.

"A day?"

Laughing darkly, he turned to her. "Why am I not surprised you overvalue your worth? An annum."

The bucket clanked on the tile as though to punctuate his answer. Then in a quick smooth movement that stole her breath, he dragged his shirt over his head, revealing the broad expanse of chest with the narrow sprinkling of hair that she'd caught sight of earlier.

Spinning around, she headed for the threshold. "I'll leave you to your bath."

"Not so fast, Phee."

She paused, the words delivered in a tone that would brook no argument. And waited. Waited. Not breathing. Not certain her heart even beat. She heard the rasp of more cloth being discarded and her body responded with alertness, like a deer spying the hunter, frozen, yet ready to dart quickly away without further thought if needed.

"You wash my back," he said.

She heard the distinct sound of water being disturbed, lapping against copper.

"You can't be serious." Her voice sounded tiny, uncertain, and it infuriated her because she recognized the tinny thread of fear. It had squeaked out before, in another place, another moment, and she had learned to hold it in check, to not reveal her terror.

"I can't reach it myself," he said. "Do close the door to keep the warmth in the room. I don't wish to become chilled."

She considered closing it with herself on the other side of it. But something inside her would not allow her to retreat. Somewhere, somehow she had learned that retreat equaled defeat. As long as she wasn't defeated, she could carry on. She could survive.

Where were these thoughts coming from? But the knowledge was clear. It left no room for doubt. Lessons learned, but not in a classroom.

"Phee? Come along now. Don't be shy of a sudden."

Had he taught her the lessons? Should she conk him over the head and run for her life?

No, just as last night she hadn't feared him upon awakening, so she didn't fear him now. He was not a danger, and where was the harm in simply scrubbing his back?

Turning on her heel, she came up short at the gorgeous sight, the mixture of colors that greeted her. She'd have never imagined something so remarkable.

"Is that dragon painted on your back?"

Chapter 8

Inwardly Drake cursed. A flaw to the plan that he'd not considered. He never shared his back with anyone—not because he was ashamed of it, but because the dragon was private, personal. He owned it. It was part of him.

"Will it wash off?" she asked softly, with awe. "If I scrub it, will it disappear?"

He stared at the far wall, realizing that a portion of her was captured in the oval mirror hanging there. Had she ever looked so innocent, so disarming? He didn't like her looking like that. It made her approachable, made her appealing. He did not want her appealing. He wanted her to see him across a ballroom floor and remember that she had once washed his back. He wanted her blushing when he sat across from her at a dining table. He wanted her stammering when next she sought to remind him of his nonexistent place in Society. He wanted to snap at her to get on with washing his back. Instead he heard himself explaining far too reasonably for a man experiencing such inner turmoil, "No, the ink is beneath the surface."

"How did it get to be there?"

"Needles."

The door clicked shut. The rustle of skirts. She sank from view and he didn't want to envision her going to her knees. Blast it. The bathing chamber created an intimacy he'd been fool enough to misjudge. He had anticipated it affecting her, not him.

"Did it hurt?" she asked on a breath that was more whisper than substance. Her fingers lightly touched his lower nape—where the top of the dragon's head curved—stealing his voice, his thoughts, his purpose. They felt like fire, and it was as though once again something was being scored into his flesh, only this time it was burning, branding. He didn't know if he'd ever be able to forget the feel of her fingers against his flesh.

He fought to regain his control. "Yes."

The solitary word was all he could manage, but manage it he did. He supposed he could relish some victory in that. Even if his voice sounded rough and foreign to his own ears.

Her fingers traced the outline of bridge, snout, mouth before trailing in a featherlike touch across red, blue, yellow, black.

"Why fire? Why does it breathe fire?"

To destroy my demons.

Not that he was about to confess that. For once he had the upper hand with her and he wasn't about to give it up. He didn't want to provide her with any fuel that she could use against him when her memory returned. No, this one day was about him obtaining the means to put her in her place . . . eventually.

"So I can use it to frighten small children."

She laughed. Not the haughty caustic sound with which he was so familiar, but a sweet tinkling of bells at Christmas. Oh, he'd heard the sound before when she was with Grace . . . No, this was different, unguarded.

He'd never heard the like coming from her. Had she never revealed her true self, even to Grace? "I don't see you being that unkind."

Outlining the spread wings now, she seemed to slow her movements as though in reverence. He could hardly blame her. When he was a lad, a dragon had caught and held his attention, had changed his life.

She stopped where the water lapped at his ribs. The dragon reached down to his buttocks, but he supposed reaching her hand into the water to touch it would create a familiarity with which she was not quite ready to deal. Hell, he wasn't certain he could handle it.

"It's beautiful, and yet why would you put art upon your back?"

He considered telling a lie, but when her memories returned, he had little doubt that she would be able to guess a good part of it.

"I was an orphan on the streets. A woman took me in. Her husband had a dragon tattooed on his back. When I first saw it, it frightened and fascinated me. I was a bit of a scamp, prone to misbehaving. He painted a dragon on my back, initiated me into the order of the dragon, and told me the woman was the queen of the dragons and I must always obey her. He used watercolors that eventually washed off, although it was some time before I realized it, as I couldn't see my back and wasn't prone to standing in front of mirrors. But by then, I had learned that I gained much more by behaving than misbehaving. I wanted to stay with them, because of the dragon. Because of them, I am a different man than I might have been otherwise."

"But you said it was painful. I suspect it was agonizing. Why go through that?"

"One must always know pain in order to appreciate beauty."

"That's rather morbid. Are all your thoughts so dark?"

"Not all of them."

"Does it hurt now?"

"No. However, it must be washed." Reaching for the soap, he grabbed it and handed it back. He sensed her hesitation rather than saw it, and wished he had angled the mirror so he could view her. He heard her swallow, felt the slight tremble in her fingers while they skimmed over his palm as she took the soap from him. Now his palm knew her touch and he found himself balling his hand into a fist as though he wanted to hold on to the sensation.

He couldn't blame her for trembling. Touching him was one thing. Washing him brought with it a more complex and deeper level of familiarity. Wrapping his hands around the lip of the tub, he leaned forward to give her easier access.

And felt the ball of soap gliding across his shoulders. Not at all what he wanted. He wanted soft. He wanted silk.

"It's better if you use your hands," he told her.

"How do you suppose the soap is moving if not with my hands? With my mind?"

The tartness in her voice made him smile. The dragon's allure had obviously dissipated; unfortunately for him, hers was merely increasing. He should send her on her way, but he was enjoying this on many more levels than he'd anticipated. "You know what I mean."

"I'm afraid I don't. Whatever instincts seem to come to me, they don't involve washing you."

He peered over his shoulder. "Shall I turn around and demonstrate?"

He couldn't see all of her, but he saw enough to know

she paled. Her memories might be questionable, but she seemed to know what was inappropriate.

"No need. I'm certain I can deduce the proper way to do it."

Taking satisfaction in her answer, he faced forward. Waited. Expectation heightened his senses. He didn't bother to analyze why he wanted her touch. He only knew that he did.

The water splashed as her hands dipped into it. He heard the faint sound of soap slipping over skin, imagined her small hands rubbing at the hard ball. His body tightened, stiffened in anticipation. When was the last time he'd anticipated a woman's touch with a burning need that threatened to reheat the water? Why was he anticipating hers?

Not because he desired her, because God knew he didn't. But because of what her actions portended, the knowledge that would always be between them. The weight of it would keep her nose from jutting into the air, her chin from lifting.

Then the touch came, so different from her earlier exploration of the ink. Not a finger outlining, tracing, but fingers and palms, pads and heels, perhaps even a grazing of wrists. Slowly gliding over his shoulders, pressing into his muscles as though she were as fascinated with them as she was with the tattoo. It took all his resolve not to flex his shoulders, bunch his muscles.

Not to lay his head on his knees and simply glory in the enticing caress.

He'd expected her to be quick about it, but she took her time, skimming her hands over skin that suddenly seemed incredibly sensitive, incredibly aware. He barely noticed when he washed his own body. It was a task to be completed. A vigorous scrubbing intended to remove the filth from his flesh and his heritage from his soul. Her touch was lighter, more tender, and yet it seemed to cleanse more deeply.

He swallowed hard. He'd not expected that.

Over his shoulders she went, again and again and again. In circles, figure eights, up and down, down and up, side to side. A corner of his mouth hitched up as he realized she was stalling.

"As lovely as that feels," he said, striving hard to keep the laughter from his voice, "my back encompasses more than my shoulders."

"Yes, well, they just seemed particularly dirty."

Not likely when he bathed every evening, and sometimes in the morning as well, depending on the night he'd had. Definitely tomorrow morning. He wondered if he should tell her before he left so she could ponder on it through the long hours before his return. Or should he just surprise her with the chore the moment he arrived?

Surprise. Surprises were always fun. Her eyes would widen, her mouth would part . . . it would all be so delicious. Besides, he didn't want her to consider leaving while he was away. He needed to ensure she felt safe so he would find her here when he entered his residence shortly after dawn.

"Should I use a brush?" she asked, and he heard the hope in her voice.

"No, the dragon requires a special touch." He didn't know why he'd said that. Her touch wasn't special, but even as he thought it he knew it to be a lie. He'd never had the caress of a lady, an aristocrat. He'd limited his sexual explorations to commoners, to those whose roots mirrored his. He wasn't about to taint a lady.

In spite of the fact that his family and their friends treated him as an equal, he knew he wasn't. Not really.

He was his own man, proud of his accomplishments, but he didn't have a history of service to the Crown, men of noble birth, women of strong character behind him. He didn't come from noble stock. He came from pain, blood, murder.

Her hands left him. He heard the swishing of the soap. She would be appalled when she learned the truth. He tried to envision the satisfaction, the sight of her stunned expression, but then she was touching him again, and all he seemed capable of was becoming lost in the sensations of silken skin over slick flesh. She possessed no calluses, no scars, no rough edges. Her hands were velvet, softer than any linen he'd ever had next to his flesh.

Women had stroked his back, of course, but it happened in the shadows and they were coarse, with him for one purpose: pleasure. Theirs more than his. They had no interest in leisurely exploring what he had no interest in revealing. Theirs was a mating with him giving far more than he received in an effort to wash away the sins of his father.

Her fingers dipped below the waterline, stroking the dragon's lower tail, stroking his buttocks. A groan, deep and feral, escaped through his clenched teeth.

Her hands flew out of the bathwater, raining droplets over his shoulders, over the floor.

"I think I'm finished," she said, a slight quaking in her voice that matched the tremors cascading through his still form.

He had not expected to be so affected by her, didn't want to be. But he was as hard as marble, aching with hunger barely leashed. He suspected when he unclenched his hands from the sides of the tub, he was going to discover impressions of his fingers in the copper.

"Yes," he ground out. "You can see to my dinner now."

The door opened and closed so quickly that he was surprised she'd had time to pass through it. He submerged himself. He required cold water, frigid water, ice. A trip to the Arctic.

Good Lord, he could still feel her touch. How was that possible? She was gone, but it was almost as though she had brought the dragon to life. It was breathing fire, not at all happy that she'd left without providing him with surcease. He didn't even like her. It was pure lust. A man's carnal needs. Any woman could have brought him to this state of agony. It had been far too long since he'd had a guest in his bed.

Too much work and not enough play. He could remedy that easily enough.

He came up out of the water, searched for and found the soap. Scrubbing at his body, he fought not to envision her touching all of him in the way she had of bringing each nerve ending to life. His arms, his chest, his legs, his feet—his feet! When had he ever cared about his feet? Cupping him, squeezing—

Once more he dropped beneath the water. This little prank or whatever the devil he wanted to call it was supposed to affect her, not him. It was madness. It was the water, the slickness that increased the intensity of the sensations. That was all.

The need rampaging through him had nothing at all to do with her, specifically.

So why the hell did he feel as though he were lying to himself?

Phee could hardly countenance that her legs had managed to carry her into the kitchen, where she practically fell into the chair, trembling and weak. At first she had been mesmerized by the dragon, the splendor of it spread across the broad expanse of his back, wings unfurled, fire licking at his side. The faded colors that she imagined had been quite brilliant when first applied: red, blue, green, yellow, various shades.

But then she had touched him and become fascinated with his velvety skin and the steel muscles beneath it. Had she ever caressed anything quite so firm, so utterly masculine?

She must have if one of her duties was to wash his back, but of course she had no memory of it and that seemed almost a sin. To not recall the pleasure of stroking her fingers across the breadth of him, the length of him. She had wanted to move beyond his back and explore every inch of him, his chest especially. Feather her palms over the sprinkling of hair, press her fingers into the defined muscles. Touch to her heart's content.

If she were not a maid, she suspected she might be a light-skirt. She came up short at the thought. Had she lived another life? Was that the reason she was out at night, the reason she ended up in the river?

Chuckling low, she buried her face in her hands. No, that did not suit at all. She knew that. That sort of wickedness was not she. And yet she could not seem to get the sight of his nakedness out of her mind. She quite relished it being there, quite enjoyed thoughts of examining it more closely.

She shoved herself out of the chair. He would be here any moment. He couldn't find her in this state of want. She needed to prepare his dinner, something quick that would have him leaving as soon as possible. Then she could settle down somewhere and scrutinize these thoughts, try to make sense of them, put them in perspective.

Spotting the cheese beneath a dome of glass, she decided that would do nicely. She placed it on the table along with some bread. She considered searching the icebox but she didn't want to face the knowing lifeless eyes. He would have to fetch his own milk. She placed a plate, knife, and fork on the table.

Hearing footsteps, she glanced up and stilled. He stood in the doorway, nearly filling it, properly dressed in black trousers, white shirt and cravat, dark blue waistcoat, black jacket. So little skin visible now, only his face and hands. Yet he seemed more dangerous, more alluring.

She realized she'd only seen him bared or in shirt and trousers. She'd not considered that he would appear so in control, so powerful, so confident when he was fully clothed. A gentleman. A man of worth.

The hair that had been unruly was tamed. The previously shadowed jaw was sporting no whiskers whatsoever. He should have looked more civilized and yet he didn't.

"No pheasant?" he asked, his voice sounding light and normal, as though he were unaffected by what had happened in the bathing room. But she had heard the growl of a wild beast that was tired of being caged.

"As I stated earlier, I don't know how to prepare it. I thought cheese would suffice for tonight."

"I'm afraid I require something a bit more substantial. I'll eat at the club."

"They serve food there?"

"They serve every sort of indulgence there."

"And you manage it."

"Quite well."

She interlaced her fingers, hard, until they ached. "You've probably told me all about your work before."

"We've never discussed it. I assumed you preferred not to know."

He hovered in the doorway, not approaching her. She

didn't know if it was because he sensed her discomfiture after bathing his back or if he experienced a bit of it as well.

"When may I expect your return?" she asked.

"Sometime after dawn. My hours are determined by how things go at the club throughout the night."

"Are there troubles?"

"Sometimes."

She didn't know why it bothered her to think of him having to manage difficult matters. He was her employer. Theirs was no doubt a very impersonal relationship. "You'll bring the letters of reference?"

It happened so quickly that she couldn't be certain but she thought he flinched.

"Yes."

"What do I do while you're gone?"

"Sweep out the hearths, arrange wood, make my bed. I'm certain if you'll simply look around, you'll figure out what needs to be done."

Cleaning out the hearths brought images of soot and ash. "Where is my apron?"

He became incredibly still, a living statue. "I don't believe you have one," he finally said.

"That's rather odd, isn't it? A housekeeper without an apron?"

"I don't pay attention to your clothing. You're merely a servant. Perhaps you misplaced it."

Merely a servant. The words stung, angered her. She shook her head. "I'm still not understanding why none of this seems familiar. I don't recall doing any of these chores. They're not second nature like the waltzing."

"I can't explain your condition, but I must be off. Enjoy your evening."

With that he turned on his heel and disappeared down the hallway. She almost went after him. Enjoy her evening? He expected her to work. How was there ever any joy in labor?

This was such an odd circumstance. It made no sense. Still, as she'd gone to the trouble to set the table, she took a chair and nibbled on cheese and bread while pondering her dilemma. She wasn't going to sweep out the hearths. She wasn't going to clean anything until she remembered doing it.

If Drake Darling wanted his house properly tended, then he was going to have to be a bit more forthcoming with information. She didn't know why she had the distinct impression he didn't truly want her to regain her memories. What was it he didn't want her to remember?

Chapter 9

It was ridiculous that he was sitting at the massive desk in his office, striving to write a letter of reference for a woman who didn't truly exist, who was merely a charade for his amusement. He had a gaming hell to run.

Besides, he was going to tell her the truth when he returned to the residence. So the letter was unnecessary. He would reveal everything and watch as shock washed over her lovely features—

The satisfaction would be less because she didn't remember him. Didn't recall the number of times she'd snubbed him, what her true feelings for him were. That Lady Ophelia Lyttleton would have never touched the tip of his little finger, let alone his entire back. Not only touch it, but do so with such glorious exploration that even now he could feel where her fingers had pressed.

He needed her to remember who she was, who he was. But no time remained for a leisurely confession. Her family was no doubt frantic by now. If Grace discovered what he'd done, she would never forgive him. Hell, he suspected none of the duke's family would forgive him. He imagined the disappointment in the duchess's eyes.

He had worked so damned hard to be worthy of them taking him in, and Lady Ophelia, the little chit, had caused him to embrace pettiness in order to exact revenge against all the slights she'd delivered over the years.

He was a better man than this.

Leaning back in his chair, he tossed the pen onto the desk. It was late, she was no doubt already abed, otherwise he would return her home now. Stupid to let her prove that he was exactly as she'd alluded all these years: beneath her.

Had the duke not taught him to always hold to the high ground? At Eton, when aristocratic nobs had shoved him in hallways, taken food from his plate, stripped his bed of its coverings in the dead of winter, he'd not fought back. He'd mastered the art of giving them a look that said that they were small, petty, not worth his attention.

Then the Duke of Lovingdon had come to Eton and everything had changed, because the duke considered Drake a friend. Their families often got together for outings and weekends in the country. To treat Drake unkindly was to earn the duke's disfavor, which was to be avoided at all costs, because it had always been apparent that Lovingdon—even at a tender age—held the power and influence of his title. Not to mention that he was as rich as Croesus.

But young Ophelia Lyttleton didn't care about earning the duke's favor, perhaps because she'd always known that Grace loved Lovingdon. So she wasn't above striving to remind Drake of his true place—as though he could ever forget it.

Reaching behind him, he grabbed a bottle of whiskey, poured himself two fingers, and downed them in one swallow. As a general rule he did not drink when he was at the club, because he wanted his mind sharp and he didn't want anything clouding his judgment. But tonight he wasn't concentrating on the club, and that needed to stop immediately.

He'd seen to matters when he first arrived, but, unfortunately, he'd spent the past three hours striving to create a false letter of reference. So far he'd merely written, "She is . . ."

He kept trying to describe Lady Ophelia Lyttleton instead of the fictional Phee. If he stated the truth: "She is opinionated, irritating, haughty," then Phee would wonder why in the blue blazes he'd hired her. He needed to describe her as sweet of temperament, a dedicated worker, a woman with the means to shatter a man while he took a bath.

After tossing down two more fingers of whiskey, he shoved back his chair and stood. He was done with her. In the morning. At that particular moment, he needed to take a leisurely stroll so he could estimate the night's profits. It was a little game he played, judging the mood of the members who were in attendance and determining what their contributions to the night's take would be.

He strode out of his office, down a hallway, and up a flight of stairs to a shadow-shrouded balcony. Standing off to the side, well-hidden behind a heavy velvet drapery, he scoured the gaming floor. An assortment of card games, hazard, dice, roulette—any game of chance that favored the house, and they all favored the house—was available to the membership. Liquor was served, glasses filled as soon as they were empty. A small expense for impaired judgment that resulted in greater profits for the club's partners. Considering that one of them was an earl and two of them were married to nobility, he would have thought they would not be so quick to fleece those with whom they rubbed elbows. But like his, their formative years had been shaped by life on the streets. They knew what it was to be hungry, cold, and frightened. They knew what it was to do without clothing, food, shelter, and shoes. They'd risen above all that, then reached back and grabbed a scrawny lad of eight by the scruff of his shirt and dragged him along with them.

He owed them all a debt he could never repay. But he especially owed the Duke and Duchess of Greystone. They had established children's homes with the duchess's share of the club's gains. They could have left Drake at one of them, to have been possibly overlooked. He'd been an angry child. Instead they had given him a place at their table, in their home, within their family.

Sometimes the anger still seeped through into the man, but he had learned to hold it in check. Especially here with the nobs and swells, with those who had much in the coffers and gave it up so easily with the whisper of a turning card or the clack of dice landing.

He knew all these faces. Lords, second sons, third sons. He knew their value, their worth, their habits, their weaknesses. He knew which ones would walk away from the tables with empty pockets and then seek out an heiress so he could return to the games. Dukes, marquesses, earls, viscounts. Within these walls rank didn't matter. They were all equal.

He gave his gaze the freedom to roam over them, to judge how loosely they were playing, to—

He came up short at one of the poker tables. What the devil was Lord Somerdale doing here? Why wasn't he out searching the streets for his sister? Yes, it was dark, but lanterns were invented for a reason and a good many gaslights warded off the dark throughout London. Even if it were impractical to search at night, especially if fog was rolling in, shouldn't he be at home worrying rather than here gambling what he could ill afford to lose?

"I'm of a mood for a private game. With Lovingdon off on his marriage trip, I might actually win a hand or two." The Duke of Avendale came to stand beside Drake, wrapped his fingers around the railing, and leaned forward.

"We'd rather not bring attention to the fact that we observe them," Drake said.

"They are well aware they are watched. I see no point in trying to be so secretive about it. By the by, what's holding your attention down there?"

He didn't want to explain, because he would have to explain too much. He'd never been particularly close to Avendale. The man tended to keep himself apart from the others. "Simply watching the money coming into our coffers."

"Hmm." He looked at Drake with brown eyes, his dark brown hair falling across his brow making him appear like Lucifer himself. "Going to join us for a private game?"

They had a secluded room where the sons—and on occasion the daughters—of the owners and their closest friends played cards. Avendale came to the group through William Graves—another former street urchin—who married Avendale's widowed mother.

"Invite Somerdale to join us."

Avendale's eyes widened at that. "The man's pockets aren't flush enough for him to play on our terms."

Their games tended to be high stakes and ruthless. And very often involved cheating. The street influenced them all.

"I'll extend his credit."

"Trying to find a way to get even with his sister for her treatment of you at the wedding ball?"

At every turn more like. "I barely gave her any notice."

"Bollocks. The little chit was very deliberate in her insults, and you didn't discreetly signal for us to take the other ladies away without some plan in mind. What exactly happened in the alcove?"

He discovered her tongue wasn't nearly as tart when engaged in something other than speaking. Again, not something he intended to share. Like the ink on his back, his ruination of Lady Ophelia Lyttleton was a private affair. It was enough for her to know that he'd won.

"We're short a player. Somerdale will suit. I don't know why you're objecting. You're bound to win with him at the table."

"I'm not objecting. I'm simply striving to determine your motive."

"Money, it's always money."

"Not with you, it's not. Just as it isn't with me. I know we've never been particularly close, but we're more alike than you think." As though he'd sliced open his soul and revealed something blackened within, Avendale scowled and looked back over the gaming floor. "I'll see that he joins us."

"Good." Drake felt as though he needed to say more, as though he needed to acknowledge the confession. He and Avendale were nothing alike. The man lived for sin. While it might be Drake's purview to encourage it within these walls, he'd never fancied himself a sinner. The son of a sinner, without a doubt, but it was his father's darkness residing inside him that gave him pause. "If you ever want to talk—"

Avendale laughed, dark and low. "Talking is for ladies. Drinking, fornicating, gambling are all that interest me." Then he was storming down the hallway as though he needed to escape the words spoken.

It occurred to Drake that they were all striving to

escape something. He dropped his gaze back to the floor, back to Somerdale, and wondered what Lady Ophelia Lyttleton might have been trying to escape.

The backroom of Dodger's Drawing Room was legendary. Entrance required an invitation. The giant at the door opened it only if the carefully guarded password was given. The inner sanctum was divided into two distinct parts. In the front, a lounging area where the losers could nurse their pride with liquor. Beside it, behind heavy drapes, the heart of the sanctuary, where exorbitant amounts of money—and sometimes nonfinancial wagers—exchanged hands on a regular basis. They played at a baize-covered table. The linen-covered sideboards along the wall sported crystal decanters, overseen by half a dozen footmen who were quick and silent when providing refreshment.

As he shuffled the cards, Drake acknowledged that they didn't require so many to attend to them, but then Dodger's had always been generous when it came to providing work to those in need. None of those employed came with references. They came from the streets or prison. Some as orphans, some sold by those who claimed to be parents in want of coin. They grew into adulthood and remained.

New names were given, new lives were begun. It had always been thus, and Drake had carried on the tradition begun by the owners. But Dodger's also had the reputation for never forgiving a transgression, not that there had ever been one as far as he knew. Those who worked here were a loyal lot, their loyalty bought with handsome salaries. But then considering how much money the club raked in each night, it was no hardship to pay their employees well.

Jack Dodger had believed that a man had no cause to

steal if enough coins lined his pocket. But Drake had to admit that the man's ruthless reputation had no doubt also contributed to well-behaved employees.

Those standing at attention within this room were trusted not to reveal anything that was discussed. Those seated at the table were equally trusted. Well, except for Somerdale. They would all no doubt be watching their words tonight. He did not share their knowledge of the streets. He was not raised by someone who had once engaged in questionable activities that skirted the law.

Drake dealt the cards to Langdon, Somerdale, Avendale, and Grace's older brother—the Marquess of Rexton. The game was stud poker. He didn't deal himself a hand because his mind would not be on the game, but rather on Lady O's brother.

He waited until they were several hands in and luck was running with Somerdale before asking, "So how is your sister, Somerdale? Recovered from all the activities involved in Grace's wedding?"

He was well aware of the other lords snapping to attention, studying him with interest. They never mentioned individual ladies, because speaking of a particular female might indicate an interest in her, which might portend a trip down the aisle. They were all confirmed bachelors. At least until they were ready to obtain an heir. For years they had bemoaned the fact that his untitled state kept him free of such responsibility. He would never be required to marry, to take a wife. He never had to suffer through lectures on his duties to his heritage.

Strange, though, how they craved his carefree bachelorhood that would never have to come to an end while he would have given anything—gladly taken on a wife—to possess their untarnished bloodlines.

"I suspect so," the earl murmured distractedly, studying the displayed cards.

"You don't know for certain?" Drake didn't bother to hide his skepticism, although he managed quite well to disguise his irritation at the less than satisfactory answer.

"She's off caring for an infirmed aunt." Somerdale picked up several chips and tossed them into the pile. "I'll raise fifty pounds."

"When did she leave?"

"Mmm. Late last night. Uncle arrived shortly after we returned home. Apparently Auntie is quite ill. She and Ophelia are rather close, always have been. Ophelia spent considerable time at Stillmeadow growing up."

"Stillmeadow?" He was generally more adept at conversation but he wanted to get to the matter at hand as quickly as possible.

"Our uncle's estate. A few hours north of London. He's the Earl of Wigmore."

"And they arrived safely?"

Somerdale finally looked up, his green eyes—not quite the intense shade as Ophelia's—homing in on Drake. "I should think so, yes. I've not heard differently. Why the interest?"

Because I dragged your sister out of the Thames hung on the tip of his tongue, but he held it back. Instinct. Preservation. He couldn't quite put his finger on it, but alarm bells were ringing. Somerdale could be lying. A little tale he'd made up after trying to do his sister in. Only why would he try to kill her? She came with an appealing dowry, but as Avendale had pointed out, Somerdale's own pockets weren't all that flush. Their parents were gone. They had no other siblings. Her dowry would no doubt go to him if she died. People had killed for less. His father had.

"Thought perhaps he'd be keen on having a membership in the club if he's only a few hours away." Distance was no deterrent to those who indulged in vice. Although he did hope Somerdale would fail to notice the erratic course of their conversation, that when it had begun Drake could not have known it would end here. Considering how much scotch Somerdale had downed, Drake was surprised the man could follow the cards, much less the direction of their discourse.

Somerdale chuckled. "Not Wigmore. He doesn't gamble, he doesn't drink. He's quite the paragon of virtue."

"Still, I should like to send him an invitation." He removed a small black book and pencil from his jacket pocket. He used it to keep a list of things that needed to be tended to around the club. He opened it to a blank page and passed it across the table. "If you would provide the details for the post."

With a shrug, Somerdale took the offerings in hand and began scribbling out the address. Drake would send a message, determine if the uncle was safe at home. If not, he would alert Scotland Yard that they needed to search the river for another body. It was quite possible that leaving in the late hours of the night, they'd been set upon. Or perhaps Somerdale was not the gentleman he appeared.

When Somerdale handed back over the book and pencil, Drake tucked them away.

"May we get on with the play now?" Avendale asked laconically.

"Actually, I just remembered a matter that needs my attention." Drake signaled to one of the footmen. "Randall, take over dealing."

A spark lit the man's eyes. They all wanted to become dealers or croupiers. This was the first step.

"Surely whatever it is can wait," Langdon said. His father, too, was a murderer. The knowledge should have made Drake feel more equal to the heir of the Claybourne title. But the Earl of Claybourne had killed a man who justly deserved killing. The same was not true of Drake's mother. She'd deserved nothing but kindness and it had been denied her.

"Your responsibility is to begat an heir; mine is to see that the club makes profits. Yours is a far more pleasurable task." He stood. "Gentlemen, enjoy your play." He jerked his head toward another footman. "Gregory, I have need of you. Come with me."

With Gregory trailing behind him, he strode through the room, down the stairs, and into his office. His pitiful attempt at a reference letter remained where he'd left it. He balled up the nonsense, tossed it in the wastebasket, and began anew.

This time involved the careful penning of an invitation to the Earl of Wigmore. He placed it in a vellum envelope that bore the emblem that represented Dodger's Drawing Room. Then he sealed it with wax. He handed it over to the young footman. "I want this delivered to the Earl of Wigmore personally, to no one else. Only him. If he's not there, I want you to ferret around until you discover if he ever returned from London."

"Yes, sir."

Taking the small book from his pocket, he found the location of the earl's estate and passed it over to Gregory. "You're not to tell anyone that I asked you to do this or to say a word about the additional information I seek."

"Yes, sir."

He didn't need to remind the footman that his position here depended upon his discretion. Drake had the power to hire, let go, and promote. He was obeyed without question, had been since he'd taken over the reins of running the establishment from Jack Dodger.

He then retrieved some coins from the safe and dropped them into Gregory's waiting palm. "For your journey. Whatever is left over is yours to keep." Considering the amount he'd handed over, a good deal should remain. "Hire a horse. Based on the distance, I expect to have your report tomorrow evening."

"Yes, sir."

"Be careful."

The man did little more than nod, before leaving.

Shortly afterward, Drake left as well. It wasn't often he lied to his friends, but tonight the club's profits were the last thing on his mind. First and foremost was unraveling the mystery of Lady Ophelia Lyttleton.

Chapter 10

It was half past two when he unlocked the door, crossed the threshold into his residence, and halted. Something was different. Perhaps it was that he was seldom here at this time, last night being an exception. But even as he considered it, he knew it was more than that. It *felt* different. It didn't seem as empty. A lamp had been left burning on the first step of the stairs, as though she'd thought—or perhaps hoped—he'd return early.

He hadn't planned to. He'd gone to Scotland Yard to inquire after any murders that might have taken place the night before. He'd spoken with Sir James Swindler, a friend of the family who wouldn't question Drake regarding his strange curiosity. The inspector confirmed, unfortunately, that some killings had occurred, but all the victims had been identified. None apparently was the Earl of Wigmore.

Drake had gone to the coroner's. No unclaimed corpses there. But that didn't mean anything. The attack could have happened elsewhere, could have been handled by other police, other coroners. The attack could have happened and the victim not yet discovered.

Perhaps it wasn't an attack. Only an accident. A careless driver losing control of the horses, the coach spiraling off a bridge. A spoke breaking, causing a carriage to careen off the road and into the river.

A hundred possibilities existed. Only someone with his past would immediately jump to the conclusion of foul play. From the moment Frannie Darling had taken him from the streets, he had been sheltered, but images of pain, suffering, and fear had already been branded into his consciousness. The loving arms and gentle smiles could not erase the horrors he'd witnessed, could not prevent the nightmares from rising up on occasion.

He was no doubt a fool not to tell Somerdale about his sister, to return her to her brother's keeping. Yet he was picking up the lamp and ascending the stairs to check in on her, confident he would find her asleep. In his bed, no doubt. Lady Ophelia Lyttleton would not sleep on a cot.

He imagined rousting her from slumber, sending her to her bedchamber. The satisfaction of it, the delight of putting her in her place was tempered by the worry at the edge of his mind. He didn't like not knowing what had happened to her. If Somerdale was telling the truth—if he was not—either way, something dastardly seemed to be at play.

Reaching the top of the stairs, he opened the door to his bedchamber, surprised to find the bed empty, but not at all surprised to see the bed remained tousled; the ashes from last night's fire were still a heap in the hearth.

Had her memory returned? Had she tried to make her way home? He tore down the hallway to the corner room and shoved open the door.

She was there, curled on the cot, a lit lamp on the floor. The relief that swamped him was unwanted and disconcerting. He wasn't supposed to care about her well-being, and yet for some unfathomable reason he did. But she was safe, not running hither and yon about London. He should leave. Return to the club and see to its profits.

Instead he approached quietly, and only as he neared did he realize that she was trembling as though he'd only just pulled her from the river. She wore one of his shirts again, the linen falling just above her knees. Her eyes were squeezed shut tight. Her breaths were harsh pants as though the air she required was elusive and distant. Her arms were crossed closely over her chest, her hands balled into knots.

"Phee?" Lightly he touched her shoulder and she struck out, arms flailing about madly.

"No, no! Don't touch me. Don't!" A shout, then a whimper, a tiny cry as she folded in on herself.

He remembered the words from last night, how he'd assumed they were directed at him. Perhaps they were directed at someone else. An attacker. Thieves could have tried to rob them. He could quite see her sticking that pert little nose of hers up in the air and informing them that their behavior was inappropriate and not to be tolerated.

She continued to shiver. Tears rolled down her cheeks. Sweat beaded her neck. She was constrained on that horrible tiny uncomfortable cot. What the devil had possessed him to think it would be fun to force her to sleep there when a perfectly good bed sat unused in his bedchamber in the evening?

All thoughts of lessons and retribution fled. All he wanted was for her to feel safe. To be safe.

"Phee?" He kept his voice calm, gentle, a tone he used to settle nervous horses. He'd always had a way with the great beasts, had even for a time considered becoming a stable boy, then a groom, but he was the ward of a duke and duchess who had grander plans for him. Bending his knees, he slipped his arms beneath her. "Shh," he whispered when she responded with a mewling. "It's all right. I won't let anything happen to you."

Lifting her up and cradling her against his chest, he realized her bare legs graced his arm with the wondrous feel of her silken skin. It was completely inappropriate to be thinking of her skin, of her flesh touching his.

With her fingers tightening around the shirt he wore, she snuggled her head into the nook of his shoulder. Her breaths lengthened as she drew in great drafts of air, as though she were delighted by a fragrance. His.

Ridiculous. Whatever was wrong with him that he would have such inane thoughts? She was no doubt simply relishing the warmth from his body, feeling as though she were tucked into a safe cocoon. No harm would come to her while he was near. Somehow she must have sensed that. Which should have made him feel better but didn't.

He carried her to his room and set her down gently on the bed, cursing his eyes for noticing how the hem of his shirt had ridden up her thighs. In spite of her short height, she had long, slender legs and the most delicate ankles. He was half tempted to place a kiss there. Instead he flipped the covers up over her, surprised that she hadn't awakened. Apparently she was an incredibly deep sleeper, even when nightmares flourished.

He went to the fireplace, crouched, and did what she should have done earlier: swept out the ashes, arranged the coal and logs. Then he struck a match, lit the kindling, and watched as the fire took hold.

He heard a sob being choked back. Damnation. Unfolding his body, he strode back over. She was restless again, rolling her head from side to side, murmuring to be left in peace, but she didn't sound as though she would find any peace this evening.

Leaning in, he touched his fingers to her cheek. "Phee?"

She inhaled deeply, once, twice. "You returned."

"Yes."

Her eyes fluttered open, and her lips lifted up into the smallest of smiles. "You chased away the monster. You and your dragon."

He felt as though he'd taken a hard punch to the gut. Her words, her smile. She never smiled at him like that, nor could he recall seeing that smile bestowed upon others. Yet there was an honesty in it. No artifice. No pretense. No role playing.

"What monster?" he asked.

"I don't know. I couldn't see him clearly. Perhaps I should have a dragon inked on my back."

He imagined a dragon in flight over her slender back, what she would endure to possess it. "It's a very painful process. Once you begin, you can't stop. What good is only a piece of the dragon?"

"I suppose you're right." She pressed her lips together before gnawing on the lower one. The action went straight to his groin. It was the shadows, his shirt draped over her skin, her in his bed.

"I have so many questions," she said, distracting him from dangerous musings.

"We'll get to them in the morning. You need to sleep now."

"I don't understand my clothes."

"Have they been talking to you then?"

Her smile grew slightly. "No, but they're wrong. I don't have a nightdress."

"We'll discuss it all later, after you've rested." He was delaying the inevitable, but he didn't want to lose the way she was looking at him, as though she accepted him, as though she didn't distrust him.

She shook her head. "I don't like to sleep."

"You were having a nightmare. No one, nothing here will harm you. I'll keep watch."

"None of this, my being here, makes sense to me."

"It will, very soon, I'm sure."

She studied him as though striving to ferret out the truth, but he wasn't lying. He would tell her everything tomorrow evening, after Gregory returned. Meanwhile, he would have another day of her scrubbing his back.

"I'm so cold," she said quietly. "It's as though I'm frozen throughout."

He couldn't make the fire any larger, and he had no more blankets, blast it all. He supposed he could heap his clothes on top of her. Or he could give her warmth in another way. "Don't be alarmed but I'm going to lie on top of the covers and hold you. All right? I can warm you that way."

She nodded. Removing his jacket, he spread it over her hips. He tugged off his boots. So the buttons wouldn't scrape her, he draped his waistcoat over the chair. For his comfort, he unfolded his neck cloth and set it aside. Then he climbed on the bed, stretched out beside her. She came into the curve of his shoulder as though she belonged there, her hand curling against his chest. Placing his arm around her, he drew her nearer. With his free hand, he rubbed her back down to her waist, down to where the covers had gathered. He didn't want to consider how close his hand might be to the bared flesh of her thighs.

"I can't decide if you like me," she said so softly he almost didn't hear her. "You seem to care for me, like now, and other times you have no patience with me."

"We just don't know each other very well I suppose."

"Then tell me a story."

A story. Yes, he supposed he could do that. He'd told a good many to Grace when she was a child. "Once upon a time there was a cobbler and his wife—"

Laughing with that sweet sound that he had only discovered she possessed, she lifted her head and met his gaze. "You are not on the verge of telling me the story of the cobbler and the elves."

"You know it?"

She gave him a pointed look. She'd given him many in the past, but none like this. It was teasing, amused. It made him want to plow his hands into her hair, bring her down for a kiss that would warm her, scorch her soul. It made him want to keep her here. It made him want to know her. It unsettled him to think she could be very different from what he had always known.

"Of course I know the story. I don't want you to tell me a fairy tale, silly. I want you to share something about you. Tell me a story about you."

Silly? He was far from silly. He considered castigating her, employer to employee, yet he didn't want to lose this moment. For the life of him he didn't know why he wanted to hold on to it. Share something with her. He had spent his life erecting a wall that only a select few could peer over, but none could see through completely. He even held things back from the Mabrys. He didn't believe anyone could accept him completely as he truly was. He could give her something to use against him, so he had to be very careful in what he shared.

She settled back down, nudging her head in the hollow of his shoulder until it fit perfectly.

"Warmer?" he asked.

"Yes. But I'm still waiting for the story. Tell me something from when you were a boy."

Those tales would satisfy the Brothers Grimm. "As

I mentioned earlier I began my life on the streets. I survived by skill, cunning, and quickness. But still food, clothing, warmth were scarce. I remember the first time I ate until I was full. I was eight at the time. Meat pies. Then I promptly brought them all back up."

"Ew! I think I would rather hear the cobbler's tale."

"I thought you might."

She was quiet for a very long time. He thought perhaps she was drifting off. Then she said, "I can't imagine that my life is very happy. I can't seem to feel any joy in being here."

An awful thought jarred him. Had she deliberately jumped into the river intending to do herself harm? Had his kiss so repulsed her—no, her plunge in the river had nothing to do with him. Nor with her wishing herself harm. If he knew anything at all about her, it was that she thought too highly of herself to deny the world her existence. Her loss of memory was simply disorienting to her.

"You take great pride in your place," he said. True, even if it was her place in the aristocracy to which he referred.

"Do I?"

"Yes. You are well versed in your duties. You carry them out with extreme diligence. You've set an example for others that few can imitate." Again, all true, although he'd never considered the merits of them, but they were there even without his recognizing them.

"Are those words from my letters of reference?"

"Only my observations."

"Did you bring the letters?"

"I seem to have misplaced them, but I shall find them."

"Why did you return early?"

"Because I was . . . concerned for you." Because she

was driving him more mad without her memory than she ever had with it.

"I'm warm now," she said. "No longer shivering."

He supposed that was his signal to leave her. He should be incredibly relieved. Instead, he found that he enjoyed holding her, inhaling her unique scent, speaking low with her—even about nothing of significance—while shadows danced around them. Disturbing her as little as possible, he eased off the bed.

With her head on the pillow, she tucked a hand beneath her cheek and regarded him. "I like this bed better. It's more comfortable."

"You may use it when I'm not here."

"But you're here now."

"Yes, but I won't be sleeping."

He stood there until he was relatively certain that she had drifted off. Then he pulled over the chair, sat, and began his vigil.

Only because she was Grace's friend, and his sister would never forgive him if something awful happened to her. His remaining had nothing to do with the glimpse she'd given him of a lady he had never before met.

She awoke disoriented on sheets that weren't quite as soft as those to which she was accustomed. The pillow was harder, the mattress firmer. She tried to latch on to what she could barely recall, but it was like trying to capture fog and it slipped through her grasp. Everything had slipped away, all of her memories, and yet . . .

The man was familiar. His scent, the strength in his arms. He was sitting in one of those awful hard chairs, his head tilted to one side, his eyes closed, long lashes resting on sharp cheekbones. His legs were outstretched, crossed at the ankles, his arms folded across his chest. She marveled that he hadn't toppled to the floor. His neck would no doubt ache when he awoke. She would massage it when she washed his back.

Because he hadn't left, because he'd kept watch as he had promised.

He shouldn't have returned until after dawn, and yet he'd arrived last night when she needed him. It seemed he was always there to rescue her: when she was drowning, when she was cold and frightened, when dreams terrified her. How many other times had he been there? How many other times might he have consoled her and eased her fears?

He opened his eyes, and she found herself staring into the dark depths. So black that they should have been unsettling. Blacker than his hair, darker than the shadow on his jaw. Nothing about him was light or carefree. Everything had a dangerous edge to it, and yet she knew she was safe with him. Had she always known that or had she once been afraid?

He didn't say anything. He simply studied her as though he wasn't quite certain who she was or how she might respond to his presence.

"I'm rather embarrassed about the spectacle I made of myself last night," she began.

"You shouldn't be. Dreaming of monsters can be upsetting. Do you recall anything else?"

She was lying on her side, one hand beneath the pillow, the other curled around the blankets. She considered sitting up, but she thought any movement might break whatever spell was presently between them, creating an intimacy she didn't understand. He hadn't moved either, as though he sensed it as well.

"A man. He was trying to hurt me, and I was fending him off."

"Who was he?"

"I don't know. He was shadow, dark, foreboding, sinister. No features. But he loomed over me. I was suffocating. I couldn't move, and I wanted to. Desperately. I screamed but no sound escaped no matter how hard I tried to make the noise, so no one could hear me. I was terrified that this time he'd have his way."

"This time?"

She sensed the alertness in him, as though his entire body had suddenly awoken. She rubbed her brow. "I must have had the dream before. Something about it was familiar. Or perhaps that was simply part of the dream, thinking that it had happened before. Perhaps a dream within a dream."

"I want you to tell me if you remember anything else about it, about the attacker."

She couldn't help but form a smile. "Are you a dream slayer then?"

He was looking at her as though he'd never seen her before. He blinked, looked down at his bare feet. His shirt was as it had been yesterday, loose and unbuttoned. But now she knew the corded muscles he hid beneath it, the ink that resided just below the surface.

A corner of his mouth finally curled up. "I'm not but the dragon on my back is."

"Is that why you had him inked? You had nightmares as well?"

He was studying her intently again, and she thought he might not answer. Yet she wanted him to, badly. She wanted to know everything about him, everything she'd forgotten. While she understood—but could scarcely accept—that she worked for him, she couldn't help but believe a bit more existed between them. They had some sort of history. She was certain of it, because why else would she not be alarmed that she was in his bed, with his linen shirt gathered at her hips, her legs bare while he was sitting there completely comfortable with half his clothing gone? It involved more than the fact that she bathed his back. While that had created a startling closeness, she knew the familiarity wasn't foreign to them.

In spite of their lack of attire, her bare legs, his bare feet, he wouldn't suddenly pounce onto the bed, he wouldn't take advantage. She knew that, but how the devil did she know?

It was so frustrating to know only pieces of him when she wanted to know the whole.

He unfolded his arms, leaned forward, planted his elbows on his thighs, and met her gaze. "During my time on the streets, I witnessed horrors that still sometimes visit my dreams. When I was younger, I did have the rather juvenile thought that the dragon would fend them off." His lips formed a self-deprecating smile that caused her chest to tighten. "But I've come to believe that only we can conquer our demons."

"Have you conquered yours?"

"Not to my satisfaction."

"Are we not also our own worst critics?"

"Perhaps."

"We always want something different from what we have." She furrowed her brow. "Why do I think—no, why do I know that with certainty? I wanted something different, but what did I want?"

He didn't say anything, only held her gaze as though he had the power to draw the memory, the truth, from her. She trusted those eyes, the depths of them, the sincerity. He was not a man who ridiculed or taunted.

"I believe I may have unraveled the mystery of my clothes," she said.

One dark brow shot up. "Oh?"

She didn't know if he was reacting to her sharp

change in topic or was truly interested in the answer. "I must have packed everything into a valise that night, all except the most hideous of my clothing. I must have lost it in the river. That's why I have no apron or nightdress. Although I don't know why I didn't leave the apron behind, because I think I was striving to escape this life. As I see no value in it."

"The life of a servant?" he asked, as though she could possibly be speaking about something else.

"Yes. I can't imagine awakening every morning and knowing that my day would be naught but dealing with dust and dirt."

"The value in it is a salary, satisfaction in a job well done. Ensuring a residence is pleasant to live in. The family with whom I lived—they were well off. One must eat. They could have prepared their meals. Instead they hired someone to do it for them. While that person cooked, they were out doing good works. The cook, while preparing nourishment for them, allowed them to have the time to do their good works. It's all interconnected, it all has value. If you're not seeing it, it's because you're not looking at it properly."

His words were laced with passion, his voice teeming with it.

"I spend long hours providing entertainment for gentlemen," he continued. "Having a servant means that I'm not distracted by household concerns. I can concentrate on increasing profits. More profits means we can hire more employees so more men can provide for their families. They purchase more meat for their table so the butcher has more income. He buys more meat. The farmer has more income. I could go on but I believe I've made my point. It may seem but a small drop, but it ripples out and affects so many. You may not see it, but even the lowliest servant has value, purpose, worth.

Everyone has a place and none of those places should be diminished."

As though suddenly embarrassed, he closed his eyes, shook his head, and leaned back. She wondered if she'd been aware of all the points he'd made, if she'd agreed with them. But if she had why would she have been running away?

Although in truth she didn't know if she had been. She was only speculating about her clothing. It was the only explanation that made sense.

"I suppose I should get to it then, shouldn't I?" she asked.

"I'll prepare breakfast for you while you dress." He unfolded his long, sinewy body, and an image of him prowling toward her flashed through her mind, kicking her heart against her ribs. It was an incongruous thought that didn't fit with the man before her, the man she knew, but then how well did she really know him? A day of memories was hardly sufficient to create a complete picture, and yet he'd been patient and understanding. Quite remarkable when in essence he'd lost his housekeeper.

He strode from the room, his movements neither stiff nor formal, but relaxed. He was in his element here, although she suspected he was within his element everywhere. He wore confidence like a cloak.

Tossing aside the covers, she scrambled out of bed. While it was disconcerting to know no more than she did, it was also reassuring to consider that he valued her, that she could lighten the load he carried.

As Drake slammed pots around the kitchen, he soundly cursed himself, wondering what the devil had possessed him to utter such nonsense about value, and purpose, and worth. He believed it of course, absolutely. But to wax on boringly about it was beyond comprehension. It was as though he was striving to beat the sentiment into her, to make her understand that her pedestal only remained upright because of the work of others. Ironically, she didn't know she'd placed herself on the blasted pedestal.

To make matters worse he was preparing the damned creamed eggs for her. He'd spoken to the cook at Dodger's about them and received the directions. They weren't all that difficult to make as he whipped them around the pan, adding cream, butter, and seasoning. But still, she was supposed to be cooking for him. That had been the plan. To have her waiting on him.

But when she looked at him so innocently, so trustingly, with her hand tucked beneath the pillow, the collar of his shirt turned up against her neck, lying all snug in his bed, he felt this irrational urge to protect and care for her. The ludicrousness of all this was not lost on him. Yet he couldn't return her home, not yet, not until he heard from his man, until he was certain that he wasn't leading her to the lion's den. Nothing made sense, especially his desire to please her at breakfast. He should feed her nothing except toast and water, should make her realize that not everyone had the luxury of creamed eggs—of any sort of eggs.

"Creamed eggs?"

The wonder in her voice had him glancing back. She looked positively delighted. Her face was still pink from the morning scrubbing she'd no doubt given it. Her plaited hair draped over one shoulder. She wore the other dress he'd found in the missionary bin. It draped off her like a sack. He fought back the notion that she deserved better, that she deserved morning gowns that outlined every dip and curve. That she deserved clothes sewn just for her figure.

"I thought after the night you had that a little treat was in order. Don't get used to it." He poured the mixture over the toast he'd prepared earlier and set the plate on the table.

"Aren't you joining me?" she asked.

"No. I'm going out for a bit to see to some matters. I expect you to begin managing your chores while I'm gone."

"You are quite the tyrant, aren't you?"

Teasing laced her voice and he didn't like the way that it made his chest feel tight and uncomfortable. "I've been lax because of your situation but understand that I expect an honest day's work for an honest day's pay."

She pleated her brow. "I suppose all that is subjective."

"My subjectivity is all that matters since I'm the one paying for the services. Now, enjoy your meal and then see to the dishes."

He charged up the stairs and into his bedchamber. Of course, the bed linens were still askew, the pillow had yet to be fluffed, so it carried the imprint of her head. He was tempted to cross over and straighten everything, but it was her job. He'd leave it to her.

In the bathing chamber, he found water in a bowl, none in the pitcher, so he used the water she'd used to wash up. He reached for his brush, halted, his fingers only inches away from it. Long blond strands were woven throughout the bristles, just as they'd been yesterday. The intimacy of it was unsettling. Tunneling his fingers through his hair, he decided that would do for now. He donned fresh clothing. It wouldn't do to arrive at Mabry House untidy, to give the appearance that his life was suddenly unsettled.

Chapter 11

The first time Drake entered Mabry House, it had been through the chimney flue. He'd been Peter Sykes that night. His father hoisted him up into a tree, and then as nimbly as a little monkey, he scrambled up the branches until he was able to leap onto the roof, where he made his way to the chimney, and down he went.

The duke, in residence at the time, had caught him. While he hadn't managed to unlock the door to let in his father, he had enjoyed a feast of meat pies and been introduced to Frannie Darling. Because of her and the duke his life had taken an unexpected turn.

Now he walked boldly through the front door without knocking. He had a room within the residence, had grown up within these walls as well as at the duke's numerous estates.

"Master Drake," the butler said. "They're already in the breakfast dining room."

Of course they were. He was late for his weekly morning visit. "Thank you, Boyer."

He wandered down the familiar hallways, stopping once to gaze on the portrait that featured the duke and duchess and all their children. Drake stood at the end, a head taller than the others. They had never differentiated between him and their true children, had never made him feel as though he wasn't part of the family. They had given him a great gift; he understood that readily enough. They had embraced him. Yet when he studied the painting, he saw himself on the outer edge, included but holding himself separate.

He marched on. The doors to the breakfast dining room stood open. Only a few steps in after crossing the threshold, he was enveloped by the duchess, who had come out of her chair before anyone could assist her. For as long as he'd known her, she always greeted children—her own and every orphan who crossed her path—with a hug. Whether they were returning from a term at school or a jaunt to the park. Her arms wrapped tightly around him as though she wanted to hold him forever, but as always, she eventually let him go. Let them all go, even though he knew how difficult it was for her.

"I was beginning to worry," she said, her blue eyes scanning his features, striving to determine if something was amiss.

"Just running a tad behind this morning."

"Rexton said you left the club last night."

Looking over her shoulder, he glared at the Greystone heir, who merely shrugged. "I went to see you after the game ended, and you weren't about."

"Just some business. Nothing to worry over."

"Then prepare your plate," the duchess insisted, "and join us at the table."

If she wasn't hugging them, she was stuffing food into them. Like him, she was not a stranger to hunger. The sideboard was laden with all sorts of offerings, the aromas wafting around him. Quite suddenly he realized he was famished. He refused to feel guilty because he'd left Ophelia with nothing more than creamed eggs and toast. Hadn't she said it was what she preferred? No sense in giving her an assortment of choices when most would be discarded. Although he knew that whatever was left over here would be taken to a mission to be served to the poor.

After heaping an assortment of selections onto his plate, he took his usual chair beside the duchess. Andrew, the spare, sat across from him. The duke sat at the head of the table, with Rexton to his left, beside Drake. The chair to the duke's right was Grace's. It was odd to see it empty.

"Have you heard from Grace or Lovingdon?" Drake asked.

"No," the duchess said, "and I doubt we will until they return in a fortnight, which is the way it should be."

"They're so disgustingly in love," Andrew said.

"With any luck you will be as well one day," the duke said.

"I don't need an heir, so I'll never marry. Drake and I are going to be bachelors until our dying days, aren't we, Drake?" he asked.

"That's the plan," he admitted.

"We swore to it," he said. At twenty-one he was young and full of himself. Drake couldn't recall ever feeling that young. He'd always been older in experience as well as years.

"That's a silly thing to swear to," the duchess said. "You can't control your hearts."

"Your mother has the right of it there," the duke said, smiling softly. "Love will have its way."

In the beginning, Drake had marveled at the kindness the duke had shown his wife. He never yelled at her, never raised his fist to her, never strove to intimidate her. They discussed issues; her opinion was as important as his. For no reason at all, he plucked flowers to give to her, bought her gifts, and spent an amazing amount of time kissing her. Drake appreciated the softness that lit her eyes whenever the duke walked into a room, the sweetness of her laughter. He had no memory of his own mother's laughter. He knew her tears, her pleading, her screams. Under the duke's influence, it hadn't taken him long to come to the realization that his father had been a brute. And that a man treated his wife better than he himself wanted to be treated.

A niggle of guilt regarding Ophelia pricked his conscience but he ignored it. Unlike the duchess, she didn't treat people kindly, she didn't engage in good works, she didn't put others before herself. He'd caught her berating servants, knew she was easily displeased. Patience and appreciation of others were strangers to her. She cared only for her own wants, comfort, and pleasure.

She cried out in her sleep.

"So how goes business at Dodger's?" the duchess asked, interrupting his thoughts, thank God.

"Profits are up ten percent this month," he said, digging into his eggs Benedict. "I approved the membership of an American."

"American?" Rexton repeated. "Good God, does Dodger know?"

"I didn't seek his permission before making my decision, if that's what you're asking," Drake said. "The American is embarrassingly wealthy, enjoys gambling now and again, and increases our profits. From what I understand, more Americans are beginning to spend their time in London as they strive to marry their daughters off to the peerage." He gave Rexton a pointed look. "Perhaps you'll even marry one. I hear they rather like dukes."

"It'll be a good many years before I'm a duke. Besides, I'm sure they will have grown bored with us by the time I'm ready to take a wife. By the by, in the future don't invite Somerdale to join us for a private game. He trounced us rather badly."

Conversation moved on to the orphanages. It was odd not to have Grace there inserting her opinions, sharing gossip, talking about her various plans with the ladies. Drake never realized how much he depended on her for information. She was insightful and gave him an edge when it came to little wagers regarding the various happenings in Society—who was courting whom, who was likely to marry whom. Although few had suspected she would wed the Duke of Lovingdon. The man had been an unrepentant rake, but also wise enough to fall in love with Grace.

Following breakfast, Drake took a stroll through the garden with the duchess, her hand nestled in the crook of her elbow.

"Are you happy?" she asked.

"Yes, of course."

"You seem troubled."

She would notice that his mood seemed a bit off. She noticed everything, but then most thieves did. It was the key to survival. "I have a lot on my mind."

"Lady Ophelia, perhaps."

He nearly stumbled on the cobblestones. "Why would you think that?"

She gave him a sly look. "It didn't escape my notice that you disappeared into an alcove with her at the ball."

He cursed soundly. He'd been so angry with her that he'd not taken precautions to protect her reputation. The last thing he wanted was to find himself permanently tied to the harridan. Although the woman in his bed last night . . . He mentally shook his head. They were one and the same. He needed to remember that. "Did anyone else notice?"

"I don't think so. I've heard no rumors."

He needed Grace. She would know with certainty. Ironically, so would Ophelia if she possessed her memories.

"I've long thought she fancied you," the duchess said.

Drake barked out his laughter. "Lady Ophelia Lyttleton? No. I'm the last person on earth she would ever fancy. And I most certainly do not fancy her."

"Something about her always struck me as tragic."

He stopped walking and faced her. "A woman who walks with her nose so high in the air it's a wonder sparrows don't perch on it? A woman who can give a cut direct to a fellow without anyone else noticing? A woman who harangues her lady's maid if a hair falls out of her coiffure? Are we talking about the same woman?"

"For being a woman you don't fancy, she certainly doesn't seem to have escaped your notice or scrutiny."

"She's been underfoot, a friend to Grace since she was old enough to walk. I could scarcely not notice her."

Her lips curled up. "Oh, I suspect you could have if you tried." She placed her hand on his elbow and began guiding him back toward the residence. "It's her eyes. They're haunted."

"Haunted by what?"

"I wouldn't know. That's the thing of it. We can never know everything about another person, and sometimes actions are a defense." She squeezed his arm. "I know she has slighted you on occasion, but I think perhaps you frighten her."

"How the bloody hell did I frighten her? Because she is Grace's friend, I've been remarkably cordial whenever our paths cross."

She chuckled faintly, as though amused by something he could neither see nor hear. "The duke terrified me when I met him."

He couldn't imagine it. Even when the man had caught Drake trying to steal from him, he'd merely fed him. "What monstrous thing did he do?"

"He drew me to him in ways no other man ever had."

Lady Ophelia Lyttleton was not drawn to him. The thought was ludicrous. The duchess was getting up in years, fancied herself a matchmaker for her sons, but she had atrocious taste when it came to who would suit and who would not. Still, Drake loved her, knew she meant well, and it took all his self-control not to laugh until his belly hurt. Ophelia. Drawn to him. When pigs flew.

After they returned to the house, he excused himself to talk with the housekeeper as he had some questions regarding his new residence. The duchess had seen it, of course, when he purchased it, but he hadn't invited any of the family back over for a visit. He wanted to wait until he had things in order. So she wasn't surprised by his desire to speak with Mrs. Garrett.

"Mrs. Beeton's *Book of Household Management*," the elderly housekeeper told him now as they stood in her office below stairs. "The very best resource for learning how to manage a house properly. Mrs. Beeton believed that an untidy house led to marital discord. Her guidance has saved many a marriage, I assure you."

He had no interest in saving any marriage. He didn't even know why he was seeking her counsel. Ophelia would no doubt be returning to her residence tomorrow morning. But he would soon be hiring a proper housekeeper, and it seemed he needed to have an idea regarding the knowledge she should possess.

Leaving Mrs. Garrett, he went in search of a sweet little maid who had come to work here a few years before. He found Anna making the duke's bed.

Blushing, she curtsied. "Master Drake."

He had told her numerous times that she need not curtsy for him, but still she did the little bob. Taking a moment, he outlined details of her form as discreetly as possible. She was perfect for his needs. "Anna, I was wondering if you might be able to help me."

"If I can, sir, anything at all. You need only ask."

"I know a woman who has fallen on hard times. She is approximately your size. I was wondering if you might have any clothing you were considering disposing of. I would gladly pay you a hundred pounds for it."

Her blue eyes widened. "Oh, you don't have to do that, sir. I'm more than happy to help those in need."

"I insist on recompense. She requires quite a bit, actually. A uniform, an apron. Some unmentionables." He grinned. "Which I just mentioned, didn't I?"

She laughed. "You're such a tease, sir."

She made him smile, and he thought she was the sort to whom he should be drawn, a commoner like himself. Yet she was too sweet for the darkness that resided inside him.

"A nightdress if you have it." He had to get Ophelia out of his shirts, because he would never be able to put them on without thinking of the linen touching her skin. "Perhaps an old dress that you'd wear when you have time off?"

"I believe I have some things. Won't take me but a minute to fetch them."

It actually took her a good half hour, not that he was going to complain. She met him at the back door, large bundle in her arms. He handed over the coins he'd promised, knowing she'd gotten the better end of the bargain, but then he'd been raised to be generous. If one possessed fortune, one shared it.

Then because he had a few more errands to see to, he decided to make use of one of the duke's carriages. It would hasten his return to his townhome. Not that he was anxious to again be in Ophelia's company, but he didn't want to leave her alone for too long. And it was long past the hour when he normally went to bed. It was practicality that had him having a carriage readied.

Not any desire for haste so he could sooner look into her green eyes and see if they were indeed haunted.

Phee washed the dishes. Simple enough task. She'd dusted somewhat yesterday so she didn't think she needed to attend to that chore again. Trying to recall what other duties Drake had told her to manage, she wandered through the residence. He really needed to acquire a very comfortable chair in which she could curl. As housekeeper was it her responsibility to inform him regarding what was needed? Yes, she believed so, as it seemed he hadn't really a clue.

Walking into the front parlor, she tried to envision what all it should contain. Chairs, a sofa. Brightly colored fabrics, yellow and green. No, not for him. Something darker. Burgundy, perhaps. He was a dark wine with a bitter edge that dried the mouth.

How did she know wine? Because she enjoyed its flavor. She needed to search the kitchen for some bottles. It was strange, the things she recalled, the things she didn't.

She'd heard him laugh, but it didn't seem to contain any joy. She didn't think he was particularly content with life, and while she knew she needed to be striving to remember her duties, she was more interested in remembering what she knew of him.

Perching her hip on the wide windowsill, she gazed out on the street and wondered if it was possible to move forward without a history. Did she truly need to recall her past? Obviously it wasn't anything special or she wouldn't now be a domestic.

Recalling Drake, though, had the possibility to be much more interesting. While she instinctively knew it was wicked, she could hardly wait for his evening bath, to once more have the opportunity to trail her fingers over his firm back. Not an ounce of fat resided on his person. His body was all sinewy muscle.

She couldn't decide if she preferred him in his carefree attire of only shirt and trousers or in his proper dress with waistcoat, jacket, and perfectly knotted neck cloth. As he had no valet, he was quite masterful at dressing himself. Why didn't he have a valet? Funds, she supposed. No doubt the reason he had only one servant. It was costly to have domestics.

Of course with a residence that echoed its emptiness, she didn't have a great deal to manage just yet. She had it quite easy, shouldn't really complain. Still, she would like to see some furniture in here. The room had such potential. She imagined the paintings that would go on the walls, daisies and landscapes—

No, they should be storms. Gray and untamed and brutal. The art should reflect her employer. It was more than his black hair and eyes that made him appear dark. It was his swagger, the intensity of his gaze, the past that he reluctantly revealed, one comprised of shadows that haunted him, because even in sleep he didn't seem at peace.

She wanted to explore those shadows, explore him, inside and out. He intrigued her. Or perhaps she was simply trying to limit her boredom with thoughts of him. Because presently she missed him. For some minutes she had stood in the kitchen doorway watching as he prepared her breakfast. Efficiency marked his brisk movements. Confidence rolled off him. She couldn't imagine there was anything he couldn't conquer.

Including her.

The thought tumbled through her mind, but before she could examine it more closely, a very fine carriage rattled to a stop in front of the residence. As with everything of late she didn't know how she knew what she knew—why she didn't know what she didn't know—but she knew without question that it was a very fine carriage indeed. With a liveried driver and footman, the latter hopping down to the street and quickly opening the door.

Drake stepped out in one fluid movement that belied the fact he was holding an assortment of parcels. The footman made a motion to relieve Drake of his burdens, but her employer simply shook his head, uttered something, and the footman let him be, clambering back onto the carriage, and off it went.

Rushing to the door, she threw it open and couldn't contain her smile. "You're home."

He staggered to a stop, appearing at once confused and disconcerted, as though he hadn't expected her to be here. Then his features settled into a mask of disgruntlement as though he weren't at all happy to see her. "A servant should open the door with a bit more decorum."

She was stung by the words, by his displeasure when it had so delighted her to see that he'd returned. Giving a quick bob of a curtsy, she said, "My apologies. What have you there?"

He edged by her. "A servant doesn't question her employer."

"I wasn't questioning you."

"A sentence beginning with *what* and ending on an elevated note generally implies question."

"Fine." She slammed the door, jerked up her chin. "I suppose a servant doesn't close doors with a bang either."

"Quite right. They shouldn't be heard at all and seldom seen."

"I suppose they shouldn't be overjoyed to have their master return." She couldn't keep the pique from her voice, which she supposed was another failing. Servants no doubt talked in modulated tones so no one ever knew precisely what they were thinking.

He didn't seem to have an answer for that, but studied her for a moment before jerking his head to the side and saying, "Come to the kitchen."

She didn't like being ordered about, didn't like it at all. It didn't sit well, and a small seed of rebellion deep inside her wanted to rise up and protest. But she tamped it down and followed docilely behind. Maybe not quite so docile. Her hands were fisted, and she was half tempted to plant one in the center of his back, right in the dragon's heart.

The silence stretching between them was awkward, but everything she thought to say was a question. How was your morning? What all did you do while you were away? Did you see anything interesting, hear any juicy gossip? She was craving gossip.

But she bit her tongue and kept from speaking. When they reached the kitchen, she thought he might praise her for her restraint, but he merely set the packages down and waved a hand over them.

"Open them."

"They're for me?" She growled at the words that had escaped without thought. "I know. I'm not supposed to ask questions."

She caught the barest twinkle in his eyes. "I'll overlook that one."

She had the oddest desire to see him overjoyed, happy, laughing. At ease. Not in the way he was comfortable with his surroundings, but deeper, at ease with himself, at ease with her. He must have liked her. He'd hired her. She couldn't blame him for his impatience with the recent turn of events. She had to relearn everything. He'd not bargained for that. "You should release me."

She didn't think his eyes could have grown any wider if she'd punched him in his flat stomach. "Pardon?"

"You should dismiss me. Hire someone who remembers how to tend to her duties, how to open the door properly—"

"At this precise moment all I require is that you open packages properly."

His impatience was tempered this time, and she was glad he wasn't letting her go. How would she even begin to make it on her own when only a chasm of emptiness existed where knowledge should be?

She tugged on the bow of the string that held the brown paper around a large package that seemed to contain something soft and malleable. Parting the wrapping, she uncovered clothing. She grabbed the dress by the shoulders, lifted it up, shook it to unfold it, and held it out for inspection. A plain frock of dark blue with buttons up to the starched white collar. Long sleeves. She peered over it at him.

"Your uniform," he stated succinctly. "You were mistaken with your assumption that you had packed your clothes into a valise. You arrived with few possessions. I should have made arrangements for you to purchase things."

Nodding, she set it aside and unfolded a white frilly apron. Tears stung her eyes.

"You'll no doubt be more pleased with this package," he said, shoving another toward her.

"I'm not displeased. I've never had such a thoughtful gift."

"You've had lots of gifts."

Cocking her head to the side, she studied him. "Have I?"

"I can't know for sure, of course, but I'm certain you have. One does not grow up without receiving any gifts."

"I can't recall a single one. It's truly like starting my life all over."

"Some would consider the chance to start over a blessing."

"But that's the thing of it. I don't know if I should or not." She didn't want to focus on the troubling notion that maybe she should be grateful so she turned to the next parcel. It contained a gray dress, again with buttons to the collar, but the skirt contained several short ruffles on the backside.

"Another uniform?"

"No, I just thought you might have a need for regular clothing."

"Do I get a day off?"

"From time to time."

How grand! "When is the next one?" she asked enthusiastically.

"The next what?"

"Day off, silly. I should like to go to a bookshop. And gardens. I like to walk through gardens. Speaking of gardens, you really should hire a gardener."

He appeared completely flummoxed. "Did you call me silly?"

Of all she'd said, he was going back to that? "I meant

no insult. I suppose I shouldn't be so informal with my employer."

"No, you should not."

"I'm only to tend to your residence?"

"Precisely. And the packages I brought you."

She considered prodding him about the gardener but perhaps she would have more success if she brought it up another time. She would so love to have flowers to brighten up the rooms. But as he seemed most anxious for her to examine the contents of the packages, she returned her attention to them.

Setting aside the frock, she lifted other items, realizing they were underthings, much finer and softer than what she was presently wearing. The heat scorching her face, she shoved them beneath the dress.

"No need to blush," he said. "I'm well acquainted with women's undergarments."

She had no doubt there, but she didn't much like the cockiness in his words or the satisfaction in his smile. She didn't want to think about women draped over him, stroking his dragon, his chest, any part of him. "Do you bring your ladies here?"

"No."

Taking some comfort in his not parading them past her, she wondered why it mattered. She was his servant, nothing more. Yet it seemed there should be more.

With the undergarments stuffed aside, one more item remained. A nightdress. She would no longer have to sleep in his shirt. The thought didn't bring as much joy as it should, but she didn't want to examine the reasons either, because they were mocking her, reminding her that she didn't want to be here, and yet she did.

He then nudged what appeared to be a box toward her. But when she untied the string and folded back the paper, she discovered *The Book of Household Management*. If the uniform hadn't succeeded in reminding her of his expectations, the book did, glaringly so.

"The housekeeper of the woman who raised me assures me that Mrs. Beeton, the author, is the authority when it comes to proper management of a household," he said.

"I see."

"It also includes recipes so you'll have more success at preparing my dinners."

Flipping through the pages, she couldn't imagine anything that would be less joyous to read. After setting it aside, she reached for one of the two remaining packages.

"No, this one first."

Inside were four more books, but these . . . Reverently, she trailed her fingers over two leather-bound works by Austen and two by Dickens.

"Thought I might as well give you something to dust on the shelves," he said.

She peered up at him. "So these are yours, not mine."

He shrugged. "You're welcome to read them while you're here."

"You say that as though you don't expect me to be here for long."

"No, it's just that—"

"I can't blame you. I'm not what you thought when you hired me."

"Your position is secure," he said impatiently, shoving the last package into her hands.

Discarding the string and paper, she revealed a sturdy leather box. Setting it on the table, she lifted the hinged lid. Inside, nestled in velvet, were a silver hairbrush, comb, and hand mirror. Flowers were intricately carved into the back of the brush and mirror. "They're beautiful." *And costly*, a little voice in the back of her mind whispered. She didn't know how she knew but she knew. "I hardly know what to say."

"There's nothing to say. I noticed you used mine and that won't do."

Of course it wouldn't do. She was his servant. She should have used her fingers or simply let the tangles have their way. "You can take these out of my salary if you like."

"Don't be ridiculous. They're a gift."

"I can't accept it."

"You most certainly can."

"When you take no delight in giving it? When you're being so curmudgeonly?"

He sighed heavily. "I want you to have it. It will please me immensely if you take it, and keeping your employer pleased is what you should want above all else."

To what extent did he expect her to keep him pleased? He hadn't made any unwanted overtures, certainly didn't appear to be interested in anything other than her cleaning skills. But would accepting such a lavish gift make her beholden to him? If she discovered it did, she could always give it back. Besides, she wanted the silver set. It made her feel elegant, above her station.

"Thank you," she said simply.

"You're most welcome. Now it is time for me to retire. You remember when to wake me?"

"Yes, at five for your bath."

He tapped Mrs. Beeton's book. "Spend the afternoon relearning how to care effectively for my residence."

"You said the housekeeper of the woman who raised you recommended it."

"Yes. She's an exceptional housekeeper, been with the family for years."

"So you were with your family this morning."

He seemed to hesitate, to weigh his words. Nodded. "We have breakfast together once a week."

"Have I a family?"

She didn't know it was possible for a person to go so completely still. Not a blink. Not a breath taken. She wondered if his heart continued to beat. He slowly shook his head. "No, you're an orphan."

She marveled at the relief she felt, curious as to what prompted it.

"They've been gone a long while I believe," he said somberly.

She smiled at him. "You needn't worry that I'm going to go into uncontrollable sobbing. They could have all died horribly two days ago, and it wouldn't matter. I don't remember them. I suppose I should mourn the not remembering. It seems people in our lives should always be remembered."

"I'm certain they cared deeply for you."

Narrowing her eyes, she scrutinized him. "I didn't think you knew anything about my past."

"I don't, but I can't imagine you not being loved by someone."

"High praise indeed. Yet you are so often put out with me."

He sighed heavily once more. "A servant should not argue or point out when her employer is not acting himself." He again tapped the book. "Hopefully within these pages you will find a list of rules for proper housekeeper comportment. I'll see you at five."

Drake marched into his bedchamber, slammed the door, and paced. He'd told her the truth: she was an orphan. Her mother had died ten years earlier, her father two. She did have a family, her brother, but he hadn't wanted her to seek out her family, not that she would have known where to begin, but she might have asked him again for her employment papers. It was simply easier to omit that little detail. It didn't sit well with him, but then this whole affair was beginning to gnaw at his conscience.

He shouldn't have purchased her the blasted silver grooming set, spent a small fortune on it when she would be leaving in the morning. But the long blond strands of her hair mixed in with his darker ones had been unnerving, as though they belonged interwoven into his brush like that. He couldn't have her using his things. He wished she hadn't looked so damned grateful for everything in the packages. Well, except for the book on housekeeping. She'd obviously not been delighted with the reminder of her place in his life.

Grinning, he sat in the chair and tugged off his boots. He should deliberately step in horse manure and trample it through the house, make her clean his boots. That would lessen her gratitude.

He didn't know why he was so out of sorts. It was the manner in which she'd flung open the door and greeted him as though she were truly happy to see him. Her broad smile, the sparkle in her eyes had hit him like a solid blow to the chest and nearly had him staggering back. He'd wanted her, with a fierce longing that had nearly unmanned him. He'd wanted to take her in his arms and carry her up the stairs to his bed. He'd wanted to explore a body that he had bared only two nights ago but to which he'd given little attention. He'd wanted to settle into her velvety heat and watch the warmth in her eyes smolder with passion.

Raking his hands through his hair, he stood and stormed to the window. Desiring her was the last thing he'd ever do. He couldn't be fooled by her innocence.

The woman in his kitchen was not Lady Ophelia, but that she-devil was lurking just below the surface, and at any moment she was going to burst forth with her memories intact and her icy façade that could burn him if he attempted to get close.

He needed to remember that. But gazing out on the street, he seemed capable of only remembering her smile that warmed, her tart voice and words that amused more than irritated, her clinging to him as she fought the demons of a nightmare.

"You haven't much in the way of cleaning equipment, have you?" Marla asked.

Phee felt rather embarrassed by the pronouncement. She'd been thumbing through Mrs. Beeton's book, striving to grasp more coherently what her responsibilities entailed, when Marla knocked on the door, ready to keep her promise from the day before to help her remember her chores.

"I must have just used up everything," Phee said.

Marla smiled brightly. "It's a good thing I brought what we'll be needin' then. What all have you seen to today?"

"I washed the dishes after breakfast."

"That's good. What else?"

Phee thought about it. Surely she'd done something. Marla widened her eyes as though she thought that would assist Phee with finding the answer. "I opened packages."

Marla laughed lightly. "Did you now?"

"Drake brought me some things—books and clothes and a hairbrush." She couldn't stop her smile at the last.

"Drake?" Marla asked.

"Yes. Drake Darling. He lives here. I told you that yesterday."

"You should refer to him as Mr. Darling."

But he didn't seem like a Mr. Darling to her. Drake or Darling seemed to fit better. Perhaps because she'd awoken in his bed. "All right, then, yes, Mr. Darling."

"Why would he be bringing you a hairbrush?"

"Because I haven't one."

"Why not?"

"I don't know. I seem to be without a good many things. I think perhaps I was going somewhere when I fell into the river."

"You fell into the river?"

"Yes, I told you that."

"Nah, you said you hit your head."

"Well, I fell into the river and now I can't remember anything. Although I sense I'm being rude. Would you care for some tea?"

"We haven't time for tea. Mrs. Pratt only gave me an hour to help you this morning, so we'd best get on with it. Have you swept the front walk?"

"No, why would I?"

"Because leaves and dirt and such are on it. You can't expect Mr. Darling to walk through the muck."

"It seems a waste of time. The wind will only blow the leaves and dirt and such back onto the path."

Marla shrugged. "Which is why we do it every day." Without asking, she opened the pantry door, peered inside, and removed a broom. Then picked up her bucket that was filled with rags, bottles, and tins. "Come on. I'll show you how it's done."

"I think I can manage sweeping."

While Phee proved her skills in that regard, Marla went back into the residence and returned moments later with a bucket of water. Phee supposed she should have been a bit more cautious about Marla going into the residence but it wasn't as though Darling possessed anything of value to be taken. Besides, Marla was a housekeeper and domestics were trusted. She had no reason to pilfer. She had a salary.

With her hands on her hips, Marla walked along the pathway from the door to the gate like someone inspecting troops. How did Phee know that? Had she seen troops being inspected?

"You did a fair job," Marla said.

"Fair? I did an excellent job."

"You missed a few bits here and there."

"I didn't miss them; the wind blew them back, just as I predicted it would."

Marla glanced around, up and down the street where people were going about their day. "I don't feel any wind."

"Well, it's not blowing now, but it was a moment ago."

Marla's smile, with her crooked teeth, made her look so young, too young to be doing all this. "You don't like being told things, but if I don't tell you how will you remember?"

"I said the same thing to Drake—" Marla's eyes bugged out, which Phee took to be a reprimand. She supposed there were worse punishments. "—Mr. Darling, that he needed to tell me things but he said I needed to figure it out."

Marla shrugged her shoulders. "He has his way, I have mine. I'll scrub down the front step there while you polish the door. I've got what we need in my bucket."

Looking at the dusty door, Phee could only think of one thing to say. "I'm not a very good housekeeper, am I?"

"Don't be so hard on yourself. There's only you taking care of things." She handed Phee a cloth, then opened a tin. "We can only do so much in a day. Here now, use the wax to polish the door."

Marla went down to her knees, took what looked like a brick from her bucket, and began scraping the front step.

"You can just tell me what to do," Phee told her. "You don't have to actually do it."

"I'm not a fancy lady to stand around doin' nothing all day. Besides, friends help each other, don't they?"

"I haven't known you long enough to be your friend."

Squinting up at her, Marla grinned her crooked toothed grin. "Friendship isn't measured by time. It can happen in the blink of an eye when you meet someone you like."

Phee felt an uncomfortable and unfamiliar tightening in the center of her chest. "You like me?"

"Course I do. Wouldn't be here otherwise. Haven't you ever met someone and straightaway you knew you'd be friends?"

Had she? Did she have friends? Before she could answer, Marla carried on. "Then sometimes you meet someone and you immediately think, 'Cor, blimey! Not if she was the last person on earth.' And don't you be worrying. I'm going to tell you plenty of things you can do after I leave."

"Thank you, Marla. I truly appreciate your help. You're very kind."

"Doesn't take any more effort to be kind."

But it did. The girl was taking time from her own schedule to assist Phee, someone she hardly knew at all. Would Phee be as generous with her time and knowledge? She liked to think she would, but she didn't know.

Marla nodded toward the door. "Start polishing."

Turning back to the chore at hand, Phee thought about how surprised and pleased Darling—Mr. Darling—would be the next time he used this door. She did wish that she'd polished it up all nice and glistening for him this morning before he'd returned with the packages. As she ran the cloth repeatedly over the wood, she decided it wasn't a completely unpleasant task and she liked watching the way her actions transformed the wood from something murky to something clean and pretty. She wished life could be cleaned so easily, but it was far too complicated. Even with no memories, she knew that.

"I'm assuming your Mr. Darling has a laundress," Marla said.

"Why would you think that?"

"Your hands." Marla held up her own. "Mine are all rough-looking."

They were red, chapped. Phee thought they looked years older than the housemaid's face. While her own were so white and soft.

"You might ask him about the laundress," Marla said. "To get clothes really clean the water's got to be hot. When I was first being trained for service, they made me stick my hands in near boiling water."

Horrified, Phee stopped polishing and simply stared at Marla. Surely she hadn't heard correctly. She couldn't think of any response, except "No."

Marla nodded. "Yeah. You gotta get used to working with the hot water."

"That's barbaric. How old were you?"

"Twelve."

Phee knew her eyes grew as round as saucers. "But you were a child."

Marla shrugged in a way that made it appear she was rolling Phee's words off her back. "Me mum had eight kids, another coming. I had to start earning my own way. How long have you been in service?"

Phee could hardly believe that Marla was so accepting of the treatment she'd endured, but obviously she wanted to move the conversation along, so Phee obliged her.

"I don't know. Supposedly I've been here for a fortnight." She studied the door. "Do you think I've polished this since I set foot in the house?"

"Doesn't look like it, does it? Windows need washing, too."

Oh God, that was going to be a chore. She'd have to get a ladder. Was she afraid of heights? "Maybe Mr. Darling doesn't care about the windows and doors."

"Of course he does. All the middles care about appearances. It's why they hire servants."

"The middles?"

Marla laughed. "You have forgotten a lot. You know, those who aren't poor, but they're not the upper swells either. Like Mrs. Turner. They hire at least one servant for appearances' sake, so people know they have *some* money. Most have two or three domestics, whatever they can afford. We make them feel rich."

Was that why Darling had hired her? For appearances? No, he didn't strike her as giving a fig about what others thought of him. He was quick enough to put her in her place if he didn't like what she said. "All right then. Windows. What other chores do I need to see to?"

"Oil lamps have to be cleaned and prepared every day. Some households have a gent and that's his sole job. He's in charge of the oil lamps."

"Our furnishings are rather spartan at the moment so that chore shouldn't take an inordinate amount of time. What else?"

Phee polished while Marla began listing all the things she needed to tend to. Oddly, she didn't find it overwhelming. Instead, she thought her chores would make the day go rather quickly, but more she imagined how rewarding it would be when Drake Darling noticed her efforts. The next time a fancy carriage rolled to a stop in front of the residence, the driver and footman would see a gleaming door.

And just maybe Drake Darling would smile at her, revealing that intriguing little dimple.

Chapter 12

He awoke to a light nudge, late afternoon sunlight spilling through the windows, and arresting green eyes. Why couldn't they be as black and uninteresting as his? Why did they have to reflect expectation? Why did they have to make him wish he could gaze into them for the remainder of his life?

It would forever haunt him that he saw them this warm and welcoming, knowing that on the morrow they would once again be frigid and hard when meeting his.

"Your bath is ready," she said, her voice low and enticing. He could clearly envision it whispering endearments in his ear, urging him onward as he pounded into her while she gripped his buttocks, meeting him thrust for thrust.

His cock was so damned hard at that moment that he could have driven nails into wood with it, but it was only because he was awakening and it always stood at attention first thing. It had nothing at all to do with the woman in the dark blue dress and ruffled apron leaning over him. She could have been a crone for all it cared. Was a crone beneath the silken skin and the long dark lashes that didn't match her hair and inviting red lips that were slightly parted.

"Then leave so I can make my way there." He hated the irascibility in his voice, the slight dimming of delight in her eyes. Which made no sense as he was doing all this—

He didn't know why the bloody hell he was doing it. His mind was foggy from sleep, and he couldn't concentrate with her so near, so unlike the Ophelia he knew.

Then she tipped up her pert little nose in that gesture that never failed to irritate—thank God, thank God, thank God—tilting his world back onto its rightful axis. "Of course. Pardon my intrusion."

He watched the swing of her hips, the apron ties swaying, as she made her way from the room. She may not have slammed the door in her wake, but it closed with a definite resounding click that conveyed her pique.

He covered his eyes with his arm and wondered why clothing that left so little skin revealed was so incredibly enticing. He wanted to see her wearing naught but the apron. Where had that thought come from? What was the matter with him? Tomorrow was not soon enough. Perhaps he should return her tonight. As soon as he was convinced she was in no danger. No sense in prolonging the inevitable.

Tossing back the covers, he rolled out of the bed, coming to a halt as her words finally hit him. She'd prepared his bath. He shouldn't be surprised that she'd managed to learn by observing him the day before. He'd always known she wasn't an idiot. Still, he was taken aback that she hadn't feigned ignorance today, that she hadn't garnered some excuse to avoid the chore. A chore that wasn't truly hers.

He wondered if it had felt foreign to her or if she'd conjured images of others doing the task for her.

He went through the door that connected the bathing chamber to his room. No steam arising. He climbed in, settled his head back against the lip of the tub. The water wasn't as blistering hot as he preferred it but—

Who the devil did he think he was—*her?*—complaining about something that had been done for him? The temperature of the water didn't matter, didn't undo the effort that had gone into preparing—

Click.

He stilled. The door was opening. He glanced over his shoulder.

She gave him a tentative smile. "I'm here to wash your back."

"Right." He shoved himself up, waited as she settled behind him.

"I was listening at the door, trying to hear you getting into the water. I felt rather perverted. Perhaps we should get a bell for you to ring when you're ready for me."

No need when this would be the last time she'd ever touch him. Not that he was going to tell her that. He simply held his silence and anticipated the first caress of those gentle fingers.

She reached around him for the soap, and cotton brushed up against his skin. The frill of her apron or the cotton-covered swell of her breast. All the blood drained from his head, went elsewhere, and for a second he was hot and dizzy, grateful the bathwater was not as heated as he was accustomed to.

The water made a slight splashing as she dipped her hands into it. He heard a sharp hiss, twisted in time to see her grimace.

"Sorry," she said. Biting her lower lip, she rubbed her hands over the soap, flinched.

"What the devil?" He grabbed her hand. The soap plopped into the water, but he barely noticed as he gazed at the red, raw blisters on her palms. He cursed soundly, imagining her carrying the buckets of water, the handles digging into her soft flesh, rubbing, scoring, tearing the satiny skin.

"It's all right," she said, fighting to wrench free while he refused to let go. "I can see to my chore here."

"Like hell you can. Go into my bedchamber and wait for me."

Finally managing to break free of his grip, she glared at him. "You can't order me about."

"Of course I can. I'm your employer."

She blinked as though she'd forgotten that, and he realized that in anger she was more the Ophelia he knew. Best not to anger her until he was ready to deliver her to her brother's doorstep, lest her memory come roaring back. He had a feeling his life would be in danger if it came back while she was here.

The thought almost had him laughing, welcoming her fury directed at him. He'd never realized how much her fire could appeal, excite. Damnation, but he didn't want to like her, yet he was seeing shades to her that put her in a different light. If they could be friends, he thought they might very well enjoy each other. But as they weren't, and she was hurt, he needed to tend to her. "Go. To. My. Bedchamber," he repeated.

If looks could kill . . . well, hers might wound him, but it wasn't going to be the death of him. She punctuated it with a little huff before shoving herself to her feet and disappearing through the threshold and slamming the door behind her.

He couldn't help it. He chuckled at her pique. God, it was a damned good thing that she wasn't his servant in truth, because she would drive to him to madness. Searching the bottom of the tub, he located the soap and scrubbed up as quickly as possible.

It wasn't until he was drying off that he realized he hadn't brought in any clothes, but then he never did. He washed up in here, then strode as naked as he pleased into his bedchamber to dress. Why should he change his habits for her?

Because the choices were the uncomfortable chair or the bed, she chose the bed, sitting on its corner on top of the rumpled blankets, a pillow at her back. A pillow upon which he'd slept and upon which she would sleep later. A pillow that smelled of him. She knew because she'd buried her face in it before placing it behind her back.

She cursed her hands and her inability to hide the discomfort. She had so wanted to wash his back again, to glory in it. She'd been too self-conscious the day before to enjoy it as much as she might and she had planned to rectify that mistake today.

While he was a mixture of kind and curt, she suspected there was more to their relationship than was proper. The clothes he'd brought her today fit her as though they'd been made for no other, as though he knew her precise measurements. She didn't want to consider that he had spent so much time in the company of women that he had an eye for sizing them up, although that was probably the truth of it. She was probably no more than a servant.

But why the novels? Why the silver brush? Why the concern over her hands?

He strode out of the bathing room with a towel around his hips, held firmly in place at his waist by one hand clutching it. Without a word, he snatched up the trousers and shirt that were draped over the chair and disappeared back into the bathing room.

When he again emerged, the shirt was tucked into

his breeches but not buttoned. He set an assortment of items on the table beside the bed, before sitting down on the edge of the mattress. He took her hands, turned them palms up, and scowled at them. While she found herself staring in wonder at how small her hands were when compared with his. His were rough and lined with faint scars that must have been part of him for an eternity.

"How did you come to have the scars?" she asked.

His scowl deepened before he released his hold on her hands and reached for a jar. "They're from when I was a lad."

She hadn't thought he'd answer. He was always surprising her. No more so than when he gently applied the salve on her broken skin. She imagined those fingers gliding over all of her, with such reverence and care. "You would think my hands would be tougher," she said, "accustomed to carting pails of water."

"I usually prepare my own bath."

"I thought you said I prepare it." Had he? Or was her memory faulty on that score? Perhaps her brain had somehow been damaged. Would she constantly be confused and forget things?

"If I did, I misspoke. You're not to do it again."

"You're angry with me."

Releasing a deep breath, he began to fold a strip of linen around her hand. "No, but you were never supposed to get hurt. I don't want you doing any chores that cause you pain."

"Perhaps you should hire a footman to assist me."

"Eventually I will." He began wrapping the other hand.

"And a valet."

"I need my money for other things right now."

"What things?"

He concentrated on his task.

"Not my business, I suppose," she said tightly.

"No, it's not."

"Then you shouldn't have spent your money on the silver brush set."

"It wasn't that much."

"It was very costly. I recognize quality when I see it. I don't know how I do but I do. Like the carriage that brought you here. It was very fine indeed. Is it yours?"

"No, it belongs to the man who raised me."

"Why don't you refer to him as your father?"

"Because I'm not worthy enough to be his son."

"Why not?"

She wasn't surprised that he didn't answer, that he merely tautened his jaw and concentrated more diligently on his task. The relationship between an employer and a domestic was such that they didn't share secrets and dreams and yearnings of the heart. She should let it go, but she seemed unable to follow her own counsel. "Are you saving your funds to purchase a carriage?"

Finished with the wrapping, he gave her a pointed look. "No."

"What then? Another residence?"

"You're quite the busybody, aren't you?"

"It's not fair. You know nearly everything about me and I know nothing at all about you."

"If you knew everything about me, I daresay you would not be impressed."

"Did I know nothing about you before I came to work here?"

He skimmed his fingers along her cheek, catching stray strands of her hair and tucking them behind her ear. "We didn't talk much."

"I suppose I was more concerned with impressing you than having you impress me."

"Something like that."

His fingers lingered at her ear, circling the delicate shell. "You're not to do anything else that causes you discomfort, is that clear?"

Nodding, she thought she could sit for hours while he touched her like that. His finger skimmed along her neck. She was incredibly tempted to mimic his actions, but she feared if she did that he might stop.

Even without her distracting him, he stopped. She wanted to shake her head until her hair came loose again, so he would put it back into place. She thought if he had ever touched her like this she would have remembered.

"Perhaps we didn't talk much because I was shy," she said.

He barked out his boisterous laughter then, and the quiet moment between them shattered. "You are anything but shy."

Coming off the bed, he gathered up the items that he'd used to treat her hands. "These will be in a cabinet in the bathing chamber if you have need of them."

He began to walk away.

"Drake?"

He stopped, turned back, something dark in his gaze, and she wondered if she should be addressing him as Marla had instructed her, but it just didn't seem right.

"Will things change between us when I remember everything?"

"Yes."

He walked from the room, leaving her to wonder why he seemed saddened by the admission.

Drake. She'd never called him by that name before. It shot straight to his gut, caused it to tighten. He liked the way it sounded on her lips. Christ, if he were honest, he liked everything that came from her lips since she'd awoken in his bed. Even the tart tones were starting to have an appeal. She had backbone. He had to give her that.

He tried to imagine what it would be like not to know anything at all about oneself. It would be like falling into a great unknown. How many people, he wondered, would simply stay abed and pull the covers up over their heads until they remembered something? But not her.

She straightened her spine and charged into the fray. Oh, she'd grumbled and questioned, but he could hardly hold either of those reactions against her. He suspected he would have been pounding his fists into something. He would not have graciously accepted his circumstance.

She'd already left his bedchamber when he returned from the bathing room. After changing into fresh clothes, he headed out. He caught the fragrance of polish. Apparently, she'd done more than just prepare his bath. As he neared the kitchen, lovely aromas wafted around him. Had she actually cooked?

Stepping into the kitchen, he found Phee bustling around, setting items on the table, where the roasted pheasant sat, browned and glistening. His mouth actually watered, but it didn't stop him from being irritated with her. "I ordered you not to do anything."

"This was already in the midst of being prepared when I went upstairs to awaken you. And you're most welcome."

He came up short at the reprimand in her tone. He deserved it, blast it all. She had gone to all this trouble. He couldn't help but be impressed by all she'd accomplished. He'd never considered her stupid, but she was quite the quick learner.

She pointed to a chair. "Sit. Enjoy."

"You'll be joining me," he said, pulling out a chair for her and waiting.

"That's being quite unconventional, isn't it? To dine with the housekeeper?"

"Do I strike you as someone who follows convention?"

"To be honest, no, you don't."

She took the chair and he sat opposite her. Doing away with formality, they served themselves. Then she sat, poised on the edge of her seat, waiting for him to sample her cooking. She'd probably poisoned it. No, she didn't know yet that she should.

He took a small bite. To his immense surprise, it nearly melted in his mouth. "It's quite tasty."

"You were correct. Once I got started seeing to matters, I remembered what was to be done."

She remembered something she'd never known? He was fairly certain she'd never prepared pheasant in her life, had no doubt never boiled an egg. He almost questioned her on it. Instead he let it go because he would have to explain how he knew she'd never made her way about a kitchen.

"You'll be leaving for the club soon," she said.

"Yes."

"And you'll be gone all night?"

He recognized the trepidation in her eyes. "Yes, but no worries. Sleep in my bed. The nightmares won't bother you there."

"How do you know?"

"Because it's a very comfortable bed and based on your previous times beneath my covers, you shall sleep most soundly."

A faint blush rose into her cheeks, mesmerizing him.

He had no idea Lady O possessed the wherewithal to blush.

"Perhaps I'll purchase a new bed with my wages," she said.

That would be quite the trick, considering he wasn't truly paying her wages. "Your employer provides the bed."

"When will mine be arriving?"

He sliced off another bit of pheasant. "Your memories are quite erratic. You should recall that you have one."

"I have a cot, not a bed," she stated very succinctly. "It's ghastly uncomfortable."

"Yes, I know. I slept on it when I was waiting for my bed to be delivered."

"Then why give it to me?"

Because I wanted you uncomfortable, because I didn't think you'd be staying more than a day. Because I hadn't expected to find myself caring about your well-being.

"Because I'm an unkind employer."

She skewed her mouth and he had the insane thought to unskew it by kissing it. Why did she have to look completely adorable sitting across from him, striving to work things out, to make sense of them? Why did her brow have to pleat slightly? Why did her green eyes have to take on a faraway look as though she were traveling a path toward enlightenment? God help him when she did uncover all the answers.

"Your actions don't match your words," she said. "I'm left with the impression that you are striving to deceive me, but for what purpose?"

Because he didn't truly want her to know him, his hopes, his dreams, his secrets. Why then did he find it so difficult to accept that perhaps Lady O had felt the same, had distanced her true self from him, had created a haughty veneer to protect the woman within? "A puzzle to think about while I tidy up in here."

"That's my duty, to clean up."

"Not while your hands are blistered. You don't need them in dirty water."

As he removed the plates and glasses from the table, wiped it down, washed the dishes, he could feel her watching him, striving to understand him. He wasn't even certain he understood himself any longer. He could only hope that Gregory would provide him with the answers he sought so he could return Phee home before she drove him mad.

"Lord Wigmore was there?" Incredulously, Drake repeated the words that Gregory had just told him. He wasn't certain what he'd expected, but it wasn't that, not really.

"Yes, sir." Gregory stood straight and tall as though insulted by Drake's doubt. "I delivered the invitation to his hand."

If Wigmore was there, then had Somerdale lied? Had he wished Phee harm, and thought no one would look for her at her uncle's? It was a tale too easy to check. But if she'd been traveling with her uncle, what was she doing here? "Was there anything odd about him?"

"Odd?"

"Did he look as though he may have been set upon by ruffians?"

"No, he appeared quite well. He was a bit impatient with my presence and I believe insulted by the invitation. He merely muttered, 'When hell freezes over,' and had me escorted out."

It made no sense, although he was relieved that he didn't need to notify Scotland Yard that they should be out searching for a missing lord of the realm. But it still left the mystery of how Phee had come to be in the river. With her having no memory, he didn't know how he could uncover the truth. He wasn't comfortable returning her to her brother without ensuring she would be safe with him.

"Will there be anything else, sir?"

Looking up at Gregory, he was disconcerted to realize he'd become so lost in his thoughts about Phee that he'd forgotten the man was present. "Job well done. You can return to your duties."

"Yes, sir."

After Gregory left, Drake walked to the window and gazed out on the street. Nothing made sense, in particular his relief that he might not be returning Phee to her residence in the morning. That she might stay with him a bit longer, might again wash his back. With a sigh, he pressed his forehead to the cool glass.

He couldn't keep her. It was unconscionable behavior. Even if he had enjoyed sharing his dinner with her. That sentiment confounded him. He didn't like her so how could he enjoy her company? Blast it all!

Spinning away from the window, he headed out of his office and into the gaming area. He'd not made his early night walkthrough, his need to talk with Gregory taking precedence over everything else. The partners wouldn't be happy about his distractions, his priorities of late. He owed them for the opportunity they'd given him to make something of himself. He had to see this personal vendetta put to rest as quickly as possible.

Out of the corner of his eye, he spied Somerdale nearing one of the tables, changed his course, and quickly intercepted him before he reached his destination. "Somerdale."

"Darling."

"I heard you made out like a thief last night."

Somerdale chuckled. "Lady Luck did seem to be with me. I look forward to another invite into the sacred lair."

Ignoring the subtle request for an immediate offer, Drake asked, "How is your sister? Heard from her since she went to your uncle's?"

"Not a word."

"Are you certain she arrived safely?"

Somerdale scowled. "I should think I'd have heard if she hadn't."

"No letter from her informing you of her arrival, to lessen your worry?"

He chuckled lightly. "Ophelia has never been one for writing or caring about my worry."

Yes, he could see that, too clearly in fact. "When do you think she'll return to London?"

"When Auntie Berta either improves or dies, I suspect."

"How ill is your aunt?"

"Fairly ill, based on Uncle's assessment."

"I can't imagine Lady Ophelia missing even a few balls of the Season to comfort another."

Somerdale tilted his head to the side, reminding Drake of a dog trying to determine if a bird was nested in a tree. "Are you interested in courting her?"

"What? No. Absolutely not. I simply find it difficult to believe she would give up this Season when both she and Grace were so set on finding a match."

He shrugged. "She's very close to Auntie. Spent a good many summers with her when she was younger, especially after Mother passed, as Auntie Berta is mother's younger sister."

"But Lady Ophelia could find herself on the shelf, in spite of her substantial dowry."

"I'm quite surprised you would care."

"It's not that I care, I simply . . ." Damnation. Did he care? Of course not. He was striving to ferret out information in order to determine what Somerdale might know. "I simply find it odd is all. Unselfishness is not at all like the Lady Ophelia I know."

"Perhaps you don't know her as well as you think. Regardless, she's had quite a number of suitors, although she hasn't expressed much interest in any of them. I'm not sure what she's searching for exactly in a chap, but her dowry ensures she'll be fine if she's not here for the entire Season. She won't be overlooked next. Now if you'll excuse me, I need to get to the tables, see if my luck from last night continues."

Drake watched him go. He didn't sound like a man who would wish his sister ill. But then neither did he appear to care a great deal if she were happy. Fine? She would be fine? She deserved to be more than fine.

He growled. No, she didn't. She deserved to marry a toad. As a wife, she'd be a shrew. Her dowry was what drew men to her, not her temperament. He'd never understood what Grace saw in her.

Although he had been surprised to discover she was a stubborn little minx, continuing to carry up buckets of warm water even after her skin split. He would have thought she'd have set the bucket down as soon as she realized how heavy it was. That she would have knocked on his door and ordered him to *fetch* the buckets. Not to mention she'd been willing to wash his back again. He cursed the buckets for denying him that pleasure. He could still feel her fingers outlining each aspect of the dragon, up and down, curving—

"Imitating a statue, hoping not to be noticed?" Avendale asked.

Drake schooled his reaction not to reveal that he'd

very nearly leaped out of his skin at the unexpected deep voice at his back. Calmly he turned. "Simply observing, pondering, contemplating. Why aren't you enjoying some cards?"

Avendale shrugged. "They seem rather boring of late. Damn, but I miss Lovingdon. Can scarcely wait for his return. There's little enjoyment in going in search of sin on one's own."

Drake laughed low. "I would wager his days of sin are behind him."

"Yes, I've no doubt Grace will have him chained at her side."

"It's a chain he willingly wears."

"I've no doubt, but still I find it incredibly disappointing that he fell so easily." He gave Drake a once-over. "Care to become my new partner in sin?"

"I don't have to go looking for it when it's all around me."

"But you don't partake."

"Not here, no. And not during the busiest hours. I'm sure you can find someone to accompany you on your excursion."

"I shall give it my best. I am curious, though. Why all the questions regarding Lady Ophelia last night? If I didn't know how often you two are at odds, I'd suspect you invited Somerdale to the game simply to quiz him about her. You're not on the cusp of falling as well, are you?"

His meaning was like a slap. "In love? No, not with her. Never with her."

Avendale raised an irritating dark brow. "A bit overmuch on the protesting there."

"She and I would not suit. Now, if you'll excuse me, I have a gaming hell to run here."

He left Avendale standing in the middle of the

gaming floor. Ludicrous that both he and Somerdale had questioned Drake's interest in Ophelia. He had no interest in her whatsoever, other than determining how she had arrived in the river.

Chapter 13

Drake waited impatiently in the foyer of a modest townhome while the butler fetched the owners. He could hardly fathom that he was here when he needed to see to business. Hearing the footsteps of more than one person, he tensed. He wanted to make this visit as short as possible.

Sir William Graves exited a hallway, his wife at his side, her face etched with concern.

"Is it Avendale?" she asked, clearly worried. "Has he been hurt?"

He knew she was really asking if he was dead. The former Duchess of Avendale was no doubt well aware that her son was not always cautious when it came to his partaking of sin. On more than one occasion Drake had wondered if the man's goal was to acquire an early grave. As Avendale frequented Drake's world, it stood to reason Drake would be the one to deliver the unwelcome news. "He's quite well. I saw him earlier at Dodger's, looking for sport."

Relief washed over her features, even as she gave him a skeptical look. "My son is searching for a good many things, but I'm not sure sport heads his list."

"I assure you that he's fine."

"Is someone in the family ill?" Sir William asked. Years ago, he'd been knighted because of his exemplary care of the queen.

"Everyone is well, but I wondered if I might have a private word."

"Yes, of course. Come back to my study."

Reaching out, his wife squeezed Drake's arm. "It's good to see you."

He wished he could assure her that her son would remain well, but he was convinced Avendale's demons existed in greater numbers than Drake's. So he settled for a reassuring smile before following the doctor to his study. He took the whiskey and chair that were offered. Graves sat in the chair opposite him, studying him intently as though he had the ability to diagnose with little more than an outward assessment.

"So what brings you to my door?" Graves asked.

Madness. Utter and complete madness. Revenge gone awry.

Drake sipped the whiskey. Now that he was here, he didn't quite know how to handle things. Showing up at the doctor's door had been a rash decision, but that seemed to be the way of things for him where Phee was concerned. "I know a gent, took a tumble in the river a couple of nights ago, and he seems to have left his memory there."

"You're having difficulty remembering things?"

"No, not me. Why would you think that?"

Graves gave him a small smile. "I often have patients describe a *friend's* ailments when they are uncomfortable with their own symptoms, but I assure you that everything you tell me is held in confidence and you have no reason to be embarrassed. I do not sit in judgment."

You bloody well might if you knew exactly what I've

done. "I'm not the one who has no recollection of his past. I'm wondering if his health is at risk."

"I shall have to examine him—"

"He won't come. He has a fear of physicians."

"Thought he'd lost his memory."

"Not all of it. He remembers little pockets of information. How long before he'll recall everything?"

Placing an elbow on the arm of the chair, Graves rubbed his chin in thought. "Difficult to say. I have to admit that I've not had much experience dealing with catastrophic loss of memory. Some patients are a bit disoriented after a head injury but usually everything comes back to them shortly. I've had a few patients who never regained the memories they lost."

"There's no cure?"

"Not to my knowledge. Although I did hear about a fellow who fell from a roof and couldn't remember how he'd come to be there. Nor could he recall that he had a family. But when he was taken home the familiarity helped him to remember. I assume this man you know is already home."

"He can't remember where his home is."

"That's unfortunate. I wish I could be of more help. The mind is terribly complicated. It can forget what it doesn't wish to remember. Sometimes memory can be triggered by something odd: the aroma of a particular fowl cooking, an experience, a person. But I have no magical elixir."

"But being back in a familiar setting might be all that is needed?"

"Might be. No guarantees. A French physician is doing some amazing studies in neurology but I've not heard of any specific conclusions regarding amnesia. I could pen him a letter, attempt to gather some more information. Meanwhile, see if you can talk this gent into coming to see me. It sounds as though he might be a fascinating study."

Fascinating indeed.

Because the most comfortable piece of furniture in the entire residence was Drake's bed, Phee was curled up on it, a mound of pillows behind her back, while she read *Pride and Prejudice*. She knew that Elizabeth Bennet and Mr. Darcy belonged together. She knew scandal was involved, although she couldn't recall the details. It was an odd thing. As she read each page, it was as though it caused her to remember reading the page at another time—curled in a little nook or sitting beneath the boughs of an elm. Why had embracing her duties today not caused the same thing to happen?

She wondered if it was truly important to know the past, especially as she felt somewhat lightened by not knowing it. What had it entailed?

Setting aside the novel, she reached for the book on household management that she had placed on the bedside table earlier. It was dry reading, but necessary. She wanted to please her employer. No, that wasn't quite true. She wanted to please Darling.

For all his gruffness, he possessed a tenderness that took her by surprise at the oddest moments. Sometimes she thought she recalled him from before, but the images that flickered through her mind were not those of the man she was coming to know. His were small kindnesses, but they touched her deeply. While he often seemed impatient with her, he also appeared to care for her well-being. Wrapping her hands, excusing her from carrying out her duties. Had she a servant, she didn't know if she would be as thoughtful.

Sitting up straighter, she concentrated. Had she had a servant? It seemed she had, but that made no sense. Had she once been well off but fallen on hard times?

Settling back down, she opened the book. She considered skipping over the chapter that addressed the duties of the mistress of the house, but as he had no wife, she decided those responsibilities belonged to her as well. As she read the pages, she was surprised by how familiar the tasks of the mistress were, as though she'd once carried them out. Had she been mistress of a household? Was she a widow? Had she come into service because her husband died and left her with nothing?

Scrambling out of bed, she hurried into the bathing chamber and studied her face more closely in the reflection in the mirror on the wall. No lines, no sagging skin, no jowls. How old was she? Not old enough to be a widow surely.

Had she overseen her father's house? Squeezing her eyes shut tightly, she concentrated on bringing forth images, but nothing was there. In frustration, she smacked her hand against the wall. The past didn't matter, it couldn't matter.

She wouldn't let it.

She returned to the bed and curled up with Mrs. Beeton rather than Jane Austen. She would embrace her duties, perform them to the utmost of her abilities. Darling would be grateful she managed his household. His residence could be so much more than it was. She would see to it, even as the section on housekeeping began to overwhelm her. So much to oversee, so many tasks that needed to be tended to. She wondered that she had a moment to breathe, much less find herself in the river. It appeared the evening was the only time she would have a few minutes to herself.

She was quite surprised when she read the portion

that explained how she was responsible for a household budget, for purchases. Shouldn't she have remembered such a significant detail? She was supposed to have a book where she recorded expenses. Where would she keep that? According to Mrs. Beeton, she should have a housekeeper's room from which she oversaw the household. Darling hadn't indicated a room for her purpose. Perhaps they shared his office. Based on the size of his desk and the fact that he was sadly lacking in servants, that made sense to her.

She wondered about the extent of the monies that she might oversee, on what she was expected to spend the funds. If she were extremely frugal, could she purchase a comfortable chair, hire a cook, secure a housemaid? Those thoughts excited her with possibilities. She needed to find her book.

Sliding off the bed, she reached for her shoes, then decided that she didn't need them. She was the only one about. Who would be offended by her stockinged feet? She wandered out the door and down the stairs. It was so incredibly quiet, yet she didn't feel lonely. Rather she relished the silence. Every little thing she noticed was a new discovery about herself. It was such an odd thing not to know everything that she liked and enjoyed. It was as though she'd only just met herself and was slowly unveiling the mystery of who she was, developing a friendship with herself. Did she have friends? Would they be missing her, wondering why they didn't hear from her? Would they come to visit?

If she only knew who they were, she could go to them. As it was, she would have to wait for them to come to her—then perhaps they would answer all the questions that Darling didn't. She did hope they wouldn't be too long in paying a call. If they had been here before, perhaps they would visit soon.

Reaching the library, she turned on the gaslights and took a moment to appreciate the three books that presently sat upon a shelf. She would add the other two when she was finished with them. She imagined the satisfaction she would feel with books on every shelf. Perhaps she would delay the purchase of a chair in order to gain more books. She imagined the musty fragrance they would give the room, a scent of knowledge, power, journeys that knew no bounds. She could see herself spending a good deal of time in here, sitting in a stuffed chair before the fire, reading. Darling, doing the same, sitting opposite her.

She blinked. No, a servant and an employer would not sit together in companionable silence. If he were here in the evenings, she would be relegated to her room while he enjoyed the fire, the books, the calm setting she worked to create. Not fair, not fair at all.

Going to the desk, she sat in the comfortable leather chair, allowing it to ease the aches in her body. Her hands were still wrapped, protected. Perhaps an employer who took such care with her hurts would welcome her sitting with him in the evenings. Surely with only the two of them here, they weren't as formal as they would be otherwise.

She turned her attention back to her task at hand: finding her book of accounts. She opened one drawer after another, finding most of them empty of belongings. Truly this man lived a most spartan existence. She couldn't imagine doing the same. She paused. Based on her meager belongings, she did exactly the same. Not by choice. She was not one to do without. So why was she?

Again, no choice. The reasons behind her lack of choice were the mystery.

She went back to work, opening the last drawer. Inside was a finely crafted wooden box. Taking it out, she set it on the desk so she could see more clearly into the depths of the drawer. But again, nothing that would serve as a ledger of accounts.

Odd that she would know precisely what it should look like, so perhaps she had been a housekeeper for some years. Well, not too many as she didn't think she was that old. A housemaid perhaps who had been in training to become a housekeeper.

With a sigh, wondering where else she might look for her account book, she rose from the chair. In the kitchen perhaps. After taking two steps, she stopped. She couldn't leave his things lying about. She returned to the desk, studied the box. It wasn't very large, but perhaps it contained her ledger. Maybe her ledger was small. Glancing around cautiously, she knew she should simply put it back. He'd placed it in a bottom drawer for a reason. Something private, perhaps even personal. A good servant knew her boundaries, but as she had no memory of her duties, surely she had no memory of her boundaries. She released a little laugh. She could get away with things she might not otherwise.

Slowly, half inch by half inch, she lifted the hinged lid and peered inside. Nothing more than what appeared to be a yellowed-with-age clipping from a newspaper. Because it seemed brittle and fragile, she removed and unfolded it with care. It was an article concerning the hanging of a Robert Sykes. Why would he have this in his possession? Why would he keep it shut away, and yet within easy access?

"What the devil are you doing?"

She should have screeched, should have at least been startled, but she was becoming accustomed to that booming voice intruding when she was in the midst of contemplation. Besides, she was too enamored with what she'd discovered. She glanced to the mantel, but no clock rested there. Somewhere in her life was a mantel with a clock. A gold filigreed clock. A hideous thing that ticked far too loudly.

"I wasn't expecting you," she said.

After snatching the clipping from her fingers, he refolded and returned it to the box. "You have no right to go through my things."

"I was looking for something and found that instead. Who is Robert Sykes?"

"A murderer."

"Yes I rather gathered that from the newspaper account, but why would you keep it as though it were a treasured keepsake?"

"Perhaps I'm macabre."

"No, I don't think so. I believe it's something personal, something with meaning."

Slamming down the lid, he glared at her. "I do not explain my possessions. You are to leave them be."

As he was avoiding her questions, she could only assume it was indeed most personal, but he wasn't going to share it with her, no matter how many times she asked. She decided it was best to justify her actions, or at least those that could be justified. "I was searching for my account book."

"Your what?"

"According to Mrs. Beeton, I'm supposed to keep a detailed record of things ordered, purchased, received. I don't even know what my budget for the household is so I'm at quite a loss regarding what I can purchase."

"I handle all the purchases."

"But I'm the housekeeper."

"You have enough duties without worrying about that."

"You don't trust me."

"I am very particular about how my money is spent."

He studied the desk for a moment, then walked over to the shelves, reached up, and placed the box on a shelf that she would be unable to reach without a stool. She didn't bother to point out that it wasn't safe there. If she wanted to look at it again, she could drag in a chair.

"I don't understand our relationship," she said instead. "I think you're purposely keeping things from me in order to ensure I don't regain my memories."

He prowled toward her. An image flashed through her mind of his doing that while shadows closed in around them. She dropped down into the chair, pressed her back into it. Stopping, he hitched his hip onto the edge of the desk and leaned forward slightly. "What would I gain by such underhanded tactics?"

"You've come at me before like that."

"Don't be ridiculous."

"You were—" She shook her head. "In formal attire. That makes no sense. I wouldn't be at a formal affair . . . unless I was serving, I suppose."

His gaze roamed over her, taking in each detail. She remembered that action from another time as well. In the background had been music . . . a waltz. But she didn't fear this man. She trusted him. So why this sense of discomfiture? Especially after all he'd done for her, all she'd done for him.

Abruptly, he stood. "You'll need your shoes. We're going out."

"Going out? Where?"

"In search of your memories."

Chapter 14

He'd hired out a hansom cab. She couldn't recall ever traveling in one although she couldn't put much stock in her recollections since most were missing. She was, however, acutely aware that it was an incredibly small vehicle. He sat beside her, leaving no room between their hips, thighs, shoulders.

"I know etiquette," she said quietly, the small confines immersing her in his intoxicating masculine scent with its hints of tobacco and whiskey. But beneath it all was the distracting fragrance of rugged man, his unique blend. "And proper comportment. In a carriage, the gentleman travels backward, allowing the lady to travel forward."

"You're assuming I'm a gentleman."

"Aren't you?"

"You've called me a scoundrel on occasion."

"And still you kept me in your employ?"

He flashed a self-deprecating smile. "I don't know what possessed me," he uttered.

"You needed someone to tidy up after you."

He chuckled low. "Have you not noticed I am the one doing most of the tidying up?"

She had noticed. He was very particular about it, constantly picking up her discarded articles of clothing and folding them neatly, putting them away. It occurred to her that he wouldn't have a cluttered home even after he finally began to fill it with furniture. He would have only the pieces he needed. He required space; he required order. He required someone more adept at caring for things than she'd been since her tumble into the river. If she didn't regain her memories soon he might be forced to let her go. Although she'd made some progress today with Marla's assistance, she wasn't certain she'd made enough to be valuable.

"So where precisely do you think we're going to find my memories?" she asked.

"I'm not really sure. I spoke with Dr. Graves earlier—"

"Graves? What an unfortunate name for someone who is supposed to keep people *from* the graves."

"Yes, I suspect there are times when he regretted choosing such a somber name."

"Wasn't he born with it?"

"I doubt it. He began his life on the streets during a time when names were changed on a whim. Regardless of that, however, he is remarkably skilled, so I sought his counsel. He suggested the familiar might stir your memories back to life. I thought it worth giving a try."

"But shouldn't you be at the club?"

"It's still early in the evening. Most of the business comes later and this shouldn't take long."

She could tell by the curtness of his words that he was still out of sorts about the newspaper clipping. "I'm sorry," she said quietly.

She felt his gaze home in on her. "I beg your pardon?"

Had he not heard her or were apologies from her foreign? Had he never heard her utter one before, as the words did seem odd on her tongue? Or did he not know what she was apologizing for?

"The box. I should have never opened it, should have left it be."

"Yes, you should have let it alone. I suppose you have no recollection of Pandora and the harm she caused."

She felt light-headed for a moment with the realization that she did indeed know the story. "Why would you keep that particular clipping and no other?"

Reaching up, he opened a hatch and shouted, "Here!"

The hansom came to a stop, and she wanted to scream because she knew he would ignore the question now. She heard the clank of the driver releasing the levers, and the doors sprang open. Drake stepped out, then reached in and took her hand. She'd placed her foot on the first step when he squeezed her hand, stilling her actions. They were on eye level now, something she doubted they often were. Little light was out this time of night, save the lantern hanging on the side of the cab, but it was enough for her to see into the coal-black depths of Drake's eyes, to see his battle, to recognize when it had ended, and to wonder briefly why it appeared he'd lost.

"While you are striving to recall your past," he replied quietly, "there are parts of mine that I would rather forget, and yet I believe it imperative that I not."

"Was this Robert Sykes a friend of yours then?"

"No, never a friend."

"Who then?"

"Leave it be, Phee."

Only she didn't know if she could. His eyes had held more than anger at her opening the box. She'd seen torment there. She wasn't certain how she'd recognized it, only that she had experienced it herself before—shame, humiliation, pain. She wanted to console him, but instinctively she knew that would only worsen things between them. He was a man of immense pride, a man with demons.

After handing her down, he took the lantern from a hook on the outside of the conveyance and led her off the road onto a path. As she spied the river, a shudder went through her. Taking her arm, he stopped her progress.

"There," he said, pointing. "That's where I found you."

She could see the water lapping at the bank, so dark, so shadowy. It was a wonder he'd seen her at all. "How did you get me to your residence?"

"I carried you," he said offhandedly. It wasn't far, but still she thought it a great distance to carry someone. "Is anything familiar?"

"No." She looked up and down the river, glanced around. Shook her head and repeated, "No." She peered over at him. "Why were you out here walking?"

"This exercise isn't about me." He spun on his heel and started off so quickly that it took her a few seconds to realize he was done here. Perhaps he was done with her. She hurried after him, not able to catch up until he was already at the cab and hanging up the lantern. He held the door open for her.

"You can be quite vexing," she said as she stepped into the conveyance and settled on the seat.

"St. James," he called up to the driver before settling himself beside her.

This time without alarm or disquiet she accepted his body touching hers. She wouldn't admit it to him but she found comfort in his nearness. Being so close to the river had unsettled her, formed a cold knot in the center of her stomach. Something had happened there, something she didn't think she wanted to remember.

"Perhaps the secret to unlocking the door to my

memories is through you," she said. "If you were to share more about yourself, rather than striving to remain so mysterious, everything I know might suddenly gush forth."

"Nice try, sweetheart." She could hear the humor laced in his voice. She liked it. She liked when he wasn't quite so somber and serious.

"Sweetheart is an endearment and I don't believe I am endeared to you in any manner whatsoever."

"Yet here I am giving you time that should go to my club."

"Because you want me properly tending to your needs."

Since they were crammed together, she was quite aware of his stiffening beside her, and she wondered what in her words had caused the reaction.

"What do you know of my needs?" he said, his voice low and dark.

"I know you need your clothes laundered and your bed made and your boots polished. Mrs. Beeton obviously had a dislike for idle hands. Mine shall be truly busy from dawn 'til dusk and then some."

"You're not to do anything that causes you to hurt yourself further. I don't have time to be tending your wounds."

"You're so gruff, but I believe you're all growl and no bite."

"Oh, I bite, sweetheart. Ladies beg for it."

Something dark and tempting wove through his rough voice and caused a pleasant shiver to race through her. She should let it go, and yet, curiosity, the cat, and all that. "Why would ladies want to be bitten?"

He lowered his head, as much as he was able in their cramped confines, and she inhaled the maleness that was him, all him. "Doesn't hurt. A little nip on the lobe, the lips, the collarbone. It can be quite provocative if done right."

"Bite me and you'll find that I scratch."

Chuckling darkly, he straightened. "As though I didn't already know that."

"Have you tried to bite me?"

"If I had you'd have remembered."

"When I had forgotten everything else, I'd have remembered that? Are you that arrogant?"

"I'm that good of a lover."

She was finding it very difficult to draw in air. How had the conversation gotten off course? "Why St. James?" she asked, striving to sound nonchalant, not to give the impression that she was on the verge of asking for a nibble. "Why are we going there?"

"Some of your references came from people who lived in the area. I don't know the exact residences but I thought perhaps you would see something that would spark a memory."

Taking a shaky breath, she wondered why she was suddenly dreading what she might discover.

It took everything within Drake not to yell up to the driver to release the blasted doors so he could leap out and run until his muscles ached, until he collapsed in exhaustion, until he was too tired to be so acutely aware of the woman next to him. He'd never been coiled so tightly in his life. She didn't have her perfume and yet he could still smell the orchids. Her thigh, her hip were pressed to his. When they hit a rut in the road, his arm brushed up against her breast. When she had mentioned taking care of his needs, his mind had raced up a path that it should have steered clear of. He'd almost taken that lobe that was visible—because her hair was pulled back in a braid—and worried it between his teeth until she was moaning for him to never stop. The Ophelia he knew would have slapped him for his innuendos but Phee—Phee, bless her—was too innocent to know better.

He had no business talking to her as he had.

Until she regained her memories she was too naive, too easily taken advantage of. For all of Ophelia's harshness, she was no fool. She knew how to stand up for herself. Until he knew for certain she would be safe, he couldn't return her to Somerdale. He had considered taking her to the Duchess of Greystone, but a part of him wasn't yet ready to let her go. She was in no danger as long as she was with him.

With her there, his residence echoed less. He found himself beginning to like the woman who was in the hansom with him. Perhaps being with him was dangerous after all—dangerous to them both.

They traveled through random streets. He didn't feel that he could very well point out the home in which she resided with her brother because then he would have to explain about her brother and she would no doubt want to go inside. Nor could he point out Mabry House where she had often visited with Grace. Pointing out anything at all meant explaining. If she remembered on her own, he would release her. If not—

She cooked one hell of a pheasant.

"There's a park near here, isn't there?" she asked, dragging him from his thoughts.

"Yes. Do you remember it?" He wanted to help her remember, and yet he experienced a tinge of disappointment that perhaps tonight he would return her home. That her fragrance would no longer be wafting through his residence, that she would no longer smile at him. That everything between them would return to what it had been.

"Not really. But can I see it?"

He called up to the driver to take them to St. James Park. This time of night it would be fairly empty. When the cab came to a stop at the park's entrance, she simply sat staring at it, not moving a muscle, and yet he was acutely aware of the tenseness vibrating around her as though she dreaded regaining her memory.

What the bloody hell had happened?

Finally she released a long slow breath through slightly parted lips. "Perhaps it would help to walk for a bit."

Her voice was faint and he wondered if she was hoping he wouldn't hear her.

"We can if you want to," he said. "Or we can carry on."

She turned to him. The streetlamps provided enough light that he could see the well of tears in her eyes. His chest tightened painfully. He didn't want to see her as vulnerable. He didn't want to see her scared.

"I'm not certain I want to remember," she said softly. "Yet I don't want to be a coward. For some reason, it's more important to me not to be seen as cowardly. I think I've done things before that I didn't want to do, but I did them because I was told that I must." He heard her swallow, saw her nod. "I must go into the park."

Her resolve astounded him. Had she always possessed it? "I'll go with you."

"You don't have to."

"Whatever demons you think you might face in there, you're not going to face them alone. Besides, my legs are cramping from these close confines. They're in need of a stretch."

"Why do you strive so hard not to appear kind when you are indeed very nice?"

Because he had spent a lifetime living in a world

where he had feared revealing his true self. With her especially he'd put up an additional wall. It kept threatening to crumble and he had to re-erect it. Rather than answer her, he knocked on the roof and the driver released the latch holding the doors secure. Drake stepped out, handed her down, then grabbed the lantern. Without thought he offered her his arm. Without thought she took it.

Phee took it. Ophelia never would have. Where did one lady end and the other begin? Were memories so crucial?

They walked in silence for long moments. He assumed she was drinking in her surroundings. He wasn't concerned that the people they passed would recognize her. She was not dressed as a lady. He was not dressed in aristocratic finery. No one would give them a first glance, much less a second. Besides, most of the aristocracy would be at some dreadful ball or boring dinner tonight. Her absence would be noted. Her brother would explain she was in the country.

He should have had Gregory check with a servant on the health of the aunt. He supposed he could send him back. Or he could wait and see if she remembered.

He enjoyed walking beside her, this woman who did not hold her posture so stiffly and yet she did not slouch. He imagined she had spent long hours walking with a book perched on her head. A slackness characterized her gait as though she knew she wasn't on display, being watched. She had no need to put on airs. He wondered if he'd ever known the true Lady O. He'd questioned why Grace would hold her as a dear friend. Perhaps they each saw a different side of the same woman.

"Is it familiar?" he asked.

"Yes, I've walked here before but I can't remember

with whom. Someone I cared for. Only if I really cared for him would I have forgotten him?"

"Dark hair?"

"I can't recall his features at all. To be honest I don't even know if it's a man. Could be a woman. I know I laughed. I yearn to laugh again. I love to laugh. I'd like to hear you laugh."

"I laugh."

With a wry smile, she peered up at him. "No. Your throat rumbles but you don't laugh. I'm talking about the sort that causes your belly to ache and makes it difficult to draw in breath. The kind that brings tears to your eyes and lasts forever. It makes you feel so good that you don't want it to stop. When someone hears you laugh they start laughing. They don't even know why you began chuckling in the first place. It's the best sort of contagion. Better than gossip or snide remarks. It makes you glad to be alive. I've not heard you laugh like that."

He wasn't certain if he ever had, not to that extent. Oh, he'd certainly joined in laughing with his family from time to time, but tears in his eyes? Tears were not for men. Even tears of mirth. But he would laugh when her memory returned and she realized all she'd done in his company. He'd laugh then.

But he doubted it would make his sides ache, or his breath catch, or his eyes water. It wouldn't be joyful. It would be revengeful.

Phee didn't deserve it. But when her memories returned, she'd fade away and leave Ophelia standing there. And Lady O deserved a bit of time in his company. He would not feel guilty about it, and he'd keep telling himself that until it became true.

However, before her memories returned, he hoped to God he heard her laugh like that. He thought it might very well be a sound he'd carry with him until the day he died. But once she recalled everything he'd certainly never hear it again. He imagined looking at her across a room, catching her gaze, reminding her that he knew her laugh. That once she'd given it to him freely. It might hold more value than her washing his back.

"What would make you laugh?" he asked.

She shrugged. "I don't know. It's not something you can force. I fear you know nothing at all about laughter if you think you can."

He knew dark and dangerous things. Laughter was far removed from his world. Laughter had been part of the Mabry family. His father had laughed, but it had been a cruel sound. He almost told her about his father. Almost. But the risk was too great that she would use the knowledge against him. That she would catch his eye across a crowded ballroom and give him a look that said, *I know your darkest secrets.*

She stopped walking, half of her lost in shadows. He wondered if he was all shadow to her. He needed to remain an enigma. Needed to maintain the upper hand. Releasing her hold on him, she faced him. "I need to confess something."

"You remember?" He didn't know why he was at once disappointed, but relieved.

"No, I think this exercise as you call it is going to prove futile. However, you should know that I didn't prepare the pheasant. Mrs. Pratt did."

"Who the devil is Mrs. Pratt?"

"Mrs. Turner's cook."

"And who the devil is Mrs. Turner?"

"The widow who lives next door," she said. "I asked her cook to prepare the pheasant."

"Why didn't you just tell me that earlier?"

"Because I've not been able to do much correctly, not

anything that you've noticed at least, and I just wanted something I did to impress you, something that didn't have you grumbling at me."

"I don't grumble."

"Of course you do. I prepared you a lovely bath. You didn't even bother to thank me for it. You simply snapped at me because I hurt my hands doing it."

Had he? He had. Was he no better than she?

"So I took the credit for dinner," she continued, "because I liked the way it felt to do something right. Although of course I'm not the one who did it."

"The cook prepared the pheasant with no recompense?"

She lifted her shoulders up to her ears, dropped them back down. "I shall beat rugs for her tomorrow."

"The bloody hell you will. You can't hold a broom with those hands."

"Of course I can."

"Don't be stubborn about this, Phee. Talk to her, find out what her services are worth, and I'll pay her."

"But you shouldn't have—"

"It'll come out of your salary."

"Oh." That stopped her protests cold, but she didn't seem particularly happy about it. "If you would hire a cook you would pay her and it wouldn't come out of my salary."

"No, it wouldn't. You're quite right. I'll pay her out of my pocket." Which he would have done anyway since he wasn't really giving her a salary. The argument was moot but quite fun. He shook his head. He didn't want to have fun with her.

"Perhaps we should have her prepare all our dinners," Phee mused. "I'm sure she wouldn't mind the extra income. It was tasty pheasant. You said so yourself."

"All our dinners? And what will you do with your day?"

"According to Mrs. Beeton, quite a bit. I shall talk with Mrs. Pratt on the morrow. And you need not worry. I shall ensure the terms are fair."

As though she'd know what terms were fair. Narrowing his eyes, he couldn't help but believe she'd manipulated him somehow. But he didn't care. He wouldn't take this victory from her. He liked too much the way triumph lit her eyes. They held no arrogance, but a spot of teasing. She *had* manipulated him. He was rather sure of it.

The question was: Why wasn't he angry about it?

She was quite right. The exercise had proven futile. She knew buildings: Buckingham Palace, Parliament, the Clock Tower. She recognized the clanging of Big Ben. But beyond that, she recalled little.

"Perhaps it would be different if we went during the day," she said as they entered the foyer. He'd ordered the hansom cab driver to wait, so she knew he was going to head to his club, to see to his duties there. She wished he'd stay here, that he'd ward off the nightmares she feared were lurking in the shadows of her mind, ready to spring as soon as she drifted into slumber. Turning, she faced him. "But I don't think so. I appreciate your efforts, though. I know my situation is quite bothersome. You hired a competent servant, and find yourself burdened with one who can't even recall how to properly polish furniture."

"You're not a burden. You're safe here in this residence. You know that, don't you?"

She nodded. "Yes. It's one of those odd things I know by instinct. I knew the moment I opened my eyes and saw you. Even though I didn't remember who you were."

"Phee . . ." It appeared he intended to say more, but he merely shook his head. "I must return to the club. Sleep well, sleep late."

"According to Mrs. Beeton, a body is supposed to arise early. It is the only way to accomplish anything of worth."

The dimple formed in his cheek. "You're truly reading that book?"

"I must earn my keep lest you let me go."

"I'm not going to let you go." He seemed startled and bothered by his words. He settled his hat on his head. "I must be off."

He left then. She locked the door, leaned her back against it. She'd seen larger houses tonight, fancier ones, palaces. During odd moments, she'd envisioned herself inside them, waltzing. She imagined being courted by nobility. No doubt a dream shared by all housemaids.

Strange how she realized that it wasn't what she wanted, wasn't what she'd ever wanted. She'd wanted something . . . more. Pity she didn't know what the *more* entailed.

Chapter 15

As the hansom rattled through the streets, Drake cursed himself. He'd nearly told her everything, everything he knew about her and who she was, everything she'd once known about him. But telling her meant ending the farce. Ending the farce meant her leaving his household.

He'd been quite arrested by her tonight. Her courage, her determination. Her description of laughter. He wanted it. Balling a fist, he pounded it against his thigh. He did not want to be intrigued by her, did not want to get to know this woman who lived in his residence. He wanted to be rid of her. And he would be as soon as he had a better grasp of how she'd come to be in the river.

The driver pulled the cab to a stop in front of Dodger's Drawing Room. For the first time in his life, Drake was not focused on his responsibilities here. He always worked from dusk until dawn and beyond. Phee was serving as a distraction he could ill afford. His obligations, his life took place within the walls of the gaming establishment. Beyond it, his life entailed eating, sleeping, existing. It was only at Dodger's that he truly lived.

But he'd never laughed uproariously within those walls.

Suddenly he had an insatiable desire to laugh until his sides ached.

The hatch above his head opened and he handed up the money to the driver, who then released the latch on the door. Drake leaped out, charged up the steps, and crossed the threshold into the building that had the power to destroy and rebuild. Fortunes were lost here. Fortunes were made.

He'd taken only three long strides inside when he knew—*knew*—he was being watched. Jerking his gaze up to the shadowed balcony, he was unable to make out any form or figure, but he knew Jack Dodger was up there. The man's presence was so bold and powerful that it could be felt even when he wasn't visible. In his day he'd managed Dodger's with an iron fist, and on occasion he returned to stretch his muscles. Tonight was apparently one of those occasions.

By the time Drake reached his office, Jack was sitting behind the desk pouring whiskey into two glasses. Even now, dressed in the finery of a gentleman, Jack had the look of the streets about him. Gray feathered through the dark hair at his temples. His eyes were dark, alert, assessing.

Drake wasn't about to take the chair in front of the desk, to place himself in a subservient role. He was the overseer here, and while Jack might be the majority partner, the public face behind Dodger's, Drake was now responsible for its management. Taking the offered glass, he walked over to the window and gazed out. Jack intimidated many, but not him. Like the man at the desk, Drake was a product of the streets. He was not one to be frightened, cowed, or bullied.

"I wasn't expecting you," Drake said.

"That's the whole point, to see how things are managed when one doesn't know that I plan to stop by."

Drake glanced over his shoulder and held Jack's gaze. "And how do you find it managed?"

"Quite well. No complaints." Shrugging, he leaned back in his chair. "Well, one perhaps. Membership to an American? The purpose here has always been to fleece the nobility—as legally as possible."

Turning, facing the man fully, Drake pressed his shoulder to the hard edge of the window casing. "The nobility is not what it once was. Many are impoverished. Lord Randolph Churchill's marriage to Jennie Jerome is going to change everything. Others will turn to the Americans to replenish their coffers. It seemed a sound business decision to get a jump on allowing them to replenish ours as well."

Jack grinned. "So you're going to allow more in?"

"As many as I can entice. Presently they are an untapped source of revenue."

"More money in our pockets. I can't complain." Jack downed his whiskey.

Drake had yet to touch his. "Then why are you here?"

Jack set his empty glass down deliberately, yet slowly, so it didn't make a sound. "When I ran the place, I spent a good deal of my time in the balcony, looking out over my fiefdom, feeling like a king. I don't feel like a king so much anymore."

"You will when you see the increase in profits. I have other plans I intend to implement. Your coffers will be overflowing."

Jack narrowed his gaze. "Perhaps, but I've been thinking of late that Dodger's has had a good run, but all runs must come to an end."

Everything within Drake tightened, stilled. "You're closing it?"

"You said it yourself: Times are changing."

Drake took a step away from the window. "Yes, but we can adjust, adapt."

Jack stood, tugged on his red brocade waistcoat. "I believe a meeting with the partners is in order. My residence. Friday next. Half past two. Bring your ideas. We'll go from there."

Drake stood in the balcony and gazed out over his fiefdom. He understood Jack's sentiments because they so mirrored his. Only he couldn't imagine any of this going away. He'd given years of his life to it. The majority of the hours of his days. Even after he'd purchased his residence, he usually slept here, ate here—until Phee. He'd been caught up in her and not devoting himself to the management of the club as he had before. Had Jack sensed his loyalty waning? It was only a temporary disruption. He could assure the partners of that without providing details regarding his distraction.

A distraction that even now called to him more than the sound of ivory and cards. He thought about returning to his residence to watch her sleep, but what sort of madness was it that he couldn't go an hour without seeing her? He would return to his residence when his obligations here were finished. That he managed to get everything taken care of two hours sooner than usual was mere coincidence.

As he walked up the path to the door, he refused to acknowledge the disappointment he felt that his arrival hadn't heralded Phee's. She was no doubt still abed. He had not been anticipating her greeting him at the door, smiling at him. Damnation. Of course he had. He might not be completely honest with her, but it was imperative that he remain honest with himself. He could make up all the excuses he wanted for why he hadn't sat her down and explained everything to her last night, but the truth was that he wasn't quite ready to have her dislike him once again.

As he inserted his key, he noticed the sheen of the door. When had she polished it? Had the task contributed to the damage to her hands? He hadn't expected her to embrace her duties.

Stepping over the threshold, he went in search of her. His bed was made, no evidence at all that she'd slept there. Except for her lingering fragrance, the true essence of her. He should purchase her some orchid-scented perfume. He went into the bathing chamber, halfway hoping he'd find her in the tub. He found only her brush, mirror, and comb set out neatly beside his. He realized her bedchamber contained no mirror. He should remedy that.

Why, he chastised himself, when he would be returning her home any day now?

But somehow her brush resting beside his looked . . . right. An odd thought. It didn't look right at all. Because it was completely and unmistakably wrong. It didn't belong there. She didn't belong here. He would tell her all as soon as he located her. Perhaps the truth would return her memory, and he could determine if Somerdale was indeed speaking true about the blasted uncle and the ill aunt.

Phee wasn't in her bedchamber. She couldn't possibly be preparing him breakfast, as he'd arrived earlier than expected. Still he headed down to the kitchen and staggered to a stop in the doorway at the sight that greeted him.

Had Drake ever conjured up images of Ophelia on her knees, he'd have never pictured her as she was at that precise moment with her bottom tilted up in the air, moving forward and back, side to side as she scrubbed the stone floor of the kitchen. He imagined lying beneath her, having her engaged in those same motions above him, her clothing discarded, her breasts filling his hands.

Whatever was wrong with him? When had he ever considered bedding Lady O? The answer was simple. Never. She had never appealed to him—

Yet he had kissed her at the ball and been shaken to his core.

And now he couldn't deny the enticing picture she made, so hard at work. He had to give her credit: when she set her mind to something, she gave it her all.

"You shouldn't be doing that," he barked, more to bring himself back from his fantasy than to chastise her. "You'll damage your hands further."

Sitting back on her heels, she peered up at him and with a quick breath, blew the hair that had fallen across her brow, sending it off to the side. Why did that small action cause his gut to clench tightly? Then she smiled, and he almost dropped to his knees beside her.

"Good morning to you as well," she said brightly.

"It won't be such a good morning if you're hurt."

"I wrapped them with extra linen and I'm not putting them in the water, only the brush bristles." She blew at the wispy strands again. "Shall I prepare you some breakfast?"

"An early luncheon would be better as I'm expecting a delivery of furniture at any moment."

"Truly?"

"Assume if I tell you something that it's true." Even if the majority of what he'd told her thus far were lies.

"I can't wait to see it," she said with enthusiasm that unsettled him. "Which rooms?"

"The only ones I'm presently using. My bedchamber and the library."

"Then I should sweep them, make them ready. I do wish you'd said something yesterday." Quickly she shoved herself to her feet, but apparently she'd forgotten about the wet stone, because one of her feet flew out from beneath her, she reared back, her arms flailed—

Snaking one arm around her, he saved her from a hard tumble, had her pressed up flat against his body, and was staring into her wide green eyes. Why did they have to be so beautiful, like spring leaves after a bitter winter? If he wasn't careful they'd seep into his soul, take root there. He'd never rid himself of her.

Ophelia he could gladly drag out of his residence kicking and screaming. But it wasn't Ophelia in his arms at that moment. It was Phee.

For reasons he didn't completely understand, he was loath to give her up. This woman possessed a warm smile, always seemed so damned glad to see him. He returned to the residence earlier than normal because he couldn't stand to go another moment without seeing her, although he'd expected to find her still abed. But here she was scrubbing his floor and delighted by the prospect of the arrival of furniture. He wished he'd purchased enough for every room.

With his free hand, he cradled her cheek and stroked his thumb over the softness. The wayward strands of her hair had refallen across one eye but she refrained from blowing them back. He almost asked her to because he liked watching the movement of her lips, imagined her puffs of air stirring the hair at his temple, on his chest, his belly, lower. He almost growled. This woman in his arms left him in a perpetual state of needing to groan with want and desire.

It was ludicrous to yearn for her touch when he knew what a spoiled, bored miss she truly was. But this woman wasn't spoiled. She was something he didn't understand.

She affected his judgment, made it questionable. She had him doing things he didn't normally do. She had him doubting his little act of revenge. She had him wanting what he couldn't have, not for the long term. When her memories returned, so would the woman he could scarcely stomach. But for now she was nowhere in sight, for now her breasts were flattened against his chest and she didn't protest. Her bandaged hands rested on his shoulders, her eyes searched his. She didn't flinch at his touch. She merely waited.

She would have been better served by protesting.

He lowered his mouth to hers. She welcomed him, parting her lips, giving him access to the honeyed depths. She tasted the same, the shape of her mouth was as he remembered, but the eagerness of her tongue as it parried with his was new. The sweet sigh, the low moan, the rising up on her toes as though she couldn't get enough, as though she craved more—that was new. Her fingers scraped along his scalp, her arms tightened around his neck. He deepened the kiss, exploring each nook and cranny with a freedom that had been lacking before. He took his time, reveling in every aspect. Her enthusiasm matched his. She wasn't shy or repulsed or horrified.

He knew she wouldn't exhibit any of those emotions when he pulled back, but he wasn't quite ready to end the kiss, not just yet. It was wrong of him; he was taking advantage, but he couldn't quite care that he was exhibiting not only bad behavior, but horrendous judgment. Surely, eventually, her memory would return. She would remember this kiss. He was determined that she would remember it.

That she would recall her tongue sweeping through his mouth, her body moving against his as though she could crawl inside him, the tightness with which she held him near. She would know that his mouth had been latched on to hers for long minutes, devouring, possessing, conquering. She was willingly taking what he was offering. No slapping this time. No fury. No cutting words.

He should have felt triumphant. Instead he questioned who was truly winning here.

Drawing back, he fell into the green depths of her eyes, marveling as the wonder reflected there slowly evolved into suspicion.

"You kissed me before," she said quietly. "I remember. Is that the reason I ran away?"

Slowly he released her. It hadn't occurred to him that kissing her would cause her to remember him or at least something she'd shared with him.

"I don't know why you ran away." Truth. Or even *if* she had run away. Although it seemed more likely that she had—from either Somerdale or Wigmore. Neither had reported her missing, so her disappearance was going to reflect badly on one of them. But which one?

"But we have kissed before," she said, more statement than question.

"Yes."

"Is there something between us?"

How did he answer that? Dislike, distrust, pride—his, perhaps hers—was between them. "Anything between us would be inappropriate."

"Of course. You're a gentleman; I'm a servant." She angled her chin, squared her shoulders. "Thank you for rescuing me from the tumble."

"I'm certain you would have caught your balance."

"Why do you never take credit for your kindnesses?"

Because I'm not kind and you'll realize that soon enough. She brought out the worst in him. She surely did.

A hard knock on the door saved him from having to answer. Thank goodness. Not that he would have, but a distraction from her questions was in order and he welcomed this one. He opened the door to a bulk of a man.

"Mr. Darlin'? We've got yer furniture, sir."

Through the gate, he could see the large wagon in the mews. "Bring it in."

Stepping back, he glanced at Phee. "They shouldn't be here long, if you'd rather be elsewhere in the residence."

"I can see to it if you like. Besides, I'm rather curious as to whether I was correct in my assessment regarding the type of furniture you would select."

"I had this furniture specially made."

A corner of her mouth eased up, teasing in her eyes. "Heavy wood. Dark. Mahogany, I'd wager. Dark fabrics. Burgundy. Perhaps forest green."

He didn't much like that she was spot-on with her assessment. Ophelia never would have known him so well. Or had she? Was that the reason that she'd always known how to rattle him?

"Very astute, Miss Lyttleton." He realized his mistake too late, when her eyes widened and her mouth—that very kissable mouth that was still swollen from his kiss—formed a slight O.

"Lyttleton. I never thought to inquire regarding my surname. Phee Lyttleton. Do you know what the Phee is short for?"

It might assist her in regaining her memory, in recalling what happened that night. And with her memory, she would know him for the bastard he was. "Ophelia."

She scowled. "A character from Shakespeare. I can remember something insignificant but not recall my name. It is the oddest thing."

A bang sounded as one of the deliverymen misjudged the width of the door opening.

"Careful there," Drake barked. He'd paid good money for that sofa.

Phee squeezed his arm, her face a wreath of delight. "Burgundy. I knew it. I'll remember everything I know about you before long."

Dear God, he hoped not.

Ophelia's assertive nature had always irritated Drake, but as he stood off to the side in the library allowing her to be in charge, he could not help but be impressed and to see the benefit of having at his disposal a lady who was not a wallflower. The duchess and Grace were equally confident but they were tempered with warmth and softness that he'd always found lacking in Ophelia.

But Phee was not overly cocky. She simply knew exactly how the furniture should be arranged and was intent on having the deliverymen set it in place to her satisfaction. What amazed him was that she correctly identified which pieces belonged in which room, which gave him the unsettling thought that they had similar tastes. The furniture for the sitting area in his bedchamber had already been carted upstairs. Now they were arranging a sitting area in front of the fireplace in the library.

Phee pointed, here, there. She gave orders, the tone of her voice allowing for no disobedience. She might not remember who she was but *what* she was reverberated through every fiber of her being, and for once he admired it.

He imagined her sitting in one of the chairs that she'd had set before the fireplace, he in the other, carrying on a discussion in a civilized manner with no tartness in her voice, no upturn of her nose as though she'd caught scent of a ghastly smell. He imagined her laughing, making him laugh.

From the moment he'd learned the treasures that a woman's body held, he'd never contemplated extending the pleasure into something more permanent, had never considered taking a wife. He liked the solitude of his life, liked not having to share the dark thoughts that sometimes troubled him. He savored the decision to not carry on the heritage his father had passed on to him. He'd grown up in a family where births, deaths, marriages were recorded. On cold winter nights, they would gather before a fire in the parlor and the Duke of Greystone would wax on about his ancestors and their accomplishments. He had instilled in his children an appreciation for those who had come before them.

Drake had no such tales of his ancestors to share. He had known only his father, his mother. His father brutal, his mother weak. One did not tell children about large hands wrapped around a slender neck. Sometimes when he looked down at his own large hands, he wondered if a woman would be truly safe from them. What if he was more like his father than he realized? What if his temper flared, what if he struck out with his fists?

What if he couldn't control his anger?

He'd once threatened to kill Lovingdon if he hurt Grace. He'd meant the words. He knew he was capable of destroying a man. Others knew it as well. It was the reason that he managed Dodger's with such success. No one wanted to have a confrontation with him. Although he suspected one was waiting when he discovered who was responsible for Phee's dip into the river. He thought it very unlikely that it had been her choice.

She came to stand beside him. "What do you think?" she asked.

"Perfect."

She smiled up at him, clearly pleased by his word. Those smiles were an addiction. Having seen one in its true form, he wanted to see a thousand, a million. He wanted to be the reason for them.

Obviously he was overwrought and overtired. He'd not had a good day's sleep since he'd found her. His thinking was off-kilter. He saw the driver and his assistant out. When he returned to the library, he found her sitting in the chair, a book on her lap, her eyes closed.

"Taking a holiday today?" he asked.

Slowly she opened her eyes. Even more slowly her lips curled up into a smile that nearly dropped him to his knees.

"Simply testing it out. It'll be much lovelier with a fire this evening."

For the first time since he'd begun working at Dodger's more than a decade earlier, he regretted that his nights were spoken for, that he couldn't give them to her.

Straightening, she moved to the edge of chair. Her smile withered, her features settled into somberness. "You said anything between us would be inappropriate, but you didn't exactly say nothing was between us."

Were they back to that now? He thought they'd ended the unwanted conversation.

"Are we lovers?" she continued.

"No. We've only kissed twice and in both circumstances, I took advantage of an opportunity. It won't happen again. You're safe here, Phee. I would never force myself on you."

"I'm not quite sure it's you I'm worried about in that regard. I rather liked it."

He didn't know what to say. This woman, her candor. She had to represent Ophelia's very soul. How had he never seen beneath the surface? How had he never understood what a complicated creature she was?

His original lie, implying she was a servant, was a travesty. He needed to tell her the truth now. He would live with the consequences. He needed to help her remember, needed to assist her in determining what had happened that night. He was halfway to the chair opposite hers when he heard the ringing of the bell signaling someone at the front door.

"That'll be Marla," Phee said, coming to her feet in one smooth movement.

"Marla?"

She gave him an exasperated look. "Do you not pay attention to my words? She's the housemaid across the way."

"Right, with the cook who is going to prepare our dinners."

"Better. She's going to teach me how to prepare them. I decided this morning that you hired me to cook your meals so I must have known how to do it at one time. I should think it would come back fairly quickly."

Perhaps if there were something to come back. "Phee—"

He'd never seen such anticipation in her eyes before. He wanted it to stay there, didn't want to be the one to douse it.

The ringer sounded again.

"I must get that before she gives up and goes on without me. We're going to the market. I'm looking quite forward to fresh tomatoes and asparagus."

He doubted she had a clue regarding what fresh tomatoes and asparagus should look like. She was accustomed to having it served to her, not selecting it from a bin.

"But I don't know how much I'm allowed to spend," she continued.

"I'll get you some coins while you open the door."

She smiled brightly. "Thank you."

Then she was rushing by him, their discussion regarding the kiss apparently forgotten. Her step contained a lightness he'd never before seen. So much about her was a revelation. He went to a shelf, pressed the wall behind it, releasing a door that matched the woodwork. Withdrawing a key from his pocket, he opened the safe and removed some money. He wasn't concerned that anyone in this area of London would recognize her. Certainly no one would look into the happy face of a servant and see a lady of quality.

She was back in a flash, her apron gone, her braid wreathing her head. She needed a hat. Ladies didn't go out without a hat.

He handed her the pouch. "It's a goodly sum. If you require personal items, purchase them."

"I shall be frugal."

He was surprised she knew the word. "Buy what you need. I'm not a pauper."

"You're irritated with me again."

"No, I just—" *Fear I've done you a disservice.* "Do be careful."

"I shall stay clear of the river." That smile again, the one she'd given him from the chair, the one that made him want to take her in his arms and ensure no harm ever came to her.

He escorted her into the hallway where a young woman with dark hair and startling blue eyes bobbed a quick curtsy as soon as she saw him.

"No need to curtsy for me, girl," he said.

"Yes, sir."

"I'll wake you for your bath," Phee said, before brushing by him and leading—Marla, was it?—out the door.

In three quick strides, he was at the entryway window

gazing out. The ladies were walking toward the street. Marla said something, Phee smiled. She would be fine. No one would accost her, no one would recognize her. All would be well.

He was exhausted. He needed his sleep. He had the club to worry over. And his own future should the partners indeed decide that it had outlived its usefulness. He'd taken three steps toward the stairs before turning on his heel, retrieving his hat, and heading out. He wasn't going to interfere, but he intended to follow them. She was his responsibility.

He was beginning to wish he'd left her in the bloody Thames.

Chapter 16

"He is a handsome devil," Marla said as they walked along the street. "Much better to see him up close, rather than looking at him through the window. So large. I don't know if I've ever known anyone as tall as him."

"I barely noticed," Phee lied. She hadn't expected Marla to be so enamored of Drake. He was all she'd spoken of since they left the house. She wondered what Marla would think if she confessed that he kissed her. But she knew that kisses were not to be talked about. Like everything, she didn't know how she knew, but she knew it would put her reputation at risk. But who was there to care?

"He seems rather dark and brooding, though," Marla said. "Like Heathcliff."

Wuthering Heights. Phee almost shouted out the title. She knew the character. She knew the book. She had feared she'd appear to be somewhat of a nitwit on this outing. But she decided she could hold her own. More, though, she *wanted* to shop. Had this intense yearning to purchase something.

Now she had coins jangling in her pocket—she

needed a reticule. And a hat. And gloves. Good Lord, she was out in public without gloves.

"Before we get to the market, will we pass any shops?" she asked.

"Yes, just over there." Marla pointed, although houses prevented Phee from seeing any shops. "I like to look in the windows."

"Don't you go inside?"

"Hardly ever. No point in it when I won't be buying."

"Why don't you purchase things?"

"I have to put away my money for a rainy day."

"You shop when it rains? Are the prices better then?"

Marla laughed. "No, it's an expression. Do you just not remember it?"

"I don't recall saving my coins. It seems if I want something I should purchase it."

"We have to hoard our pennies. When Mrs. Turner passes, where will I be? I have to find other employment and I don't know how long that will take."

"Drake Darling isn't going to die anytime soon. He's young."

"And strong. And virile," Marla said on a sigh. "You are so fortunate. I read a novel just last week where the girl in it was a maid. She fell in love with her employer. Terribly romantic."

"But it was all made up. It wasn't real. Maids don't marry the masters of the house." Even if he did kiss her in the kitchen until her knees turned to jam.

"Somewhere they might."

Phee felt badly for what she'd said. Apparently Marla was hoping to marry a gentleman, but it seemed so unlikely. "Perhaps I'm wrong. I hear every story is based on a bit of truth."

"Where did you hear that?"

Phee released a bubble of laughter. "I haven't a clue."

"That must be so odd not to remember things."

"It was at first, terribly odd, unsettling, but I've resigned myself to the notion that I might never know. Perhaps that's not such a bad thing." Maybe Darling had the right of it, that she had forgotten for a reason.

"I have to admit I'd prefer to forget some things in my life. M'dad lost in drink mostly. Bein' in service is not such a bad thing."

Perhaps not such a bad thing, but Phee wanted to do more with her life. While the specifics eluded her, she did know that she wanted to make a difference in some manner. "Have you always wanted to be in service?"

"It's better than working the farm. The vicar helped me. I was only twelve but I was sweet on him. I used to imagine that when I grew up I'd meet someone like him, someone to take me away from all my chores."

Did everyone yearn for a different life—the wealthy, the aristocracy, the royals? What did she yearn for? Independence flashed through her mind. She wanted to be free to do as she pleased, not that Drake was a harsh taskmaster, and she was beginning to enjoy caring for his house, but something was lacking. She wanted *something*. "Have you a beau now?" she asked.

Marla released a light chuckle. "No. Few domestics marry. Seeing to our chores is supposed to be our life's work, our priority. You have forgotten a lot, haven't you?"

Phee couldn't imagine that she would care about chores more than anything else in the world. Even as she considered how best to care for Drake's residence, even as she wanted to arrange the furniture and purchase more of it and give the place a pleasant atmosphere, she couldn't see herself caring about only those things. If she had a chance to dance, she would leave scrub brushes behind without a second thought. She'd rather purchase a new frock than repair an old one. She wanted to wear a different dress every day, not the same old drab uniform.

Embracing her present life wasn't nearly as appealing as stretching the boundaries and searching for something new. Just as at that moment, new gloves called to her.

She'd barely noticed they'd come to a street of shops. Marla stopped in front of a window, almost pressing her nose to the glass as she peered in. "This is my favorite shop."

Phee glanced inside. She could see why. It was a ladies' boutique, specializing in the various personal items a lady needed. "Let's go inside, shall we?"

"Oh no," Marla said, stepping back, her eyes wide. "Can't go in if we're not going to purchase anything."

"Who said I wasn't going to purchase anything?"

Before Marla could object, Phee had opened the door and stepped inside. For the first time since she'd awoken in Drake's bed, she felt remarkably at home. The gent behind the counter came to attention, seemed to take them both in with a sweeping glance, before relaxing his stance and looking down the long, knifelike bridge of his nose.

"May I help you?" His condescending tone almost had her taking her business elsewhere, but she was far more interested in putting him in his place. She didn't like him, shouldn't give him her business, but was quite sure she'd dealt with his sort before.

She angled her chin, did her own looking down, and said as distinctly as possible, "I need to see what you have in the way of gloves."

His head gave the tiniest of jerks as though he couldn't quite believe his ears. "As you wish, madam."

"It's La—" Was she going to say lady? Why would

she say that? Had she been a lady in another life, before she became a servant? Was she hiding from something before the river? Such strange musings. "Miss."

He turned to a set of drawers, tugged one out completely, and set it on the counter. An assortment of gloves awaited her perusal. Cotton. Some with a bit of lace. She lifted one, examined it, dropped it. "These are poorly made. I want kidskin. Your finest, most supple kidskin."

"I doubt you can afford it."

"I doubt, sir, that you have the barest inkling as to what I can afford. Now be quick about attending to my needs lest I go elsewhere."

She was much more pleased with the leather selections. She had rewrapped her hands before leaving on the outing, covering the broken skin only twice with linen strips, but still it was a challenge to put the gloves on in order to determine the proper size. Finally she was satisfied. "I'll take a pair in white and tan."

Then she noticed Marla's gloved hands resting lightly on the counter. The cotton worn and frayed. "I'll also be taking a pair for my friend. Marla, which ones would you like?"

Phee was relatively certain she'd seen a full moon, but she didn't think it could have been any bigger than Marla's eyes, round with surprise.

"Don't be daft. You can't purchase me gloves."

"Silly girl, Darling will be paying for them." She removed the pouch of coins from her pocket, started to open it, and stopped. It didn't feel quite right. One did not pay for gloves with coins. She looked at the clerk. "Everything we want is to be charged to a Mr. Drake Darling. I shall give you his address and you're to deliver the items there this evening. He'll pay you at that time."

"I don't know a Mr. Drake Darling, so I'm afraid, *miss*, that I can't extend you credit. You have to pay for your purchases."

That wasn't the way it was done. She knew that. Even though she had coins in her pockets, those were for the market. In a shop, she did little more than sign her name. She straightened her spine, brought back her shoulders, and delivered her best fuming glare. "Drake Darling is a man of influence and wealth. I daresay he has rubbed elbows with Bertie. You do know who Bertie is, do you not?"

"Not personally, but—"

"Well, Darling does know him personally." She didn't know if he did know the Prince of Wales personally, but it sounded good, and she was determined to set this man in his place. As she couldn't very well shorten the long nose he looked down at her from, she would have to bring his conceit down to size. "Do you know who I am?"

He started to shake his head. She pounced before he could utter any words. "I am the woman who is going to purchase enough items today to pay your bills for a month. I am accustomed to purchasing on credit and shall continue to do so. Should Mr. Drake Darling have to come in here to personally see to this matter, he will not be at all happy. You, dear sir, do not want to be the reason for his unhappiness. Now I wish to see what you have in silk underthings. Be quick about it. I do not suffer sluggards well."

He was quick about it, very quick about it. Phee took perverse satisfaction in how solicitous he became. Half an hour later, wearing bright smiles, she and Marla walked out of the shop.

"You sounded like a bloody nob," Marla whispered. "Are you sure you're not a lady of quality?"

"I'm quite certain. A lady would not end up in the river."

"What if your Mr. Darling doesn't want to pay for those things?"

"He will. He told me to purchase what I needed."

"But those aren't things that are *needed*. Just things we'd enjoy having."

"It'll be fine, Marla. I'm relatively certain he's quite well off. Now, is there a milliner in the area?"

Ebenezer Whistler stared at the pile of silk nothings that the lady had determined she required. He'd never had one customer purchase so many items during one visit. Silk stockings for every day of the week, chemises of the softest cotton, satin nightdresses, lacy shawls. One of anything was not enough for this woman, but he had not objected after she'd taken him to task because she spoke as though she were someone who might take tea with the queen.

But she dressed as a common laborer. He looked at her signature in his ledger beside the total amount owed to him. No gent was going to pay that much for his servant's madness. He shouldn't bother the fellow. He should have stopped the lady before it got this far, but fool that he was, he kept hearing coins dropping into his palm. He should simply put everything back in its place.

The chimes above his door tinkled as it was opened. A tall, broad-shouldered man walked in, his long strides bringing him to the counter before Ebenezer had a chance to properly greet him. This man was not in want of money. His clothes were well tailored, his mien one of success. He nodded toward the pile of items.

"Are those the things the lady who was just in here wished to purchase?"

Ebenezer nodded. "Yes, sir."

The gent arched a brow at the book. Ebenezer turned it his way. "I'm afraid, sir, that she may have overreached."

Without hesitation, the gentleman took the pen from the inkwell and scrawled his name—Drake Darling—beside hers. "Oh, I suspect this is paltry compared to the damage she'll do before the day is done."

Drake was grateful that he had decided to follow them. He'd been peering in the shop window when he'd seen Phee's back stiffen. The aristocratic lady that she was had risen to the fore. She'd spoken with such authority that he'd been able to clearly hear her. He suspected the clerk initially hadn't known whether to shake in his shoes or laugh. Based on the items he'd given her leave to purchase, Ebenezer Whistler had shaken in his shoes.

Drake very well might have too. He'd made arrangements for the items to be delivered to his residence. Later, he would send a note to his man of business warning him of several unusual bills that would be coming his way. His man would think he'd taken on a mistress. He had little doubt a mistress would be less expensive.

Phee was in her element now: shopping. It was how ladies of quality spent their afternoons and she was apparently remembering quite nicely the specifics of how it should be done.

For a heartbeat, he considered catching up with her and stopping the madness but he was rather enjoying the lively bounce in her step, the smiles he occasionally caught a glimpse of. It was equally obvious that the little maid traipsing along beside her was having a grand time. He didn't want to spoil their fun.

It also occurred to him that this little adventure

might accomplish what last night's hadn't: bring back Phee's memories. He wanted to be nearby if that happened, because he suspected she would be quite disoriented as she began piecing things together.

It was an odd thing: the desperation with which he wanted her to remember, the desperation with which he didn't. Her being in his care needed to come to an end—swiftly and immediately. And yet . . .

She'd purchased gloves for the little maid. While the money wasn't coming out of her pocket, but out of his, he was still surprised that she'd thought to do it at all. It seemed each day, no, each hour, he learned something new and unexpected about her. Something that intrigued him and made him want to know more.

So he followed at a discreet distance, collecting bread crumbs of information, like some pauper in search of any scrap of food to appease his hunger. But where she was concerned, he possessed an insatiable appetite. He feared he might never satisfy his desire to know everything about her.

"You can't keep purchasing me things," Marla said, as they neared the market.

"It makes it more fun." They'd had the best time ordering hats at the milliner's and shoes at the cobbler's.

"But your employer will not be happy about it."

"I can handle him." Although she didn't think she would have to. He wasn't going to object. She didn't know why she knew that but she did. And if he did object, she would simply have the cost of the items for Marla taken out of her wages. He was going to have to take something out of her wages anyway. They had walked past a shop that displayed blown glass figurines in the window, and Phee had spotted one that she wanted—desperately. She would cancel all the other items she'd purchased if need be to obtain this one intricate piece of glass. The delicate piece was now wrapped and secured in a reticule she'd purchased after convincing the shop clerk Drake Darling was good for the items.

She seemed to have a way of convincing shop clerks of a good many things. Marla said it was her tone, that she would not take no for an answer. Perhaps it was. Phee never once considered that her requests would be refused. She wasn't accustomed to not being obeyed. Perhaps that was why Darling had hired her to be his housekeeper, even though she was relatively young. He knew she'd brook no disobedience from her subordinates—once she had subordinates.

"I don't think I've ever seen so much money spent in one outing," Marla said.

"I daresay those with the means to spend are not often appreciated, and yet without them Society would crumble."

"How so?"

"Everything we purchased today put coins in someone else's pocket. They in turn will spend those coins on bakery goods or some such. If you look at it that way, we are really obligated to buy things."

Marla laughed. "You do have an odd way of looking at things."

"I suspect the shop clerks greatly appreciate my dedication to duty." She paused her thoughts. Something about duty . . . There and gone before she could grasp it.

As they wandered from stall to stall, Phee decided bartering for vegetables wasn't nearly so entertaining as shopping for trinkets and clothing. Examining asparagus, tomatoes, cabbage was quite tedious. She listened with only half an ear as Marla explained how to determine what was ripe, what had yet to ripen, and the signs that produce was overly ripe.

"I don't understand why it should fall to us to ensure the produce is perfect," Phee told her. "It should only be made available when it is. Someone who works with it all day would be a much better judge than I."

"Perhaps, but that's not the way it's done," Marla said. She glanced at the watch pinned to her bodice. "My word, we've been gone much longer than I thought. We need to hurry here."

"We can dispense with the lessons then, and you just tell me which items to purchase."

They were approaching the last stall when Phee heard a horse whinny in distress. Moving past Marla, she spotted a wagon loaded with crates and a man sitting on the bench, flicking a whip over and over at the poor beast's back.

"No!" she yelled, dropped the bags that contained the produce they'd purchased thus far, and raced toward the wagon. She leaped onto the step, reached up, and grabbed the man's arm. "No!"

He flung her off as though she were little more than a child's rag doll, and she landed on the ground in a sprawl just like one. She scrambled back to her feet, rushed forward, and stepped up again. With her fist, she pounded his thigh, his side, anything she could reach.

"Blast ye, woman!" The weight of a meaty hand snapped her head back and she tumbled, bracing for impact—

She landed hard against something sturdy, sturdy and familiar, strong arms cradling her to a firm, broad chest. Looking into black eyes, she pleaded, "Stop him."

His features set in a furious mask, Drake Darling growled even as he set her on her feet as though she were delicate glass. She watched as he bounded onto the wagon, ripped the whip from the man's hand, and delivered two hard punches to his face that toppled him over.

Hurrying to the horse, she grabbed the bridle with one hand before rubbing the horse's neck with the other. "It's all right," she cooed. "It's all right. He's not going to hurt you again."

Suddenly she was aware of Darling beside her, breathing heavily, anger rolling off him in waves. Turning to him she said, "Purchase him."

The tension in his face eased a little as incredulity worked its way through him. "Pardon?"

"Purchase the horse. He's so scarred, has been abused so horribly. Please purchase him."

"Phee, he's not our responsibility."

"Please. I'll work a year without a salary, two years. However long you say. But we can't leave him to that brute."

He squeezed his eyes shut. She could see him struggling, so she implored quietly, "Please, Drake."

He popped his eyes open. "You will be the death of me."

Recovered from his fall, the driver was trudging forward, his hands balled into tight fists at his side. Drake spun on his heel. "How much for the horse?"

Chapter 17

The last thing Drake had expected of his day was to be walking back to his residence with a lumbering horse in tow. The man had found a place to park his wagon until he could secure another beast. They had agreed on a price and Drake had given him instructions to be at Dodger's Drawing Room at four to receive payment. Fortunately, Dodger's reputation was such that the man didn't question he would indeed be paid.

As for Drake, he was a blasted fool. What was he going to do with a horse that was too old for service? It plodded along beside him as though each step might be its last. Whereas Phee walked quietly beside him. The little maid was somehow even quieter, as though she didn't wish to be seen, as though the temper he'd exhibited terrified her.

He'd spent years holding his temper on a tight leash but when he'd seen the driver shove Phee off the wagon, not once but twice, he'd wanted to put the man into a coffin. The fury that had ratcheted through him had nearly blinded him to reason. All he'd seen were his father's fists flailing, all he'd heard was the sickening thud of flesh hitting bloodied flesh. For a moment he'd been eight years old, hovering in a corner unable to save his mother, too terrified to try—

He barely recalled climbing onto the wagon and taking his fists to the man. If the man hadn't tumbled backward, he wasn't certain he'd have ever stopped hitting him. Phee's face was already bruising, her eye swelling. The anger he'd felt had died down from a blaze to a simmer, but it was still there. And something more. If he didn't know better he'd have thought he'd been terrified of losing her.

It hadn't improved his day that she looked up at him with tears welling in her eyes. Lady O whom he hadn't even thought capable of weeping. All because of a horse.

"What the devil were you thinking?" he ground out through clenched teeth. "That man was twice your size."

"The horse couldn't fight back. He'll beat the next one he has, won't he."

Not a question, a statement, because she knew the answer. Just as he'd known when his father finally stopped hitting his mother that he would beat her again. All he could do was be grateful his father hadn't turned his fists on him yet. As young as he was, he'd known he should have stepped in front of his mother, he should have stopped his father. The guilt over his cowardice had eaten its way into his soul. "I'll have a word with him when he comes for his money."

"You don't think he knew what he was doing was wrong? If your fists don't stop him, I don't see how your words will."

He peered over at her. "Have some faith in me."

"I have complete faith in you."

His gut tightened. He didn't want her to have that much. Only a smidgen. It was all he deserved. She'd realize that once her memories came back.

"What were you doing at the market anyway?" she asked.

He was hoping with all that had happened, she'd have not been so inquisitive, would have just accepted his arrival in the nick of time. He considered fabricating some tale, but he was still struggling to get his anger in check after first seeing her tumbling from the wagon. Catching her the second time she went flying should have helped ease his fury except that he'd gotten a rather close view of her reddened face and the imprint of the driver's hand. Morris, his name was. Drake didn't know if it was his first or surname and he didn't really care.

"I followed you," he admitted.

"Why?"

"I feared you might find yourself in a bit of a bother. It appears my fears were well-founded. You seem to call to trouble."

"You thought I might end up back in the Thames."

"Morris was certainly contemplating putting you there. Do you make a habit of attacking large men?"

She gave him an impish smile—or started to. It ended with a grimace. "I don't know, but perhaps. Brutus is grateful, though."

"Brutus?"

"That's what I'm going to call him, the horse."

"He is a she."

She blinked, glanced back, peered down, reddened. "Why, yes, I suppose you have the right of it there. Daisy, then," she said. "You're going to enjoy our garden, Daisy. Lots of tall grass for you to eat."

"We can't keep her in the garden."

"Why not?"

"Because it's simply not done. I'll have to make arrangements at a stable."

"Not for a few days. Give her a chance to know she's safe."

He couldn't very well deny her that request when he'd purchased the blasted horse for her. "Two days."

"Thank you." They walked on in silence for several moments before she said, "I made several purchases at different shops today."

"I'm well aware. I went in and confirmed the arrangements after you left." She had such a smug look of satisfaction, a look that had once irritated him and now only served to charm him. How could he view her in an entirely different light after only a short time? Who was truly altered here?

"You're quite my guardian angel, aren't you?" she asked.

He didn't answer. He was fairly certain a day would come when she would see him more as her guardian devil.

"I couldn't believe it," Marla muttered as she bustled around the kitchen. She'd come inside, wanting to tend to Phee's injuries while Drake saw to the horse. "Just couldn't believe it. First you running off and attacking that man. Then Mr. Darling."

Her blue eyes wide, she held up an ice pick. "I thought he was going to kill him."

"I wouldn't have blamed him if he had. I can't abide someone abusing animals."

Marla knelt in front of the icebox, chipped ice, and placed it on a linen cloth. "I've never seen anyone so furious. Or so frightened."

"Frightened? Darling? I doubt anything frightens him."

Marla peered up at her. "You didn't see his face. I think he fancies you."

Phee started to laugh off the words, but then she thought of the kiss, felt her cheeks grow warm. "Our life is not a romantic novel."

After folding the cloth over the chipped ice, Marla stood, worry in her eyes. "The way he looks at you, the way he talks to you, letting you spend his money on your own pleasures—he doesn't treat you like a servant. He treats you like an equal."

"Only the two of us are here, and so we've become—" *Close* was the word that came to mind.

The door opened and Drake walked through, bold and confident. The joy that his presence brought was unmistakable. She did feel close to him, connected in a way she couldn't explain. But with his arrival, she wouldn't have to defend their relationship to Marla.

"I chipped off some ice," Marla said, holding up the cloth. "Thought it would help the swelling on her face. I can't believe he hit her."

A corner of Darling's mouth eased up. "I can't believe she hit him."

Marla grinned. "She was awfully brave. And you were, too."

"Foolhardy more like," he said, holding out his hand. "I'll see to her injuries. I'm sure you're needed elsewhere."

Marla gave him the linen-wrapped ice chips, bobbed a quick curtsy. "Yes, sir."

"If you're reprimanded at all for your delay, let me know and I'll have a word with your employer," Drake told her.

"Thank you, sir." Turning, Marla gave Phee a hug. "Take care."

"I will. Thank you for everything."

"I didn't do nothing."

"You rescued my packages." Winking, she grimaced

at the discomfort. "I'll let you know when our purchases arrive."

With only a nod, Marla left.

"Sit," Drake ordered.

"I'm not a dog to be commanded about," Phee said.

"Phee, my patience is on a short tether."

"I'm sorry. I don't mean to be obstinate."

"I think you mean everything you do and say."

"I suppose." But she did sit.

He drew a chair near and sat. She winced as Drake gently placed the cloth-wrapped ice against the side of her face. The concern in his eyes almost brought tears to hers.

"You're going to have quite the black eye in the morning," he said.

"I think I might have had one before."

"When you were nine and fell out of a tree after trying to rescue a mean-spirited cat."

"How do you know that?"

He swung his gaze to hers, and she saw a mixture of emotions: confusion, aggravation, worry.

"You mentioned it in passing once."

"Was it my cat?"

"No, it belonged to a childhood friend. At least that's what I recall you saying."

"What else did I mention?"

He shifted his attention back to the side of her face, as though if he didn't watch it, the ice would wander off. "You had a scruffy mutt that barked at anything that wasn't wearing a skirt."

"I suppose it would have barked at you then. I wish I could remember it." She thought for a moment. "Probably best not to. Might just make me sad. Anything else?"

"You like to ride, but Daisy will not be suitable for riding."

"I have no plans to ride her. I just want her to have a life without care. You'll need to get her some oats."

"I'll take care of it before I go to the club."

"I'm quite the bother, aren't I?"

"I've known more bothersome wenches."

"You are such a grumbler, even when you're trying to make me feel better."

He smiled, and without thought she reached up and touched the small dimple that formed in his cheek. His lips started to close. "No, don't stop smiling. You don't grin nearly enough. And you have such a lovely smile."

"Lovely? Lovely gets a bloke beat up."

"Not you. I never doubted for a moment that you would put that awful man in his place."

"I broke his nose. And his jaw, I think."

His voice contained no boastfulness, but she heard regret.

"He deserved it," she said with conviction.

"Aren't you bloodthirsty?"

"I think I am, rather. When it comes to animals." She placed her hand over his where it still held the ice to her face, and lowered it to her lap. "Your knuckles are grazed and swollen. We should put ice on them for a bit."

"They're big and ugly. Ice isn't going to help that." As though suddenly uncomfortable, he got up briskly. "I should see to the oats before trying to get a few winks."

It hadn't even occurred to her that it was the middle of the afternoon and he'd not yet had a chance to sleep. "It can wait. You must be exhausted."

"I've gone longer without sleep. I'll be fine."

He headed for the door.

"Wait, I have something for you."

"A list of other things you need?" He was teasing her.

She could tell by the twinkle in his eyes. She thought she could easily fall in love with that twinkle. Wouldn't that be a disaster? As she'd told Marla, servants did not marry their employers.

"No, something else." She reached into the reticule that Marla had rescued after she'd dropped it and pulled out the small wrapped parcel that was as big as her hand. Hearing a clink, she frowned. "It may have broken."

Still she pushed it across the table toward him. He approached it as though he expected it to bite.

"It's a gift," she told him. "Surely you've had gifts before."

With care, he slowly unwrapped it and simply stared at the glass-blown red and blue dragon, with wings spread wide as though about to take flight.

"It's a dragon," she pointed out.

"I can see that."

"Unfortunately, its tail chipped when I dropped it. I wasn't thinking about anything beyond the horse. Why are people so cruel?"

Very tenderly he cradled her bruised face. "I don't know. Yet sometimes they are very nice indeed and it's just as confounding. I like the dragon a great deal."

"You will need to hold back a portion of my wages as I want the purchase to come from my purse not yours."

His lips twitched. "Yes, your wages. I'll adjust them accordingly."

"See that you do."

His grin grew ever so slightly. "You can be quite bossy."

"I'm the housekeeper. I'm supposed to be bossy."

"So you are. I'm going on to the club to prepare for the meeting with Morris."

He couldn't have said anything that would have disappointed her more. She wasn't ready for him to leave. "What about your sleep, your bath, your dinner?"

"I have rooms at the club. I'll bathe and eat there. See that you ice your eye some more." With that, he picked up the dragon and left.

Leaving her with the sense that she had done or said something terribly wrong.

He didn't want her giving him gifts. He especially didn't want her knowing how touched he was by the dragon. Or how unsettled he was that she had known such an item was perfect for him. Few knew about the dragon on his back, even fewer knew the reasons he had changed his name to Drake.

She made him feel vulnerable, exposed. And he'd been stupid enough to tell her about the black eye she'd acquired when she tried to get Grace's cat out of a tree. And Phee's mutt of a dog that had always bared its teeth at him, as though it were charged with protecting her from all things male.

He'd forgotten those stories about her, but now he viewed them slightly differently. Had she rescued the dog from a man who beat him? She'd bravely gone up to get Grace's cat, just as today she'd braved a brute of man in order to stop him from taking a whip to a horse that was too old to be pulling a wagon as weighted down as that one had been.

Now that brute of a man, belligerent and angry, stood before him while Drake counted out the coins. He considered offering Morris a job in the club that would ensure he never had a need to hitch a horse to a heavy wagon, but he didn't much like the man and didn't think he would be an asset to Dodger's. One didn't solve one problem by creating another.

But he'd made Phee an offhand promise that this man would never again beat another horse. Another aspect to his day that he'd never imagined—giving a vow to Lady O. But the simple words *I'll see to it* had been an assurance, a promise, a vow. He would honor his word. To her. For her.

When the final coin was set down, Morris reached for the pile.

"Not yet," Drake commanded, the tone of his voice brooking no disobedience, the possibility of the coins being snatched back into his coffers hovering between them. He made a notation in a ledger. "I'll need your mark here indicating that the horse now belongs to me."

"Ye say that like I can't write me name proper."

Drake merely arched a brow. Morris scowled, took the offered pen, and scrawled two X's joined by a half moon. Then he glowered. "I got the better end of this deal. Won't be long before you'll be calling for a horse slaughterer."

It was an honest trade, a licensed trade, governed by laws. The city was teeming with horses. They needed to be mercifully put down when the end of their life came. Drake momentarily wondered if when the time came for Daisy—which he didn't think was in the too distant future—Phee would still be with him or back in the world where she despised him.

"Some whiskey to close the deal?" Drake asked.

"Don't mind if I do."

Leaning back in his chair, Drake reached for the whiskey and poured it into two glasses. With this man he didn't have to stand in order to dominate, to prove his position of power. In fact insolently lounging conveyed the message much better. And he had been correct. He'd broken the man's nose. His jaw, however, seemed intact. He should have struck a bit harder.

Before Morris could enjoy the taste of fine whiskey, a knock sounded on the door that Drake had closed earlier. This was a personal matter and he'd not wanted to be disturbed—until now.

"Come."

The door opened and a large bruiser of a man entered. "Gregory said you wanted to see me."

"Yes." He waved the man in. "I want to introduce you to Morris."

Morris's head didn't reach the bruiser's chin. "Morris, meet Goliath."

Morris chuckled, revealing two rotten teeth that Drake wished he'd knocked out of the man's mouth.

"That ain't really 'is name."

"Probably not, but it's what we call him around here. Notice his hands. How large and strong they are. He's going to become your shadow."

"Me shadow?"

"That's right. The next time you take a whip to a horse, he'll be there. He's going to count each lash against horseflesh. When you're done, he's going to take those incredible hands of his, ball them into fists, and introduce them to your face as many times as you struck the horse. I daresay he's going to eventually destroy those good looks of yours." A generous assessment of the man's features considering he closely resembled a toad.

Morris paled. "That ain't fair."

"Of course it is. You have a choice here, which is more than you gave the beast today. Either lighten the load of your wagon or use more horses to pull the weight, but stop abusing them."

"It's because of that bitch—"

Drake came up slowly, menacingly. Morris must have recognized his error as well as the fury that was no doubt glinting in Drake's eyes because he quickly took three steps back. "I'll stop 'urtin' me 'orses."

"Good."

Slouching, Morris slipped in and scraped the coins on the desk into his hands. "I'll be off now."

"You should know that you probably won't see Goliath keeping watch, but rest assured he'll be there, because I don't like you, Morris."

"Don't think much of you either."

"That bothers me not in the least."

Morris scurried out like the rodent he was.

"Do you really want me to follow him?" Goliath asked.

With a sigh and shake of his head, Drake dropped back into his chair. "He's a bully. The threat is no doubt enough."

"That's good 'cuz I'm not much good at counting." He gave Drake a pointed look. "And I don't hit. You know that."

Drake grinned. Goliath was a giant of a man, but a gentle one. "Morris doesn't have my inside knowledge."

Goliath indicated the untouched glass of whiskey on the edge of the desk. "May I?"

"Absolutely."

Goliath took it in that large paw that Drake had used to intimidate Morris and tossed back the amber liquid. He smacked his lips. "So who's the bird?"

Drake stiffened. "I beg your pardon?"

"What do you care if he abuses his horses? You're doing this to get the attention of some lady."

"A rather inept ploy considering she's not here to witness my good deed."

"Perhaps." He set down the glass. "I'd best get back to the kitchen. A good many hungry lords tonight."

"I'm going to be leaving for a while. Pack up some

dinner that I can take with me." He cleared his throat. "Enough for two."

Goliath grinned, pleased as punch. "Shall I include a bottle of our fanciest wine?"

Drake had wine in his residence, but it wasn't the fine vintage that Dodger's had on hand. He shrugged. "Wouldn't hurt."

Chapter 18

He found her in the library, in a chair beside the fireplace, her legs tucked beneath her. The burgundy fabric would absorb her scent. When she was no longer here, it would no doubt become his favorite chair in the residence.

He didn't think he made a noise, but she looked up and smiled at him, her lips forming the slight curve that he had begun to crave. "I wasn't expecting you back tonight."

"I wanted to ensure the horse got fed properly." Walking to the fireplace, he set his elbow on the mantel, striving to ignore her bruised and battered face. He should have hit Morris once more, just for good measure. No, twice more. A dozen times more.

"How did things go with Morris?" she asked, as though reading his mind.

"He and I came to an understanding. He won't be abusing any more horseflesh."

Her smile widened, gratitude filled those lovely green eyes, and he felt like a rotten bastard. He should tell her everything now. Take her home. Before he'd left, he'd seen Somerdale on the gambling floor. He would only gain access to her dowry if people knew she was dead. He was either patiently waiting for her to wash ashore, not knowing she'd already washed up, or he didn't know she'd been in danger of drowning. The latter seemed more likely. Which meant he was probably telling the truth about the uncle. But why was the uncle not trying to find her?

If she regained her memories, she might know what had happened. If he told her what he knew she might remember—and in the remembering he would lose her. "Have you had your dinner?"

"No. I didn't want to go for my lesson when I knew packages would be arriving. By the time they were all delivered, I was quite exhausted from the day. I had a bit of cheese."

The silk, satin, and lace he'd spotted on Ebenezer Whistler's counter was in his residence, might even be on her person if she'd been impatient about feeling it next to her skin. He imagined skimming his hands over silk and flesh, slipping things off, slipping things in. Christ, he should return to the club before his imagination prodded him to do something they'd both regret. He saw her again, bravely facing down Morris. Courageous girl. Foolish but courageous.

He didn't want to admire her, but dammit all to hell, he did.

I'm back off to the club was what he'd meant to say. But what he heard coming from his traitorous mouth was "I brought some food from the club. Care to join me?"

They spread a blanket in the garden, set the large wicker basket at one end, and served themselves. Twilight eased in around them as the bustling noises from the streets quieted, creating an intimacy that Phee wasn't certain she could ignore. While he didn't have a proper garden with flowers adorning it, she no longer minded. Daisy wandered along the brick wall where the grass was tallest, nibbling here and there, obviously content with her lack of duties. Phee was equally content.

Drake still wore his jacket, waistcoat, and neck cloth. She wished she had changed out of her uniform, but she wanted to save her other clothing for a special occasion, although tonight seemed rather special. Marla's earlier words echoed through Phee's mind, and she couldn't deny that an unusual camaraderie existed between her and Drake that seemed to defy the societal conventions of master and servant. If it wasn't allowed for her to have tea with Mrs. Turner, how was it that she could enjoy a picnic with Drake? She didn't know quite how to define their relationship. She knew only that she was terribly glad he was here.

She was also extremely grateful for everything that had come from the basket. The wine was superb. The beef was the most tender she'd ever eaten. Or at least that she recalled ever eating. She thought she should be more bothered by her lack of memories, and yet new ones were being created and she wanted to treasure them.

"I don't understand why you don't dine at the club every night," she said. "It seems it has the most incredible cook."

"I did eat there before you came here," he said.

"I think you should return to eating there, and just send dinners 'round for me. This"—she held up a Brussels sprout she'd speared—"is remarkably tasty."

"I suppose I could consider altering your duties."

"A smart man would, as it will take me forever to learn to prepare food that is this delicious."

"Forever? You have no doubt you'll become an amazing cook?"

"I believe I can do anything I set my mind to." She stopped, considered. "Yes, I really do believe that. Sometimes I have a thought and it feels as though it's part of my soul, something I pulled up from deep down in that well of nothingness. Like today with Daisy. I knew I could not stand by and watch that horse be abused. I saw people walking by as though nothing were amiss, and I just couldn't do the same, carry on as though I wasn't witnessing an injustice."

"I had no idea you could move so quickly. One moment you were examining asparagus and the next you were loping toward that brute. At first I thought you'd caught sight of someone from your past, that your memories had returned." Grinning, he peered at her over the lip of his wineglass. "But then you were terrifying the poor gent."

"He's hardly a gent, and I don't believe I terrified him in the least, but I was so angry. I didn't know I had it in me to be that furious. I've been thinking about it, though, and I'm rather certain I've done it before."

"Beaten men to a bloody pulp?"

She smiled, so enjoying the ease with which they conversed. She could tell him anything, trust him with her deepest secrets. If she had any. "Rescued animals. I think that's why I had such a hard time with the pheasant, looking at me as it was." She thought some more, nodded with certainty as images came to mind. "I want to have a place in the country where I can nurture animals that are broken in body or spirit." She beamed with wonder. "Yes, that's my dream. I knew I had one but I couldn't remember it. But that's what it is. I know that's what it is."

"Most ladies dream of marrying."

She shook her head, conviction in the depths of her soul. "I don't want to marry."

Stretching out on his side, resting on an elbow, he studied her as though she were an odd specimen he'd found beneath glass. "I suspect when your memories return, you'll feel differently."

Again, she shook her head, more forcefully this time. "No, I'm quite sure. I will not marry. I have no desire to do so. Perhaps that's the reason I chose service. Marla told me that few in this trade marry."

"I suppose that's true enough. I've known of couples in the same household marrying but it's rare."

"So I shall never marry and I shall hoard my wages until I can acquire a place in the country."

"Based upon the number of purchases you made today, it will be a long time before you realize that dream."

"We'll see."

"Yes, I suspect we shall."

She didn't think he was mocking her, but rather had as much faith in her convictions as she did. She might be an old woman, bent over with a walking stick, but she would acquire her dream. She had no doubt of it.

When she was so full that she thought she might burst, she lay down and gazed at the darkening sky. "I'm rather glad you don't have a proper dining room. If you did, I suspect we'd eat there, and this is so much more pleasant."

"Yes, it is." His voice was low, and it contained some emotion she couldn't quite identify.

Rolling her head to the side, she found him studying her intently. She was fairly certain he wanted to kiss her. She knew she wanted to kiss him. She also knew that Marla was correct: her relationship with Drake flirted at the edge of being something more than servant and employer. Had she always been drawn to him like this? Had they enjoyed more moments like these? It seemed a tragedy to have experienced them, and then to have forgotten them. She knew that if she asked him to elaborate about their relationship, their past, he would simply inform her that she needed to remember it on her own. She wondered why he didn't want to influence her memories. Had they once been in love? Did he want her to fall in love with him all over again? She thought she could tumble quite easily.

"When is my day off?" she asked.

He seemed surprised by her question, and she wondered if he recognized it for what it was: a distraction from dangerous places where her thoughts should not journey.

"I'll have to check the schedule."

"Which I suppose is in your office at the club."

With a nod, he took a sip of wine.

"Not very efficient of you," she told him. "The way you keep everything at the club. Especially as you have such a nice desk here."

He studied his wine and she didn't want to consider that perhaps she shouldn't have taken him to task, that she might have ruined what had become a most enjoyable evening, nor did she want to admit her reluctance to consider that the reason he kept everything at the club was because he didn't trust her. Not that she blamed him, as she had looked into his box, even knowing that she shouldn't have.

He shifted his gaze to her. "What would you do with a day away from here?"

"I'm not quite sure, especially as now I'm saving my pennies."

"Pretend money would be no object."

"Oh, well, in that case"—she smiled brightly—"I could go anywhere."

"Anywhere," he repeated. "So where would you choose?"

She couldn't imagine it, being able to go anywhere in the world. "The seaside I think."

Surprise crossed over his features. "Not someplace exotic and faraway?"

She rolled her head from side to side. "No, I prefer simple, familiar, someplace that makes me feel safe. I've been to the seaside before. I can see the ocean, hear the rush of the waves and the cry of the gulls. I like the seaside. Have you been to faraway, exotic places?"

"I've traveled a good deal of the world, thought I'd seen everything of beauty." Setting aside his wineglass, he leaned over and trailed his fingers along her chin. She wasn't certain how they'd come to be so near one another. "Your courage humbled me today, when you went after a man twice your size."

"I wasn't being brave," she said softly. "I was just angry. If I had stopped to think, I don't believe I'd have gone after him like I did."

"I think you would have. I'm seeing sides to you that I never imagined existed." He stroked his thumb over her lower lip, causing warmth and pleasure to weave through her limbs. She wasn't certain she'd be able to move them if she tried. Not that she wanted to move. She didn't want to break the spell. "You're far more complicated than I ever realized."

"Isn't that true of everyone?" she asked.

"It seems especially true of you."

With his nearness, butterflies were fluttering madly in her chest. She feared as much as she anticipated that they were on the verge of doing something entirely inappropriate. But she didn't want him to cease his attentions, to stop touching her.

"Where would you go?" she asked. "If money were no object and you could go anywhere?"

"I would remain right here." He lowered his mouth to hers, his tongue teasing her lips to part, before thrusting deep and sure.

In the farthest recesses of her mind, she worked to decipher his words, wondering if the *here* he referred to was his garden, London . . . her. Her, she decided as the kiss became hungrier, all consuming. Something strong and potent existed between them. She might not remember it, but she knew it with certainty. He would no doubt claim that he had taken advantage again, but how could he deny them this when it seemed so right, when everything within her yearned to be nearer to him? He'd saved her, he'd saved Daisy. This gruff man who seemed irritated with her most of the time, who seemed so unwilling to share himself, was doing so now in a most intimate and thorough manner. She relished the barriers between them dissipating. Perhaps she had a bit of Marla's romantic bent within her. Even though she knew no good would come of this. Their status was vastly different, an immeasurable chasm separating their places within Society. He had means, influence, and power. He ruled over a gentlemen's club while she ruled over dust and cobwebs.

Yet he never made her feel less. He never made her feel beneath him, even though at that precise moment, he shifted his weight and she found herself quite literally beneath him. He managed to hold himself so he wasn't crushing her. One hand cradled her cheek while the other skimmed along her side until it settled on her hip, strong fingers kneading. Clutching his shoulders, she wished he'd discarded the jacket and waistcoat earlier, would not have even minded if the shirt were gone. Would he consider her completely wanton if she began loosening his buttons?

She knew proper etiquette and comportment; she understood fully that her actions represented neither. But who was to care? She had no family, no stalwart friends to embarrass. Marla wouldn't object. Phee thought if given the chance, Marla would change places with her in a heartbeat, although she had no plans to give Marla the opportunity.

She loved his throaty growls, the eagerness of his mouth. Her heart sped up, her body warmed. Twilight had given way to darkness that brought a cooling to the air that should have chilled her and had her wanting a wrap. Instead she was fevered, discovered she wore too many clothes. He made her long for things she instinctually knew no respectable woman would yearn for. Yet she didn't seem to give a fig that her reputation was at risk.

She wanted him to know that she desired his kiss. She didn't want him to apologize for it afterward. She wanted him as captivated by this vortex of madness as she was.

It was madness, total and complete madness. Drake knew it even as he seemed unable to stop himself from tasting her again and again. She intrigued and fascinated him, this woman who would go to the seaside if she could go anywhere. When she traveled to Paris simply to order her gowns. This woman who didn't complain about her limited wardrobe, when he suspected in her other life she had dozens of dinner gowns, ball gowns, morning dresses, walking dresses, riding habits.

They'd shared a dinner on a blanket in an untended garden, yet contentment eased in around him as surreptitiously as night washed away day. She had shared her dreams, her aspirations, which were not at all what he would have expected of her. Marriage to a duke or a prince, queen of a realm. Not a spinster's life tending broken animals.

She smiled and his gut tightened. She laughed and his chest grew taut. She sighed and something deep, feral, and possessive growled within him. He couldn't explain any of his reactions, didn't want to analyze them. She touched him in ways no other woman ever had. She made him yearn for things he'd thought beyond his grasp: wife, children, home.

He had no business kissing her, and yet he could no more deny himself this pleasure than he could cease to breathe. It didn't help matters at all that she welcomed him with open arms and pliant mouth. This warm, willing creature beneath him was nothing at all like the frigid, stiff—

A hard nudge to his shoulder had him breaking off the kiss. Enough light remained that as he looked back he saw the silhouette of the blasted horse. It lowered its head and bumped his shoulder again. "See here!"

Giggling, actual giggling, wafted toward him, creating that tightness once again in his chest. Turning his attention to Phee, he was torn between amusement, frustration, and relief. The madness was abating, his senses were returning. Things never should have gone this far.

"Sorry," she said, not sounding sorry at all. With her hand, she covered her mouth. "I know it's not funny, but it is rather."

"Don't apologize. You saved her this afternoon, she saved you now." He shoved himself to a sitting position and began putting the items back into the wicker basket.

"What do you mean by that?" Phee asked.

"I had no business kissing you."

She pushed herself up. "So you keep saying. Are you married?"

"That's a ridiculous question. If I were, my wife would be here."

"Would she?"

"Yes, of course."

"Am I married?"

"No."

He could feel her gaze boring into him. Why were there so many dishes to be put away? Why was it taking forever to end this ghastly mistake? He should have never returned here with dinner. He should have stayed at the club.

"Is it because of the difference in our positions?" she asked quietly.

"Yes," he answered succinctly. Tossing in the last of the items, he thought he heard a plate crack. Lovely.

"Our different places in Society matter to you," she said.

"They matter to you." Twisting around, he faced her. Feeling a need to lessen the tartness of his earlier response, he trailed his fingers over her cheek. "You'll remember that someday." He was quite sorry that she would.

Heaving himself to his feet, he reached down, offered his hand, and helped her stand. Before he could step away, she was cradling his cheek.

"Why would it matter to me?" she asked.

Placing his hand over hers, holding it in place, he turned his face and pressed a kiss against the center of her palm. "Because in spite of how it might all appear, you believe me beneath you."

"It makes no sense. Why would I think that?"

"Because of who and what I am."

"I think you're wrong."

"I know I'm not." Bending over, he hefted up the basket. "I need to return to the club. Deliveries arrive there in the morning. I shan't return here until almost noon."

"Then I shall sleep in and you will never know."

The tartness in her tone alerted him that she was moving on from what had just passed between them. He should be grateful, but as an image of her sprawled in his bed flashed through his mind, he wished for other things, uppermost that he could join her there, without guilt or remorse. "Sleep well."

Then he walked quickly from the garden before his resolve left him. How was it that Lady Ophelia Lyttleton had become the most important thing in his life?

Chapter 19

Over the next few days they settled into a routine. Or at least she did. He was leaving the club earlier, returning later at night, loath to give up moments with this woman who intrigued him more and more. The hours spent at the club were the longest of his life. Chores he'd once enjoyed—inventorying, receiving goods, marking statements to be paid, discussing strategies with employees, ensuring all was running smoothly—now seemed tedious and time-consuming because they kept him away from Phee. All he could think about was returning to the residence for breakfast, listening as she waxed on about her plans for the day—which more often than not included trips to the market with Marla. He'd made her promise no more altercations or attacking men. While she had given her word quite reluctantly, he needed to sleep sometime and so he trusted her not to get into any trouble. Probably foolhardy on his part.

This particular morning after returning to the residence, he walked into the kitchen to find an urchin who couldn't have been more than eight sitting at the table munching on bacon.

" 'Mornin', guv'ner," the lad said, jerking his head so the long thick strands of his hair momentarily weren't falling over his eyes.

Phee turned from the counter where she was pouring milk into a bowl. "Good morning. I wasn't expecting you for another hour or so. This is Jimmy. I'm paying him a shilling to clean up after Daisy."

He'd yet to make arrangements to move the horse to the stables. He couldn't make himself deny her the pleasure of the beast. "A shilling? That's robbery."

"I suppose you could clean it up," she said.

He considered reminding her that she was the one who wanted the creature, but what was the point? She knew as well as he did that he wasn't going to make her shovel manure.

"I'm the best at cleaning up horse manure," the lad boasted. "I know where to sell it. She says I can keep that."

"You may indeed," Drake said.

She set the bowl on the floor and a scrawny white cat crawled out from beneath the table and began lapping at the milk.

"Who is that?" he asked.

"Pansy. Because of her eye."

When the cat looked up, he saw that one eye had a black marking around it that might possibly—with a good deal of imagination—resemble a pansy.

"Why do we need a cat?" he asked.

"We don't. She needs us. She showed up at the door the last couple of evenings. I gave her a little milk. Last night I let her in, and discovered she's terribly sweet and wonderful company."

He would not feel guilty because she was alone at night.

Picking up a bowl filled with meat scraps, she headed for the door.

"Where are you taking that?" he asked.

"To feed Rose."

"Rose?"

He followed her out to the terrace. She set the bowl down in front of a dog that was more bone than muscle. She patted its head. "She followed me home from the market."

"She is a he."

She peered beneath the dog. "Oh. You're ever so good at noticing that sort of thing."

He was amazed she wasn't, but then ladies were not generally in the habit of peering at an animal's private quarters. "So I'm not certain the dog will appreciate being called Rose."

"Short for Rosencrantz," she said with another beaming smile. "That'll work."

She went over to Daisy and petted her.

"We're not keeping a menagerie here," Drake told her.

"Of course not." She walked back over and stood before him. "Kick them out whenever you feel like it."

The woman was manipulating him again. He wasn't going to kick these pitiful creatures out and well she knew it. As she opened the door to go in, Jimmy sauntered out, his cap pulled low over his brow, keeping the hair out of his eyes. Drake was surprised Phee hadn't taken scissors to it. He most certainly didn't want to remember that he'd been skinny as well at that age. For the briefest of moments he envied Phee her inability to recall the past.

"Be seein' ye, guv'ner," the boy said.

"Clean up after the dog as well. We'll pay you two shillings."

The boy grinned broadly. "Me pleasure. See you, missus." He tipped his hat before racing for the gate at the back.

"That was nice of you," Phee said.

"He's too thin."

"I thought the same thing."

He suspected she'd feed the boy whenever he showed up. Drake couldn't fault her for that. He didn't like admitting that over the past few days he'd found very little fault with her. "I suppose he followed you home from the market as well."

"See, there you are sounding all grumbling again when I know you don't mind. But yes, our paths did cross at the market this morning. Marla and I went fairly early."

"I suppose that cost me another fortune."

She smiled, and he wouldn't have cared if it *had* cost him a fortune. "Only went to the market this time."

She walked into the kitchen. "Give me a few moments to prepare your breakfast."

Dammit all. He was willing to give her all the time in the world.

He awoke earlier than usual, stared at the ceiling. What was he doing? Why was she still here, a week after he'd discovered her in the Thames? Why was he putting off uncovering the truth? Why was he delaying returning her home?

He needed to redouble his efforts to determine exactly what had happened the night he found her in the river. Oddly, Somerdale had not been in the club for the past two nights. He needed to seek him out, sit him down, and talk with him—get to the bottom of this entire matter.

And he would, after his meeting with the partners on the morrow. He needed to prepare for it. That was the reason he'd awoken with a start. Had nothing to do with guilt over Phee possibly being lonely in the evenings and seeking out a cat for company. Had nothing to do with the unfairness to her.

He had no clock, no pocket watch, but still he knew he'd awoken early. He'd bathe, head to the club, eat there. Reestablish his schedule.

Rolling out of bed, he found himself instinctively listening for the sounds of her moving about the residence—the creak of stairs, the moaning of a floorboard, the closing of a door. The house was more alive with her in it. He would barely notice when she was gone, however, as he would return to his habit of spending most of his time at the club. Everything would again be as it should be. His bed would no longer smell of her. He would sleep without dreaming of her being beneath the covers with him. He wouldn't fantasize about touching her skin. He wouldn't think about kissing every inch of her.

After drawing on trousers and shirt, he checked the bathing room to ensure she'd not filled the tub with water. He'd forbidden her to bring up the pails, not that his orders ever seemed to carry much weight with her. She did as she pleased. That part of her character seemed unchanged. Odd how it didn't irritate him as it once had.

He jaunted down the stairs, came to a stop in the foyer. A narrow black and white marble-topped table was set against the wall. Hideous thing with scrolled iron legs and a chipped corner. A gleaming black vase held a bouquet of red roses.

Where the bloody hell had that come from? She was purchasing furniture for him now, was she? He'd have never selected that particular piece, yet he couldn't deny that it somehow seemed to belong. He wondered where she'd found the flowers.

Stepping forward, he took a petal between his fingers and rubbed it. He should see about acquiring a gardener. Then she could have flowers all around the house, inside and out.

He jerked back his hand. She didn't need flowers here. She would be leaving soon. She wasn't a permanent resident.

Yet as he headed toward the kitchen, he couldn't deny that he'd become accustomed to having a housekeeper about. He'd have to hire one. But even as he made a mental note to do so, he knew he would find her lacking simply because she wasn't Phee.

As Phee dragged the brush through Daisy's mane, she marveled at her own contentment, amused that she had fought so hard against believing she was actually a servant. While none of her cooking lessons seemed to bring forth any memories, she was mastering the task, and she could scarcely wait to serve this evening's meal to Drake. She was purchasing little odds and ends for the residence, but she wanted to speak with him about purchasing more. She wanted to make his residence more homey—even if it meant more dusting and tidying for her. She didn't mind it so much, well, most of it, anyway. The windows still needed cleaning and she didn't fancy the scrubbing and polishing of floors. She would suggest they hire someone to assist her as the chores increased. It seemed only fair.

"Is that your brush you're using?"

Jumping only a little at the brusque tone, she turned to Drake. His shirt was mostly unbuttoned, his feet bare, his hair tousled, his jaw shadowed. She loved him like this, when he came down to begin preparing his bathwater, before he tidied up. Although if she were completely honest, she loved to look at him just as much when he was tidied up. Scoundrel, rake, or gentleman. He always fascinated her.

"I just finished bathing her," she told him, "and I wanted to get the tangles out of her mane. I didn't see that I had any other choice except to use yours and I didn't think you'd appreciate that at all."

"It's silver." He said the words in a manner that suggested they explained everything.

"Well, yes, I'm quite aware of that. I know it was costly, but—"

"You're using it on a horse? A *horse*?"

"Her mane was so snarled. I was feeling badly about it. You've set up a trough for her water. You feed her. I wanted to pamper her for a bit."

"Why didn't you say something? I could have purchased what you required."

"You were already abed. I'd finished my chores, and it just hit me that I wanted to do it. Besides, she's already cost you a fortune. I didn't want to be a nuisance."

His eyes widened. "You? Not be a nuisance? That is like saying the sun does not shine."

"Well, thank you very much for that."

"You don't use a lady's brush on a horse."

Was he going to rant about it forever? She'd had quite enough of it.

"And your hands. You're carting buckets of water after I told you not to."

"They've healed," she said. Rough and a bit callused but healed.

He didn't seem to be listening to her, he was so caught up in his own fury. "You don't think things through," he carried on. And on. And on. As though she'd done something monstrously unthinkable.

She hefted the pail that contained the leftover water she'd planned to use on Rose. Doing exactly as he accused, she didn't bother to consider consequences or ramifications as she tossed the contents at him.

His diatribe came to an abrupt halt as he jerked back, blinking at her while the water dripped down his face, caught in the stubble at his jaw, soaked his shirt and trousers.

She released a small laugh. “I didn’t mean for it all to hit you. I only wanted a bit—”

He narrowed his eyes at her. “You’re going to pay for that.”

With a low growl, he charged. She shrieked, dropped the bucket, and ran. Or intended to run. She’d barely taken three steps before he scooped her up and tossed her over his shoulder.

“I’m not a sack of potatoes!” While she tried to sound indignant, it was a little difficult to do when she was laughing. She didn’t know why it struck her as funny. Perhaps because he was always so somber and serious that she had rather enjoyed catching him unawares and eliciting such an unexpected reaction from him.

“You’re going to be a *drenched* sack of potatoes,” he said, striding across the grass with purpose in each step.

Pressing her hands to his back, she lifted herself just enough to cast a quick glance over his shoulder, to determine his destination. The water trough? Surely not. “You wouldn’t dare.”

“Oh, I believe I would.”

His hand came to rest on her bottom. The world suddenly went topsy-turvy, grass, sky—

Rosencrantz leaping up—slamming into Drake.

As he lost his balance, somehow he twisted, released her, tumbled into the trough while she landed on the ground with a soft thud. She scrambled to her knees. “Are you all right?”

Soaked, he sat in the small trough, his legs sprawled over the sides, water dripping from his hair, droplets gathering on his face. He appeared so disgruntled, so . . . adorable. Not a word she would have ever thought to associate with him.

"I'm fine," he groused.

"Serves you right, for wanting to dump me in there."

He narrowed his eyes at her. "Careful, sweetheart, you don't want to poke the tiger."

The words, the tone, the menace were familiar. He'd said the words before. Why? In what situation? Because what she did know was that she did want to poke him, did want him to react. She was hoping for laughter, but she thought she would settle for anything other than the politeness, the careful questioning and answering that indicated he always watched his words with her, ever since their kiss in the garden. He was so cautious, distancing himself, and she hated it. It didn't matter that he seemed to come home earlier and leave later, he was too watchful, too civil.

He started to pull himself up. Rose jumped up, placing his huge paws on Drake's shoulder, and Drake went down again. Slapping her hand over her mouth, she chortled. She couldn't help it. When he glared at her, she chuckled all the harder.

Rose began stroking his large tongue over Drake's face and neck—

Sitting back on her heels, she laughed outright at the sight of the unhappy man and the incredibly happy dog, his tail wagging so forcefully that he was whipping up a wind.

"Help me get out of here," Drake grumbled.

She swallowed back her amusement. "Yes, all right."

After shoving herself to her feet, she shooed Rose away. The dog lumbered off, caught sight of a squirrel, and they were forgotten as he raced after it. Drake held up his hand. She wrapped hers around it, expecting to provide him with some leverage. Instead she felt an insistent pull, shrieked, fell forward—

She landed on his belly, water soaking her hips and torso, her legs over the side of the trough, her hands on his shoulders buffering her fall. Deep laughter echoed around her. Rather than protest her position, his ploy, she marveled at the richness of Drake's throaty laughter, the sight of his head thrown back. She would weather a thousand dunkings for that sound. Smiling broadly, she joined her chortling with his, until her eyes watered, her sides ached. She laid her head on his chest.

His laughter died, hers withered.

Very slowly she rose up. He was so near. His nose nearly touching hers. Whatever mirth he'd been enjoying had dissipated. Within his smoldering eyes, she now saw desire and longing. She could feel the yearning in his tense body, almost quivering like a tightly strung bow with the arrow notched and pulled back—she was an archer, a corner of her mind whispered. But she let the memory go because nothing in her past mattered as much as he did. Nothing was more important than this moment.

He was going to kiss her again. She knew it with everything in her heart. She wanted him to kiss her, wanted to feel the luxurious movements of his mouth over hers. She wanted it desperately, even as she knew another kiss would lead them further into temptation and she didn't know if she was strong enough to deny them the journey.

"I love your laughter," she whispered.

"It's been a long time since I've heard it. I'd forgotten—" He shook his head, swallowed. "We need to get you dry."

Just like that the spell was broken, and she wondered if perhaps she'd imagined it. Shifting his weight, placing his hands on her hips, he managed to boost her up until she was again on her feet. Her clothing clung to her. She'd have to change into the scratchy clothing she'd first worn upon awakening with no memories, but she didn't mind.

He worked his way out of the trough. Before he could step away, she cradled his jaw, his cheek. "I wish I remembered everything I knew about you."

"You wouldn't like me much if you did."

"I find that rather difficult to believe, because at this precise moment I like you a great deal indeed."

He liked her a great deal as well.

Gazing in the mirror as he knotted his neck cloth after his bath, Drake knew that was a problem. She wasn't supposed to make him laugh. She wasn't supposed to care so much about a blasted horse that she used her silver hairbrush to groom it. She wasn't supposed to make him want to kiss her senseless. She wasn't supposed to make him wish that she never regained her memories, that they could carry on like this forever.

He sank into a chair and lifted a boot that had been buffed to such a shine that he could fairly see his reflection in it. She had done that. She was doing so much more than he had ever initially intended. He couldn't keep her. He had to tell her the truth, return her to her life.

Shoving his foot into the boot, he decided that he would confess all and take her home before he went to the club. He was fairly certain Somerdale hadn't meant her any harm. She would be safe with her brother.

As he yanked on his other boot, he wondered if *fairly certain* was certain enough to ensure her safety. He shook his head. He was striving to convince himself to delay the inevitable. Surely arguing with himself was a sign of madness.

She had driven him to it.

He'd almost kissed her when they were in the water trough. If he took her mouth one more time, he didn't know if he'd find the strength to stop until he'd taken all of her.

Standing, he stomped his feet to get them situated in the boots the way he liked them. He tugged on his waistcoat. It was time to set the matter right. He needed to prepare for his meeting with the partners and she merely served as a disruption to his life.

"Right, then," he muttered. "Now is the time." She would be furious with him, things between them would return to normal, and he could cease having these damned moments of enjoying her. He much preferred the haughty nose-in-the-air Lady O. He knew precisely where he stood with her. The woman in his residence now was far too layered, far too intriguing, far too distracting.

He strode from his bedchamber with purpose in his step. It would be freeing to have his life as his own again, to not be worrying about her, what she might discover or remember when he wasn't around, how frightened—or angry—she might be.

He was halfway to the kitchen when the aromas assailed his senses. The dinner she was preparing for him. He had thought to humble her by having her catering to his wants and desires. Yet he was the one being humbled, that she would strive so hard to please him. He had expected her to instinctually complain the entire time, to ignore her duties, and sit around twiddling her thumbs. He hadn't expected her to step into the role with enthusiasm, to embrace the challenges of learning to care for his household.

Tunneling his fingers through his hair, he decided he would reveal the truth after they'd eaten. It would be unkind to allow this evening's efforts to be wasted.

He walked into the kitchen in time to see her removing a dish from the oven. Straightening, she gave him a warm smile that arrowed through him, from his head to his toes.

"Perfect timing," she said, setting the dish between two burning candles on the linen-covered table. White wine filled two glasses, waiting for them. "It's a chicken pie. Not fancy, but I made it all myself. Well, with Mrs. Pratt providing the direction, but she didn't do a thing, not even cut the vegetables. I did it all."

She sounded so remarkably pleased with herself. He wanted to add to her joy, her sense of satisfaction.

"It smells delicious." And it did. Steam was rising through holes in the crust.

Reaching back, she untied her apron, removed it, and hung it off a peg on the wall. "I hope you don't mind that I added the cloth and candles to the table. It just seemed wrong to eat on a bare table. Of course, once your dining room is furnished, it'll all be moot."

By the time that happened, she'd not be here. She wouldn't see any of the other rooms furnished or notice the changes he planned to make to the residence.

"I don't mind at all," he said, pulling out her chair.

With another one of those impish smiles, she sat. He took his place opposite her. She scooped pie into a bowl for him and then for herself.

While he waited for his to cool, he said, "You seem to enjoy taking care of things."

"I do rather. So odd that when I first awoke without my memories I couldn't imagine myself doing any of this."

She fairly glowed. He was not looking at all forward

to that glow turning to red rage when he told her everything after dinner. Nor was he anticipating taking her home. His residence would seem empty, lack energy, become bereft. It was a blasted building and he was acting as though it lived and breathed, as though it noticed her presence as much as he did.

He was mesmerized by the way the light from the flames reflected in her eyes, over her hair. She wore it in a braid circled about her head. Such a simple style, one he would have said wasn't suited to Lady O, and yet it seemed perfect for Phee. The two distinct ladies were blending into one that he was becoming increasingly taken with. To distract himself from the way she lured him, he said, "I noticed the addition to the foyer."

She laughed lightly, and he realized that not being distracted by her was going to be impossible. Every aspect of her fascinated him.

"I discovered the table at a little shop. I argued down the price because of the chipped corner." A pleat appeared between her brows. "Did you notice it?"

He'd been dishonest with her from the beginning. Why stop now? "No."

She gave him another one of those brilliant smiles. "I'm glad to hear it. I didn't think it was too noticeable. Hopefully it will be the flowers that garner attention."

She dipped her fork into the pie. He followed suit, noticing that she had yet to place the food in her mouth. So he took a bite, grinned. "Very tasty."

And it was. Exceedingly so. The last thing he expected was for her to master preparing food.

"I'm so glad you're enjoying it. Something else you would have no doubt enjoyed was watching Marla and me as we struggled to bring that table here."

"You carried it yourself?"

"Only for a bit. Then I stayed with it while she fetched Rob, Mrs. Turner's footman."

"Mrs. Turner?" He held up a hand when she pierced him with her gaze. "The widow."

"Yes. I wish you could afford a footman."

He could. He could afford a host of servants. Obviously she was a housekeeper who spoke too freely what was on her mind, without mincing words or striving to save her employer's sensibilities. What the bloody hell was he thinking? She wasn't a servant at all.

"I'm supposed to wash the windows," she said, poking at a piece of chicken with her fork. "But I've put it off. I don't know if I like ladders, don't even know if you have one. I suppose I could borrow—"

"You're not to climb ladders."

"But what of your windows?"

"I'll hire someone to wash the blasted windows."

"I won't try to talk you out of the expense as I don't truly want to do them."

He had the feeling of being manipulated again. He should be angry. Instead he was rather amused. He was losing count of the number of times she amused him. "Where did you get the roses?"

"I stole them from Mrs. Turner's garden."

He arched a brow. "So you're a thief now?"

"Marla said she wouldn't notice them missing. She never goes into the garden, no one ever comes to visit. Which I find rather sad. I thought about calling on her, asking her to take tea with me among the roses, but apparently servants aren't allowed to visit with those who hire servants."

Her compassion astounded him. Was this the woman Grace saw, the woman with whom she was friends? Why the cold façade, the distance? He wanted to explore her, not only with his hands, but with his mind, to know and understand every aspect of her.

The minutes were ticking by. He needed to tell her. Tomorrow. He would find time for it tomorrow. No sense in ruining her enjoyment in a day of accomplishments.

As Drake sat at his desk in his library, it occurred to him that today he wasn't doing anything that he was supposed to do. He'd left Phee in the kitchen, tidying up, thinking that he was headed to the club. He'd thought the same thing himself until he walked to the end of the street. Then he'd abruptly turned around, borrowed Mrs. Turner's footman, and paid him to deliver a message to Goliath at the club, informing him Drake would be in residence this evening. He told himself it was because he could think better here, it was quieter, he was less likely to be disturbed.

But he knew the truth of it. He was loath to leave her alone with the company of only a cat, knowing this would be her last night in his residence, that following his meeting tomorrow he would tell her everything. This little farce had gone on long enough. It was time to put an end to it. But first he had to concentrate on the meeting.

Yet it was so silent. Had he ever realized how quiet it was when darkness fell beyond the windows? He heard the occasional crackle of the fire, but that only added to the sense of isolation. And he'd left her here alone, night after night, a woman whose evenings had been filled with balls, dinners, and gaiety. He doubted she'd ever spent an hour completely alone before she'd ended up with him. Not that she remembered all her social obligations, but he knew of them, and that somehow made it all the worse.

He refused to acknowledge the gladness that swept through him when the door clicked open and she stepped into the library, the cat brushing against her skirts as it sauntered in with her. Surprise lighted her features.

"I thought you'd gone to the club."

"I decided to work here tonight."

"Oh." She hesitated, glanced around, held up a pad of paper. "I was going to sketch for a while. Do you mind if I do it in here?"

"No, of course not." It wasn't as though she had an abundance of choices, so he couldn't very well be selfish about sharing the room.

She closed the door, which created an intimacy that he hadn't expected in a room as large as this one. It was silly really when they'd been in his bedchamber together, been in his bathing chamber. It was the laughter in the garden, he thought. It had changed things between them, knocked down walls he'd strived so hard to keep erect, opened windows he would have preferred remain shut tight.

Coming to stand before the desk, she gazed at the paper before him, the pen in his hand as though she expected to be privy to some great discovery. "What sort of work can you do here that doesn't require you be at the club?"

"I have a meeting with the partners tomorrow. I'm trying to organize my thoughts."

"What are they? Your thoughts?"

"I'm not quite sure as I've yet to organize them."

Blinking, she stepped back. "I'm sorry."

"No." He held up his hand, cursing himself for his terse words earlier. "I stayed here because I expected it to be quieter than the club, and I need to concentrate."

"Perhaps I should go elsewhere."

"No, I—" *I want you here.* "I've already built a fire, and it's cozy over there with the new chairs. You should enjoy them."

"I shall be as quiet as a dormouse."

She took the chair that was turned so it faced the desk. If he leaned forward slightly, he could see her clearly with her legs tucked beneath her, the pad on her lap, the pencil moving across the paper with a speed that should match that of his pen.

Then she stopped, looked up, opened her mouth, and snapped it shut. He wasn't near enough to see her blush, but he suspected it was there, a faint pink that hinted at warm passions. Perhaps a measure of embarrassment, because she'd been on the brink of disturbing him with a comment or a question. She returned to her drawing.

He tried to return to his notes, but he was acutely aware of her, of each of her movements, of her soft sighs, the faint scratch of her pencil, its falling into silence. Discreetly he would peer over to see her looking in his direction, gnawing on her lower lip. Sometimes it appeared she was carrying on a conversation with herself, in her mind, and he found himself yearning to know the thoughts that visited her.

The cat that was supposed to keep her company had made itself a berth on a lower shelf. Not such a friendly creature after all, although he'd never favored cats. Dogs were more to his liking, even when they were big and clumsy and toppled him over. He hadn't planned to dump Phee into the trough. Only carry her over, pretend his intentions were sinister, have her shriek for him to stop, and at the last moment set her feet on the ground. Instead, Rose had ensured he got what he wanted—Phee's laughter wafting around him. It didn't matter that he'd been soaked and made to look the fool. Her eyes had sparkled, her smile bright. He thought he could fall in love with this woman. Only what a disaster that would be.

Scraping back his chair, he stood.

"Are you finished?" she asked.

He hadn't even begun, but suddenly he wanted this time with her. He walked over to the table in the corner, poured whiskey into two glasses, wandered over to where she sat, and handed her one before taking the chair opposite hers.

"Careful," he warned. "It can burn going down if you're not used to it."

She brought it to her nose, inhaled deeply, took a small swallow, smiled the smile he was coming to love. "It's very familiar. I've had it before. Was I wicked once, do you think?"

Where she was concerned he didn't know what to think any longer. "Perhaps."

She took a sip of the whiskey, licked her lips in a manner that made his throat go dry.

"Did you get your thoughts organized?" she asked.

They were more scattered than ever. "You were too distracting."

"I wasn't talking."

"You were fidgeting."

With a sigh, she rolled her eyes. "I kept thinking of things to tell you, but I knew you wouldn't appreciate it."

"Tell me now."

"I shouldn't bother you with it."

Nothing about her was a bother. When had that happened? So slowly, so irrevocably. "I'd like to know what you're drawing."

"All right then. I've been designing your front parlor."

Leaning back, he stretched out his legs. "My parlor?"

She nodded with enthusiasm, but he was beginning to realize she did everything with enthusiasm. "I don't know why but when I walk into one of the empty rooms, I can envision how it should look. So I thought if I sketched it out that it might help you when it came time to furnish the room."

"What should my parlor look like?"

"At first, I thought it should be bright—yellow or lavender—but that's not you. It needs to be dark, yet elegant. Black and gold, I think. Here, I'll show you." Setting aside her glass on the table beside the chair, she rose, walked over to him, leaned in, and held her pad in front of him.

The front parlor she'd sketched was a remarkable likeness to the room in his residence. But it had furniture, a large mirror above the mantel, designs over the wall. She was explaining things but he was only catching fragments—black velvet, edged in wood, black and gold paper on the walls—because most of his attention was focused on her breast pressed against his shoulder. Soft and pliant. She wasn't wearing a corset. Only thin material guarded her flesh from his touch, and he could dispense with it easily enough. If he reached up, cupped her breast, she would feel the heat of the fire that she built within him so easily. She was a temptress who didn't know she possessed the power to turn him into a mindless dolt.

When she was near, he couldn't concentrate on anything save her: her fragrance, alabaster skin, flaxen hair. He wanted to unravel her braid, comb his fingers through the long strands. She didn't need a silver-handled brush. His fingers would suffice. Over and over. A hundred strokes. A thousand if she wished it.

Sometimes when he let his guard down, he would have flashes of images of the night he'd undressed her, when he had strived to be a gentleman. But the scoundrel within him had looked. He knew her long legs and narrow hips. He knew the flatness of her stomach. Or he thought he did. He'd been quick about removing her clothes, had taken no liberties, but he knew she was comprised of glorious satin.

"Drake?" Her tone was terse, impatient. He lifted his gaze to her face, so near his, her brow deeply furrowed. "What do you think?"

That I should like to carry you up to my bed again, only this time I would take long moments, hours, to undress you.

Clearing his throat, he directed his attention back to the drawing. "It's very nice."

Scoffing, she stepped away, and his tormented pleasure came to an end. Thank God. He'd come close to doing something they would no doubt both regret.

"You're only saying that to be kind. I've bored you with my prattling." She returned to the large plush chair that had been made for a man's comfort, and brought up her feet, tucking them beneath her. Curled as she was, she reminded him of a cat, with her oval green eyes, exotic in the way they captured the flames from the fire and glittered.

"No, I do like it. I can see it quite clearly. You've put a lot of thought into it."

She angled her head, studied him, sipped the whiskey. He didn't want to admit that he could see himself doing this every night, being with her, whether with words or without. She was turning his world, his expectations upside down, inside out.

"It's not really my place, I suppose. Your wife will no doubt want to decorate the rooms to her taste."

"I've told you that I don't have a wife."

"But you will one day."

"No. You and I are alike in that regard: I have no intention of marrying."

"Why ever not?"

It was such a simple question with such a complicated answer.

"My bloodline needs to end with me."

"That seems a rather drastic reason."

But there was more to it than that, and he could tell by the arching of her delicate brow that she suspected as much. For once, she wasn't questioning, poking, prodding, insisting that he provide information. She was merely waiting, giving him time, giving him room. It was so easy to forget who she was, the true nature of their relationship. He could ignore her if she were nagging at him, harping, tilting up that bent little nose and staring down it at him.

But she was looking at him levelly, equally. Not a servant to her master, not a highborn lady to street-born man. Almost a friend to a friend, or perhaps something a little more. He wasn't quite certain how to define what was between them anymore. Perhaps it defied definition because much of it wasn't real, but was simply a farce, a ruse, a deception.

He should tell her the truth of who she was now while whiskey warmed her blood, relaxed her thoughts. But he'd held so much in regarding his own truth for so long, a burden he'd not dared speak about to anyone, a weight beneath which he sometimes felt he might suffocate. For who would truly understand? Perhaps she who was now almost a blank slate.

Leaning forward, he dug his elbows into his thighs and held his glass between both hands, noting how the liquid paled and darkened, depending how the light from the fire hit it. Life was comprised of the same shadows, weaving in and out. He'd spent too much time with the shadows.

He shifted his gaze to the shelf, to the box that

contained his heritage. "You asked me about Robert Sykes."

"The murderer."

He brought his attention back to bear on her. He wanted to trust her, wanted to believe that this woman residing in his residence was the true Lady O. That the other had been a fabrication of Society. Steadily holding her gaze, he spoke the words he'd never uttered aloud.

"He was my father."

Phee fought not to show any reaction, but she was fairly certain she'd grown pale because her skin suddenly felt cold and clammy. "How old were you when he . . . died?"

"I was eight when he was hanged."

He said the words so casually, as though he'd just informed her of his age the last time his father went out for a walk.

"I overheard the servants talking about the hanging that was to take place the following day. I collected newspapers for days and hoarded them away. I couldn't read, but I knew that one day I would and if there was anything about my father in the paper, I wanted it. It was perhaps a year and a half later when I clipped that article"—he jerked his head toward the shelves where he'd placed the box after she'd discovered it—"hid it away. I never wanted to forget from whence I'd come, never wanted to forget that I came from brutish stock."

"What of your mother?"

Leaning back, he took a long swallow of his whiskey. "He killed her."

She was horrified. "I'm so sorry."

He met her gaze. "It wasn't your doing. I'm the one who failed her."

He was so damned calm about the whole thing. She

wanted to get up and shake him, make him show some reaction, but then she noticed the hand holding the glass, the knuckles so white from his grip that she could see the outline of his bones. She was surprised the glass didn't shatter. He wasn't at all unaffected by the tale.

"How could you have possibly failed her?"

"He would hit her." He shook his head. "No, *hit* is too tame a word. Beat her. He would beat her. His hands balled into meaty fists." He held up one of his hands, turned it over, turned it back, examining it. "I have his hands."

"Don't be ridiculous. Those are your hands. They've nothing at all to do with him."

He lifted his gaze to hers, and she could see anguish within the dark depths. "You hurtled yourself at a man for mistreating a horse. I should have done the same to my father when he took his fists to my mother, but I cowered in a corner, afraid that if he remembered I was about, those massive paws would land on me next."

"You were a child. Your mother didn't expect you to protect her. I daresay, it would have broken her heart, caused her more pain had you been hurt as well. You can't blame yourself for his ugly behavior."

Taking another long sip, he shifted his attention to the flames. "I went to his hanging."

"Oh my God. Someone took you? A child? They should be horsewhipped!"

A corner of his mouth curled up ever so slightly as his eyes came back to hers. "You don't believe in whipping horses."

"I believe in whipping people when they behave badly. You should not have had to witness your father's death, no matter how horrible he was. You should have been spared seeing him die."

"No one took me. I went alone. I grew up on the

streets, knew my way around, didn't fear getting lost. Never told anyone."

"It's not a place for a child." Not a place for an adult. She had no memory of ever attending a hanging, but she could well imagine the gruesomeness of it. Her heart ached for him, that he had seen something so horrendous. That it had been his father up there made it all the worse.

"Quarter of a century ago, it served as entertainment. I was only eight, but still I recognized that I should be ashamed. I stood in that crowd and looked up at those gallows and was mortified that the creature up there with the noose about his neck—like an animal—had anything to do with me. And worse, I wept, because I loved him. I hated him, I despised him, knew the brutality he was capable of, knew he had killed my mother, and yet, somehow, to my mortification, I still loved him."

She couldn't help herself. Too much distance separated them. She rose, crossed over, knelt before him, and took his free hand. Feeling the tenseness in it, she stroked the long callused fingers, the wide palm. "I believe we can love a person without loving the things he does. He was your father. A bond existed between you."

"A bond. Yes." After he downed the last of the whiskey, he set aside the tumbler. Then he cradled her cheek. "His blood courses through me. And that, sweet Phee, is why I will never marry, why I am unworthy of a wife or children or the family who took me in. Because of the legacy he left to me. I can't impose it on others."

Tears welled in her eyes. That this man should believe those things was unconscionable. "You're not your father."

He laughed low, darkly. "Did you not see the way I went after Morris? I have my father's hard hands and his harsh temper. I've spent my life trying to keep it under control, but it's always there, seething beneath the surface. I can't escape it."

"Morris deserved your temper and your fists. It would have taken me much longer to beat him as he deserved, so I was very grateful you were on hand to handle the task for me."

He chuckled, a relaxed sound that reverberated through her. She didn't want him harboring these dark thoughts, going to these shadowed places where his past would haunt him. She wished she had the power to make him forget about his father, all he knew, all he'd witnessed. Perhaps there were some things that a person should not remember.

"You were quite the hellcat," he said.

"Tempers serve a purpose." Pressing a kiss to his knuckles, she repeated, "You're not your father."

"I wish I could believe you."

"You can. You must." She sighed deeply. How could she explain it? "I know I don't remember you from before, and that you make little cryptic comments from time to time that indicate we might not have been the best of friends—I don't know why, and I don't care. Because I know you now. I know who you are. I know how kind you are. You let me keep a horse, a cat, and a dog. You bring me supper and take me on picnics in the garden. You don't shout at me even though I'm an awful housekeeper. You don't complain that I purchase things for Marla with your coins. You try to help me remember, and you're patient with me when I don't." Reaching up, she combed her fingers through his hair. "I refuse to believe that there is anything of your father in you. You are your own man. I find you to be quite remarkable."

With a growl, he pulled her onto his lap, took her mouth as though without it, he might die. It was a sentiment she completely understood because she had not wanted to go another moment without kissing him. She had been so glad to discover he was still here. She thought she would never have enough moments with him. She'd come to despise the moon because when it rose in the sky, he departed. She much preferred the sun because it brought him back.

Pulling away, he gazed into her eyes, and within his, she saw burning desire that sent her heart to galloping. He plowed his fingers into her hair, held her still.

"This between us is so dangerous," he said, his voice rough and raw.

"You won't hurt me."

He pressed his forehead to hers, shook his head slightly. "You should not be here."

"I don't want to be anywhere else."

"I'm on a frayed tether."

"What does that mean?"

Drawing back, he gave her a wry smile. "That I want to be with you in ways that an honorable man would not. I won't ruin you. I won't."

She thought he was trying to convince himself more than convince her. Was it wrong of her to be flattered that he desired her? Did it make her wanton? Probably, but she didn't care. She wanted to encourage him to throw caution to the wind, but then she recalled why he was here. She'd promised not to distract him, yet she'd managed to do just that. "Can you tell me about this meeting you're having with the partners?"

He seemed relieved by her question, that she was willing to change the subject, lead them away from temptation.

"The club that I manage—Dodger's Drawing Room. Is the name familiar?" he asked.

She shook her head. "Should it be?"

"It's quite well known. You knew I oversaw it. I

just thought—" He shook his head. "Doesn't matter. Anyway, it's owned by three partners. One of those partners is the woman who took me in and raised me as her own."

Blinking she released a startled laugh. "A woman owns a gambling hell?"

"She was once the bookkeeper. Thirty years or so ago, London was very different, darker. Before that, more different, more dark. The three partners survived the streets, became successful. I owe her my life. I owe all of them for what I now hold. But I believe the purpose of tomorrow's meeting is to decide the club's fate, and I fear that they might decide the time has come to close it."

"What will you do if that happens?"

"I'm not sure. I hope to persuade them otherwise."

"And if you can't?"

"I shall open my own establishment. Begin anew."

"I can't imagine all it would take to start over." She furrowed her brow. "Although I suppose in a way I am."

"I'll have an advantage, though, if I must start over. I already know everything involved, everything I'll need to do. The notion of beginning again rather excites me. I've long wanted to own my own place, but my loyalty is to them. That's why I need to organize my thoughts, to convince them there is still money to be had, and that I can keep them in the flush."

"You'd sacrifice your own dream for them?"

"I doubt I'd be around to dream at all if not for them."

How could he possibly think he was anything like his father, a man who had ended his life at the end of a noose? "I know I don't remember you from before, Drake Darling, but I know you now and I can say with utter confidence that you haven't a shred of your father in you. Your loyalty to those who have helped you along the way, your kindness to me . . . You are a man who deserves all the good in life. I hope you acquire it."

"You humble me, Phee." He cradled her cheek. "You are a distraction I can ill afford."

"Will you return before your meeting?"

"Afterward."

Leaning in, she kissed him deeply, thoroughly. When his arms closed around her like tight bands, she broke away and scooted off his lap. "That was for luck," she told him with a grin. "Whatever you need to accomplish at your meeting tomorrow, you will succeed. I have full faith in you." *I love you*, she almost added. Could she love him when she had known him only a short time? Did she need her memories to know him fully? She didn't think so.

She started to leave him, had only taken three steps when he called out to her. She turned back to him.

"You, Phee, are an incredible woman. I'm not sure I ever realized that before."

"Perhaps you'll give me a day off then."

He laughed deeply, richly. "Perhaps I'll do more than that and take you to the seaside."

"I'd like that very much." Smiling brightly, she walked from the room. Even if she had all her memories, she doubted she'd recall a moment when she'd been happier.

Chapter 20

Their meetings were always held at a square table in a corner of Jack's library. Drake assumed it was their rendition of a round table. No head. No foot. They each had a side. They were all equals. From the moment he'd become the manager of Dodger's, he'd had a place at this table. When he was seventeen, he'd thought he'd be here forever.

Jack Dodger sat across from him. Frannie Mabry was to his right. The Earl of Claybourne to his left. More than thirty years had passed since they opened Dodger's. Not much had changed in all those years. A few games added. Women no longer worked on their backs. But for the most part, it was as it had begun, and that, Drake realized, was the issue at hand.

After Phee had left him the night before, he'd returned to the club, stood in the balcony, and organized his thoughts among the clatter and clicking of vices being enjoyed by men of quality. He couldn't see Dodger's going away, not when business was thriving. But he did believe some adjustments were in order.

Jack lifted his glass of whiskey, beginning the meeting as he always did: with a salute. "To Dodger's and the life it has given us."

They clinked their glasses together. Dodger's had given Drake a good life. He wasn't a partner, but his income was derived from the profits, and they were extremely handsome.

"I called this meeting," Jack began, "because times are changing and I don't know that I'm willing to change with them."

"That would be foolish," Drake said. Within this circle, he'd never hesitated to give his opinion on matters. They listened to him. They didn't always agree, but they listened.

Jack arched a dark brow. "Would it?"

"If you want your profits to continue to increase, you must be willing to adapt."

"Dodger's has had a good run. Besides, adapting has never been my strong suit."

Drake felt his stomach drop to the floor with the finality of Jack's tone. "However, it is mine. Dodger's caters only to the aristocracy. But more of our members are struggling. For many of them, the family coffers are not what they once were. Industrialization is changing everything. Those with the wealth now are not titled. They are visionaries. They are in manufacturing and railways and land. They are architects, inventors, builders. They are looking for validation, because for all their wealth, their blood is not blue, and that matters here. We open Dodger's to them."

Jack leaned back. "You're rather passionate about this."

"Yes, I am, because I understand it." He glanced around the table. "You all should. We have an opportunity here to expand our resources, to perhaps make a difference and knock a few bricks off the wall that separates the aristocracy from the common man."

"Don't you desire something more than managing a gaming hell?" the duchess asked, her blue eyes earnest. He'd always loved the way she met his gaze head-on.

"I'm suited to it, and I enjoy it. The only thing I would want more is to actually own one."

"Then why don't you?" the Earl of Claybourne asked.

Drake glanced around the table. "Because I owe each of you for the chance you gave me to better my life. I'm not going to show my appreciation by going into competition against you."

Claybourne gave Jack a pointed look. Jack merely shrugged. "I told you."

Drake furrowed his brow. He didn't have a good feeling about this. He liked even less the sense that something more was going on here than he'd thought. "Told him what?"

The duchess reached across the table, placed her hand over his, and squeezed. "Jack thought you were sacrificing your own dreams for what you perceived to be ours."

"I'm not sacrificing anything."

"Then you won't mind that we're ending the partnership," Jack said.

The words contained finality. "You've already discussed it, made your decision?"

"We have."

"You're closing Dodger's?"

Jack nodded. "I suspect it will cease to exist."

Drake thought of all the hours he'd poured into it, all the labor, the effort. The plans he had hoped to implement. "I'll purchase it from you. I have money set aside. Name your price."

Jack looked incredibly pleased. "You owe me five quid, Claybourne. I told you he'd want it."

"Why wouldn't I?" Drake asked. "Unless your own sons would rather have it."

"What would they do with it? They're not from the streets," Jack said. "They have no interest in the work it takes to run a place like this. Besides, we were all in agreement, from the moment you took over the reins, that if you had a knack for managing the place, someday we'd offer it to you. You have a knack, boy, and then some."

"Then this meeting—"

"Was to see if you'd have it."

"You couldn't have been a bit more direct?"

"You should know me well enough to know I wouldn't give it up without putting you through a little gauntlet. You've managed it well, but still I needed to be reassured you had the passion for it. You convinced me."

Drake felt his chest expand with relief, his thoughts explode with possibilities. "What's the price?"

"My share goes to you free and clear. Consider it your inheritance," the duchess said with a smile.

It was too much, far too much. He wasn't worthy. He needed to explain that to her, but then he heard Phee's insistent tone, *You're not your father.* Still, he shook his head. "I can't take from your own children."

"You're my child."

"The law does not recognize me as such."

She glowered at him. "Do you think I give a fig about what the law recognizes? I was a thief and a forger long before I was a duchess."

"And stubborn," Claybourne said. "Accept her gift with grace, lad."

Drake looked at the duchess. "You've given me so much."

She smiled softly. "You've given me more."

"Then I welcome your generous gift with more gratitude than I can ever express."

He negotiated with Claybourne and Jack for their shares. They seemed surprised by his shrewdness, but part of his preparation for the meeting had involved anticipating that he would make an offer for the business.

Whiskey was poured to seal the deal. Drake stood. "I am quite overwhelmed. I had hoped to convince you not to close Dodger's. It has a reputation tied to you. I will change it to fit the times. If you've no objection, I'd like to change its name in order to truly make it my own."

"You are now its owner," the duchess said. "You are to do with it as you please."

"I'll make you proud," he promised her.

"My darling son, you have made me proud since the moment you became mine."

It was silly for Phee to sit on the edge of the windowsill in the parlor and gaze out on the street waiting for Drake's return. He'd said he would come to the residence after the meeting, but she had no idea how long it would take or how soon after he would come. For all she knew he would stay at the club to work for a spell, to see about his business there.

She wasn't his wife, his lover, his friend. She was his housekeeper, his servant, his laundress, his boot polisher, his back scrubber. Even if she'd only had the pleasure of doing the last once. Her hands were healed enough that she could wash his back again. Although maybe she would wash a tad more: his hair, his arms, his chest. She would probably stop there. The remainder of him far too intimate, but maybe . . .

She'd braved a park that for some reason terrified

her. Why would she not brave exploring him? She thought it would be a far more pleasant task.

Sighing, she pressed her forehead to the glass. She had chores that needed to be attended to, although at the moment she couldn't recall a single one; cooking lessons to be attended to, although at the moment she didn't know if she would ever eat again, her stomach was such a knot of nerves.

She didn't want them to rebuff him or scold him or make him think he couldn't accomplish what he most certainly could. She didn't want them to hurt him, undermine his confidence. She wanted to be in that room and shake anyone who made him feel less.

Not that he needed her to stand as his champion. He was perfectly capable of handling the matter on his own. It was simply that she wanted to be his partner, wanted to be involved in his life, his plans, his dreams.

Good God, she sounded like Marla with her romantic tale of servants and masters of the house. The next thing she knew she would be imagining Drake declaring undying love for her.

Silly, foolish girl.

She saw a hansom cab pull to a stop in front of the residence, saw him leap out—

She rushed to the door, opened it, and nearly rammed into him when she darted outside. His quick reflexes, folding his hands over her shoulders, were the only things that saved her nose, his chest. She looked up at him, studying him as she tried to decipher the answer in his eyes but he was closed up as tightly as shutters during a storm.

"Well?" she demanded.

"You're looking at the new owner of Dodger's." Laughing, picking her up, holding her tightly, he swung her around until she was dizzy.

When he finally set her down, she asked, "But how?"

"It's a long story. I'll explain later. We're going out to celebrate."

She wished she had something in satin and silk to wear but at least she'd been saving the skirt and blouse that he'd brought her that second morning for a special occasion. The sleeves were long, the buttons of the bodice went to her throat. She felt rather plain and unadorned. No jewelry, no pearl combs for her hair. Even though, with the help of Marla's attentive hands, the blond locks were pinned up into an elegant style that she thought was befitting any ballroom . . . or tavern.

She couldn't recall ever being to a place where people were quite so boisterous, but surely she had. She and Drake were sitting at a back table in the corner, each with a tankard of ale, waiting for their shepherd's pie to be brought out.

"Sorry it's not very fancy," he said.

She smiled. "I wouldn't know if it was or not. I haven't anything to compare it to, but I adore the joviality here. Do you come here often?"

"For a pint every now and then."

She wanted to reach out and brush his hair off his brow, hold his hand, hug him. He looked as though he carried no burdens whatsoever. Strong, handsome, sure of himself, the world, and his place in it.

He had told her everything about the meeting, the wonder of them giving or selling him their portions of the club. She was amazed at his humility, how touched he was by their generosity. He took nothing for granted.

"Will you call the club something different? I think you should. It will be yours."

"I was thinking of calling it the Twin Dragons," he said.

"I like it, but why twin dragons?"

"Because I want it to represent the old and the new. Presently, you must be part of the peerage to even qualify for membership." He rolled his shoulders into a shrug. "Well, I did make an exception for an American, because I can see what's coming. The peerage is not what it once was. There is a new elite forming. Those without titles but with wealth that most can't even imagine. But we still have a class system, with which I am extremely familiar because I was raised within it. The family who took me in—he is a duke. She is a duchess."

Phee widened her eyes. "You were raised by nobility?"

She'd always thought he had a polished edge to him, but he also possessed an undercurrent of something rough and dangerous. It was odd that she found herself attracted to both aspects of him.

"I was. They treated me as one of their own, but beyond their walls, their sons are lords, their daughter a lady, and I am Mr. Darling. In spite of the fact that they never made me feel less, Society never accepted me as being equal. I don't resent it. I'm not angry about it. But I understand it. All these newly wealthy gentlemen are standing with their noses pressed to the window wanting in . . . and I want to give them the way in."

"By taking their money at cards."

"In a game of chance everyone is equal. Fate cares not one whit about rank, title, or class."

"What of women?"

He stared at her, clearly confused. "I'm only interested in managing gambling, not prostitution."

She gave a caustic laugh. "I'm not certain whether to be irritated or unsurprised to discover that's the direction your mind would take. I was referring to women gambling in your establishment. Surely they stand with their noses pressed to windows. Why not let them in as well?"

"Radical notion. I'll consider it as I'm renovating."

"You're going to renovate it?"

He nodded. "I want to modernize it a bit. I want to give it its own character. It's my dream, and I want it to reflect my values, my beliefs."

She could see that he would make it someplace special.

"I'm glad you shared your plans. It's a wonderful dream, owning your own place, making a difference to so many. It's much grander than mine."

"All dreams are equal. They can't be measured or weighed against someone else's. They're too personal. Their value rests with the person who owns the dream."

"You very much believe in things and people being equal don't you?"

"Yes, I very much do. At least for others." A shadow crossed over his features. Reaching out, he took her hand and stroked his thumb over her knuckles. She'd worn her kidskin clothes but removed them to eat. She was glad they were tucked away and that his skin was touching hers. "Sometimes I envy you not remembering your past."

"You mustn't let memories of your father ruin this night or taint your accomplishments. The original owners of the club entrusted you with something they built from nothing. They have faith in your abilities. I do as well."

He slammed his eyes closed, shook his head. "Phee—"

Her heart lurched. "Don't ruin it."

He opened his eyes, and she squeezed his hand. "Don't tell me that when my memories return I won't like you. Because I don't believe it. I won't believe it. I know what I feel for you now at this very moment, and I know deep within my heart, to the depths of my soul that I will never care for anyone as I care for you. Let us have tonight to celebrate the realization of your dream. Dance with me."

A band of three was playing fiddles. People were swirling around in another corner of the tavern.

"It's not a waltz," he said.

"But it looks like a great deal of fun."

He pulled her to her feet and led her into the midst of the dancers. While the music was wrong, completely wrong, they waltzed. Or tried to. There was no room to be swept over the floor or to be circled about. But he was grinning, that dimple winking. She loved that smile, loved that dimple. Loved the way his eyes glinted.

He was a man striving to let go of his past, while she had none. She no longer cared about what had come before. She only cared about now, about being with this man. This man who knew what it was to press his nose to the glass, a man who was opening the door for others. Who weighed all his actions against a past she had only glimpsed.

A remarkable man with so much good in him, good he failed to recognize.

As the crowd pushed them together, she rose up on her toes and kissed him. Maybe it was the ale she'd drunk, the music, his broad smile, but she wanted his mouth moving over hers. She didn't care that he was her employer and it was wrong. She didn't care that she was his servant and nothing permanent would come of anything between them. She didn't care about his past or her lack of one.

He pressed her closer as his mouth greedily welcomed hers. She was aware of whistles and cheers. When he drew back his eyes were darker than she'd ever seen them, smoldering with desire, burning for her.

She needed memories, craved them. She wanted tonight to leave her with ones she would never forget.

With his arm around her, holding her near, he was quiet in the hansom cab that returned them to the residence. He was quiet as he unlocked the door and led her inside. He was quiet as he prepared a bath. He was quiet as he lifted her into his arms and carried her upstairs.

It was only when they were outside the bathing chamber that he said, "I've dreamed of bathing you."

His eyes held hers. She saw the earnestness there. Warmth swirled through her. She nodded.

"I've dreamed of much more than bathing you," he said quietly.

Her heart was thrumming like some mad thing, but she seemed incapable of doing little more than nodding again.

"If at any time we are going further than you want, you need only say no."

"I don't think that word will be in my vocabulary tonight." Words at last, words that encouraged, gave permission.

With a low feral growl, he took her mouth. She ran her hands up into his thick black hair. He was a man of many talents, it seemed. He held her, kissed her, carried her into the bathing chamber as smoothly as a skater moving over ice.

An image flashed of her skating over a frozen pond in the dead of winter with snow-laden branches overhead, but she shoved it back into the farthest recesses of her mind to be examined later, much much later. This wasn't a time for memories to intrude. This was a time for memories to be made.

Slowly, slowly, her body unfurling and gliding against

his, he lowered her feet to the floor and drew back from the kiss. "We'll leave your hair up so it doesn't get wet," he said.

"I should like for you to wash it sometime."

"Tomorrow." He began undoing her buttons. "I tried very hard not to notice what you looked like as I undressed you the night I found you in the river."

"Did you meet with success?" she asked breathlessly as he parted her bodice.

"Your legs were my undoing. You are not tall and yet they are incredibly long, and I very much like long legs."

"Yours are long as well. I noticed that right off about you."

He laughed, deeply, richly. "They aren't all that's long."

She felt the heat suffuse her face, because she was fairly certain, based on the wicked glint in his eyes, that he was being naughty. Leaning in, she buried her face against his chest. "I don't know if I can joke about this."

Cradling her face, he tilted it up. "I want you very, very badly, Phee. But I won't force you and I won't do anything that makes you uncomfortable."

"I know. I'm not uncomfortable, I'm not even hesitant. I want you as well. I just don't want you to be disappointed."

"I won't be."

He removed her clothes slowly, provocatively. Shoes, stockings, silk underthings that he pressed open-mouthed kisses to before removing, coating her skin in dew. Then he was crouched before her, looking up at her. "It's like seeing you for the first time."

"Except for my legs."

He grinned. "Except for your legs."

He skimmed his large hands, warm and rough, up them, sending shivers of delight through her. Unfolding his body, he took her hand and helped her into the tub.

As she sank into the water, she smiled. "A shade past warm."

With his eyes never leaving hers, he removed his jacket, waistcoat, and neck cloth. He unbuttoned three buttons of his shirt and his cuffs, rolled up his sleeves, and she wondered why that last action seemed so remarkably sensual, more so than if he'd stripped himself of his shirt.

Kneeling beside the tub, he slipped a hand into the water and glided it over her toes, her arch, her ankles, up her legs, her thighs and back down. Up again, a little higher, and back down. "You're silk," he rasped.

"You're velvet."

"More like sandpaper."

She shook her head. "No."

His hand went higher, brushing over a hip, dipping in at her waist, gliding over her ribs, higher still until he was cradling a breast as the water lapped at it. Leaning over, he circled his tongue around her nipple, and once more her hands were in his hair, holding him near. With his hand kneading, he closed his mouth around light pink.

She was grateful these hadn't been memories to lose. They could not have done this before if he thought it was like looking at her for the first time. They had kissed, yes, but they could not have gone farther. Surely this would all feel familiar, surely there would be flashes of memory.

But there was nothing except the wonder of the sensations, as though she were only now being introduced to them. He trailed his mouth up to the curve of her neck, nipped at the delicate flesh with a satisfying growl, and she wanted to curl in on herself even as her head dropped back to give him easier access.

His hand skimmed back down, lower, lower, until his fingers were parting her and pleasure speared her. She released a little cry that was part moan, part sigh.

"Not yet," he grumbled, and she didn't know if he was talking to her or himself, but his fingers and lips left her.

She opened her eyes to see strain in his features as he reached for the soap. He concentrated on rubbing it over his hands. Lifting her foot from the water, he worked the soap between her toes, over her heel. Rough silk over smooth satin. The soap added a texture that delighted, yet she longed for his bare hands.

He washed her slowly, every line and curve, every nook and cranny, taking his time, exploring every aspect of her as though it were truly the first time he'd laid eyes on her. She watched the appreciation lighten his eyes, the passion flow in to darken them. Once more, she reached out and sifted her fingers through his hair. She wanted to touch him, needed to.

"Join me," she said.

He peered over at her. She flung some water droplets at him. "In here. I can wash you while you wash me."

Leaning in, he blanketed her mouth, his tongue exploring with the same intensity that his hands did, as though he could unearth something new about her. Their relationship would change. She knew that, but then it had already changed.

She didn't do her chores around the house because they were her duties. She did them because she wanted to please him. She wanted him happy. She wanted him to want to come home to her. She wanted to greet him with a smile and a kiss. She wanted him to take her into his arms. She wanted him to return at midnight, slip into bed beside her, and cradle her. She wanted him to sleep beside her, his breaths matching hers.

It all seemed right. From the moment she had awoken in his bed, some things had seemed correct and others had felt wrong. He had felt right. He had always felt right. Her feelings for him were the only thing she truly trusted. They were real, they were absolute. They carried with them no doubts.

Drawing back, he stood and pulled his shirt over his head. Although she'd seen that chest before, she still marveled at it. And the flatness of his stomach. He removed his boots and then his trousers. Oh yes, he was a man comprised of astonishing lengths.

He stepped into the tub, his feet on either side of her. Lifting her feet, she placed them on his chest as he lowered himself into the water, which rose and threatened to spill over. Taking her foot, he kissed her toes, her ankle, her calf.

The devil was in his eyes. How she loved that devil.

Locating the soap near her hip, she picked it up and rubbed her hands over it. She rose up on her knees and began washing him. "I think I was a silly girl to only ever wash your back," she said, skimming her hands over his chest, his arms.

"I was the fool for not insisting you do more." He braced his hands on either side of her ribs, his thumbs grazing the underside of her breasts as he brought her nearer and peppered kisses over her.

"You're distracting me from my purpose here," she told him.

"Concentrate."

But how could she when he was eliciting such marvelous sensations? Lowering her hands into the water, she stroked them over his hips. He stilled.

"Oh, I have your attention now," she said.

"You've always had my attention."

She moved her hands around, wrapping her fingers around the heat of him. He growled low in his throat and she felt the vibrations going through him.

He came up out of the water, pulling her with him. He stepped out of the tub, then assisted her out. He dried her, his actions tender but quick before he roughly ran a towel over himself.

When he was done, he lifted her into his arms and carried her out of the room, took her to the bed, tumbling her onto it, following her down, once again exploring her as though he'd never set eyes on her before.

He worshipped her with hands, mouth, tongue. He nibbled on her lobe, her neck, her shoulder, her breasts, lower.

He was right. If he'd done this with her before, she'd have not forgotten. She'd have not forgotten the heat, the passion, the groans. She'd have remembered the feel of his skin gliding over hers as he moved lower, the sensation of velvet rasping over her as his tongue swirled over her most intimately. She'd have remembered crying out as he took her on a journey of pure, unadulterated pleasure. She'd have remembered the smug look of satisfaction on his face when he rose above her, a look that should have angered her, but only endeared him all the more.

A man who made promises and kept them.

Yes, if she'd ever been with him before she'd have remembered.

She'd have remembered him filling her inch by slow inch. The weight of him, the fullness of him, the way her body closed so tightly around him. The deep groan he uttered as he buried his face in her hair.

Yes, she'd have remembered.

He lifted himself up, captured her gaze, and began

to rock against her, long, slow, deep thrusts. Until the pleasure once more began to mount. She could see the strain on his face, the strain in his arms. He lowered his head, took her mouth, the tempo of his movements never faltering. His taste was somehow darker, richer now. He was darker, more passionate.

Breaking off the kiss, he began to move faster. Rubbing her hands over his back, over the dragon, she lifted her hips, met him on equal terms. Their breathing became labored, their skin slick. Pleasure exploded through her. She cried out his name, heard him growl hers as he slammed into her one last time, his body trembling, his jaw clenched.

Keeping his weight off her, he pressed his forehead to hers, their breathing calming, even as tremors of pleasure continued to undulate. Lethargy crept in, and she thought she might never move again.

She also knew that she would never ever forget this night.

Rolling to his back, bringing her up against his side, Drake knew he would never forget this night. The fire in her, the passion. Dear God, she was his dragon.

Hearing her soft snoring, he realized she had gone to sleep. Reaching down, he managed to snag the blankets, pull them up, and tuck them around her.

Never in his life had he known a woman like her. Never in his life had he wanted a woman as much as he wanted her.

Closing his eyes, he relived the sight of her as she was revealed to him, a gift to be unwrapped and savored. The feel of her in the water, the wonder of her touching him. The journey to the bed. The madness that followed.

The taste of her, the scent of her.

The readiness of her when he had slid into her . . .

She was tight, God she was tight.

Yet he had slid into her unimpeded. The truth dawned sharply and without doubt.

Lady Ophelia Lyttleton had not been a virgin when he took her.

Chapter 21

It was late morning by the time she awoke, while he'd not been able to sleep at all. Various scenarios regarding his discovery had run through his mind. One being that she was in love with someone, that Drake had taken her when she had given her heart to another. Perhaps she'd been running off to be with him, eloping even. Maybe there had been a tragic accident. Somerdale had said she had numerous suitors. Had one caught her fancy?

She smiled at him, the impish smile that he loved, that caused his chest to tighten. "Good morning," she said sweetly.

"Morning." There was no point in asking her, because she wouldn't remember if she loved someone else. It was more imperative than ever that she regain her memories.

She rolled to her side, flattening her breasts against his chest, reached up, threaded her fingers through his hair, and guided him down until her mouth could capture his. His resolve threatened to dissolve like sugar encountering a cup of hot tea. He loved the straightforwardness with which she came to him, the feel of her sleek skin pressed to his. He loved her sighs and moans, the way she shifted and eased her knee between his thighs.

Dear God, but he ached to toss her onto her back, slip inside her, and stay there for the remainder of the day, the week, his life. It was possible she might never regain her memories. He could move her to the country, let her shelter animals there, visit her as often as he could—

But it wouldn't be enough. He wanted her every day, every night. He could not settle for scraps, although it was quite possible that he already had. He never should have taken things this far. He never should have given in to temptation. He thought he knew everything about her, when in reality he knew nothing all.

Pulling back, she studied him as she trailed her fingers over his face. "Why are you scowling?" she asked. "Did I do something wrong?"

"No, God no."

"Don't you want me anymore?"

With an anguished groan, he buried his face in the curve of her shoulder, inhaled her unique fragrance now laced with the musky scent of sex. "If at all possible, I want you more."

"Then what's the matter? Something is. I can tell. And you're frightening me."

Drawing back, he moved strands of her hair from her face. He wanted to do that every morning, tuck strands behind her ear. He skimmed his finger across her collarbone.

"Drake?"

"I'm not ready to give you up, and I know it's wrong of me."

She smiled at him. "How can it be wrong when I'm not ready to give you up either? Shall we stay abed all day?"

Knowing what he knew, he couldn't in all good conscience take her again, no matter how tempting she was. They needed to talk, but not yet. "Let's go to the seaside," he said.

Her eyes widened, green pools in which he thought he might drown. He didn't know why it seemed imperative that they have one more day together before he told her the truth. Especially as tomorrow he would no doubt think the same thing.

"On the railway?" she asked.

They would travel in the least expensive seats. No one would know her. Anyone she knew would be traveling at the front of the train, waiting for their servants to bring them refreshments when the train stopped. Only he didn't want her sitting at the back of the train. He didn't want to hide her. He cradled her jaw, could feel her pulse thrumming against his fingers. "We need to talk first."

"Yes, all right."

Where did he even begin? With his discovery last night? With his discovery of her in the river? Before that, with the kiss she almost remembered, the kiss in the alcove.

He heard the door chime. Phee gave him a questioning glance. "Are you expecting someone?" she asked.

"No." He rolled out of bed, walked to the window, and glanced out. The Duke of Lovingdon's coach was in front. Dammit. The timing could not have been worse. What the devil was he doing here? He should not have returned for another week. Drake could ignore his friend—

The bell chimed again. Or perhaps he could seek counsel from Lovingdon.

"I'll get it," Phee said, climbing out of bed in all her naked glory.

"No, I'll see to it," he told her. He strode quickly into the bathing chamber and snatched up his trousers and shirt from last night and hastily donned them.

Then he was out of the room and pounding down the stairs. He opened the door to find Grace standing there. Apparently, things could get worse.

"Lady Ophelia Lyttleton has gone missing," she announced, before she swept over the threshold, causing him to step back.

"What?" He stared at her with incredulity. How had she come to discover that?

She faced him. "She was supposed to be caring for her aunt, but when Somerdale went to Stillmeadow to see her, Wigmore told him that she'd run off. He thought she'd returned home, which is why he didn't notify Somerdale of her leaving. But I find it all very odd."

Very odd, indeed. Somerdale had been telling the truth, which meant he was innocent in all this. But what of the uncle?

"As she hadn't returned home, Somerdale wrote me to see if I knew where she might go, but I haven't a clue. So Lovingdon and I returned straightaway. We arrived only this morning. He's gone to find Avendale, because God knows the company he keeps these days might come in handy. I thought you might help as well."

"Grace—"

"I know you don't like her, but Somerdale is trying to keep this as quiet as possible to protect her reputation. You know the darker elements of London." She rubbed her brow and began to pace with agitation. "I don't know why she would run off. Not willingly. She didn't fancy anyone, so it's not an elopement. The only thing I can imagine is that Vexley kidnapped her as he kidnapped me, and Wigmore was too lazy to pursue the matter. I've never liked him."

He hadn't even considered that Lord Vexley would be involved. Vexley had tried to force Grace into marriage in order to gain her dowry. Had he succeeded with Phee, consummated the marriage? Rage shot through Drake with the thought. It would explain things. At her first opportunity, she would have run away from Vexley. But it might have come too late.

Grace stopped her pacing and grabbed his arm, her eyes imploring him to put aside any ill feelings he might have toward Phee. "You will help, won't you? We'll start with Vexley's estate."

"Grace." He couldn't have them traipsing over the country when Phee was here. He would have to explain everything to Grace, and if she didn't kill him first, perhaps she might help him reveal everything to Phee.

"Please, Drake, she is my dearest friend in the entire world. If he is involved—"

"Grace!" Phee exclaimed from her midpoint on the stairs. She was in the clothes from last night. Apparently they were easy to don quickly. She looked so positively happy, so delighted, while his chest was caving in on itself. How did she recognize Grace? "Oh my God. It's you who's come to see us."

"Ophelia?"

In spite of Grace's stunned expression, Phee hurried down the stairs and embraced Grace heartily. "It's so wonderful to have you visit. I was so hoping you'd come. I've missed you terribly. Oh my God!" She held Grace at arm's length. "I know who you are. You're Lady Grace Mabry. No, no. You were. But you married the Duke of Lovingdon. You're a duchess. I saw you and I just knew who you were. No one has your shade of red hair. And I am Lady Ophelia Lyttleton." She released a bubble of laughter. "My brother is the Earl of Somerdale."

Spinning around, she gave Drake the brightest, most

joy-filled smile he'd ever seen, and it nearly tore him in half. "I remember. I remember everything. The wedding, the ball, my Season. Oh my God, I'm not a servant." Turning back to Grace, she grabbed her hands. "I don't have to scrub floors or prepare meals or polish boots. And I have clothes. Dozens of gowns and shoes and hats. I have servants! I don't have to do anything. I remember! I remember it all. This calls for a celebration. Boy, fetch us some champagne!"

He didn't know it was possible to remain standing when possessed of a heart that no longer beat. Grace was obviously stunned and confused to discover her friend here, to listen to what sounded like the mad ravings of a lunatic. But Phee, the look on her face was pure devastation as she slowly turned to him again.

"I remember everything," she whispered, clearly horrified. "I remember you, who you are, what you are."

"Phee." Holding out his hands, he searched for adequate words, but none existed to explain the horror of what he'd done.

"You told me I was your servant. You made me clean your house, wash your . . ." Her voice trailed off. Her gaze darted up the stairs. "Oh my God!" she rasped. "Oh my God."

Her hand covered her mouth as tears welled in her eyes and she stumbled back.

How could he explain the unexplainable? How could he articulate how he had come to care for her? "Phee, I swear to you that I never meant for things to go as far as they did." He held out a hand imploringly.

"No! Don't you dare touch me." She scrambled back, hit the table, causing the vase to wobble and topple over. With a crash, it shattered and spilled its contents of water and roses over the floor. "I remember everything. Everything. Every touch, every squeeze, every ugly whisper." She made a gagging noise. "I think I'm going to be ill."

"Sweetling," Grace said, taking a step toward her, but Phee held up a hand to stay her actions, her eyes never leaving Drake.

"You knew who I was all this time. You didn't tell me. You took me to your bed."

"You wanted to be there," he said.

She shook her head. "How could you believe that when you knew everything that I didn't remember? I didn't know who I was. I didn't know who you were. You could have told me everything. You could have helped me remember."

"Phee—"

She released a sad, heartbreaking laugh. "You made me your whore."

"No, it wasn't like that. You must believe me."

She pressed her hands to her face. "I want to forget again. I want to forget everything." She turned to Grace. "You mustn't tell Somerdale. He must never know what happened."

Grace shook her head. "No, we won't tell him. But your uncle told Somerdale that you ran away. He's searching for you so we must tell him something."

"I have to think about it. He can't know that I was touched, that I'm . . . wicked."

"You're not," Drake said, stepping forward. "Phee—"

"Don't you call me that. Don't you ever call me that. Not after what you did. To you I am Lady Ophelia Lyttleton. You'd do well to remember that." Closing her eyes, she took a deep breath, and then another. Her spine straightened, her shoulders went back.

He realized he was watching a transformation. When she opened her eyes, he found himself staring into icy green. She tilted up her nose, lifted her chin, and suddenly Lady Ophelia Lyttleton was standing before him.

"You were trying to teach me a lesson, like at the ball when you kissed me, trying to bring me to heel."

"Maybe at first, but things changed. You changed. You were different."

Slowly she shook her head. "While you were who you have always been."

No, I changed, too. You changed me. But he held tight to the words because he knew she was too wounded to listen, to believe him.

"I trusted you," she said. "I trusted you with . . . everything. You took advantage, you betrayed me. All I wanted for you was wonderful things."

"I wanted to share those wonderful things with you."

"You must forgive me if I don't exactly believe you. What you did is . . . unforgivable." Angling her head haughtily, she said, "Grace, can you please take me away from here?"

Then he watched as Lady Ophelia Lyttleton strode from his residence, from his life.

And it took everything within him not to drop back his head and howl. As a boy on the street he'd been beaten savagely, starved, come close to dying a time or two, but never in his life had he been in as much agony as he was now, because he'd hurt Phee—thoughtlessly and irrevocably. Revenge was a double-edged sword, and at that moment it was slicing his heart to ribbons and he regretted deeply that it was slicing hers as well.

Lady Ophelia Lyttleton did not look out the coach window, did not glance back to watch the residence disappear from sight. She simply stared straight ahead at the leather that lined the inside of Lovingdon's coach, while everything inside her screamed at Drake's betrayal. He had taken her to his bed, knowing who she was. He had touched her, kissed her, joined his body to hers . . . made her cry out his name with pleasure. She had wanted what he offered, wanted him. She was as she'd once been told by another: wicked. She tempted men into wickedness. While Drake had not hurt her physically, she was still devastated emotionally because she would have never gone to his bed if she had remembered who she was. He had to have known that, and he kept the truth from her in order to seduce her. She had no doubt.

"Where would you like to go?" Grace asked gently, kindly.

She didn't know, she couldn't think. Her head was beginning to hurt. She desperately wanted a bath, needed to wash away his touch, scrub away his caresses. "Could I stay with you until tomorrow? I have to give some thought to what I'm going to tell Somerdale. I've been alone in a bachelor's residence, a scoundrel's residence, for days, nights. I won't marry him, Grace."

Leaning across the expanse separating them, Grace took Ophelia's ungloved rough, scarred hands in her gloved ones. Ophelia felt soiled without the trappings of a lady. They had always provided her with a measure of protection. With them she could pretend that she wasn't what she was.

"No one would expect you to," Grace said. "I shall send word to Somerdale that I think I know where I can find you, and that I shall have you home tomorrow. To lessen his worry."

Phee nodded. As much as she loved Somerdale, he was not one for taking charge. He would accept Grace's letter with relief, leave the matter to her, and return to his club.

Grace continued, "I believe I've pieced together what

might have happened between you and Drake, but I'm confused regarding how you came to be there."

"I don't wish to talk about it. Not yet." Not ever.

She'd been happy, blast him. For a while she'd been truly happy. But it had all been only an illusion. None of it had been real, and now she would have to deal with it.

She'd welcomed his touch, encouraged it. She wanted to curl into a ball and weep for all that she'd allowed, for everything that he'd done. Instead she kept her spine straight and stiff. She fought not to reveal the depth of her hurt. She had become quite skilled at hiding pain. Her proficiency at it would come in handy now. It would protect her, ensure that no one knew what she'd suffered.

More importantly, it was imperative Drake Darling never realize how he affected her. She would not allow him to have power over her. She would not let him destroy her completely. She would find a way to piece herself back together, to carry on.

She'd done it before. She would do it again.

Chapter 22

"Where did you take her?" Drake stood in the Duke of Lovingdon's front parlor. His best friend was nowhere to be seen, but his new wife was not at all happy. Not that he blamed her. He wasn't particularly happy with himself either. Phee's face crumpling with the realization of what he'd done would haunt him for the remainder of his life. She believed him worthy. He'd proven her wrong.

"She's here, at least for tonight. Sleeping. Dr. Graves came to examine her."

"And she's all right?"

"Depends on your definition of all right. I've a good mind to smack you. What were you thinking, what were you hoping to accomplish?"

Charging over to the fireplace, he pressed his forearm against the marble mantel and stared into the hearth, wishing for a fire so he could envision himself writhing within it. "You'd never understand."

"Why don't you try to explain it anyway? I know you, Drake. I love you as a brother. God help me, I love you *more* than I love the brothers who share my blood. I'm trying to give you the benefit of the doubt here but it's exceedingly difficult when my dearest friend in all the world cried herself to sleep."

He grimaced, despising himself for being responsible for her tears. "It was childish."

"I believe that goes without saying. The question is why did you do it?"

He sighed heavily, considered pounding his fist against the marble, but the rage he felt would be behind the blow and so it was likely he'd damage the mantel. "I know you're not aware of it, but at every opportunity she slighted me."

"Of course I'm aware of it."

Dumbfounded, he stared at her. "And yet you remained friends with her, after just telling me how much you love me?"

Grace perched on the arm of a padded brocade chair. "Of course I did. Because I believed I understood what was behind her actions."

"Insulting me?"

"Attraction to you."

He felt as though he'd taken a full body blow, as though the house had just toppled down on him. "What? Are you mad? She never had a kind word for me."

She smiled softly. "I don't recall you having very many for her either. You two skirted around each other as though you feared if you ever got too close there would be a conflagration."

God, there had certainly been that. They'd scorched and singed each other with their passion and desire. Unfortunately, in the process he might have destroyed her. "She irritates the devil out of me."

"Which was her purpose. I think she was frightened—possibly terrified—by what she felt for you."

"Only because she considers me beneath her."

"Perhaps. Or mayhap she sought to convince you

both of that so she wouldn't have to deal with what she felt. It's also possible that she wanted the distance because she didn't consider herself worthy."

He laughed at that, a deep harsh bark that reverberated through the room. "I have never known anyone who put herself so high up on a pedestal."

"When one is that high up, Drake, she can't be touched. I have always wondered why she put such distance between herself and men. Not only you. I suspect that if word got out about your little ruse, several men would cheer."

He'd flatten each one who did. "I'm not telling anyone. What happened is strictly between Phee and me," he ground out.

As though considering, she cocked her head to the side. "I like the way you say her name, as though she's special to you."

She was special. Not that he could admit it without coming across as a total ass. Had he known how remarkable she was, he would have treasured her from the beginning.

Grace rose, walked over to a small table of decanters, and poured a splash of rum—her spirit of choice—into two glasses. Hers had been an uncommon upbringing. She swore, cheated at cards, smoked cigars, and drank. She could survive in a man's world if she needed to. The duchess had seen to that.

Now Grace brought him a glass, then clinked hers against his, before taking a swallow. He was not as delicate. He downed his contents in one gulp. He had an irrational urge to prove he wasn't a gentleman, to be barbaric, uncouth, uncivilized.

But she wasn't watching him. She was staring at the amber liquid, tapping her dainty finger against the side of the tumbler. "As close as Phee and I are, I know that she has never shared everything with me. To be honest, there are things I haven't shared with her, so I'm not faulting her for her discretion. But when she was younger, before we had our coming out, she would spend a good deal of the summer with her aunt. She would always invite me to join her there, would insist upon it actually. I was given my own bedchamber, treated like a princess. After all, I was the daughter of a duke. But without fail, Phee would always slip into my room near midnight, crawl into the bed, and snuggle against me. She would be cold and shivering, no matter how warm the weather. She forbade me to ask questions or to say anything about her presence there. I was young, naive, but I often wondered what it was she feared in the night. To this day, I haven't a clue. I've never pressed. We all have our secrets."

He needed more rum, a full tumbler this time, because he could not help but believe that something was dark at Stillmeadow, something that had been responsible for her journey into the Thames.

"Did she explain how she came to be in the river?"

Slowly she shook her head. "She doesn't recall that part. Dr. Graves doesn't believe that to be unusual. It was no doubt traumatic, and he believes that sometimes our mind strives to protect us from bad memories. He's treated men returning from wars, survivors of railways disasters. They might remember what happened before or after, but not during."

"Vexley wasn't involved," he said with conviction. Considering when he'd found her, he knew she hadn't had time to arrive at Stillmeadow, hadn't had time to be abducted.

"No. Lovingdon went to see him only to discover the man somehow financed his way to America. So what happened that night is still a mystery. Although right now, Phee's biggest worry is striving to come up with an explanation for Somerdale. She's quite insistent that he not learn where she spent the past several nights. She fears it would be disastrous."

"That Somerdale would force her to marry me?"

"There is that possibility. In the heat of the moment you both said things that left nothing to my imagination."

"I need to speak with her, Grace."

She nodded. "I assumed that was the reason behind your visit, but I'm not certain she's yet ready to see you. Perhaps you should give it a few days."

"A few days won't lessen how much she despises me. I daresay a year, a decade, a century will not be long enough as far as she's concerned. But I need to see her tonight, before she talks to Somerdale. And we need to be alone. I won't go near her, I won't touch her. If I could think of a way so she wouldn't have to breathe the same air that I do, I would make it happen. It was never my intention to destroy her, and I know I can't put things right. But I can make amends."

Reaching up, she touched his cheek. "You need to know, Drake Darling, that in spite of everything, I still love you as a brother. I trust you. We can only hope that my belief in you is enough for Phee." She lowered her hand to her side. "Let's see if I have any luck at convincing her to give you a chance."

Phee peered from behind the curtain onto the front drive. Why hadn't he left yet? She'd seen the hansom arrive, had been looking for it actually, although she'd have never confessed that to anyone, but she had known that sooner or later he would come here. He would try to talk with her. She knew so much about him. How much easier it would all be if she didn't. If she didn't know the feel of his hands gliding along her throat, over her breasts, across her stomach. If she didn't know the sensations created when his mouth followed the same path. If she didn't know what it was to spread her legs for him, to have him rising above her—

She slammed back the memories, wouldn't recall everything that happened in his bed. But it was so hard not to consider every moment spent with him, every minute detail of her time with him. Unfortunately, she saw it all in a different light, now. It was no longer beautiful and joyful. It was tainted by his deception, by whatever game he'd been playing.

She knew all about games and the ugliness that initiated them.

Still, she'd not been able to look away as he walked from the cab to the front steps. He was properly decked out like a gentleman. Jacket, waistcoat, neck cloth, hat, gloves. So handsome in his rough way. She wanted to rush down the stairs into his strong arms, wanted him to hold her. Everything had seemed right with the world while she'd been with him—until her memories had returned.

All along he'd known who she was, what she was. Had known what she wasn't. All along he'd lied. He'd led her to believe she was someone other than who she was. That he was someone different.

She could forgive the chores. A very tiny part of her might even acknowledge that perhaps she deserved it, for an hour. But not for days. And no part of her could accept that she had deserved to be seduced by him. With her memories, she'd have never visited his bed. It didn't matter that he had taken her on a glorious journey. There had been no honesty in it.

At the sound of the door opening, she turned as Grace walked in.

"He hasn't left yet," Phee announced as though Grace might not be aware that Drake still lingered in her residence.

"He wants to speak with you."

"No, absolutely not. You were supposed to tell him I was sleeping."

"I did, but I don't think he believes me. Besides, I'm not convinced it would be such a bad thing for you to see him."

"He's a silver-tongued devil, that one. I want nothing more to do with him." She turned back to watching the drive. If she stayed up here long enough, perhaps he would grow weary with waiting and leave. She needed him to leave. When he was here she couldn't stop thinking about all that had transpired between them. She could find no peace.

The bed groaned as Grace sat on it. "What are you afraid of, Phee?"

Not being strong enough to resist tumbling back into his arms. "He took advantage, did things, unforgivable things, things I did not want . . . ever. If I'd known who I was, if I'd possessed my memories, I'd have never allowed it to happen."

"Are you saying he forced you?"

She shook her head. But he'd made her want him, damn him. She stared harder at the drive, willing him to appear, to walk out the door.

"He promises not to touch you, not to go near you. He wants only to speak with you. I think you owe it to him to at least hear what he has to say."

"Owe him? I scrubbed his floors. I polished his boots. I *worked*." She could voice all of that, but not the worst of it. The humiliation, the shame, the mortification. The degradation of desiring him.

"I know he has regrets," Grace said.

"As well he should."

"I also think he cares about you."

She scoffed. "If he did, he wouldn't have done what he did."

Grace got up off the bed and walked over to her. "Phee, I know we are taught that we are not to be intimate with a man before we marry, but if it makes you feel any better, I shared a very special night with Lovingdon before I even realized I would marry him. Desire is not a horrible thing."

The weight of all that had happened was exhausting. It was taking all her strength not to crumble. Phee turned to her. "But you knew who you were. You knew who he was."

"Yes, there is that, I suppose. Still, I love you both," she said solemnly. "I think you're both hurting. Perhaps a small chat will ease some of the pain."

"It'll only make it worse."

"He's stubborn and prideful, Phee. He's not going to leave without seeing you. You know that as well as I do."

"I can be equally stubborn and prideful."

"But what is to be gained?"

As he stood by the fireplace, staring at the boots she'd recently polished, the minutes dragged by one after another. The only reason he didn't give up hope was because Grace had yet to return to inform him that Phee would only consent to see him when he was rotting in hell. He doubted she would accept that he was there now.

Hearing the soft footfalls, he glanced up. Nearly doubled over with relief. She stood in the doorway in a light green satin dress with dark velvet striping. Velvet circled the collar, the cuffs, her waist, outlined the ruffles and bustles of the skirt. It had been made for her, he had no doubt of that. It didn't matter how she'd come to have it here. Her hair was gathered up into a chignon. No loose wisps to be blown away with an enticing twist of her lips and a quick breath.

She was regal in bearing. Proud. But her stance was accented by an undercurrent of hurt, betrayal, and the definite mien that she wished to be anywhere other than where she was. Yet just like that night when she had expressed dread at walking in the park, she had shored up her courage to meet with him. He wondered how often she would humble him before his life was done. No doubt every time their paths crossed.

He straightened, moved away from the fireplace, and bowed slightly. "Lady Ophelia."

"Grace said you wished to speak with me. Please be quick about it."

He tipped his head toward the sofa. "Will you sit?"

"I prefer to stand."

"Will you at least move into the room so I needn't shout and our words can remain private?"

Hesitating, she glanced around. In his residence, he found her pique amusing. Here, it only served as a reminder that she had every reason to be upset with him. Finally, she wandered into the room, stopping near the before-indicated sofa, folding her hands primly in front of her, and meeting his gaze head-on.

Had he really thought only a short while ago that memories of washing his back would have humiliated her? That he could bring her to heel so easily? How had he not recognized the depth of her pride, the strength of her backbone? How could he have not seen that she could have resided in the filthiest squalor, and she still would have held herself as though she were a queen? How had he not known that he would gladly serve as her most loyal subject?

"I make no excuse for my actions. They were reprehensible."

Her face a mask of calm, she said nothing. He wanted her to at least tell him he had the right of it, he was a beast. He wanted her to yell, rant, move forward, and pound her fists into his chest. He would wager everything he owned—*everything*, including his recently acquired club—that she knew precisely what he wanted and so she withheld it as a means to punish him. A lashing would have hurt less, but then he didn't deserve less.

"Do you remember how you came to be in the Thames?" he asked.

A flicker of emotion at last. Fear. Deep and dark. "No."

"Somerdale said you left with your uncle—"

"You've discussed this with my brother?" Fury now. Her eyes narrowed, her hands clenched at her side. Her breaths coming harsh and fast.

"No!" He held up a hand. "No. Believe it or not, in the beginning, I only planned to have you serve as my housekeeper for a day."

"But you were having such a jolly time with it that you decided to prolong it?"

"It was not as I thought it would be." He gripped the mantel to stop himself from rushing forward and taking her in his arms, comforting her with his touch, with soft whispers, with tender kisses. "It would be much easier if you sit down and allow me to explain without interruption."

"And you think I care about what is easier for you?" She held out her hands, palms facing him. "My hands are scarred now, not the hands of a lady. And I'm no longer innocent. I won't be a virgin for my husband."

"You weren't a virgin for me," he said somberly.

"You bastard!" she rasped, before tearing across

the short expanse separating them and pummeling his chest, his arms, his jaw. She was a madwoman, her fists flailing about, striking anything they could.

He didn't try to stop her, not at first. He deserved every bruise, every cut, every scrape. But then he feared she might damage herself. He folded his arms around her, brought her in close, held her tightly. "Phee," he whispered in her hair. "Phee, it's all right."

Her arms went limp as she sagged against him, great wrenching sobs causing her shoulders to tremble, her tears dampening his shirt. It seemed he was always destined to cause her pain. He would leave her if he could, but not yet, not just yet.

"Tell me," he urged gently. "Tell me what happened."

Sniffing, wiping at her eyes, she pushed away from him. Without meeting his gaze, she walked back to the sofa. "You don't know what you're talking about."

He wished he didn't. He hoped he didn't. He who never prayed, prayed to God that he was wrong. But it was the only thing that made sense, that fit with the timeline, and yet it was incomprehensible.

"The first night after I found you, your brother was at the club, playing as though he hadn't a care in the world. I couldn't understand why he wasn't out searching for you. Unless he didn't know that something had happened to you. Or unless he was the one who tossed you in the river and thought you were dead."

She rolled her eyes. "Somerdale wouldn't harm a fly."

"So it was your uncle. You were going to Stillmeadow with your uncle in order to care for your aunt. But you never got there. Yet your uncle claims you did and then you ran away. Why would he lie?"

"I've had quite enough of this." She turned to go. Lunging forward, he grabbed her arm. Wrenching free, she glared at him. "You promised not to touch me if I met you in here, yet you seem incapable of keeping your promise. I suppose I should not be surprised considering the blackguard you are."

As much as he didn't want to do it, he needed to shatter this pretense in order to get to the truth. "Your uncle forced himself upon you that night."

She heaved a sigh as though he was the most infuriating man in the world and she could hardly be bothered with him. "Let this matter go. You've done quite enough damage, don't you think?"

Oh, he hadn't done nearly enough if his suspicions were correct. "Look me in the eye and tell me that he did not force himself upon you that night."

Drawing in air through her gritted teeth, she closed her eyes and balled her fists. He thought it very likely that she was going to hit him again. But when she opened her eyes, he saw determination and steel in them.

"He. Did. Not. Force. Himself. Upon. Me. That. Night."

Studying her intently, he saw naught but the truth. The absolute, unvarnished truth in her eyes. She meant each word she'd punctuated with conviction. Relief swamped him, and yet he was still troubled. "But you had no barrier for me to penetrate."

Red crept up her throat, over her face, and he knew his words were shocking, too blunt, but he wanted an explanation. He needed to know that he hadn't done her an even greater disservice than he'd originally thought. Her reaction in the foyer had been more than anger. He couldn't quite understand what he'd witnessed.

"Perhaps I wasn't born with one," she said. "Or perhaps it somehow broke. I don't know, but surely not every virgin remains completely intact. Besides, considering how desperately you wanted me last night, were you truly in a position to notice?"

She had a point there. He'd been lost in the passion, the fire of her. Mayhap he was wrong, but something was amiss. She was striving too hard to get him off the path. While he knew he should let it go, let her go, he couldn't quite bring himself to do it.

"How did you come to be in the river?"

"I don't recall."

"I don't believe you."

"I've had quite enough of this, and of you."

Turning on her heel, she headed for the door.

"If you don't tell me how you ended up in the Thames, I'm going to confess to your brother what I did."

Staggering to a stop, she spun around and glowered at him. "You wouldn't."

"I daresay, he'll insist that we marry."

Hands balled into fists, she marched back over to him, stopping a mere inch from him, glaring, fire shooting from those emerald eyes. "You are a beast."

"Considering my recent behavior, I believe that's unarguable."

"Why does it matter how I came to be in the river?"

"Because in spite of everything, and while I don't expect you to believe it, I fell desperately in love with the woman who lived in my residence. If someone caused her harm, they will answer to me."

"If you truly loved me, you wouldn't have done what you did."

"I didn't love you when it began. Christ, I didn't even like you."

Her mouth gave the slightest twitch, and he saw the barest of nods, as though she'd made up her mind about something. With her posture, her stance, emerged the woman he'd never been able to tolerate.

"The truth? Yes, I was going to the country with my uncle. But in the carriage he described my aunt's condition in detail. We were in the midst of the Season and I was going to endure the stench of a sickroom to bathe my aunt, feed her, read to her, and hold her hand. No more dancing, no more strolls through the park admired by gentlemen, no more flirtation. Just drudgery and boredom and tedious tending to an ailing old woman. I didn't want it. I wanted balls, fine dinners, and theater. I wanted to have fun. I wanted to be sought after. So when the carriage slowed to turn onto a bridge, I leaped out. Uncle sent his footmen after me. Ghastly long legs they have. Why does everyone value tall footmen? Anyway, I knew they would catch me, so over the railing I went. I wasn't too far along on the bridge, the plunge not such a great distance that I couldn't survive it. I doubted they would follow. Better to be wet for a bit than to miss the Season. I would worry about dealing with Somerdale later." Her tone was haughty, cold, and calculating. It sent a shiver down his back.

"You're not that selfish."

"Perhaps the woman who lived with you wasn't, but the one before, the one you didn't even like? Admit it, that's precisely how selfish she was. And is. Now that I have my memory back and understand what is my due."

"Why didn't your uncle notify your brother straightaway?"

"I assume he thought I was going home so he saw no need. He no doubt expected I would explain to Somerdale that I'd changed my mind about going on to Stillmeadow."

"He didn't think it important to ensure you were safe? What sort of man is he?"

"One who cares only about his own convenience. Are we done here?"

Maybe if they were truly two different women with different hearts and different souls he'd have been convinced. But he knew and understood the woman he'd rescued. When she'd hit the water, her façade had shattered. Now she was desperately striving to reerect it. Why?

For the same reason that he had built a barrier around himself: to keep hidden something ugly from his past, something he wanted no one to ever know. But he'd shared it with her, opened himself up to her. Trusted her.

He'd betrayed her. She wouldn't trust him with it now. But he knew there was something so hideous and dark . . .

Something that gave her nightmares . . .

Something that touched her, that she fought against . . .

Something Grace said she feared in the night when at Stillmeadow . . .

Not something. Someone.

"Your uncle didn't force himself on you that night," he said.

She jerked up her chin. "Did I not just say that?"

"He raped you when you were a child."

Chapter 23

Phee wanted to remain standing, tall, erect, confident. She wanted to brazen this out, but she couldn't. Not with him, not with the sympathy and understanding in his dark eyes. Not with the certainty there. He knew her too well. When her guard was down, she'd let him in. When she'd had no memories with which to shore up walls.

Not when she found herself sinking to the sofa, her legs too weak to support her. She should have never come down here, should have never agreed to meet with him. She should have known he'd poke and prod until he got to the tarnished truth. Until he'd uncovered her deepest shame and mortification.

What Drake had done to her paled in comparison.

But his actions hurt her heart much worse because she had fallen for him. Had known his love. It was an experience she'd never thought to have, knew herself to be unworthy of. Something about her was evil. Her uncle had told her that often enough.

Whenever he came to her.

Drake knelt beside her. She couldn't look at him. Refused to. "Can't you please let this go?"

"How old were you?"

She should have expected him not to ignore her question. She should ignore his, but he was like a rapacious dog gnawing at bone. He wouldn't leave her be until he got the answers for which he'd come. She had carried the burden of the truth for so long. Perhaps if she released some of it into his care, it would lessen the weight. "Twelve when he first came to my bed in the dead of night. Touched me." She thought she might be ill. Her jaw tingled. Bile rose. "Made me touch him."

Daring to lift her gaze to his, she couldn't miss the revulsion in the obsidian depths.

"You didn't tell your father?"

She released a shuddering breath. "No. I was too ashamed. And Wigmore—he told me that I was wicked, that it was my fault he was doing these things to me. He told me that if I said anything, my father would send me to a place where they locked wicked girls away. I would be alone in the dark." Forgotten, fodder for the rats.

"What about your aunt? If you were close to her—"

"She would have hated me, known me to be the wicked girl that I was. I couldn't tell her."

"You don't think she knew?"

"They had separate bedchambers. He always came late at night, after the servants were abed. The clock would strike two and the door would open. Even at home I got into the habit of not retiring until the clock struck two. The two dongs followed by silence always jolted me awake." Suddenly so cold, she rubbed her hands briskly up and down her arms. *Let this be enough*, she prayed. *Let his inquisition end.*

"How old were you when he took things further?" he asked.

The backs of her eyes stung, but she would not give

the tears their freedom. If they began, she would be unable to stop them, and she would not humiliate herself further by weeping. She swallowed hard. "I was seventeen before . . . before he had his way completely. Had I not lost my memories . . . what happened between you and me never would have happened. I would never have subjected you to someone as defiled as I am, as impure." She wrapped her hands around her upper arms. She wanted to peel off her skin, wanted to again forget the feel of Wigmore's thick, pudgy fingers poking and prodding while his hot, wet, panting breath condensed near her ear.

"You think what he did is a reflection on you?" Drake asked quietly.

"How can it not be?"

He reached out, his hand stopping just shy of her cheek, before balling into a fist, and pressing into his thigh. She didn't know if he was honoring her request that he not touch her or if he was repulsed by the thought of touching her, of how intimately and thoroughly he'd been with her in the wake of another man. Ladies of quality were not supposed to be touched by anyone other than their husbands. But something in her called to the deviant, the sick, the perverted.

"His behavior is reprehensible," Drake said with conviction. "You are not at fault for his evil deeds. But knowing what he was capable of, why did you go with him?"

"Because I'm stupid. Because I believed he was done with me. Because Aunt is truly ill. But in the carriage, he told me how much he'd missed me. How glad he was that we could have some time together again, and I knew he wasn't done with me. As much as I love my aunt, I couldn't force myself to suffer through his touch again. So I ran." Taking a deep breath, she regained control, straightened her spine, met his gaze. "Are you happy now?"

"I am far from happy, but that will be remedied when Wigmore is dead by my hand."

He shot to his feet and was striding to the doorway before his words truly registered. She scrambled after him, nearly tripping on her hem in her hurry.

"No." She grabbed his arm and somehow found the strength to spin him around, he who was so much larger than she, broader, more muscled. She could feel the fury shimmering through him. "You can't kill him."

"I beg to differ." He held up his massive hands. "With these wrapped about his throat, I expect I'll accomplish it quite easily."

"You can't do this."

"You were right all along, Phee. I'm not nearly civilized enough for the aristocracy. You know of my past. You know that the blood of a murderer races through my veins. I am my father's son. I have his temper, and there are times when I want to explode with it."

"But you don't. You haven't. And you can't now. They'll hang you."

"Not such a loss when you consider how I hurt you. However, I shall go out with a bit more dignity than my father went."

"You won't go out at all. I won't allow it. Don't you understand what I've been striving to explain to you? I'm not worth it."

He dragged her into his arms, held her near. "You're worth everything."

"And if Wigmore won't cooperate?" Phee asked.

"I shan't give him a choice."

She had no doubts there. They were traveling in Lovingdon's coach. She thought it a testament to the duke's faith in his friend and Grace's love of her brother that neither asked for an explanation regarding why they needed to travel to Stillmeadow this hour of the night. They were going to retrieve her aunt so Phee could care for her as she wanted, out from under Wigmore's shadow.

Within the coach, they hadn't bothered to light the inside lantern. For some reason, it seemed this journey needed to be made in shadows.

"If my memory hadn't returned, were you ever going to tell me who I was?" she asked.

"I don't expect you to believe me, but I was going to tell you the night we celebrated, but I became distracted from my purpose." She heard a smile in his voice. "Then I was going to tell you before we went to the seaside, but Grace walked in and you remembered everything. Odd."

She thought she heard disappointment in his voice because Grace had been the one to stir her memories to life and not him. "Perhaps because she was always my haven. I came the closest to being myself when I was with her. When she visited at Stillmeadow I knew I would be free of Wigmore's attentions for the duration of her stay. When I saw her in your foyer, a floodgate of memories unlocked."

"That included me."

"That included you. It was never going to end well between us. You must have known that."

He sighed. "Unfortunately, knowing how things would end did not stop me from wanting you. Which makes me the worst sort of scoundrel. I quite understand you're not forgiving me. But you're to let me know if you find yourself with child."

Her stomach clenched painfully. She'd not even considered that. To have his child—

She looked out the window. Her dream was freedom, her dream was to care for animals, but another dream nudged at the edge of her mind. A black-haired, black-eyed baby nestled in her arms, staring up at her. It was a dream she wouldn't consider. How could she ever trust him fully again?

"How is Daisy?" she asked.

"Presently being cared for in a very fine stable until you're ready for her."

It was silly to miss a horse, but she did. "I shall probably take her to Somerdale's estate, so she'll have room to run. Until I reach the age of thirty and my trust is handed to me, I'm rather limited on what I can accomplish."

"What of marriage?"

"Even without my memories I knew I didn't want it. I told you what my dream was. It was strong enough not to get lost. I've only been biding my time, pretending to be on the hunt for a husband because that's what ladies of my station do." She planned to reject all proposals, all offers until she came of an age when no man would want her, until she was quite on the shelf and could live a life without being under a man's thumb. "It's odd. Marla, who as a servant is never expected to marry, desperately wants a husband. While I, the daughter of an earl, am expected to marry and I desperately don't wish to. It seems we always want what we can't have."

"It seems so, yes." His voice was laced with regret and sorrow. "I'll loan you the amount of your trust. You don't need to wait until you're thirty to have the life you want."

Her heart gave a little stutter. "You need that money to renovate your business."

"Renovations can be made at any time."

She shook her head. "No, I won't be in your debt."

"It comes with no strings, no interest. When you become of age and your funds become available to you, all you will pay is precisely what I loaned you. No more than that. I doubt you'll get a better offer elsewhere."

She thought about how lovely it would be not to have to go through another Season, to leave behind flirting and pretending interest in gentlemen. No more balls, no more dinners, no more false laughter and feigned suitability.

"I suppose guilt is spurring this offer."

"Believe that if it makes you more willing to accept it."

Unfortunately, she didn't believe it was guilt. She thought it was something much greater. Something she didn't dare trust in him or herself.

They had not sent word that they would be arriving. Drake knew a surprise visit near midnight would give them an advantage. Not that he needed one. The fury rolling through him as they stood in the foyer while the butler alerted His Lordship—who was in the library—to their presence gave him all the edge he needed. He was fairly bouncing on the balls of his feet ready to hunt down the bastard.

While Phee stood there so calmly, so stiffly, her chin up. The only indication that this was not easy for her was the paleness of her features, as though all the blood had drained from her when they crossed the threshold. He was astounded with the realization regarding the courage and fortitude it must have taken her as a young girl to come here time and again, knowing what awaited her.

"Why did you keep coming?" he asked.

She peered over at him. "My father insisted. A daughter does not disobey her father. The reprieve came when he died. My brother suggested I visit, but his suggestions were not my father's edict so I could ignore them. Besides, I do love my aunt dearly. She's my mother's sister and after I lost my mother, we became even closer. She never had any children. She treated me as a daughter. I could not fault her for her husband's actions."

Drake could. He could fault the aunt, the servants, every staff member who failed to notice the horrors being visited upon a young girl. People thought the poor were miscreants of society because so many were arrested. But evil was not determined by the absence of coins.

"Ophelia! You're alive! God be praised."

Drake jerked his attention to the hallway where a portly man emerged. His muscle tone and hair had long ago deserted him. His eyes were like two little raisins stuck in a mound of dough. It was obvious the earl thought Phee had died, so he'd never expected the tale he told Somerdale to be disproved. The sick aunt might have been too delirious to know if Phee was ever here. Servants didn't talk. Arms outstretched, he neared—

Drake's fist shot out and hit him squarely on the nose; bone and cartilage crunched as it gave way, blood spurted. Phee gasped. Wigmore landed with a thud, his eyes watering, his hand cupping his nose. Stepping forward, Drake towered over him. "Get up and I'll hit you again."

Please get up.

"Who the devil are you?" Wigmore whined as blood pooled at the corners of his mouth.

"The man who is going to make you regret that you were ever born."

"Drake," Phee said softly, lightly placing her hand on his arm. Strange how she could calm the beast within him so easily. She looked down at her uncle. Drake thought he resembled an overturned turtle. "We've come to get Auntie. We're taking her back to London."

"No need . . . do that." He coughed, sputtered. Started to roll over, but Drake took a step nearer and Wigmore stilled. He glanced up at Phee. "She's not so ill anymore."

"Still, I want to look after her until she's completely well."

"She's my wife. I won't allow it."

"You don't have an army large enough to stop me from letting Lady Ophelia do as she pleases," Drake said, the fury seething through him.

"I've got more than two dozen servants here."

"As I said, you don't have enough to stop me. Now Ophelia is going to inform her aunt that we will soon be leaving and she will accompany us." He crouched down. "Meanwhile, you and I are going to have a little chat. I believe I just heard you invite me into your library for brandy."

"Drake," she said again in that soft tone that conveyed so much. She was worried about him, worried that he'd do something rash, something that might result in him suffering his father's fate. After all he'd done to her, his deception, his lies, she still worried about him—and for some reason that hurt most of all. He'd always considered her mean and spiteful. Now he was coming to know the most generous woman he'd ever known—when it was too late.

He glanced over his shoulder at her. "As long as he cooperates, we're only going to talk. I give you my word on that."

"I'm not going anywhere with you," Wigmore blurted.

Drake shrugged. "We can talk here if you like. I'm

sure your servants are discreet. But talk we shall." Turning his attention back to Phee, he forced himself to give her a reassuring grin. "Off with you."

She hesitated. He almost laughed, because he knew she didn't like being told what to do, especially by him. Eventually she nodded. "Please be careful."

"He couldn't hurt me if he tried."

This time she was the one who smiled. "So arrogant."

"I'm only arrogant if it's not true."

He could see that she wanted to say something else. Instead she turned on her heel and headed up the stairs. He gave Wigmore a hard look. "Here or the library?"

The man was not a complete fool. He led them to the library. He did not offer brandy. He merely stood before his desk glowering, although the impact was tempered by the white handkerchief he held against his nose to stanch the flow of blood.

"I won't stand for you coming into my residence and ordering me about." With his nose broken, his voice was little more than a nasally whine. "My wife is not going anywhere with you. I shall order Scotland Yard to arrest you for kidnapping her. I shall see you hanged."

"There is not a single thing that you can threaten me with that will change my course."

"We shall see about that."

"I know what you are," Drake stated flatly. "I know what you did to Ophelia."

The man paled, then straightened his shoulders. "I don't know what the little chit told you but she lied. She's never liked me—"

"She's always had good taste. But she never lies."

"Oh, wrapped you around her little finger, has she?"

No, she'd wrapped herself around his heart.

"Listen very carefully," Drake ordered.

Wigmore opened his mouth—

"If you speak before I am done, I will be forced to break my word to Ophelia and reintroduce you to my fist. I shall place it where I placed it before and it shall hurt twice as much, I promise you."

Wigmore's mouth closed into a belligerent twist; it took everything within Drake not to slap it right off his face.

"I intend to destroy you. Slowly, over time. You won't notice at first. Your yearly income will begin to dwindle. Creditors will turn you away. Your staff will be offered better positions elsewhere. You will find yourself no longer welcomed in Society. I won't use what you did to Ophelia to destroy you as I won't have her whispered about, but I can set other whispers into play until you are a pariah among your peers. Until you are totally and completely alone. I shall take everything from you. Your position, your standing, your wealth . . . your pride. Your life will be nothing, just as you are nothing. Do you understand?"

"You're nothing more than an arrogant little whelp. You can't touch me."

"You underestimate me, my lord. I was raised by the Duke and Duchess of Greystone. I consider as my uncles the Earl of Claybourne, Jack Dodger, Sir James Swindler of Scotland Yard, and Sir William Graves, royal physician. My closest friend is the Duke of Lovingdon. Should I require his assistance, I would not hesitate to call upon the Duke of Avendale.

"I am owner of Dodger's Drawing Room, and I have at my disposal more resources than you can imagine. But more than that, I know the dark side of London, the dark side of myself. I am the son of a cold-hearted murderer. I have risen from the depths of hell and I have no qualms about returning there and dragging you down with me. Make no mistake, when I am done, you will rue the day you were born."

Drake took some satisfaction in Wigmore's withering before him. He hadn't planned to flaunt the names of those he cared about, but they were powerful and influential, and he would use all resources at his disposal to see this man brought to heel.

"You would be unwise to underestimate me," Drake said. "Don't do anything that will cause harm to Ophelia or her reputation. The only reason you're still breathing is because she asked me not to kill you."

"They'd hang you."

"I'd hand them the rope. I want you out of her life that badly. You are to stay within this room until we are gone. I want her to never again have to set eyes on you. Is my position clear?"

Averting his gaze, hunching his shoulders, Wigmore nodded.

"Good."

Turning on his heel, Drake stormed from the room. His first order of business was to find Phee and get her, the countess, and himself the hell out of here.

He was in dire need of a bath.

If this was her aunt recovering, Phee would have hated to see her while she was truly ill. She was remarkably thin, her gray skin draped over her bones. So little of her seemed to remain.

"Auntie?"

Her aunt opened her eyes, and Phee found herself staring into faded green.

"Phee?" She smiled weakly. "You came. Wigmore said you wouldn't."

Did he think no one would compare tales? "I'm taking you to London."

She yanked the bellpull. When the maid finally arrived, she told her, "Pack a small valise of Her Ladyship's things. We'll be leaving shortly." She turned back to her aunt. "Do you feel strong enough to sit up so we can dress you?"

"You've always been such a dear."

Phee glanced back over her shoulder at the sound of heavy footsteps. Relief coursed through her at the sight of Drake. He came to stand beside her and she nearly leaned into him for strength. "Auntie, this is Drake Darling. He's going to help me take you home."

"I am home, dear."

"To my home." She looked up at Drake, surprised by the intensity with which he was studying her aunt. "If you'll leave us, I need to dress her."

"Let's not take the time. I've had enough of this place, and I suspect you have as well. I'll carry her out wrapped in blankets. She can travel in her nightdress. We'll be back to London before first light."

She nodded, ready to leave as well. "Her things?"

"Leave them. We'll purchase whatever she needs once we're away."

Phee watched the gentleness with which Drake wrapped her aunt in blankets and lifted her into his arms. A pang of remorse hit her as she remembered his carrying her to his bed. Now when there were things she wished to forget, she could recall them with startling clarity. His passion, his fire . . . his tenderness. A complex man born into darkness who had risen above it. A man she had once discounted, thought beneath her. Someone to fetch her champagne when he should have been sipping it beside her.

She followed them down the stairs and out into the night. The footman opened the coach door. Drake settled her aunt on the bench, allowing her to lie across it.

"I'll pillow her head," Phee said, although she would have preferred sitting next to Drake.

His fingers wrapped around hers as he assisted her up. She was halfway inside when thunder echoed through the night. "What was that?" she asked.

"Wait here."

As though she was going to do anything of the sort. "We'll be back directly," she told her aunt, before racing to catch up with Drake. Did he have to have such blasted long legs?

A stillness hovered in the residence, a sense of disbelief, an aura of foreboding. They were in the hallway, almost to Wigmore's library, when the butler stepped out of the room, as white as a sheet.

"His Lordship's dead. He shot himself with one of his dueling pistols."

Phee stopped, pressed her back to the wall as darkness began to circle at the edge of her vision.

"Phee? Phee? Sweetheart?"

She was vaguely aware of Drake's voice, his masculine scent, his warm fingers tapping her cheeks. Then she was gazing into dark, dark eyes. "Why did he do it?" she asked.

"Because he's a coward."

"What did you tell him?"

"That I knew what he was, what he'd done, and that I intended to take everything he valued from him."

He would have done it. She had no doubt. Reaching up, she skimmed her fingers over his familiar jaw. "You're not responsible for his death."

"Not directly, perhaps. But I'm glad of it."

She waited where she was while he gave instructions to the servants regarding how the matter should be handled, where they would be able to reach the countess. She was grateful they wouldn't be delaying their departure overly long.

When they returned to the coach and informed her aunt regarding what had happened, she replied, "I never much liked him."

Then she promptly went to sleep before Phee could settle her aunt's head upon her lap. Which left her to sit by Drake. She didn't object when he placed his arm around her and nestled her close to his side. She had an incredible urge to weep. She didn't know why. Perhaps because it was over.

Almost.

She still had to deal with Somerdale.

Chapter 24

"He took his own life?" Somerdale was standing in the front parlor in his nightclothes, dressing gown, and slippers, his blond hair sticking up at odd angles.

Phee had been rather surprised to find him home and not out carousing. It would have been easier had he been up to his usual escapades. She might have avoided having to explain Drake's presence.

Her brother narrowed his eyes and gave Drake a pointed look. "And how was it you happened to be there?"

"As I tried to explain," Phee began, "Auntie wasn't improving and Wigmore wouldn't allow me to bring her to London. I thought Drake could manage to convince him otherwise."

"Uncle said you'd run off."

"I suppose he wanted drama. I don't know. I did leave for a few days, but I hardly ran off. I went to the local village, because he was being quite impossible to deal with and I was frustrated. Then it occurred to me that I simply needed some muscle, so I sent for Drake."

"Why not send for me?" Somerdale sounded peevish and hurt. She was really too weary to deal with his pride.

"When have you ever stood up to Uncle?"

Somerdale scowled. She had him there and he knew it. "But why would Darling care what you wanted? Why would he traipse out in the middle of the night?"

"Because she is Grace's friend," Drake said. "Stop trying to analyze everything, Somerdale. You'll only give yourself a headache."

"It's just odd that you were asking after her no more than a week ago, and now when she needs you, here you are. I fear something else might be afoot here. Did you take advantage of my sister?"

"He did not," Phee said. "Now will you please send for Dr. Graves so he can examine Auntie? Or shall I have Drake do that as well? She's quite ill."

Somerdale scrubbed his hands up and down his face. "No, no need to involve Darling further. I shall see to it."

As soon as he left the room to search out a footman, she turned to Drake. "I'm grateful for your assistance tonight. But you need not stay any longer."

His gaze slowly roamed over her face as though he was striving to etch every line and curve into his memory. "He's going to keep asking you questions."

"I can handle Somerdale. I have since I was born."

He nodded. "I shall miss having you in my residence."

She almost confessed that she was going to miss being there, but the wound of his betrayal was still fresh and she was confused regarding her feelings toward him. Where he was concerned, a whirlwind of emotions rocked her: gratitude for his assistance, anger at his betrayal, passion, desire, hurt. She didn't know if she had the wherewithal to sort it all out.

"I never—" he began, halted, shook his head. "I was going to say that I never meant to hurt you, but of course that's a lie. You always thought I was beneath you and I proved you right. I'm sorry, Phee. Sorry for more than I can say."

He walked out of the room, out of her life. Tall, strong, proud.

And she, who had never wept during the most horrendous moments of her life, sank into a chair and wept, feeling bereft and confused.

"Arsenic," Dr. Graves said. Phee, Somerdale, and Graves were standing in the hallway outside the room where Auntie Berta slept. "Definitely signs of slow arsenic poisoning."

"Will she recover?" Phee asked.

"Quite possibly. It depends on how much he was giving her and for how long, what damage may have been done to her organs. We'll need to keep a close watch over her."

"Wigmore said she'd begun to improve."

Graves shrugged. "Perhaps guilt began to get the better of him and he stopped."

Phee wondered if there had ever been a more reprehensible friend than Wigmore.

"Why would Wigmore kill his wife?" Somerdale asked. "He already had her dowry, her money. What would he gain?"

"A younger wife, a chance for an heir?" Graves speculated. "I don't understand the workings of the mind, only the body."

"But he was wretchedly old," Somerdale said. "Could he have even performed?"

"Does it matter?" Phee asked.

Somerdale's face burned a bright red as though he'd

forgotten his sister was there to hear the conversation about performance. "Apologies. Of course it doesn't matter. I just find this entire circumstance odd. You and Darling traipsing about in the middle of the night. Poisoning. Suicide. Skullduggery. My God, the next thing I know I'll discover a madwoman in the attic."

Laughing lightly, she rubbed his arm. "I think that's highly unlikely." She turned to Graves. "We appreciate your coming in the middle of the night like this."

"I'm sorry my services were needed, but I'm glad that it's something from which she will most likely recover. I'll come by to check on her tomorrow."

While Somerdale saw Graves out, Phee went to look in on her aunt one more time. She looked so peaceful sleeping there. Then her eyes fluttered open.

"He was trying to kill me, wasn't he?" she asked.

"We think so," Phee replied.

"I married him because my father wished it. Marry for love, Phee, as your mother did."

"Love is not so easy to find."

"Recognizing it, that's the tricky part. A man worthy of you is even harder."

Being worthy of a man, that was the most difficult. Drake knew her secrets now, and while he might have thought he'd miss her, she suspected as time passed, he would be very glad that she was no longer in his life.

She was sullied. After Wigmore she'd never again wanted a man to touch her. Yet Drake had. From him she'd welcomed what she'd thought she'd never be able to tolerate. Now she wasn't certain how she would carry on.

During the week since Phee's return, Somerdale, bless him, tried to ascertain exactly what had transpired between the moment she'd walked from his library with the understanding that she would travel to Stillmeadow with their uncle, and the moment she had returned to his residence, but his questioning was frightfully ineffectual and she suspected he really didn't want to know the truth of it. So she provided vague answers, muttered, and sighed, and he seemed content that he had at least done his brotherly duty and looked into the matter.

While she wandered through the residence striving to recall what she did with herself all day when she didn't have to polish boots, or furniture, or banisters. She wasn't up to making morning calls, not just yet, and looking after her aunt provided her with the perfect excuse to avoid all the gay affairs that were being hosted. She wasn't receiving, which was completely understandable for a woman who had lost an uncle—not that she offered that excuse. Society, as its way, simply assumed, for which she was grateful. She was having difficulty erecting the walls that she needed to move about within polite circles.

Her aunt was recovering nicely. That afternoon she took her tea in the garden.

"You're looking quite spry," Phee told her aunt as she took a chair at the linen-covered table near the roses.

"Oh bosh. I'm years past spry, but I am feeling more myself."

"I'm glad." She prepared a cup of tea and passed it over to her aunt.

"Thank you, dear. Tell me, whatever became of that handsome fellow who helped us escape from Stillmeadow?"

Her stomach tightened. "Drake Darling? He's quite busy."

"Too busy to come see a girl he's sweet on?"

"He's not sweet on me."

"Oh, I thought perhaps he was. But I was never good at it."

"Good at what, Auntie?"

"Figuring out who the fellows were keen on. I thought Wigmore fancied me. I think he did in the beginning. But what did I know? I was only seventeen."

Her heart lurched. Yes, the devil would have liked her aunt very much when she was seventeen.

"We never had much in common, and after I had the three miscarriages, well, I became more an ornament than a wife." Reaching over, she patted Phee's hand. "Don't become an ornament, dear. It's dreadfully lonely and boring as hell."

Squeezing her aunt's fingers, Phee smiled tenderly. "We'll have to see that you attend some parties."

"Oh, I've no time for that. Did Somerdale inform you that I had a letter from Wigmore's solicitor?"

"No, he didn't." She stirred sugar into her tea. "Good news, I hope."

Her aunt leaned toward her. "Wigmore left me a considerable sum. Of course, his cousin Bartlett and his wife will be moving into Stillmeadow as he is next in line for the title. Fine fellow. I like him very much. He'll be a good earl. They're packing up my things so I don't have to go back there. Ever so nice of them, I say."

It was nice of them. She'd once met Bartlett. He seemed a decent enough fellow, certainly better than the man he was replacing. "We shall have to find you a residence in London."

Her aunt's eyes widened. "Oh no, I'm not staying, dear. I'm going to travel once I'm strong enough. Somerdale assures me that I can see quite a bit of the world on the money that has been left to me."

Phee couldn't help herself. She grimaced. "Auntie, I'm not certain I would take financial advice from

Somerdale. He means well, but as I understand it, he hasn't seen after his own inheritance very well."

"What about this handsome fellow then? I wouldn't mind clapping eyes on him again before I leave."

Phee released a small laugh. God, it felt good. The last time she'd laughed . . . had been with Drake. Before she'd remembered everything, before she understood the depth of his betrayal. "He's a commoner."

"Ahhh." She nodded sagely. "I see."

Her words, few as they were, carried a measure of disappointment. "What do you see?"

"Your father believed a man was born to his place in this world and should never seek to move beyond it. I daresay you believe the same."

Phee did wish she'd already drunk her tea so she could busy herself by pouring another cup. She didn't like the earnestness with which her aunt was studying her, waiting for an answer. "Perhaps once. Now I . . . I don't know any longer." She thought of the long hours Drake put in, all the things he oversaw. He'd earned his success, earned respect from those who had trusted their business to his care.

"What does he do, this Drake Darling? He didn't dress like a commoner, so he must engage in some sort of worthwhile business."

"He manages—no, he's the owner of a gentlemen's club."

"Indeed. A businessman. Perhaps I should write to him and see if he can advise me regarding my inheritance."

Phee shook her head. "No, as I mentioned earlier, he's exceedingly busy."

"Pity." Her aunt looked out onto the gardens. "I feel up to a walk. Care to join me?"

"I'd like to very much." And she wanted to be there

to provide her aunt with support should she discover she wasn't as strong as she assumed. Helping her aunt from the chair, Phee offered her arm.

Their steps were slow and small, but they were steps. Phee was grateful her aunt seemed steady.

"Your father loved my sister very much," Auntie Berta said, "and I am thankful for that. But he was a hard man who was resistant to change, believed in the old ways. However, I say if the old ways were so good, no one would come up with new ways." She leaned against Phee. "Invite that handsome gent to dinner."

"It's complicated, Auntie."

"Most things worthwhile are, dearest."

It was not the proper time for a morning call, but then she wasn't calling on the aristocracy, although she was attired as though she were. She stood on the stoop of a townhome waiting for the door to be answered. Her gaze was locked on the residence next door. She wondered if Drake were asleep, if he were even there. Perhaps he'd gone to the club. It was best to end their association quickly and cleanly. No lingering. No more apologies or questions or regrets.

The door finally opened.

"May I help you?" Marla asked.

Phee knew that clothing could make a person look very different, be perceived differently. Still she thought she would be identifiable. "Marla."

Marla's eyes widened, her jaw nearly dropped to the floor. "Cor. Phee? I didn't recognize you."

Because she hadn't looked closely. Because she'd seen a fine dress and hat, gloves. Blond hair without a strand out of place. Lady Ophelia Lyttleton's hair did not fall across her face, did not have to be blown back with an odd twist of her lips and a quick breath.

"Did you remember who you are?" Marla asked.

"Yes. Lady Ophelia Lyttleton."

"Nobility. I knew it. You was too proper."

"Marla, I wanted to thank you."

"I didn't do nothing."

"You taught me to manage Mr. Darling's residence. You taught me how to shop for asparagus. You became my friend."

"You don't thank someone for being your friend. You just be their friend in return. I know that's not possible now—"

"I was hoping it would be. I know Mrs. Turner is elderly and I don't wish to upset her routine or her household, but when you find yourself in need of a position, I hope you will call on me. There will always be a place for you within my household." She extended her card.

Marla took it with reverence. "I don't know what to say."

"If you ever need anything, anything at all—" Then in spite of her best intentions, she shifted her gaze over to the other residence.

"He's not there," Marla said. "Hasn't been for a couple of days now. But if you want to have a look-see, for old times' sake . . ." She reached into her apron pocket and removed a key.

"He gave you a key?"

Marla nodded. "He asked me to keep a watch out. I'm not sure for what, though, unless it was for you."

Phee looked back at the residence. She'd been in a frightful state the morning she'd left. Did he think she'd return for her things? What things? was her next thought. Someone else's cast-off clothing, books that belonged on his shelves, a silver brush, comb, and mirror? Why would she want any of those items? They weren't really hers, just props for his farce.

Yet she was drawn toward it. Wanted to see it again: the floors she'd scrubbed, the mantels she'd dusted, the banisters she'd polished. She snatched the key from Marla's fingers. "I won't be but a minute."

Marla gave her knowing grin. "Take your time. I'm not going anywhere."

She'd descended two steps before Marla called out, "By the by, it's to the back door."

Glancing over her shoulder, Phee smiled. "Thank you."

She hurried down the narrow path between the houses until she came to the mews and the back gate. Opening it, she was disappointed not to see Daisy about. Even though she knew the beast was being cared for at a very fine stable, it didn't seem right that she not be here. Then her heart soared at the sight of Rose on the porch. The large dog lifted his head, shoved himself to his feet, and lumbered toward her in an uneven gait, tongue lolling out. When he reached her, he circled her three times before jumping onto his hind legs, placing his front paws on her chest, and releasing an enthusiastic bark.

Phee laughed as she ran her hands over the dog. "Look at you! You're still here, and you've put on weight. Aren't you a handsome fellow with a little meat on your bones? I daresay if I didn't know better, I'd think someone had been brushing your coat as well."

He barked again before dropping to all fours and loping along beside her as she walked to the terrace. She couldn't refrain from reaching over and petting Rose from time to time. She wondered how Somerdale would feel about having a dog at his residence, if Drake would give him up.

Leaving Rose to nap on the terrace, she went inside, halfway expecting to find Pansy lounging on the wooden table where she'd shared meals with Drake, but all she found was a very tidy kitchen. She supposed he ate at the club now. She wasn't surprised he hadn't kept the cat. She wondered if she roamed the neighborhood if she would find it. Probably not.

She wandered the familiar hallways. Nothing had changed except now a light sprinkling of dust seemed to have settled in everywhere except his desk. Did he work there from time to time? Did he think of her when he did?

In the entryway was the hideous table she'd purchased. Atop it was the vase she'd knocked over her final morning here, pieced back together, evidence that it had once shattered clearly visible. She ran her finger along one of the jagged lines. Strange how the imperfection didn't detract from its beauty. Nor did the absence of flowers. She was half tempted to snitch a few roses from Mrs. Turner's garden to brighten the entryway. Perhaps she would so Drake would know she'd been there. Where had that thought come from? What did she care if he realized she'd stopped by? She didn't want him making any more of her visit than a simple journey through nostalgia. And why in God's name was she nostalgic about the place?

It wasn't as though it had ever truly been hers to see after.

Peering into the parlor, she came up short.

"Oh my God," she whispered, pressing her fingers to her lips. Astonished, she stepped into the room.

The black and gold wallpaper, exactly as she'd sketched and described it. On the walls. Black draperies at the windows. And the furniture, black velveteen, edged in mahogany. The shape of each piece—sofa, chairs, tables—exactly as she'd sketched it, arranged in the room precisely as she'd laid it out on paper. Just as elegant as she'd envisioned it would be.

Curled on the corner of the sofa set near the fireplace

was Pansy, watching her, just watching her, with slow, slow blinks.

"No enthusiastic greeting from you?" Phee asked as she sat on the sofa and ran her fingers through the soft fur. Pansy purred deep in her throat. "That's better."

Feeling a nudge against her skirts just as she heard a mewling, she glanced down to see a small white kitten weave itself between her ankles. Laughing, she lifted it up. "And who are you? Drake Darling was most insistent there not be a menagerie in his home, so how did you come to be here?"

She stroked behind its ears, and it purred. "You like that, don't you? I'm sorry I can't stay longer."

Setting the kitten down, she rose and walked from the room. One more place she wanted—needed—to see.

She took the stairs slowly, one step at a time. Her heart sped up and she forced it back into calm with long deep breaths, a trick she'd learned so no one could tell when she was anxious or nervous. It was the reason Somerdale had not realized she dreaded leaving with Wigmore that night, the reason he and her father had never known how much she disliked going to Stillmeadow. Wigmore had convinced her that her *wickedness* must be hidden from everyone. She'd become quite adept at creating a façade to hide the ugliness she experienced in life.

It was her shame, her humiliation to bear. She had come to believe that somehow she was at fault, she brought Wigmore's attentions on herself. She was unworthy, she was impure, she deserved—

She shook off the thoughts. No one deserved what she had endured. She understood that now. Because of Drake. Strange that as much as he'd hurt her, he'd helped her as well.

Stepping into the bedroom was like stepping into a

cocoon of safety. The room was tidy, no clothing scattered on the floor. It smelled of him: dark, masculine, strong, powerful. She wandered over to the bed. The covers weren't rumpled. She saw no evidence that he'd slept there. No evidence that she'd ever been curled in that bed, nestled against his side.

Would she have been there if he'd told her who she was? Had he spoken the words, "You are Lady Ophelia Lyttleton" would she have remembered anything? Would it have made a difference? Or would she have thought it was all simply preposterous?

Hearing the creak of a floorboard, she turned her head to see Drake standing in the doorway, dressed to perfection, neck cloth knotted, waistcoat buttoned, jacket snug across his broad shoulders. Dark hair curling, dark eyes penetrating.

"Marla told me you weren't here," she said flatly, striving not to let him know how her heart was thundering, her nerves quivering.

"I wasn't. But I needed to put out some coins for Jimmy. Today is one of the days he cleans up after Rose. And I just—" He shook his head. "The residence felt different, smelled different when I stepped inside. I knew you were here."

He seemed to be measuring his words as though he thought if he spoke the wrong ones, she would run off. When in truth she despised the distance separating them. But the thought of him being closer terrified her. She wanted to run her hands over his shoulders, across his chest, through his hair.

"You've acquired another cat, I see."

"Her name is Orchid."

She couldn't help but smile with the realization that he was keeping with her tradition of naming them after flowers. "It's my favorite fragrance."

"I know."

The solemnity of his words tore at her heart. Of course he knew. He knew everything about her, all her darkest secrets. But then she supposed that was only fair, as she knew his as well.

"How is your aunt?" he asked.

"Recovering quite nicely, considering Wigmore had been poisoning her."

"Bastard. He wanted you back that badly."

Her heart lurched. "I don't think it had anything to do with me."

"You said you were close to her and you'd not been back since your father died."

She squeezed her eyes shut, her stomach roiling. Drake was right. The only thing that would cause her to return was her aunt's ill health. Wigmore had known. Then to cover his sins, he would have continued to poison her until she died so she couldn't contradict his tale that Phee arrived at Stillmeadow and then ran away. She opened her eyes. "I'm glad he's dead. We can't really ever know everything about a person, can we?"

"No, not everything."

But one could know enough, she thought, enough to fall in love. All those various emotions she felt toward Drake were still swirling about. She didn't know what to do with them, so she ignored them and turned the conversation to something that had pleased her. "I couldn't help but notice that you took my advice regarding your front parlor."

He took a step toward her. "Why are you here, Phee?"

So he wasn't going to let her lead them into casual banter. She should have known. He always asked far too many questions, always needed answers. She shook her head slightly. "I don't know."

Her gaze darted to the center of the bed, to where she had been happiest. "I keep thinking about the night we were together."

"Had I known of your past, I'd have gone more gently."

She peered up at him. He was only inches away now. "But you still would have *gone*."

"Yes." He lifted his hand and very slowly, as though giving her a chance to move away, to step beyond reach, he cradled her cheek. "But I should have told you who you were. I should have told you everything."

"You didn't know everything. And had I known everything, what transpired between us never would have happened. I've been thinking about that. Quite a bit, actually. Losing my memories for a short time was a blessing." She placed her gloved hand on his jaw. "With them, I never would have known how it should truly be between a man and a woman. I never would have—"

Taking her hand, he began loosening the buttons of her glove. Her heart thudded. "What are you doing?"

"If you're going to grace me with a touch, I don't want you wearing gloves."

"I'm not going to touch you, I'm not—"

He peeled off her glove, tossed it aside, and returned her palm to his jaw. "Much better," he said, raising his eyes to hers.

The desire smoldering in his gaze arrowed straight through her, down to her toes, causing them to curl. And he was right. It was so much better to touch, skin to skin.

"How can you want me, knowing what you know about me?" she asked.

"The ugliness was in him, not you," Drake said. "You are brave and courageous. Even as a child, you carried on when many would have crumbled. What passed between us in my bed had nothing at all to do with him."

Tears stung her eyes. "I try to convince myself of that, but it's so hard. I wish I'd never seen him again. I can't get him out of my mind. I think I came here because I wanted the memories with you to be stronger. I need them to wash the ones with him away."

Taking her other hand, he bent his head and gently began removing her remaining glove.

"Drake—"

"I can make you forget him." He lifted his gaze to hers. "Allow me to do that for you."

She shook her head slightly. "I don't know if I can, not now that my memories have returned, not now that I know everything I've done."

"Everything he did. You did nothing. I know I have no right to ask this of you, considering how we came to be here. But trust me."

"I'm afraid."

He skimmed his thumb along her cheek. "It will be like walking in the park that night. You thought there was something to fear but you stepped out of the cab anyway, and there was nothing to cause you harm. He can never hurt you again, Phee. He has no power over you, with or without your memories. Let me show you."

She realized she hadn't come here to see the floors she'd scrubbed or the wood she'd polished. She'd come here to be closer to him, to let memories of him usurp the ones with Wigmore that were threatening to take hold. But Drake in the flesh, here with her now, was so much better, so much stronger than any memory. What he was offering . . . she didn't know if she had the courage to accept it.

"What if I can't . . . what if—"

He stroked his thumb over her lower lip. "You can say no at any time and I'll stop." He freed the button at her collar. "Anytime you become uncomfortable. Whether it be the releasing of a button, the untying of a ribbon, you need only say no or wait or stop. Your command is mine to obey."

Another button loosened. Another. Another. She didn't say no or wait or stop. She simply watched as his nimble fingers made short work of the line of pearls. Her nerves tingled. She feared she might swoon. *Breathe*, she ordered herself, *breathe*.

Kneeling on one knee, he patted his thigh. Placing her hand on his head to steady herself, relishing the feel of the silken strands curling around her fingers, she set a foot on his leg. More buttons freed before he removed her shoe. His clever hands slipped beneath her skirt and rode over ankle, calf, knee, and thigh until they encountered ribbons to be loosened. Then he was rolling her stocking down so incredibly slowly that she thought she might go mad.

He moved on to the next shoe, the next stocking. No haste, no fumbling fingers. Each action was sure, deliberate. Each made her feel treasured, appreciated. Each made her anticipate the next.

In one smooth movement, he stood, took her hand, and led her over to the side of the bed. Continuing with his ministrations, he removed her dress, her petticoats, her undergarments. As more flesh was revealed so his hands briefly skimmed over it, causing shivers of pleasure to course through her. His touch was as she remembered: intoxicating. With each stroke of a finger over her skin, her body yearned for another.

When she stood before him completely bared, she thought she should have felt a measure of shame or unease, but how could she experience any sense of embarrassment when the appreciation that lit his dark eyes warmed her far more effectively than any fire might?

The pins came next, the ones holding up her hair. *Clink, clink, clink*. They hit the floor, setting the curls free, not in a tumble, but in a leisurely unfolding over her shoulders and back.

Scooping her up, he eased her onto the bed, before backing away. Rolling slightly to the side, she watched as he removed his boots, his gaze never leaving her. As he removed his clothes, his movements were slow, provocative, and she found herself almost begging him to hurry. She loved watching him being unveiled, loved the way his muscles bunched and relaxed. He was no strutting peacock. Rather, he was some sort of untamed jungle cat, moving lithely toward her. He had yet to remove his trousers, which for some reason made him appear all the more dangerous—not in a frightening way, but in a manner that excited her, that made her think her heart might burst free of its moorings.

The bed dipped as he placed a knee on it, as he stretched out beside her. He buried his face in the curve of her shoulder. "I'm so glad you're here," he rasped. "You will be as well when I am done."

She already was. She needed this, needed him. While she could not say that she had forgiven him completely, she couldn't deny that she was drawn to him as she'd never been drawn to another man, as she hadn't believed she *could* be drawn.

He nibbled on her ear and her body curled against him. He trailed his mouth along her neck, nipped at her shoulder. She scraped her fingers up into his hair. This was a memory she would cherish, that she would take out and reminisce about on long, lonely wintry nights when in the company of dogs, cats, and bunnies. These sensations—the rumbling in his throat, the vibrations in his chest—she noted them, locked them away, never to be forgotten.

Each caress, each kiss, each stroke of his tongue was unforgettable. Wedging himself between her thighs, he pressed his lips to the hollow between her breasts. Wrapping her legs around him, combing her fingers into his hair, she held him near, relishing the intimacy.

"You're so beautiful," he said.

She'd never felt beautiful, not really. Not until her memories had been lost. When they had returned, the ugliness of her life had risen to the fore. But now with him, worshipping her as he was—

"You make me feel beautiful."

"Never doubt," he whispered as he turned his head to the side and closed his mouth around her nipple, his tongue stroking and teasing, shooting glorious pleasure to the apex between her thighs. She lifted her hips to meet his, seeking some sort of surcease.

He chuckled low, the wicked sound its own aphrodisiac. She scraped her fingers over his back, over the dragon, imagined she could feel its muscles within his. He scooted lower, kissing her stomach. Lower still, licking at the hollow of her hip. Lower still, spreading her, blowing a gentle breeze over the curls.

"Drake." His name was a benediction, a plea, a question.

His eyes held hers, boldly, irrevocably without any doubt.

"Every aspect of you is beautiful," he said, before dipping his head. The first caress of his tongue nearly had her coming off the bed.

She dug her fingers into his shoulders, pressed her head back against the pillows as he nibbled and nipped, stroked and suckled. Insistent, determined. The pleasure escalating until only this moment, only he, only raw sensation existed. No memories, no other man, no ugliness.

Only beauty. Only his adulation. Only joy. Only want. Only desire.

No shame in any of it. Only acceptance.

She allowed herself to embrace it, fall into it, be consumed by it until her back was arching, her body trembling, her voice crying out his name in wonder. She was lost, lost in the bliss of it, he her only anchor—and even that added to the enjoyment of it. She had soared to new heights of awareness, had experienced incredible splendor.

A memory that put all others to shame, but still not enough.

He kissed the inside of her thigh, then eased up until he was gazing down on her, a quiet satisfaction in his eyes. How did she tell him it wasn't enough?

"I want you," she whispered.

He pressed his lips to her forehead. "Today is for you."

She shook her head. "I need you." She slipped her hand between them, felt his burgeoning hardness and wondered that he wasn't doubled over in pain. "I need you inside me."

"Phee—"

"You promised to obey my commands, so take me."

He cursed harshly, growled low. His mouth came down on hers, hungry, without finesse or gentleness. She relished his eagerness, relished the notion that she could drive him to such madness. There was no shame to be found in true, honest desire. She understood that now, understood it completely.

She almost laughed at the haste with which he removed his trousers. He rose up over her, held her gaze, and plunged swift and deep as she lifted her hips to welcome him. He stilled, his eyes sliding closed, his groan echoing between them. "I love the way you feel," he said.

Slowly he opened his eyes. She ran her hands over every aspect of him that she could reach. "I love the way it feels when you're inside me."

Words she'd never thought to say, words that made her entire body grow warm, but she would not retract them. She loved the weight of him, the fullness of him nestled within her.

Holding her gaze, he began to rock against her, slow but sure, long and deep, resparking the sensations that only moments before had nearly undone her. She wondered if it all felt as marvelous to him as it did to her, and she found herself grateful that she could give him this, that she could share it with him—openly, without remorse, without long-ago memories intruding.

It was only they, here in this bed, touching, kissing, sighing, moaning, rocking against each other. Pleasure building until they reached the summit together. Until they were both soaring. Until there was nothing except each other.

Drake thought he might have died. For a brief second at least, when the pleasure had ripped through him with an incredible force that he'd never before experienced. He had planned to give to her, and not to take, but he supposed there was a sort of giving even in the taking.

Lethargic, not certain he'd ever be able to move again, he rested on his side, facing her, his hand draped over her hip. He didn't fool himself into believing that anything had changed between them, that he would have anything more than today. When they had made love before, she had not known who they were.

Now she knew. She wasn't here because she loved him. She was here because she needed to put the past with her uncle—and perhaps her past with Drake—behind her. She was staring at his chest more now than she was looking into his eyes.

"It's somewhat of a relief," she said quietly, "to feel free of him. I didn't expect to ever know what it was to willingly be with a man. I wasn't certain I'd even be able to be so close to a man." Laughing lightly, she finally lifted her gaze to his. "I seem to have overcome my doubts."

"Does this change your position on marriage?"

"I suppose I'm not categorically opposed to it any longer, but it would have to be a true love match, based on trust." She studied him for a moment. "Why did you tell me I was your servant?"

Slamming his eyes closed, he sighed.

"Because I was always calling you boy and asking you to fetch things for me? Because I never failed to give you a cut direct whenever our paths crossed?"

He opened his eyes. "I was being petty."

"I apologize for the way I treated you before. It was wrong of me."

He'd never expected an apology from her, especially as he owed her one. "I'm sorry as well. I should have taken you home straightaway."

"You should have, yes. But if you had, I never would have had this." She circled her hand over the bed. "I can't regret it exactly, but I wish the circumstances had been different. And I do appreciate your efforts today."

It took everything within him not to curse. She was building the walls again. Not that he blamed her. She was Lady Ophelia Lyttleton and he was the owner of a gentlemen's club.

"Perhaps in the future, we'll be friends," she said. She rolled out of the bed.

He couldn't be angry that she'd used him. He'd

offered. He got out of the bed, snatched up his trousers, and drew them on. Then he assisted her with her clothing.

"This isn't nearly as much fun as taking them off," he said.

She laughed, the sweet sound that he loved. "I never thought to be comfortable with all this. I thank you for that."

"For God's sake, stop thanking me."

Nodding, she drew on her gloves. "How are things going at the club?"

"I'm going to close it down for a couple of weeks, modernize it. By the way, I decided to take your advice. I'm going to open it to women."

Her green eyes widened until he was drowning in them. She smiled brightly. "Marvelous. I might have to get a membership."

"You shall always have a membership there, with my compliments."

"Well, then, I shall definitely stop by sometime."

"I look forward to it." But he hated the increasing formality between them. "I meant what I said that night at Lovingdon's. I fell in love with you."

"No, you said you fell in love with the woman in your residence. We both know she wasn't me."

"I think you're wrong there."

"I don't think so." Edging past him, she headed for the door.

"Phee?"

Stopping, she turned, peered over at him, one blond eyebrow finely arched. "Yes?"

"I also meant what I said about if you should find yourself with child. Or if you are ever in need of anything, I'm here for you."

"I shall keep that in mind. Good-bye, Drake."

Then, once again, she walked out of his life. And he, being the fool he was, let her go.

Phee stared out the carriage window, fighting not to cry because Drake had not tried to stop her from walking away. It seemed of late she spent a good deal of time staring out windows and warding off tears.

In a manner of speaking, her loss of memory had been a blessing, had allowed her to experience something quite remarkable, even if deception had been involved. If she were to be honest with herself, she might even admit that she deserved it a little bit, a very tiny little bit.

Dammit. She had deserved it, all of it. Her treatment of Drake had been obnoxious. If their situations had been reversed, if he'd been the one without a memory, she'd have done the same thing. Only she'd have made him a stable boy shoveling manure.

She smiled. He'd always pricked her temper, sharpened her tongue. She wished she had been the lady who lived in his residence, but one couldn't change one's stripes.

On the other hand, maybe one could.

Chapter 25

"Bloody hell, I can't believe the line of people standing out there waiting for you to open the doors," Andrew said, staring out the window of Drake's office at the Twin Dragons.

Its inauguration tonight was the talk of London, not only among the aristocracy but among the wealthy who bore no titles. Entry into the Twin Dragons was by invitation only, each one hand-delivered to the elite, those who could afford membership. The aristocracy. The newly rich. Railway barons. Manufacturing barons. Those who dared to reach for something better. Americans. And the ladies. Ladies were being allowed into what had once been the men's inner sanctum. And that was causing quite the stir.

Leaning back in the chair behind his desk, Drake dared not browse the expectant crowd, because he knew if he did, he would search for her, and he didn't want to experience the disappointment that she hadn't come.

It had been six weeks since Wigmore had been put in the ground. Grace had informed him that Phee was again attending balls and dinners, concerts and theater.

She was being wooed and courted. Any day now he expected to read about her betrothal in the *Times*.

From her he had received but one missive, which said simply, "No child."

He should have been relieved. Instead he'd felt his last opportunity to regain her in his life melt away. Not that the circumstances would have been ideal. But it might have been a chance for them to start over. It might have—

"I can't believe how different the place looks," Rexton said.

Drake's brothers had arrived early, intent on sharing the reopening of the Twin Dragons with him. They held no resentment, no grudges that the duchess had handed him her portion without recompense. He was touched by their loyalty, their goodwill toward him. They embraced his good fortune as though it were their own.

"I wanted ladies to feel welcome here," Drake said. "It was too dark before."

He'd done much of the work himself, hammering, painting, papering, rearranging. The more punishing the task, the more likely he was the one to do it. Anything to make his muscles scream and ache, anything that resulted in exhaustion, so that when he finally went to bed he could sleep without dreams, without thinking of Phee.

Not that his plan garnered him much success where she was concerned. She always hovered at the edge of his consciousness and he could do little to eradicate her from his mind. It didn't help that as he oversaw the arrival of new furnishings and their placement that he envisioned her handling the delivery of furniture at his residence. A residence that was now too blasted empty, the only sound his hollow footsteps. He could smell her on his pillow, his sheets, and his desire for her would only sharpen.

"I'm not sure how I feel about playing against women, taking their money. Not very gentlemanly," Rexton said.

"Never bothered you to take Grace's money."

"He could never beat Grace," Andrew said. "I could, though."

"Because you cheat," Rexton announced.

"So does she. Did you never figure that out?"

"I wouldn't expect my sister to be so underhanded." Rexton lifted the glass dragon from its perch on Drake's desk and examined it.

"Careful with that," Drake said. Rexton arched a brow at him. "I don't want it broken."

"Pity it's already broken. Part of its tail is missing."

Not missing exactly. Rather it was nestled within a small pocket in Drake's waistcoat, so it was always with him, so he always carried a reminder of Phee.

Carefully, Rexton returned it to its place. "It's an exquisite piece. I can't imagine Jack Dodger having such whimsical objects in his office."

"But then it's not his office," Drake said with a smile. It hadn't been in some time, but tonight it truly felt like Drake's. Perhaps he was going to be able to generate some excitement after all.

"I assume he's coming tonight?" Andrew asked.

"He and Claybourne, along with their families, should be here anytime now." He'd given them a private tour the day before. They'd been impressed with the alterations. While most of the main floor would cater to both genders, he'd added private salons for each. A rather fancy dining hall created a pleasant atmosphere for a gent to bring a lady for dinner. Another room would offer dancing. He was expanding beyond vice.

A soft knock sounded.

Drake peered over at the doorway and saw the duke

standing there. He quickly came to his feet. "Your Grace."

Greystone held up a bottle. "Anyone care for some good scotch before the masses are allowed inside?"

"Absolutely," Drake said. Grabbing four glasses, he set them on the corner of his desk.

"Where's Mother?" Andrew asked, as the duke wandered in.

"With Grace and Lovingdon, ordering people about, making sure all is in order before the festivities start. It means a great deal to your mother that you allowed her to have a role in planning tonight's unveiling." The duke poured two fingers into each glass. As Drake reached for his, the duke said, "Oh, wait, something else first."

He slipped a hand inside his jacket and withdrew a small leather case. He extended it toward Drake. "Just a little something to mark your success."

Drake hesitated a moment. Fine things came in leather boxes. "I haven't had the success yet."

Greystone winked. "But you will."

Drake took the offering and slowly folded back the hinged lid. Inside he found nestled among velvet a gold pocket watch and chain. On the cover, finely etched in exquisite detail, was a dragon. He wasn't certain he'd ever received such an exquisite gift. He had no words. "It's remarkable."

"You and I have always had the dragon in common. It seemed appropriate." Greystone patted his waistcoat pocket where his own watch was protected. "A father passes his watch down to his firstborn son, so of course mine will go to Rexton."

"Not for many years yet, please, Father," Rexton said.

Greystone grinned. "Not for many years yet." Sobering, he gave his attention back to Drake. "But I wanted you to have a watch as well. Doesn't come with a storied past, but each watch must begin its tale somewhere so it can be carried on down the line. There's an inscription."

Taking the watch from the case, holding it in his palm, Drake carefully opened the cover and read the words etched in delicate script.

To my first son
—Always, with love and pride

Drake swallowed down the hard knot that had lodged in his throat. His chest tightened. His eyes stung. He lifted those eyes to the man standing before him. "I don't know what to say, Your Grace."

The duke nodded slowly, his lips curling into a slight, wry smile. " 'Thank you, Father,' would be nice."

Drake shook his head, or he thought he did. He seemed incapable of moving. His voice was locked. Every muscle in his body was locked. He had stood in a crowd and watched his father hang. He saw his father's fists, his rage, his ugliness. He saw . . .

He saw . . .

He saw the duke holding his hand the first time they boarded a ship. He'd been terrified, but hadn't voiced it, yet the large, sure hand had been there all the same, calming his fears.

He saw the duke crouched beside him, pointing out and explaining Stonehenge, the pyramids, the Roman Colosseum, the Great Wall of China. He saw the duke climbing a mountain with him and revealing the world from its summit. He saw the duke teaching him to ride a horse, correcting him with a stern voice when he misbehaved, insisting he learn his lessons, never allowing him to shirk his responsibilities, patting him on the shoulder for encouragement, carrying him on his back when he was younger and grew tired.

He saw now that the man on the gallows had merely given him life. The man standing before him had gifted him with *a* life, and a remarkable one at that. But more, he'd always shown him kindness and love.

Everything within Drake unknotted, unlocked. Swallowing hard, he held the duke's blue gaze. "Thank you, Father."

Greystone smiled, his own eyes misted, and he blinked them several times. It wouldn't do for a duke to be caught weeping or displaying unbridled emotion. "You're most welcome. A bit of advice, though. Never look at your pocket watch when you're waiting for a lady to ready herself so that you might go out. It will drive you to madness. A woman's five minutes are never fewer than twenty. Now let's get this on you, shall we? See how it looks."

Taking the watch from Drake, the duke leaned low and close, striving to hook one end of the gold chain around a button.

Drake's heart went out to him as he watched him struggle. "I can do that."

"I'm not blind quite yet."

"I'd give you my sight if I could," Drake told him.

Greystone succeeded in securing the chain to the button and stuffed the watch into the proper pocket on the waistcoat. Straightening, he patted Drake on the shoulder. "I wouldn't take it. A father always wants better for his son than he had for himself. You are well on your way. And now it's time for the toast."

Rexton passed around the glasses.

Drake's father lifted his glass high and in a strong voice said, "To your success, my son. May tonight be merely the first step of a remarkable journey."

"Hear! Hear!" Rexton and Andrew said.

They all clinked their glasses before tossing back their scotch. The warmth from the liquid going down was nothing compared to the warmth Drake felt for these men surrounding him.

He had them because he'd once been forced to climb down a chimney flue in order to steal valuables from a fancy residence.

What an odd turn of fate, that the man who sired him had in a strange way been responsible, after all, for giving him a family.

Drake stood in the shadowed balcony—one aspect of Dodger's that remained untouched—and looked down as the main floor of the Twin Dragons filled with the curious. Tomorrow more gaming tables would be added, but for tonight much of the space had been left open for dancing. An orchestra played. Liveried footmen served champagne. People drank, laughed, wandered. By all observations and accounts, tonight was a success. Yet something was missing.

Then he saw her. Phee. She'd come. He'd hoped but hadn't truly expected her to accept the invitation. She was more beautiful than ever, dressed in pale green silk and dark green velvet. Long white gloves that rode past her elbows hid hands that had once caressed him. Her hair, held in place with pearl combs, revealed a slender throat that he desperately wished to nibble. And he knew she'd have arrived on a cloud of orchids. He rather imagined that her fragrance had wafted up to the balcony, that even now he could inhale her scent. Although he knew it was impossible.

No shadows seemed to be hovering about her. She greeted those she knew with a smile. He stayed where he was because he didn't want to see that smile wither.

He didn't want to see ghosts dim the sparkle in her eyes. He didn't want his presence to ruin her enjoyment of the evening.

Even as he argued that she came knowing he'd be here, he couldn't convince himself that she'd be glad to see him.

"People are beginning to speculate that the owner of this establishment is a phantom," Avendale said as he placed his forearms on the railing and leaned forward.

"Avendale, for God's sake—"

"They know you're up here watching. I daresay you have a more potent stare than Jack Dodger. A shiver went through me every time your gaze landed on me."

"Must be guilt that caused the shivers as I wasn't giving you any notice at all."

Avendale grinned. "So who *is* garnering your attention this evening? Ah, could it be Lady Ophelia Lyttleton, returned from her uncle's? Nasty bit of business that. Wigmore killing himself while cleaning a pistol. Although I can't say I ever really cared for the man."

An accident was the story they had all decided on. Simpler that way.

"Something is different about her," Avendale continued.

"Who?" Drake asked, coming to attention.

"Lady Ophelia. I ran across her at Hyde Park, thought to stop, have a quick chat, offer my condolences. Strangest thing. While we're talking, she notices her lady's maid's nose is turning pink from the sun and insists that she use Lady Ophelia's parasol. Can you imagine a lady giving her maid her parasol?"

He could quite well imagine it of Phee.

"She is suddenly quite intriguing," Avendale said. "I've decided to pursue her."

Drake hardly had time to give any thought to it before

he grabbed Avendale by the lapels and slammed him back against the wall. Still holding the duke in place, he growled, "I'll not have her touched by the likes of you."

"The likes of me? I'm a bloody duke."

"You're a bloody scoundrel."

"What's going on here?"

Peering over at Lovingdon, Drake realized he was making quite the spectacle of himself. Unclenching his fists, he released his hold on Avendale and stepped back, but he'd be damned if he was going to apologize.

Jerking on his waistcoat, Avendale said, "I seem to have struck a nerve. Thought I might. I don't know why you won't admit you have a fondness for Lady Ophelia."

"Just stay clear of her or I'll cancel your membership here."

"I can't have that now, can I? Not when things are on the verge of getting most interesting. Ladies in a gaming hell. They shall be the ruination of us all, but what fun we'll have along the way. Lovingdon, I'm off to the card room. Hopefully you'll join me there."

"Perhaps after I dance with my wife," Lovingdon said, but his gaze never left Drake.

Avendale wandered away. Drake took a deep breath. Phee was perfectly capable of warding off the man's advances.

"Grace wondered if you were coming down," Lovingdon said. "Everyone is asking after you. They're all rather interested in meeting the enigmatic owner of the Twin Dragons."

Drake nodded. "I'll be down in a bit."

"He's not going to pursue her."

When Drake looked at him, Lovingdon added, "Avendale. I don't know why he was trying to get a rise out of you, but he has no interest in marriage."

"Neither did you."

Lovingdon chuckled. "That's true." He sobered. "Do you love her?"

"It doesn't matter what I feel for her. I hurt her badly."

"Yet she came tonight. Your moment of triumph and she's here. That has to count for something. Think about it. Meanwhile, I've been too long without my wife, so excuse me while I return to her." Lovingdon left.

Drake walked back to the balcony and gazed out. He spotted Phee immediately, as though she were the brightest star in the night sky. Suddenly he desperately wanted to hear her voice, inhale her scent. He wanted to look into her green eyes and see for himself that she was all right. That her uncle's death was behind her. That there were no more shadows, no more ghosts.

But getting to her required walking through hordes of people who delayed his passing with congratulations, and questions, and praise. He greeted them all as quickly and politely as he could, all the while striving to keep her within his sights.

She was standing in a circle of young ladies. He knew them. They had been the ladies who had been tittering around him at Grace's wedding. Ladies who found him a curiosity, nothing more. Ladies who would never consider him as a serious suitor. He was not nobility. He was a club owner, and while that club would now extend memberships to women, it didn't negate the fact that he worked. Long hours. Tedious hours.

Like half the gentlemen in this room.

Suddenly Phee stepped back and accidentally knocked into a footman carrying a tray filled with flutes of champagne. The tray upended, the flutes crashed to the floor. He heard Phee's cry of dismay right before she knelt on the floor beside the footman and began to assist him in placing shards of glass on the tray, while everyone stood around and gaped.

In two long strides, he was crouched beside her in time to hear her say, "I'm so sorry. That was extremely clumsy of me."

"It was my fault," the footman said. "I wasn't looking where I was going."

Drake waited until she set the glass on the tray. Then he grabbed her hands before she could retrieve any more. She lifted her eyes to his, and within hers, he saw the worry and concern over broken glasses and spilled champagne.

"You are a lady of the nobility," he said. "You do not clean up messes."

"I was clumsy, not looking where I was going. It was my fault. The least I can do is help clean it up."

"You needn't worry about it. I'll see to it."

She studied him, her gaze roaming over his face. She squeezed his hands. "You're the owner of this establishment, Drake Darling. You don't clean up messes either."

He grinned. "No, but I pay good money to people to do it for me."

Standing, he brought her to her feet, then turned to the crowd. "This will all be taken care of shortly. Please return to the merriment."

He gave his attention back to her. There were a thousand things he wanted to say to her, a thousand things he wanted to do with her. But he had no right to impose on her, not after his deception. He almost told her he missed her—desperately. Instead he said, "I'm so glad you came, Lady Ophelia, but I don't want to ruin your evening. I'll leave you to enjoy it."

Her mouth curled up ever so slightly. "Dance with me."

Not a question, but a command. It was her way. As it was his. One didn't ask when one thought the answer might be no, although why in the world she thought he wouldn't dance with her was beyond him.

"It would be my pleasure," he said, offering her his arm and leading her into the dance area.

She hadn't planned to come. She had stroked her fingers over the gilded invitation he sent and convinced herself it would do neither of them any favors if she attended.

But she'd been unable to stay away.

For long moments they simply waltzed, gazing into each other's eyes. She felt as though everything was being communicated, even though no words were being spoken.

"What a fool I was," she finally said, "to have rebuffed your previous invitations to dance. You're quite good at it, while I was quite insufferable."

"I won't argue with you there."

She laughed lightly. "Now you decide to be honest with me?"

"I shall never lie or deceive you again. You have my word on that."

"I shall never give you another cut direct. You have my word on that."

"I've missed you, Phee."

"I don't see how you had time. I remember Dodger's from before, when I visited once with Grace. You've made it all very elegant, but it took a lot of work. You had to have been very busy with it," she told him.

"Not so busy that I couldn't find moments to think of you. I'll redo any of it if it's not pleasing to you."

"This is your place, Drake. Not mine. It's quite the talk of the town. Now that you've come down from the balcony, I daresay, the ladies will be swarming to your side once we stop dancing."

"Then we won't stop dancing."

Something warm settled in her chest, tightened it. She didn't want to stop dancing, didn't want the other ladies fawning over him. "That would create quite the scandal after we worked so hard to avoid it."

"I don't think anyone would fault me for keeping you in my arms when you're so beautiful."

She didn't feel beautiful, not really, not where it counted. "I wasn't a very nice person before."

"You had your reasons."

"To strive to make others feel small because I felt small is hardly commendable."

"Perhaps we both suffered from the inability to see you clearly."

"I see myself quite clearly now."

"I'm not sure you do. The last time I saw you, you told me that you weren't the woman who lived in my residence, and yet I know she was the sort to kneel down to help a footman clear up broken glass."

She was certain she was blushing. "I wasn't thinking."

"You can deny it all you want, but you are the woman I fell in love with. You're strong, Phee, when you need to be strong. You're courageous. You carry on when it might be easier to crawl into bed and pull the blankets over your head. I told you that you were a servant and while you hadn't a clue regarding what you were supposed to do, you forged ahead. When your memories returned, you rescued your aunt even though it meant facing your past. You are quite remarkable."

This was the reason she almost hadn't come. She didn't want to hear of his love and devotion.

This was the reason she'd come. To be near him again, to hear of his love and devotion. And she missed him so very much.

"Without my memories, with no tarnished past"—with no memories of Wigmore to intrude—"I was free to fall in love with you. I do love you, Drake. At first I was hurt and so angry but when I take in the entire tapestry of my life, my happiest, most joyful moments have been with you."

"Marry me."

Not a question, but a command. It was his way. As it was hers. One didn't ask when one thought the answer might be no, although why in the world he would think she wouldn't marry him was beyond her.

"How can you want me knowing all you know about me?" she asked.

"How can I not?"

They were no longer dancing, but standing in the midst of dancers with his large gloved hands, his wonderful large, scarred, powerful hands cradling her face as though it were made of the most delicate spun glass. "How can you love me knowing what you know of me?" he asked.

Tears stung her eyes as she smiled. "How can I not?"

"Marry me," he repeated.

She bit her lower lip, nodded. "Yes. All right. On one condition."

"You can name a hundred conditions, a thousand. I shall meet every one."

She laughed lightly. "You don't even know what it is yet."

"I know how much I love you. I know how desperately I want you in my life. I'll do anything you ask."

"Oh, Drake. I don't know that I'm worth all that."

"I've told you before: you're worth everything. Name your condition."

"I won't be Lady Ophelia after we marry."

"You'll be marrying a commoner, but the title of Lady comes from your father. You can keep it."

"I don't want to. I want to be Phee Darling or Mrs. Darling. No more, m'lady. Just Mrs."

"You don't have to do this for me, Phee."

"I'm not. I'm doing it for me, and because I want the world to know that I'm incredibly proud to be your wife. We'll be equal, Drake. You and I. That's how it should be. How I want it."

"Then that's how it shall be." Angling her head, he took her mouth as though he owned it, because he did. He owned all of her, heart, body, soul. How had she thought that she could live out the remainder of her life without him?

She was vaguely aware of the sounds of feet brushing over the floor silencing, the final strains of a waltz drifting into silence. When Drake drew back, she was aware of all eyes upon them and her brother elbowing his way between couples.

"What's the meaning of this?" he asked when he finally reached them.

"I'm marrying your sister," Drake announced.

"Not possible."

"You haven't the means to stop me."

Somerdale sighed and turned to Phee. "Ophelia, you can't marry a commoner."

"I believe I can."

"But the terms of your trust—if you marry him, your trust is forfeit. Your money comes to me."

"Unless I'm willing to wait until I'm thirty," she said, holding Drake's gaze. "It's a considerable sum."

Slowly he shook his head. "Not even if it included the crown jewels."

For a woman who had once hoped to avoid marriage altogether, she couldn't believe how happy she was. "Don't lose it all at one gaming table, Somerdale." She turned her attention back to Drake. "Kiss me once more, my darling rogue."

Taking her in his arms, he did just that.

Epilogue

From the Journal of Drake Darling

I'm the husband of a woman adored. The father of children loved. A man wealthy beyond measure in all things that matter.

The Twin Dragons was an astonishing success. Eventually I turned its care over to another and moved my wife and children to the country, near the Duke of Greystone's ancestral estate so we could visit them easily.

Phee used the land around us as a sanctuary for animals, taking in those abused, those who could not speak for themselves. I often thought she took solace from them because she, too, had once not been able to speak for herself.

When our first child was born, Marla moved in to serve as his nanny. She oversaw the care of all our children. She also married the local vicar and had children of her own. She became one of Phee's dearest friends.

Somerdale came close to squandering what he inherited as a result of Phee's marriage to me, but then he took to wife an American heiress who possessed not only an immense fortune but a head for business. From all appearances he loved her very much indeed, and she him.

I had once thought that I was tethered to my sordid beginnings and that there was nothing strong enough to free me from them.

I underestimated the power of love. The love of a mother for a child she did not give birth to. The love of a father for a son who was not his own. The love of brothers for one who did not carry their blood. The love of a sister for a brother who was not born into the family.

The love of a wife for a husband she chose. The love of a woman for a man who appreciated her strengths and her weaknesses. The love of Phee, the center of my most precious memories, the heart of my life. The true dragon who slayed my demons as I slayed hers.

PASSION AND INTRIGUE FROM *NEW YORK TIMES* BESTSELLER

LORRAINE HEATH

LORD OF WICKED INTENTIONS

978-0-06-210003-0

Lord Rafe Easton may be of noble blood, but survival taught him to rely on himself and to love no one. Yet when he sets eyes on Miss Evelyn Chambers, an earl's illegitimate daughter, he is determined to have her.

WHEN THE DUKE WAS WICKED

978-0-06-227622-3

Lady Grace Mabry's ample inheritance has made it impossible for her to tell whether a suitor is in love with her—or enamored of her riches. Who better to distinguish beau from blackguard than her notorious childhood friend, the Duke of Lovingdon?

ONCE MORE, MY DARLING ROGUE

978-0-06-227624-7

After rescuing Lady Ophelia Lyttleton from a mysterious drowning, Drake Darling realizes she doesn't remember who she is. With plans to bring her to heel, he insists she's his housekeeper—never expecting to fall for the charming beauty.